Butterfly Cottage

ISBN Number: 978-1-7366875-0-5

Hearts Overcoming Press

United States of America

Cover Design: Evelyne LaBelle, Carpe Librum Book Design

Butterfly Cottage

By

CARRIE FANCETT PAGELS

Hearts Overcoming Press

Dedication

In memory of my dear friends
Cheryl Baranski
Regina Fujitani
Bonnie Roof
Dr. Laura Vann

&

My beloved mother
Ruby Evelyn Skidmore Fancett

Heaven is brighter with all of you there.

Endorsements

"This lovely novel, centered on three generations of women as they face a summer of change, will resonate with readers long after the last page is turned."

~~Suzanne Woods Fisher, bestselling author of *On a Summer Tide*

"WHAT A SUPERB BOOK!!!"

~~Bonny Sommert Rambarran, Christian fiction book reviewer

"Beautifully written with genuine feeling and deep truths, *Butterfly Cottage* has many breathtaking moments until that final satisfied sigh. Unforgettable characters and an inspiring setting, at the Straits of Mackinac, make for an immersive must-have summer read!"

~~Kathleen L. Maher, award-winning author of the Sons of the Shenandoah series

"*Butterfly Cottage* had my emotions all over the place. I've loved all of Carrie's books but this one spoke to my heart so many times that I continued to reach for my tissues. This one is certainly an award-winner!!!"

~~Teresa Mathews, Christian fiction book reviewer

Chapter One

Dawn
Chicago, Winter 2018

A *re you sure you're really ready to retire?*
        Dawn Charbonneau crinkled her nose at the first line of the email from the potential buyer of her travel agency. "Oh, boy." Hadn't she already answered that question? After all, Barb had been managing the place for the past few years—and she was well suited to buy Dawn out and assume full responsibility.

"What's up?" Jim, her husband of almost fifty years called from his recliner.

"Aw, nothing." She closed Barb's email and opened the next one, a long message from her last high-profile client. "Oh, boy."

Jim lowered the volume on his Bulls game. "What are you 'oh boying' about?"

Dawn hadn't booked any travel plans for her former clients since easing toward retirement after Jim's knee surgery—except this one. Barb hadn't wanted to touch the high-strung woman's travel plans but Dawn had a soft spot in her heart for this customer. "Do you remember Kay-Leigh?"

"Yup, that supermodel from Europe, right?"

"Yup." The young woman had been with Dawn since before Kay-Leigh became famous. Separated from her husband, Kay-Leigh had Dawn book a flight from Switzerland, where she was living, to Michigan in July. "It's my very last booking and I want to make sure things go well for this young woman. I made hotel arrangements on Mackinac Island."

"Hard to mess that up. Hampy will take good care of her."

Dawn cringed. "Nope. I put her at the Grand Hotel." Their friends, the Parkers, owned a resort on the opposite side of the island. They wouldn't be happy if they got wind of this. "Don't say anything to Hampy about it."

"Hampy Parker won't hear a word from me, but why not put her up over there? More privacy."

She sighed. "Her husband's family owns a. . ." she did air quotes with her fingers, "cottage near the Grand on the West Bluff."

"Ah. That makes sense then."

"Don't I always make sense?"

Jim stared at her a long time before they both burst into laughter. "Nope. No, you don't."

Dawn rose and went to him and kissed his forehead. He smelled faintly of pine soap and Coca Cola.

Her husband grabbed her hand. "You okay, my darlin'? I mean you had a busy career and now you're playing nursemaid to a grumpy old man."

"You were only a crank right after the surgery." Dawn scanned her office turned sports den. "But, yes, I do kind of miss the office." She also missed hanging out with her colleagues. Could she really sell the agency?

He compressed his lips. "No one is making you retire, Mrs. Charbonneau."

"I know, Mr. Charbonneau." She bent and kissed him again.

Jim released her hand and his gaze drifted back to his sports game. He increased the volume, again.

Conversation over. Dawn laughed to herself. She'd help Kay-Leigh out. The model had told Dawn to book the trip, and she'd pay regardless of whether she went or not. Dawn would pray that the couple could work out their differences. She sat back down at the computer desk.

If Jim weren't still going to physical therapy, Dawn could drive up and spend the entire summer at her family's cottage on Lake Huron. Unlike the mansion-like cottages on Mackinac Island, her childhood home in Mackinaw City was a simple but welcoming family home. In the past, she'd had to either keep their time at the Straits short, or she'd telework using her laptop and Wi-Fi. Wouldn't that be something if she could get Tammy and Jaycie, her daughter and granddaughter, to join her for the entire season? *A dream come true.*

But her duty as a wife came first.

Jim turned off the game and looked at her. "Ya know, Kay-Leigh isn't the only one who could be going up to the Straits. I'll be able to drive soon, and I'm fully capable of getting myself to and from PT appointments. And I can nuke soup and tv dinners. You could drive up there, and your old man will join you later." He winked at her.

When had her husband started reading her mind? They'd been together so long, though, that often he knew exactly what she was thinking. Tears pricked her eyes, and she wiped them away. "What exactly are you saying?"

"Ask the girls to spend the summer with you."

Immediate pleasure was chased by a rotting apple plunked right in the pit of her stomach—the fear of whether her son-in-law would put the kibosh on the plan. She'd never met a more contrary man in her life.

"And once you're up there, maybe you can figure out what you're gonna do next—now that you're supposedly retiring."

"Supposedly?"

"Yeah, I saw the gleam in your eye when you opened that gal's email." Jim playfully wagged a finger at her. "You haven't sold the business yet."

"True. The ink isn't dry." But her heart told her it was time. *Mostly.* What next though?

"Okay. That's all I'm sayin'. You have my blessing if you want to go. I'll drive separate once my drill sergeant releases me from PT." He clicked his sports program back on and then made a fist into the air, accompanied by a whoop when the Bulls scored.

It felt selfish to leave Jim when he wasn't one hundred percent recovered. But within a few weeks, he should be fine.

Jim popped the top on another Coke. "If you go, there'll be less nagging about my home exercises."

Dawn pushed back her chair and rose. "Jim Charbonneau, do you know what I'm going to tell your physical therapist to do to you?"

"Um, make me go to Butterfly Cottage and play Pickleball with you and our friends?"

"No." She took a step closer.

"Make me start square dancing with you, again?"

"Not right now."

Jim raised his hands. "You want her to release me so I can drive you up and devour whitefish and pasties with you every day if I want?"

"Nope!"

"What then?" His beautiful blue eyes reminded her of the first time they'd seen each other, at her high school event—the Promenade up Mackinac Island's boardwalk. He was her friend Hampy Parker's buddy and had crashed their high school formal dance. Jim had swooped in on her like a hawk. He'd never left her side; walked her up the boardwalk to the Grand Hotel, and back down again to the Iroquois.

She bent and kissed him. "I'm going to tell her to cut you no slack while I'm gone and double up the home program."

Jim clasped her hand between his. "I'll work twice as hard so I can join you and my girls."

"First we need to get them onboard."

Their two terriers scampered into the room, stopping at Dawn's feet. "What would I do with these two? How can you take care of these little rascals by yourself?"

"Little sweeties, I think you mean." Hard Rock, their Yorkie, attempted to jump onto the extended leg portion of the recliner.

"Ha. I'd take Cici. She's the sweetest pup ever." Dawn bent and patted the Silky Terrier's head. Cici allowed the pat for only a moment and then ambled off to the couch.

"If you like cat-dogs. She's more cat than dog."

"And you'd bring your pest, I mean *pet*, up later?" Dawn watched as the seven-pound Yorkie pawed at the recliner.

Jim leaned over and picked up Hard Rock. "He can keep me company until I reunite with all my sweet girls."

"Right." The one fly in the ointment would surely be her son-in-law. But God already knew that, didn't He?

Tears pricked Dawn's eyes, remembering how her son-in-law had so rudely told her that regular family trips weren't worth the expense. If only her daughter and granddaughter could be with her this summer. With Barb's suggested deadline of September first for a final decision on the sale, Dawn needed all the support she could get. This choice wasn't something she could put off any longer.

Chapter Two

Tamara
Yorktown, Virginia

Tamara popped two antacid tablets and chewed them, her "breakfast" today. She'd been blessed to teach these children this year, each one a joy. Her kindergarten students bent over their first task of the morning—math coloring sheets. She'd created a special design for each student, based on his or her interests. How she loved her sweet little pupils. If she had her way, she'd love to teach eleven months out of the year. And she'd spend every July at her parents' cottage, where she'd relax and also develop lesson plans for the following year.

The classroom door opened, and Principal Melinda Evans popped her head in, her long auburn hair immaculate as usual. "Mrs. Worth, you have a visitor."

Tamara ducked her chin. She'd not been expecting anyone, but parents were allowed to visit the classroom to observe, as were school district personnel.

She mustered a broad smile. "Send them in."

Outside the classroom, foot shuffles echoed. How many visitors were there?

"Surprise!" Melinda moved out of the way as a massive tray of yellow-frosted cupcakes was thrust forward.

Tamera stiffened. Did any of her children have a birthday that week? She'd be mortified if she'd forgotten one. But with this being the one-year anniversary of her friend, Ruby May's death, Tamara had been a little distracted. She rose, one hand pressed to her middle. This was unexpected, but she'd adapt. *This is about my kiddoes, not about me.*

"Come on in. Let's put that on our center table."

Instead of one or two parents, seven adults streamed in, laughing. Emma's mom held aloft a colorful assortment of balloons and a bouquet of flowers, including some large pink lilies. Tamara inhaled their heady fragrance.

Abishai's mother, a tiny woman no taller than Tamara's shoulder, had tears in her eyes as she thrust a turquoise envelope toward her. "Congratulations, Mrs. Worth."

What in the world?

A crackling over the school announcement system signaled the room for quiet. "Good morning," one of the fifth-grade students, who took turns with announcements, spoke clearly. "We have special news today. Mrs. Worth is our Teacher of the Year for—"

Tamara's kindergarteners and the adults erupted in cheers, and she didn't hear the next part of the announcement. Stunned, she gaped at her grinning guests. Emma's mother stepped forward and gave her a quick hug. "Thanks for all you do. You're the best."

If Ruby May were still alive, and working in her classroom across the hall, Tamara was sure her dear friend would have screamed in delight. Ruby would have roused her entire class, too, to cheer Tamara on. Tears rolled down Tamara's cheeks.

Melinda pointed to the rocking chair in the corner. "Now you go sit there, Mrs. Worth, and let us wait on you."

Hours later, having been congratulated by and seated with her peers in the teachers' lounge, Tamara pulled her sandwich from her lunch box and stared at it, unsure if she could make herself eat. It had the taste of resentment in it, no doubt.

Her stomach cramped, as if in agreement.

Across the table, her friend Susan's face, with her beautiful café-au-lait complexion reddening, reflected distress. "I wish so badly that Ruby was here, too." The three of them had been the best of friends.

"Me, too." She took a tiny bite of her sandwich. Pretty tasty ham with honey-mustard dressing on it. Again, her gut clenched. She really needed to see the doctor.

Susan leaned in. "Good thing you're saving some room, girlfriend."

"Why?"

"You'll see." A smile tugged at her friend's lips.

Behind Tamara, the door creaked open and someone cleared their throat.

Someone gasped beside her. "Is that chocolate ganache cake from the Carrot Tree?" Lyzette Velazquez, the school's new Special Education teacher, had taken Ruby's place this year. The woman was a certified chocoholic and looked as if she might start drooling.

"It is indeed." Superintendent Brown's baritone startled Tamara. She turned and he was staring right at her.

School "Teacher of the Year" awards didn't normally result in the parents coming in during school time with treats. That should have been a clue, earlier. Tamara's face warmed, and her heartbeat ticked up faster. Nor would the superintendent join the teachers at lunch time. *Oh my goodness.*

"Your colleagues and the parents agree—Mrs. Tamara Worth, you are York County School Division's Teacher of the Year."

It wasn't only for her school, like she'd thought, but for the entire large district of teachers. What a surprise. What a blessing.

Behind Superintendent Brown, one of the local photographers stepped forward, snapping pictures of what was surely her most shocked expression.

The whole thing seemed surreal. She didn't deserve it. Any one of her colleagues could have rightfully taken this honor. Yes, she worked hard, but so did they. Last year, they'd all pushed hard to get Ruby the award before she passed away. But that hadn't worked out.

Tamara glanced around at her fellow educators, all of whom were pushing their chairs away from the tables and standing, clapping loudly. Tears flowed down her cheeks. Susan fished a tissue from a nearby box and handed it to Tamara.

Well done, my child, my good and faithful servant. The words whispered to her soul lent a gravity to the situation. A strange sense of finality. Goosebumps prickled her flesh and when she told Susan later about it, she knew what her friend would call them— "Holy Ghost bumps." These words issued to her were ones she hoped to hear at the end of her time at a God-issued job. But she had a good decade to go before retirement. She swept the unwanted thought of endings aside and forced herself to be in the moment, enjoying the accolades of her peers.

That cake looked positively sinful. They'd have to pry Lyzette away from it with a crowbar.

After everyone, save herself, had enjoyed a quick piece of the cake, Tamara and Susan walked back to their classroom corridor. Her friend touched her arm. "Are you all right? You didn't even touch that cake."

They paused beneath the white and black utilitarian clock that hung on the painted concrete block wall. "I don't know. I feel a little weird, to be truthful with you."

"It's the one-year anniversary since Ruby May died. Do you think that's it?"

"I think so." Tamara had spent a lot of time with her longtime friend before she'd died from cancer. At the end, almost every bit of

Tamara's free time had been devoted to helping her and her family. But Ruby May was in a better place now. It had been difficult watching what her valiant fight had cost her family as well as Ruby herself.

Ruby had told her, "Tell anyone who will listen to you to not have the Whipple procedure."

Tamara had kept her promise. But two other teacher friends in the district had gone through with the surgery despite Tamara's sharing her friend's advice. Both were now dead. One died on the operating table and the other experienced the same horrific suffering that Ruby had.

"You look deep in thought, girlfriend."

"Yeah, I was thinking about how Ruby wished she'd have not had that awful surgery and would have fought that horrible cancer a different way. To have a little better quality of life at the end than she had." She shivered.

"Will you and Brad celebrate tonight? Ruby would have wanted you to do so!" Susan gave her a quick hug. "You deserve it."

"Maybe." She chewed her lower lip. If Ruby had lived, she'd have encouraged her.

"We've got to enjoy these little victories in life. Let that man of yours treat you to a good meal."

"Yeah." Tamara sniffed. She'd text Brad and ask him to meet her at Tuscany's. He might be tight with money, but he loved Italian food.

A dull roar accompanied the sound of the playground doors opening at the end of the hall. "We best get back." Susan linked her arm through Tamara's, and they hurried toward their classrooms.

Later, a fire drill interrupted the afternoon, after which the children never did settle back down. The sugar from the cupcakes, the excitement of the award, and the practice drill sent a buzz through the children that was almost palpable. By the time the last of her darlings had boarded the bus, Tamara could have collapsed into her classroom rocking chair and remained there for the night. Instead, she tidied her desk, set out her things for the following day, and then pushed her cell phone ringer on.

Susan popped her head in the door. "Hey, you gonna take my suggestion?"

Why not celebrate with a special dinner out? She patted her hair. "I sure could use a haircut and a style."

Susan cocked her head. "That hairdo is not too bad."

"That's a ringing endorsement." Tamara laughed. She could really use a new look. Especially with her husband working out at the gym so much. She needed a hairstyle and fashions that didn't scream, 'schoolmarm.'

"John likes my new 'do." Susan patted her stylish short curls.

"It's nice."

"I bet I could get in at the salon for a quick style." This award had lifted her spirits and a new hairstyle could help her self-esteem, which had been flagging. "Then I'll pick Brad up at the gym and surprise him with my good news."

"You go, girl!"

They high-fived. How long had it been since she'd done something spontaneous? She liked things planned out. If Jaycie had been there, that would be another story. She and her daughter loved to engage in spur-of-the-moment activities.

Oh, Jaycie, I miss you so much.

"You better get on it, if you're gonna have a hot date with your man tonight." Susan raised her eyebrows. "Shrug out of those schoolmarm duds."

"Puttin' on my red dress and heels." Tamara struck a pose and they both laughed. She owed her husband more than the listless wife she'd been since their daughter left. And she'd finally make that doctor's appointment to find out what was making her stomach feel so upset. She did not want to miss a day away from her students, but she owed it to them, and to herself.

If Dr. Joseph Forbes told her it was stress, then she'd have to go back into marriage therapy yet again, even if it meant going on her own—like the last two times. She'd always respected her husband and trusted him. She had to at least give it one last try.

Chapter Three

Jaycie
Oxford University, United Kingdom

Unless something changed, in two weeks Jaycie would board a Delta jet home to Virginia. She shifted on the lumpy mattress. No summer internship secured, no graduate assistantship for the Fall semester, and no proposal from Elliott—yet.

She had to admit that Mom was right—she should have stayed in a dorm instead of renting a flat. Arms behind her head, she stared at the cracked plastered ceiling. All the lines clustered to resemble a turtle—the symbol of Mackinac Island. The island nestled in azure Lake Huron waters near the cottage where most of her pre-college summers had been spent.

Her iPhone rang and Jaycie grabbed it from the rickety side-table. A pink-haired emoji of Hannah, another archeology student from America, showed on the screen. "Hey, what's up?"

"Guess what?" Hannah squealed so loudly that Jaycie had to hold the phone away from her ear.

"What?"

"I got the internship in Boston after all!" Her best friend at Oxford shrieked again.

Jaycie's heartbeat accelerated. "Woo hoo!"

"Yeah, let's celebrate!"

"How about—"

"Shenanigans?"

"You read my mind." Their favorite pub, Shenanigans, occupied a triangular corner only two blocks from Jaycie's flat.

Jaycie sat up and swung her legs over the side of the groaning bed. "Give me a few minutes to get my face on, and I'll meet you down there."

"In fifteen then. See you." Hannah clicked off.

How wonderful for my friend. Like Jaycie, Hannah couldn't attend grad school in the fall if she didn't raise more cash. If Jaycie didn't find a position for herself, what would she do? Dad had made it perfectly clear that he'd not fund her graduate school training. Had even gone so far as to suggest she join the military which Mom would never have agreed to since she'd been transient as a young military kid. Dad claimed that archeology was for rich kids, not her. Although her paternal grandparents were wealthy, they barely had contact with Jaycie, their only grandchild. Her maternal Charbonneau grandparents, however, had more than made up for the lack of interest from the Worths.

Maybe there would be an internship for her yet. Hope propelled her to jab at the Gmail icon on her phone and when the app opened, she scanned her new emails. Nothing from any possible internship, but one from Grandma Charbonneau. She'd check that later when she had time to fully respond. Gran didn't like short messages.

Soon, Jaycie touched up her makeup and slipped into her sparkly flats. While they were comfortable, they'd definitely never be worn on a dig. She headed out the door, down the squeaky ancient staircase and made her way to the pub. The scent of fried fish and beer wafted outside to the herringbone bricked walkway. She'd miss that smell.

Part of her had believed that Elliott might propose, a fragment of hope that was becoming more minuscule by the day as her return loomed. Gorgeous, uber-intelligent, and witty, Elliott's British charm mesmerized her from day one in the UK. And he'd hinted repeatedly that he could see them together for a long time.

At the pub, she reached for the elaborately engraved brass knob, centered in a foot-long shiny brass protective plate. A suit-sleeved arm reached past her, brushing against her as a man pulled the door open. Jaycie caught the familiar scent of Nautica Blue men's cologne and she froze. She swiveled, shock almost making her dizzy.

"Parker?" She gaped at her University of Virginia nemesis and former childhood friend.

The last time she'd seen him, one year earlier in their college town of Charlottesville, he'd been at his worst. Parker had cornered her after an early morning class, croaking out something about her mother and his, rambling incoherently. He was either hungover or on something. Later, she'd learned that all he'd wanted was for her mom to pray for his own mom, who struggled with addiction. Parker's extended family and hers all knew each other from their summers in Michigan.

Jaycie swallowed hard as she took Parker in from head-to-toe.

He'd certainly cleaned up well, with his golden hair styled and his sea-blue eyes flashing at her. No bleary eyes tonight.

"Sorry, miss, ye musta mistaken me for anotha gent." The heavy fake Labor Party accent almost had her cracking up. Almost. This was

Parker after all. The same classmate, who despite his prodigious intellect, could pass off his study group's work as his own. Quite the actor.

He opened the door, and they both stepped inside the tavern.

Jaycie frowned at him. "What're you doing here?"

Parker dipped his perfectly cleft chin and laughed. Dressed in an expertly tailored suit, fitting him in all the right ways, he looked like he'd come from one of Elliott's men's magazine photo shoots. "I do have a passport and on occasion I use it." He squared his shoulders and averted his gaze.

She exhaled. Same old Parker. Same old irritant. Same old. . .

Movement at the bar caught her attention. Hannah crisscrossed her hands repeatedly in front of her chest and then jerked her thumb back toward the door, where Jaycie and Parker stood. Jaycie frowned at her friend. Why she was acting so weird?

Jaycie angled toward Parker. "The pub isn't a crush tonight, so I don't know why my friend is making that face. Too-crowded would be her usual reason for wanting to leave."

Then Jaycie saw him.

Or rather *them*, seated at a small round table. Elliott's back was to her, his Euro-cut dress shirt clinging to his muscles. With that mop of auburn wavy hair, it was definitely him. And across from Jaycie's boyfriend sat Phillipa Cowles, her hand resting lightly atop Elliott's outstretched arm. The gorgeous student's eyes reflected the same longing that Jaycie felt for Elliott. He leaned in, and Phillipa mirrored him. They kissed.

Jaycie was going to be sick.

Parker's arm settled over her shoulder. "Are you all right?" There was genuine concern in his eyes.

Hannah weaved through the clusters of patrons toward them. When her friend reached them, she glanced between Jaycie and Parker. "Who's this?"

The Michigander removed his arm from Jaycie's shoulder and extended his hand. "Hampton Parker the third, but you can call me Parker."

Hannah and Parker shook hands.

Her friend's eyes widened. "I've heard about you."

Jaycie cringed. She'd told Hannah about all the ways Parker had aggravated her. She'd also shared how close they'd once been.

Parker shrugged. "Good things I hope."

Phillippa and Elliot were still engaged in their kiss. Jaycie's stomach roiled as a flush of deep humiliation overtook her. She made herself breathe. She couldn't break down here. Not in front of Parker. She blinked back tears as Hannah and Parker continued talking. In a daze, she could barely register their conversation. Dizziness made her rock slightly, but she steadied herself.

Worst night ever.

This could not be happening. When her year-long boyfriend, the man she thought might even become her husband ended the lip-lock with his fellow Brit, Jaycie did the only thing she could do. She clasped Parker's clean-shaven cheeks and pulled him toward her for a kiss. When she met initial resistance, she tugged at his tie and he bent forward. A thousand emotions seemed to flash over his face before he finally complied and pressed his lips to hers. She released his tie as he pulled her close to him. Closer and closer he clutched her as he committed himself to the task.

This was not the feather-light first kiss that they had shared at Mackinac Island's Arch Rock on her fourteenth birthday. This was magical. Could he ever kiss! Jaycie swayed a bit and Parker dipped her back in his arms. This felt good—and it shouldn't. She should push him away, but this had been her idea. Hoots and hollers erupted as Parker continued. Finally, he released her and beamed with such self-satisfaction that she longed to wipe that smirk off his face.

What had she done? *Oh my gosh. This is insane.* Behind Hannah's shoulder, Elliott had turned to stare at them.

Hannah jerked a thumb toward the door. "Let's get out of here."

Blinking at Parker, words flew out of Jaycie's mouth unchecked, "Do you want to come with us?"

"Aw, I wish I could, but my cousins are here. They're expecting me." He bent and kissed her cheek. As if he were her boyfriend. Which he wasn't. Not that their scorching kiss hadn't suggested they were a couple in love. "Let me see if I can get together with them tomorrow instead."

He squeezed her hand and then headed away. She touched the spot on her face that he'd just kissed. It felt warm. Her lips tingled, too.

Elliott had turned back around, then tossed back the dark ale that he favored.

Hannah yanked on her arm. Her friend leaned in and whispered, "Jaycie, isn't Parker the guy who made your life miserable at UVA?"

"Yes." She watched as Parker slowly approached Elliott and Philippa's table. He paused, his profile showing a jaw muscle jumping. He narrowed his eyes at Elliott and hesitated, then shot a glance at Jaycie. Parker acted like he knew that Elliott was cheating on her. That Elliott was her guy. Or supposed to be. And Parker also must know that she'd used him to get back at Elliott. She touched her lips, which still burned from Parker's passionate kiss.

"Oh." Hannah squeezed her arm. "Tread lightly, my friend. I can't believe he just kissed you like that. Or that you kissed him like there was no tomorrow. I don't think you've been honest with me about this guy."

Maybe not honest with herself, but she wasn't going to address that right now.

Parker continued on and then stopped at a large booth. She'd not noticed the group of posh Brits in the back when they'd arrived, having been shocked by Parker's arrival and by Elliott's cheating. The booth was filled with a half-dozen of the wealthier students from the graduate program. One of the young women shook her head vigorously. It was Lady Isabella, one of Phillipa's close friends.

"I guess the Lords and Ladies are slumming tonight." Hannah sighed. "They should stick to their own fancy clubs instead of crawling the University pubs."

Jaycie cringed at her friend's mean-spirited comment. Parker leaned in toward Lady Isabella and gestured toward Jaycie and Hannah. If Jaycie could have crawled under a rock and hid, she would have. From Isabella's cool gaze and compressed scarlet lips she wasn't too happy with Parker's request.

Two chattering couples came through the door, carrying with them the faint odor of cigarette smoke. Jaycie blew out a breath and stepped aside to allow them past.

Parker headed back toward them. He stopped at Elliott's table, leaned down and said something to him, his features pinched in anger. Elliott leaned back and away from Parker. When her fellow American archeology major rejoined them, he made a sorrowful face. "I'm sorry. I can't join you lovely ladies tonight."

He swiveled forty-five degrees toward Isabella's table. "My cousin insists I stay, and she's not used to being denied her requests."

Nor was Parker. No surprise to her that the student whose attitude of entitlement had plagued her for years was related to aristocracy. Lady Isabella and he were cousins. Why did that make her feel ill? Was it simply the icing on his spoiled rich-boy cake?

"I see." Why had her tone come out so clipped? Why should she care?

"Maybe we could see you before Jaycie leaves for America?" Hannah's wide-eyed gaze suggested that she, like so many other women, wasn't immune to Parker's good looks—his stellar appearance when he bothered to clean himself up.

His tawny eyebrows rose. "Sure thing." He fixed his attention on Jaycie and motioned his hand toward his ear, miming that she could call him.

Hannah nodded enthusiastically. "Yes, Jaycie can call you."

As if!

Hannah beamed up at Parker. "I just got offered a summer internship in Boston at the Adkins dig."

The Adkins dig was the latest archeological dig at a Revolutionary war site, and one that paid the interns decently. Hannah well-deserved this position. But once all the paying internships were gone, what would be left for Jaycie? Nothing had been offered. And she wasn't about to join the Marines, like Dad had suggested. He even sounded serious. With Mom's deep aversion to military life, she might disown her.

"Congratulations!" Parker even sounded sincere.

Jaycie swallowed. Hard. She knew what was coming. He rarely spoke about himself, but he constantly asked questions. Questions that were none of his business. There was a question coming now. She felt it.

Sure enough, he pinned her with his gaze. "What about you, Jaybird, what are you doing this summer?"

She hated when he called her that pet name. *What was I thinking? I just kissed this guy right in front of...* "Mackinac." The word shot unfiltered from her mouth. *Gran. Mom.*

"Huh?" Hannah frowned. "You never said anything about going there."

Jaycie shot her a warning glance. Right now, all she wanted was Gran, Butterfly Cottage, and her mother's shoulder to cry on. But Jaycie needed a job wherever she could find one.

Parker shifted his weight, bumping Jaycie slightly with his hip. "I thought you were working at Colonial Williamsburg this year, again."

Last April, he'd gone into a drunken rant at a local bar in Charlottesville when she'd been offered the prestigious position again and he had not been given a spot.

This year, while she was at Oxford, Parker, who had remained behind at UVA in Charlottesville, had stolen the Murray Fellowship from her, an award that would have made graduate school a whole lot easier to afford. Money he didn't need whatsoever. When she'd heard, she'd run ten kilometers and nearly got herself run over by a lorry. Then she and Hannah had devoured fish-and-chips while Jaycie had eviscerated Parker, making fun of him down to his odd penchant for mismatched socks. Granted, she'd felt terribly guilty about it, but anger sure twisted things around. Why did she even care? But she did.

She mourned the loss of the Parker she'd known on Mackinac Island.

"Jaybird, you're not workin' in Virginia, again?"

"Nope." She bit her lower lip. Colonial Williamsburg had informed her that her position had been offered to another student. Honestly, she'd thought it was Parker who'd been hired. But she certainly wasn't going to ask.

Her friend beamed at the man who irritated her most of anyone in the world. Except maybe for Elliott. "What are you doing, Parker?"

He shrugged, noncommittal—an attitude he'd possessed in work groups and social situations in Charlottesville. "That's one reason I'm here. My dad sent me to check out a hotel for him."

"Here?"

"Yes." Parker sighed. "He's trying to expand his holdings."

Jaycie's own father's "holdings" were his investment and retirement accounts whose numbers he pored over weekly, staring at his laptop like Gollum from *Lord of the Rings* would do for his "Precious"—the ring that cast a spell over him.

Lady Isabella waved at Parker and scowled like an old curmudgeon.

"I better go." Parker bent in and attempted to kiss her again, but Jaycie backed away.

She raised a hand and forced a half-smile. He'd said that his hotel visit was only one of the reasons he had come to England. So maybe he'd gotten one of the prestigious Oxford internships. Wouldn't surprise her now that she understood his connections. But she wasn't going to let that get to her. And she had to put any notions he might have about that kiss to rest.

She affected a posh accent, like his cousin used, "If you take a position here in England, you know we'll have to break up, darling. So, no more PDAs. Righto?"

He laughed. Genuinely guffawed. And for a moment, Jaycie almost liked him, again, the boy she'd been such close summer friends with over the years. Maybe England suited him. Maybe it was something else making her yearn for those old days. Like the fact that he looked so good, smelled so wonderful, and kissed like. . .

He bent in and whispered in her ear, "I would never let you off so easily. You should know that." Then he pressed a kiss to her forehead, something that reminded Jaycie of her family. Grandpa, Gran, and Mom had perfected that familial kiss of affection.

She blinked back tears. She wanted to thank him, which was plain silly. He jested, she was sure of that, but it reminded her she really was loved. Elliott was a cad. She had no internship. But there were people who truly loved her.

Home. Then Mackinac. Maybe it wasn't a lie to say she'd be there this summer.

Chapter Four

Dawn
Chicago

Dawn poured Jim another cup of morning coffee, and he pointed to the phone. "Are you going to ask our daughter, or do I have to do it?"

She glanced at the wall calendar—April emblazoned across it in a gigantic font. "I guess I better get on it." It was plain silly to be afraid that her invitation would get shot down.

"Don't put it off. Tammy will need time to pack and plan. You know how she likes to be organized."

"She learned it from the best." She wagged an incriminating index finger at her husband.

He laughed and then sipped his coffee.

Dawn sighed. "I like hanging onto the fantasy as long as I can—that they'll both come."

Jim thrummed his fingers on the tabletop. "That would be wonderful if all three of my favorite gals could make it to the cottage this summer."

Yes, it would be. "I'll call Tammy right now before I change my mind."

"Good idea, Doll."

Dawn tapped out the numbers.

"Hi Mom." Was that a sniffle?

"Hi Tammy. I can't believe I actually caught you on the phone!" Dawn's words came out in a rush as she focused on her plea. "I'm going to ask you while I can get it out. Would you please, please come up this summer and stay with me?"

Jim cupped his hands around his mouth and hollered, "And bring my granddaughter, too."

"To Chicago?" Was Tammy sniffing again?

Probably fighting a cold. That was the problem with her working in a public school all the time. *Germs.*

"No, no, Daddy wants me to go ahead and go to Butterfly Cottage, but he doesn't want me to be there by myself."

"I, um, I'm in the middle of a bunch of things here."

"Oh." Her shoulders sagged.

"But, um, next week maybe I could let you know." It definitely wasn't like her daughter to sound so wishy-washy.

"Are you worried about Brad giving you a hard time?"

"No!" Tamara's response was so quick, so blunt, that Dawn flinched.

"Oh. Okay."

Jim yelled, "I'll send ya gas money, sweetie, if you need it."

"When are you going?" The fatigue in her daughter's voice cleared.

"I'll drive to the cottage a few days before you come. And it would be wonderful if Jaycie could join us."

"It'll depend on her internship, but she doesn't have one yet."

"How could that be? She's so talented."

"I don't know why. But I've got a few irons in the fire I need to deal with here."

"Care to share?"

There was silence for so long that Dawn wondered if Tammy's phone had lost the signal. "You still there?"

Tammy made some kind of noise of agreement.

"Tell you what I can do. I'll call in a favor and see if we can't find Jaycie an internship on the island. I know just the guy to ask."

"Who?"

"I'll ask our friend, Clark Jeffries, if there might be something for her."

"Oh. Great. He's pretty amazing with all he's done for the Mackinac State Parks."

"Darn right, he is. I pray that guy never retires!" Or was Clark feeling like she was—that it was time to step back?

Dawn listened, waiting for her daughter to respond, but she didn't hear any classroom noise in the background, from Tammy's phone.

"Hey, are you home today? Is it a holiday or are you sick?"

"Um, I will be having a doctor's appointment."

"You don't have the flu, do you? You got your flu shot?"

"I got the shot. I think I'll let Dr. Forbes tell me what's going on."

"Tell him to bring his family up North, again, sometime soon." They were related, on Jim's side and had all kinds of kin living near the Straits.

"Sure, Mom." Her tone said otherwise.

Dawn chuckled. "Reminds me of how you used to sound when you were a little younger than Jaycie is now."

"Hey, let's not tell Jaycie about me asking Mr. Jeffries, though. You know how independent she is."

"Agreed." It sounded like Tammy was blowing her nose. Being a teacher definitely had its downsides.

"Thanks, sweetie."

"I've got to work on a few things this morning but I'll call you back soon so we can talk some more."

"Super."

"Love you, Mom."

"Love you, too."

The terriers both circled Dawn's legs as she put the phone back on the receiver. "I suppose you scamps think you're getting treats, don't you?"

Hard Rock's big dark eyes lit up and Cici barked as if in agreement.

"All right, all right. You were nice and quiet during the call. Stop with the puppy eyes."

Jim laughed. "Aw, Ma, give them something already, won't ya?"

She shot him a scowl. "As if I wouldn't, Pa."

She pulled two small Milk-Bone treats from the counter cookie jar and handed one to each pup. Then the two ran straight to Jim. "Traitors," she called after them.

"You know who Hard Rock loves best." Jim pulled the Yorkie onto his lap. Cici slumped at his feet.

"Cici's more my kind of pet." One that didn't require a lot of coddling.

"Well, what did our daughter say?"

Dawn clapped her hands together. "She's busy right now with something. Sounded kind of strange."

Jim scowled. "Probably that husband of hers."

"She sounded sick."

"Oh. But she didn't say no?"

"Nope." That was encouraging. "She might end up coming."

Jim gave her the thumbs up. "Let's be positive about this."

"I'm going to ask our friend at the parks to see if he can find something for Jaycie to do this summer. Still no internship."

"Wow, really? Nothing for our granddaughter?"

"Looking like it."

"But maybe Clark might have something?"

"Hope so." Dawn tugged at the bottom of her shirt to straighten it.

"I assume Brad will be working."

"She'd said a while back that he's traveling more since his headaches are resolving. But he's on a lot of business trips for a big project."

"Shipyard work can be demanding."

Demanding all right. Just like their son-in-law. "Let me go send off an email to Clark before I forget."

Dawn kicked off her shoes and padded down the hall to the home office. She powered on her computer and waited. This might really happen. She wanted to pinch herself. Tammy might come for the summer.

In the past, Brad's migraines worsened when he traveled and he usually didn't come, which also kept Tammy at home many summers. It seemed strange that he still traveled for work but not for family, but Dawn had bitten her tongue about it. She'd been fortunate to never have struggled with the debilitating condition herself.

Dawn sat down and logged onto the computer. After she emailed their friend, to ask for a spot for Jaycie, she'd make a packing list. She still needed to clear her head and make some solid decisions about selling her agency. Barb was breathing down her neck and if Dawn was up North she could claim she didn't have good internet— which was true.

She'd operate on hope. She'd need the suitcases from the basement. Not that she had to bring a lot to the cottage—they'd left lots of basic clothing there and all the linens and towels they needed. They'd even kept their bikes in the basement.

She opened her personal Gmail account and searched her emails. One from Jaycie popped out at her. She tentatively clicked on it. Dawn scanned the message.

> *Hi Gran!*
>
> *Oxford has been great but now I am packed to come back to the states. :(But I think it's time. Not that I have anything to come back to because no internship yet. Big sigh. . . Mom's praying for me, though, and I guess that counts for something. Maybe I'll go home and flip burgers—which is what Dad said a degree in archeology would get for me. :(:(*
>
> *Love you Gran!*
>
> *J*

Well, that backed up what Tammy had said. So Jaycie still had nothing. An errant heart palpitation started its trot across her chest. Ugh. Jim was right. She'd probably better see the heart doctor in Petoskey when she got to the cottage. She'd call tomorrow. Dr.

Zaitoun in Michigan had insisted that she see a cardiologist in the Chicago area, too. And she had. The local doctor wondered what Dawn was doing at her cardiology office since Dawn was in such great health. She told Dawn that heart palpitations were very common, and that Dawn should only come back if they got worse. Which they had recently.

Manage your stress. Hadn't the Straits of Mackinac always brought serenity? She'd find out soon if this summer would bring back some normalcy into her life. And help her figure out what next steps she needed to take on this new journey of retirement.

Providing it *was* only stress and not her heart.

Chapter Five

Tamara
Yorktown, Virginia

Tamara sat, cross-legged on her couch, mulling over the previous few days since her world had imploded. She should shower. Or at least think about doing so. Instead, all she could manage was to rehash the last few days.

After work, on the day when she'd won Teacher of the Year, she'd decided to celebrate the award with her husband.

For the first time in a while, she'd had her favorite stylist not only give her a new cut, but also style her hair into a little more youthful looking hairstyle.

"You look dope, Miss Tamara," the young woman assured her.

"Dope?"

"Yeah. You look good." With a nasal ring and pink frizzy hair, maybe Sarah wasn't the right person to be styling Tamara's hair. But she did a great job.

"Jaycie is supposed to be home soon."

"Awesome. We'll have to chill." She pointed a slim black comb at a picture of her toddler on the mirror. "I'll get a babysitter."

Tamara couldn't imagine Jaycie with a child. Her daughter was too adventurous—not ready to settle down. "If you can't find one, you can always call me. I'm babysitting my cousin Willa's dog when she's out of town."

Sarah's dark eyebrows rose slowly. "Woah, that's right. Isn't Willa Christy related to y'all?"

"Yes, she's my third cousin."

"Ah, I think Jaycie said that." Sarah gave a slow nod. "My boyfriend and I love her show."

Tamara was really happy for Willa to have her HGTV series, which focused on remodeling far-off resorts. "I do, too."

The stylist removed Tamara's cape. "What are you and your hubby doin' tonight?"

"I'm going to surprise him by taking him to Tuscany's to celebrate my award."

"Awesome! I love that place." She shook the cape out.

After she paid and gave Sarah a generous tip, Tamara drove home. The first dress she tried on seemed weirdly loose. She went to the guest room and pulled out a blue surplice dress that had gotten too tight. Fit perfectly now. She looked younger—more like the person she'd used to be, before Brad's constant emotional distancing had her turning to extra snacks for comfort.

She donned a pair of patent leather navy heels. For the first time in a while, she opened her jewelry case and then put on a pair of diamond earrings from Mom and Dad. Impulsively, she grabbed her charm bracelet, heavy with silver charms from various travels—mostly with her parents.

She checked in the bathroom mirror, to make sure that her makeup was just right. Dark circles still shone beneath her eyes and she put a little concealer on them. Too bad there wasn't a tool you could use to magically correct the problems in your marriage.

Finally, she was ready to leave for the Riverside Wellness Center to meet Brad. Rush hour traffic slowed her progress. The car clock showed she still had plenty of time, when she pulled into the parking lot. Since it was pretty full of vehicles from people exercising after work, she parked in the one open spot, farther back in the lot.

Tamara listened to KLove radio for a while. She touched up her lipstick. Would Brad be excited for her? She didn't doubt that he'd expect her to pay for the meal, but at this point, she needed to do whatever it took to get him to reconnect with her.

The glass door to the building opened. Her handsome husband, head bent over his cell phone exited the building. She unlatched her seatbelt. She was about to open the door, when she spied a very pregnant woman hurrying up the sidewalk toward Brad. He smiled broadly at her.

For the first time in what seemed like a year, he looked genuinely happy.

With the woman's long dark hair in curls to the middle of her back, it looked to be Gina. She was one of the young women from his office, a fellow marine engineer.

Tamara leaned forward in the car seat. Why was Gina trying to work-out in her advanced state of pregnancy? Tamara drew in a steadying breath and watched.

Brad beamed at Gina. Her husband of over twenty-five years opened his arms wide, then pulled the much shorter woman into an embrace. Heat flooded Tamara's face.

Maybe it was only a hug. Colleagues.

Tamara held her breath.

Gina pulled back and gazed up. Brad bent and kissed her full on the mouth.

Passionately kissed the other woman in a way that her husband of over twenty-five years hadn't kissed his own wife in ages.

She pressed back into her seat. Her stomach spasmed and she was sure she'd be sick. But she wasn't.

This was a bad dream. A nightmare. It had to be. All of her worst fears about Brad were coming true.

She watched, feeling like a stalker as her husband and his lover got into Gina's SUV and drove off. Tamara sat there for what surely must be hours. But when she'd checked the clock, it showed only fifteen minutes.

She pulled out of the Wellness Center and began to drive aimlessly through Newport News. When she passed a place that held special memories, she'd shed more tears. She drove on to Yorktown, stopping at places where they'd gone as a family.

She'd fought back the desire to call Jaycie in England. That would be a bad move. Tamara drove to the church parking lot at Northside, and sat there, in the dark. Pastor Larry was long gone, as were the other staff members. Still, she felt better knowing that she had a church family she could turn to.

Finally, she pulled into her driveway. All of her favorite spring flowers, that she'd lovingly placed in the gardens, were in bloom. The beauty of them taunted her. She couldn't live here anymore. Like that old song said, "Love don't live here anymore."

Instead of pulling into the garage, Tamara called Susan.

"Hey, girlfriend, did you have a good time?" Her friend's upbeat voice tripped off something in her that triggered a new waterfall of tears.

Ruby was gone. Now Brad would be, too. She stifled sobs and tried to say something to her friend. The grief she'd experienced from a year ago with her dear friend's death now doubled.

"Tamara? You all right?"

She reached for a tissue and blew her nose. Choking back sobs, she managed, "Brad. . ." then broke down into more sobs.

"What did Brad do? If he didn't go out and celebrate with you, I'll come right over there and smack him upside the head!"

Tamara shuddered out two breaths. "Caught. . . him. . . cheating."

"What?" Susan's outraged voice was so loud that Tamara had to pull the phone away from her ear.

A sudden realization cheered her up. She drew in a steadying breath. "He. . . Brad doesn't know that. . . I saw them." This gave her time to regroup.

"I'm coming over there right now and we're gonna make some plans."

And they had.

Now, two days later, Tamara had surreptitiously completed many of those actions that she and Susan had discussed. She'd scheduled with a divorce attorney but had to wait for the next week. She'd moved into the guest room, telling Brad that her stomach pain was waking her up in the night. No surprise to her, he didn't object. Just looking at him, though, made her enraged. But she had to finish some things.

At least Tamara wouldn't have to hear Dr. Forbes' advice about seeking marriage counseling again. At her appointment that afternoon she'd tell him that her marriage was over.

Tamara sipped her tea. She spilled some on her pants, the same sweats that she'd put on two days earlier. She hadn't been able to make herself return to her job. Between Brad's actions and her gut problems, she couldn't function. If she went to the school, she'd be like a zombie. A zombie who cried while teaching. A zombie who scared her kids and fellow staff members.

Utter humiliation. Her desire to teach eleven months a year had vanished. But she couldn't let Brad steal that from her.

Her phone rang. It was Susan, so she answered.

"Hey, Susan."

"How're you doing?"

"Numb. Then outraged. Then numb, again."

"I'm so sorry."

Tamara lifted her 'God is Love' emblazoned mug. "I am praying about the next steps to take."

"John and I are praying for you, too."

"Thank you." Tamara sipped her tea. "I did make a good decision right this minute."

"What's that?"

"I'm going to shower for the first time since I caught that cheater."

Susan laughed. "You go, girl!"

Those words, meant to be lighthearted, stirred something in Tamara. *You go, girl.* Mom had called and invited her up to the cottage—her and Jaycie.

"You know, I think you're exactly right." She still longed for a July spent at Butterfly Cottage. Brad hadn't destroyed that desire.

Chapter Six

Jaycie
Yorktown, Virginia, May

Still reeling from the lack of Dad's presence in their home, Jaycie stared at her phone. *Happy you got an internship.* Mom's details about Dad's absence were sketchy while Dad's text about the archeology dig job on Mackinac Island was self-explanatory.

Although she'd applied for the Mackinac job months earlier, she had gotten no response. Not even a simple email rejection. She'd been told she wouldn't hear anything unless she'd been hired. But to finally get notified at this late date? Still, she smiled to herself at her good luck.

She got out of bed and followed the scent of the strongly brewed Columbian coffee her mother favored to the kitchen. She and Elliott used to enjoy a bistro near the university that offered a huge selection of coffees, including this brand. Once again, a shot of anger, sadness, and a huge case of what-might-have-been coursed through her.

Maybe her boyfriend had publicly dumped her but as Gran and Grandpa had always said, "Roll with the punches." Grandpa would make fake jabs at the air to demonstrate his point. Maybe Jaycie was rolling, but it was more like a squirrel rolling downhill over rocks and grabbing at an acorn along the way. The Mackinac Island job was her acorn. She had something. And she'd celebrate it despite all the rocks along the way—like Dad not being there to greet her upon her return.

"Good morning, Sunshine." Mom stood by the sink, packing an insulated bag with water and ice packs.

Ugh, we're really driving up North today. "Jet lag stinks."

Mom turned and waved a hand toward the kitchen island on which sat a bowl of cut fresh fruit and a big oatmeal muffin. "Eat your breakfast. I want to get on the road soon."

The pit in her stomach deepened. "Seems weird that Dad's not here."

Her mother stood stock still but then her shoulders relaxed. "It's good that he felt well enough to travel on business, again."

"I'm sorry that he's mad at you, about us leaving before your contract is up for the year." Mom had never, ever, left before her school year teaching contract was over.

Mom, her back still toward Jaycie, stopped shoving bottles into the bag. "My wonderful principal, Mrs. Evans, totally supports us going early for your internship." Was it Jaycie's imagination or was Mom forcing cheerfulness into her words?

"After all these years you've worked there, I'm not surprised she's okay with that." She cast her mother a glance, but Mom kept her back turned.

"Well, it helps that we have a student teacher in the building who she's contracting for next year. It's her chance to prove herself on her own in my classroom." Mom swiveled around and sure enough that was one of her fake smiles that didn't even come close to reaching her eyes.

"Good thing for you, right?" Jaycie tried to gauge what was going on with her mom.

"Yeah." Mom gave her a weak smile. "She's the best we've ever had. Melinda really wants to keep her at Yorktown Elementary."

"I know you love your kids, Mom." Maybe Mom was just upset about making this decision. "And for you to leave your classroom early for my internship makes me feel special." Jaycie joined her mother by the counter and gave her a big hug.

To her surprise, her mother's body shook with silent sobs. Jaycie pulled back to see tears streaming down her mother's face. Mom pulled her close again and patted her back.

"I'm. . . so glad. . . you're back." Mom choked out a sob.

"I'm glad to be here, Mom." Sometimes it was hard being an only child. Guilt set in. Jaycie had missed her mom, too, had even shed some tears. But not enough to break down over it, maybe because she'd already exhausted her supply of tears on unfaithful Elliott. How had she missed her mother's distress over her absence? *Yikes.* She'd make sure they spent some quality time together this summer.

An hour later, Jaycie had showered and then she and her mother were on their way for a two-day journey North. They'd finally get a chance to talk. Once on the road, though, Jaycie's jetlag took on a life of its own and she'd slept every time her mother drove. When Jaycie drove, her mother napped, the tolls of her school year and the separation catching up with her. Mom often spent that first two weeks of post-school year days snoozing or binge-watching Netflix.

Hours later, they stopped to eat dinner at a Bob Evans Restaurant in Pennsylvania, Mom's favorite place to stop on road trips.

Their waitress, a smiling middle-aged woman whose loose brown curls framed her round face, slid two Mason jars full of water onto their table. "What'll you have, ladies?" She pulled her order pad from her pocket.

Mom, who'd slept the last leg of the journey, stared at her iPhone.

"Mom, didn't you say you wanted the Farmhouse salad?"

Her mother dipped her head in agreement and set her phone down. As soon as she placed their orders, Jaycie would ask what her lack of verbal response was all about.

The waitress gave her mother a curious glance.

"She always takes ranch dressing."

Mom shoved her menu away and dug in her coral Coach purse for a tissue.

"I'll have your best real American burger, all the way, and fries." Jaycie handed her menu to the waitress. "And a Coke for me and an Arnold Palmer for my mom."

The woman glanced between the two of them, concern etched on her brow. She patted Mom's shoulder. "There's no problem too deep that God can't fix it."

Mom glanced up, then nodded. The waitress departed and Mom blew her nose gently.

"What's going on, Mom?"

"Your dad," was all she managed.

Guilt struck her hard. "I'm so sorry. I should have gone first, by myself. I bet he's pretty steamed about you leaving."

Mom compressed her lips.

"It'll be all right."

Her mother fixed her with a gaze that said otherwise.

Jaycie tapped her fingernails on the tabletop. "Dad can be a pain when it comes to the finances." He'd had a cow when Jaycie had used some of her longtime savings to travel to England. He, Mom, and Jaycie had argued over the year abroad for what seemed like weeks before Grandma Dawn had gotten involved. Gran called in some favors at her travel agency and got Jaycie free airfare for her round-trip ticket. And Grandpa Jim had sent a check to cover most other expenses.

"He's. . . not happy with. . . some decisions I've made." Mom clasped her hands in her lap and closed her eyes, as if in prayer. She drew in a shuddering breath and looked up. "It's not your fault, Jaycie. This is between Daddy and me."

"You've had your share of money squabbles over the years."

"Yes, we have." Mom gave a curt laugh. "But this will be all right. *Eventually.*"

Mom fixed her with a poignant gaze, like someone did when they were about to say goodbye for a long time—but Jaycie had just come home.

A chill coursed through her. Had the restaurant staff cranked up the air conditioning? She stilled, trying to be mindful. Her mother bent her head again, as though in prayer. Mom had a strong faith, but this last week her emails to Jaycie in the UK had taken on a different tone. Kind of scary religious. Every decision Mom made she'd said she was consulting God, and she'd urged Jaycie to do the same. Which of course, Jaycie dismissed as more 'Mom wisdom' that was reaching over the top.

She needed to change the topic to something less upsetting than dealing with Dad. "Mom, you'll never believe who I saw in England." Of course, she hadn't mentioned Parker nor his kiss. She'd never have heard the end of it.

Her mother's face brightening a little. "Who?"

Jaycie made a teasing face. She needed to coax Mom out of her funk. "You have to guess first."

Her mother raised her palm. "All right. All right. Three clues."

Handsome was her first thought, but Jaycie scowled that clue away. "Irritating."

"Your dad sure didn't cough up the change to fly over there himself so, hmmm." Bitterness tinged her words. "Another clue?"

Startling blue eyes. That was three words. But one clue. But not what she was looking for. "University of Virginia."

Her mother's pretty features twisted into shock. "What? No way! He did *not* show up there."

Jaycie chuckled then swigged her water. "Yes, ma'am, he sure did."

Mom gaped. "Not Parker?"

"And you will never ever in a million years guess who his cousins are over there."

Mom's eyebrows drew together.

"Keep frowning and you'll need the Botox treatment you've been threatening to get." Jaycie laughed. "I'll tell you. He's related to some of the aristocrats who live near Oxford. No kidding."

"The Rutherfords?"

"Yeah, how did you know?"

"Wild guess."

"Mom, that is not a wild guess."

"All right. Your grandma told me that his grandmother was from some kind of aristocratic family over there." She sipped her water. "And I remembered meeting Lady Rutherford once."

"Oh." Suddenly deflated, Jaycie huffed a breath. "Anyway, I did. . ." What could she say? *I kissed him and then let him continue with abandon and I liked it? I used Parker to punish my cheating boyfriend? Or that my sad attempt to do so backfired on me?*

"You did what?" Mom encouraged.

"I. . . uh. . . it doesn't really matter. But I did see him there."

Mom's knowing eyes took on a sparkle. "Methinks thou dost protest over-much of your annoyance with Parker."

"What do you mean?"

"Over your years at UVA, I've heard enough stories about him to think that he's on your mind a lot."

"Yeah, but not in a good way." Her cheeks heated. "Not usually."

Mom quirked one eyebrow but said nothing more.

The waitress returned and deftly slid their orders in front of them. Mom led them in a brief prayer and then speared a tomato and dipped it into her side dish of Ranch dressing.

"You know what's ironic?" Jaycie squeezed ketchup on her French fries.

"What?"

"I heard from some friends at UVA that Parker will be working at Colonial Williamsburg, not even twelve miles from where Dad works."

"Where you interned? And got rejected this year?" Disgust tinged her mother's voice. Mom was her fearless advocate. "After you worked so hard for them."

"Yeah, he can enjoy the one-hundred-degree effective temperature at the site. But what's ironic is that while he's in our geographic backyard, I'll be on Mackinac Island digging up artifacts only a stone's throw from one of his father's many properties."

"God has a funny sense of humor, doesn't he?"

If God did, then the joke was on her. Because for the first time since she was fifteen, she'd actually sort of wished, a tiny smidge of a wish, that Parker would be on Mackinac when she was. Before he'd become a morose teenager and then an obnoxious college student who spent most of his weekends partying with his frat house buddies and arriving disheveled at classes, still hungover on Mondays. And why did his misbehavior bother her so much? *Because he's so much better than that, so smart, so sweet.*

But God would have to deal with him, as Mom often said about people stuck in bad behavior.

"I think He's pretty smart, actually." She bit into her burger and savored the taste.

Mom cocked her head. "Parker?"

"His Father, God. God's pretty smart." She rubbed the back of her neck, stiff from driving. "He put me an ocean away from Elliott and soon Parker will be almost a thousand miles from me."

"I'm glad you're thinking about God again."

God hadn't exactly been a priority lately.

Mom set her fork down on her plate. "Sometimes space is good."

Was Mom talking about herself and Dad or about Jaycie and Parker?

Her mother pushed her plate away. "Time apart can bring healing."

A pretty deep thought and probably true. "You, me, and Gran this summer on our own." And none of the troublesome men in her and Mom's lives.

Chapter Seven

Dawn
Mackinaw City, Michigan

Outside the cottage's expanse of windows, silver-gray clouds banked over the Straits of Mackinac, so high they seemed to touch the heavens, portending one of May's blustering showers. Dawn hung the cottage's new calendar on the wall. Unlike in summers past, she'd not be working remotely, her laptop at the ready and cellphone pinging all day long. Without Jim here, her activity consisted mostly of walking the dog and making the cottage ready for the girls.

Sometime today, Tammy and Jaycie would join her.

She inhaled the scent of the decaf Columbia brewing on the counter.

Cici pressed her tiny body against Dawn's leg.

"How did I let you talk me into bringing you with me, you little scamp?" Dawn bent and lifted the Silky Terrier. "I bet Hard Rock is missing you back home." And keeping Jim good company.

The dog looked up, her wide eyes almost suggesting that she understood Dawn's words. She carried Cici over to look out the window at the water. "If your Papa Jim was here he'd have announced, 'Another big one brewin' this afternoon!' wouldn't he?"

She set the dog down.

Regardless of any storms, she still had some spiffing up to do of this place. Dust bunnies to corral. She grabbed a pink feather duster from the counter and ran it over the oak frame case that held Jim's Coast Guard insignia and medals. She continued dusting, lightly flicking the feathers over a collage photo of them ballroom dancing, playing Pickle Ball with some locals, serving cookies and lemonade to the kids at the local VBS. *Such a full life.* They'd had a blessed life. And, according to his physical therapist, soon he'd be back in the thick of things.

Her landline rang, an olive green 1970's Ma Bell Slimline that still functioned fine. She and Jim had decided to keep it functioning, although they both had cell phones, too. But she was guilty of leaving her ringer off most of the time, and often didn't hear the cell phone vibrate. She lifted the landline receiver. "Hello?"

"Mrs. Charbonneau, it's Pastor Dave."

"It'd good to hear from you."

"You're here early this year."

She eyed the calendar and straightened it. "And for longer, too."

"Really?"

"Yes."

"Wow, then you are the answer to my prayers. That is, if you can help with VBS this year."

Dawn's spine stiffened. She sat down by the dining table. Hadn't she just been wondering about what to do with herself, too? She could find plenty of things to do with Tamara. But Dawn had been so used to working, even at the cottage. "What did you have in mind?"

Dave spelled out the needs they had. "I think you'd be best with more of the management stuff."

She rubbed her eyes. "You know I'm not yet officially retired and you're already putting me to work."

"Oh, sorry." He sounded genuinely contrite.

Was this where the rubber met the road, as Jim liked to say? She'd need to find some volunteer activities in retirement, didn't she? Could she really let go of her agency? "I'll do it." Those words flew out of her lipsticked mouth before she could even stop them.

Cici dropped at Dawn's feet and closed her eyes. Even the dog seemed to be questioning what Dawn had just gotten herself into.

"That's just great, Mrs. Charbonneau."

"Aren't we still on a first name basis? I'm still Dawn."

"And I'm still Dave." He laughed. "We'll have our first meeting this week."

"Already?" she squeaked. The girls would have just arrived. But Jaycie had to start work right away and Tammy had already said she was claiming the remote and the tv for the first week for a Netflix binge.

"Yeah, we lost a couple of our volunteers and we've got to get on top of this."

"I've got the same email address, so send me the info."

"Will do. And thanks so much."

"You're welcome." That sounded so much better than saying, 'no problem' didn't it?

Dawn hung up the phone. It rang again.

"Mom?" Tamara's breathy voice sounded much like the girlish voice she'd once possessed.

"Tammy?" Dawn pressed her free hand on the smooth tabletop.

"It's me, Mom." Tammy seemed to suck in a breath. "We're at the Ohio border already but we're stopping for lunch."

"Great!" Dawn couldn't help her excitement. This felt better than landing a corporate client had ever felt. Maybe retirement would be filled with happy new memories. And she'd learn how to incorporate volunteer activities into her life. If that didn't work out well, maybe she'd have to reconsider selling the agency.

"I wanted to ask a favor."

"Sure, anything." This was her baby girl after all.

"Well, I know you like to keep a room for guests, and Jaycie and I usually share, but. . ."

Worry niggled at her. Two of her cousins had already asked to visit. Drat that she'd drank a cup of regular coffee that morning from the bakery and now her palps were off like horses out of the gate at the Arlington racetrack. If Jim had come with her, he'd have ensured she'd chosen a cup of decaf. "Tammy, I should have thought of that. With you and Jaycie spending the whole summer, I'm sure you'd rather we don't have too many guests."

Truth be told, Dawn would rather stop operating as a B&B, too, which some of her family members seemed to think Butterfly Cottage was.

"Yeah, Jaycie needs her privacy more now that she's older."

"Sure thing." Should she tell her daughter about the cousins who'd asked to stay? She'd deal with it later.

"Jaycie can have the guest room." And she'd have to let the cousins know they didn't have room after all. She'd get put on some "bad lists" for sure.

Dawn may not be the most maternal of women, but she could prioritize. Tammy almost never asked favors. This was the least she could do for her.

"I think that's best for this summer, Mom."

The summer season ran pretty much from late June until two weeks into August. "Can you believe you'll get to stay four whole months this time?" Retirement could mean she and Jim could spend months and months up there, too.

Was that a sob? Dawn heard another one. Jaycie had called her the night before and told her that her dad was fighting with her mom over money again.

That blasted tight-fisted Brad. In contrast to herself and Jim, both outgoing people, her son-in-law was also an extreme introvert. He barely spoke to them when they had visited. An engineering manager at the Huntington Ingalls Shipyard, he worked a lot of overtime, including even when she and Jim had been in Virginia for holidays. How her sweet daughter ended up with this lump of a man, she didn't know. But she had. He'd always been emotionally detached, and they'd gone through a few rounds of marriage therapy over the years. Tammy always blamed Brad's issues on his headaches, and Dawn had never corrected her. Seeing how grumpy Jim had been since his knee surgery, she was beginning to understand how irritable Brad must get with his migraines.

"Gran?" Jaycie had taken over the phone. Her voice quavered.

"Oh honey, I wish I hadn't said anything about your mom getting to stay all summer. She's probably thinking about your dad and how normally she couldn't be here that long."

"It's all right, Gran. And I hope you don't mind about Mom needing more time to herself this year. If you need me to strong-arm the guests to keep them from getting in, I'll help."

Dawn laughed at that image. "No strong-arming needed. I'll make the two calls to cancel the ones who'd hoped to visit."

"Planned on imposing, you mean." Jaycie chuckled. "The ones who invite themselves and don't help you at all."

"Call it what you want."

"See you soon."

"Can't wait. Love you!"

"Love you, too."

She hung up the phone.

Dawn finished cleaning the living room. She glared out at the clouds, which had finally let loose.

Rain burst from thunderclouds and poured down on the mostly empty streets. A couple of tourists ran to their car and scrambled inside. Lightning jagged across the Straits of Mackinac, an awesome sight over the azure water. The storm had come, and it would go. She could count on that fact. If only Tammy's situation was as easily resolved.

Once Dawn retired she could be more available to her only child. Could spend more time with her. Maybe her daughter needed her more than her employees at the agency. She wanted to be needed, to help others, to matter.

Tamara

"Walmart, here we come!" Mom scrunched up her face in faux cheerfulness and Tamara couldn't help but laugh.

Jaycie wrinkled her nose. Her daughter hated Walmart. *Big time.*

"I appreciate you going with your grandmother to help shop." Tamara really needed to head to the island. If her mom and daughter wanted to think that she just wanted rest, that was fine.

"First we'll have a wonderful lunch together, then stroll around Cheboygan." Mom's face glowed. "After that, Walmart better look out for us! Power shoppers—grandmother and granddaughter."

"I don't think you need to worry about what you'll be doing during retirement, Mom." If only Tamara possessed that same energy.

Jaycie nodded. "We probably won't be back until dinnertime."

"We'll call and see what you want us to bring back." Mom grabbed her purse and they left.

Tamara waited until her mother and daughter pulled out of their parking spot. She could catch the next ferry if she hurried. She went to her bedroom and grabbed the mini backpack that she'd fixed the previous night. No one here to *question* what she was doing, thank the Lord. Tamara wasn't ready to explain. She'd get back in plenty of time before Mom and Jaycie returned, and they'd never know she'd left.

How would they feel if she was gone? If she never returned?

Her phone text notification buzzed as she locked the house door and left. Likely another text message from Brad. She sighed and pulled out the phone.

What did you do with my accounts?

She was tempted to text back, "Just what you deserve."

Luckily, there'd be little satellite coverage once she got out on the water. She'd only leave her phone on in case Hamp needed to reach her. If anyone understood the angst she was going through, it was her long-time friend. His wife, Amanda, had overdosed the previous year and he'd been on an emotional roller coaster. What a tragedy for Hamp and his kids.

She walked as quickly as she could to the dock. A long queue of people stood waiting for the next ferry to the island. She pulled her ticket from her wallet, glad she'd snuck out and purchased it the night before. Since she didn't have to go to the ticket counter, she strode over to the line.

All those happy families standing there. All those couples who looked so in love. What had Tamara done wrong? Why didn't she have what they had? She crossed her arms over her chest. She stood a little way back from the people ahead of her, a silver-haired woman and man. Their relaxed body language suggested they were a long-married couple.

She would not cry. Just because she'd never have a uber long marriage. . .

Her text indicator buzzed again. She drew in a deep breath.

Look at me, look at me, her phone beckoned.

I'm so weak. Tamara gave into temptation and pulled out her phone. Lately, she wasn't just emotionally weaker, but her stamina was giving out.

At least it wasn't Brad. It was from her doctor's office.

All the sound around her, all the cheerful voices, grew silent. She'd heard of this happening to people, but she'd never experienced herself. It was as though she were suddenly deaf. The next ferry angled toward the dock and although people around her jumped, she didn't react. She hadn't even heard what surely was a loud ferry horn blast.

If she opened the text from the doctor's office then everything would be too real.

Someone poked her back.

She turned.

A teenaged boy, his ballcap on backwards, pointed ahead. "The line is moving."

Indeed, the people ahead of her were now about ten feet up. She caught up with them.

When she got inside the boat, she slid onto the bench seat in the back. Then she opened the message.

Dr. Forbes asked if you scheduled your consultation in Michigan yet? Please advise us where to send your records.

She pressed her spine against the back rest, as the passengers took their seats. At least she could answer that text message easily. Not only did she have an appointment with the specialist, Dr. Thomas Austin, but he came highly recommended. She'd grab his address when she got back home to the Wi-Fi and send that info to her primary care doctor's office.

Primary care? If things went as she suspected, then Tamara would never be returning to Virginia.

Her vision fogged and she blinked.

Today she'd see an old friend, commiserate, enjoy some of her favorite things on the island. Her head told her that she should not seek out Hamp, because he had his own issues to deal with. But her soul urged her to reconnect, that there was a reason they needed to be there for each other. Ruby would have told her to *listen to the Lord and forget what man said.* Forget that her mother would have cautioned her and that her daughter would think it unwise.

There was no guarantee of tomorrow. Not for anyone. One thing she did know—God held her life in His hands. What she made of what she had of this life was between her and the Lord. And she was going to keep it that way.

Chapter Eight

Jaycie
Mackinac Island, Michigan

First day of internship or first day of a nightmare?
Acid filled Jaycie's gut as she glanced past the Director of the Mackinac State Parks, Clark Jeffries, and at the intern in the other room, bent over a map. Someone she knew all too well. Her lower jaw slacked open, then she pressed her lips back together.

"You'll be working with Hampton Parker III this summer." Mr. Jeffries smiled benevolently at her.

How could the man grin like that? Didn't he realize what he'd unloaded on her? She managed a nod.

"He prefers to go by Parker, though." His sandy eyebrows drew together. Tall, attired in pressed khakis, a starched white shirt, and a navy and gold pin striped tie, Mr. Jeffries appeared every bit the professional he was reported to be. And his stiff shoulders suggested he'd expected more of a response from her. Didn't he know? How could he not realize—she and Parker were both from the same program.

"I...uh, Parker and I..."

In the adjacent room, Parker looked up from his map and smiled at his supervisor before glancing at Jaycie. His tanned face began to pale. Then he straightened and shuffled the map on his desk.

Their director called out, "Come on in here, Parker, and get introduced."

When Parker didn't move, but stared at them, Mr. Jeffries took slow appraising glances between them. "You two are acquainted?"

"UVA," Jaycie mumbled.

Clark Jeffries feigned a palm smack to his forehead, for a moment seeming much younger than his age, which was somewhere between Mom's and Gran's. "Of course, I should have known that. Your grandmother mentioned you'd attended school in Virginia."

What did Gran have to do with this? "You know my grandmother?" Hadn't he just said so? Her cheeks heated. *No, no, no, this was not good. Didn't I get this spot on my own? Gran is gonna get an earful later. She should have told me.*

Parker languidly strolled into the room, his clothing almost a complete match for Mr. Jeffries's, which seemed odd, since Parker should be going out to the dig, shouldn't he? He extended his hand and when she clasped it, a frisson of something seemed to jump between them. She quickly released his hand and backed away, right into the director's globe, set on a high oak stand, which threatened to tumble. Parker reached past her and righted the stand before it could fall and caught the globe.

"Good catch, Parker." Mr. Jeffries grinned as if the two of them were good buddies. They probably had known each other all their lives.

"Thanks! I've often come in behind Jaycie and rescued her." Parker's lids half-closed, a smirk tugging at his perfect lips.

Jaycie fixed him with a stare. He couldn't be deliberately bringing up the incident in England. Not the kiss. "When was that? When we were ten and biking around the island by ourselves?" That had been a scary day when they'd been caught in a downpour, but Parker had taken her to a small cottage in the woods where they'd waited it out. He could not dare be implying that he'd bailed her out at college. A head of steam began to build inside her. "Certainly not at university." There, she'd occasionally assisted his study group when they'd gotten pitifully behind.

Mr. Jeffries removed his tortoiseshell-rimmed eyeglasses and wiped at the lenses. Jaycie read the motion as a caution to both of them and gritted her teeth. She needed this job.

Parker shifted his weight, his expensive loafers screaming 'privileged' from beneath his equally costly tailored khaki's. "You must have a short memory. I recently saved you in England, from. . ." He had the nerve to cock his head and offer a self-satisfied smile.

"You're right," Jaycie interrupted with forced enthusiasm. "If it hadn't been for you, I'd have been run right over." It seemed like the truth. Ok, a half-truth, but Elliott had run over her like a Mack truck.

Mr. Jeffries smiled. "You know what they say—always look to the right on the street over there, not to the left."

"Right." Jaycie squeezed out a chuckle, eyeing Parker.

"I think you mean, 'Correct'." Parker took a step closer to her. He patted her arm, condescendingly. "I'm looking forward to being your supervisor this summer."

Her stomach lurched as she swiveled to face Mr. Jeffries. "I, um, I thought Dr. Evans was the Archeology Supervisor at the sites."

Averting her gaze, Mr. Jeffries scratched his neck. "I'm not sure if either of you will actually be sent to the digs. But for now, Parker will supervise the paperwork the two of you will be doing."

Parker swept his hand toward a desk near his.

Could this summer get any worse?

Dawn
Mackinaw City

Dawn patted her completed shell-pattern baby blanket with satisfaction. Pastor Dave had asked if she'd make one for his new grandson, and she'd been happy to oblige.

The front screen door to the cottage creaked open and then banged closed. "Mom?"

Time was flying by. They'd established a couple of habits, such as Tammy grabbing their morning coffees. She had set out over a half hour ago to procure a couple of cups of coffee from the Mackinaw Bakery, which was only a few blocks down the street. This time of year, there weren't often lines out the door of the popular establishment like there were once the season really kicked off.

"I'm in the living room," she called out. Not that it would take long to find her in the small house. Cici looked up expectantly, as if she expected her own tiny cup of joe. Dawn shook her head at her dog. "Not for you, Cici."

"I've got the coffee. A decaf for you and double espresso cappuccino for me." Tammy rounded the corner from the entryway and held the two cups high.

Dawn pulled a face. "Decaf, ugh!"

"Gotta listen to your heart doctor, Mom."

"Yeah, yeah, yeah." Dawn accepted the proffered drink. She opened the lid and motioned to Tammy to pour some of hers into Dawn's. "Maybe I'll get a kickstart and be ready to play Pickle Ball this afternoon with Hampy."

Tammy ignored her and sipped her drink instead. "Maybe your coffeepot biting the dust was a sign for you."

"Sure, it was. A sign it was a decade old. That's what the old thing was telling me." Cici yipped as if in agreement, and Dawn chuckled.

"I'll run out to the Walmart in Cheboygan later and pick up one of those fancy electric teapots for you instead. Buy some herbal tea. Get you off caffeine altogether."

The superstore was the closest large grocery store to the cottage. But it was a good half-hour drive away, albeit surrounded by beautiful forest en route. "You'll do no such thing." She gave Tammy a *Mommy glare.*

"Buy a teapot or go to Walmart?" Tammy sipped some more of her fancy coffee.

"I can buy myself a new coffee pot all by myself, thank you very much. So no to both." Dawn set her coffee cup down. "Besides which, the bakery has that tea shop on the one side. Did you look over there?"

Was it her imagination or did Tamara's face pale a bit? Dawn never had been too good at decoding her daughter's facial expressions. Truth be told, she was usually too busy with her own stuff to take a lot of time figuring out what people were thinking or feeling. If folks wanted to tell her, they could do so directly was her way of thinking. "You okay?"

"Ah, I was disappointed that they didn't have something I wanted." Her daughter chewed her lower lip.

"Maybe next time." She smiled at her child and hoped her words encouraged her. Dawn lifted the baby blanket from her lap. "Look what I finished."

Tamara leaned in and lifted the bottom of the blanket. "That's so pretty. I can't believe you got it done so fast."

"I made ten of these while your dad has been recovering." Her church's Ladies Aid crocheted baby blankets for babies whose families were in need. When she'd been at the office full-time, she'd rarely been able to participate.

"Did you enjoy that? I mean, did it help?" Tammy's expectant gaze seemed to be asking far more than her simple question.

"Yes." It surprised her how she actually had, even though it wasn't a physical activity, which was what she really enjoyed doing when she wasn't at work.

"Jaycie might be right." Tamara kicked off her slide-on sandals.

"About what?" Cici plopped down on Dawn's feet.

"She read an article online that claimed crocheting activates an area of the brain associated with relaxation. That's the same portion that is lit up on those Functional MRIs they use to study people in meditation. Or in prayer."

"This is a lot of fun, too. And beneficial."

Tammy sat on the sofa beside Dawn and sipped her cappuccino. Dawn folded the baby blanket and reached for her decaf. At least it had some flavored French vanilla creamer in it, something she didn't normally keep in her own fridge. Jim took his coffee black, something he called 'an acquired taste' and a taste she'd never master herself.

A long silence followed as they enjoyed their drinks. Cici finally rose and went to her dog bed, complete with memory foam cushion, in the corner. "You are so spoiled, Cici."

Tammy's cell phone chimed in rolling bell tones. She pulled it from her pocket and frowned at the screen. Dawn discreetly glanced over. It was her son-in-law calling again.

Her daughter tapped her thumb at the green circle on the bottom of the screen, accepting the call, and raised the phone to her ear. "Hello?" Her voice was uncharacteristically sharp.

Dawn rose from the couch, wanting to give her daughter some privacy. Why hadn't Tammy gone to another room to talk with her husband? Did she want her to hear? Dawn went to the kitchen, passing the small dining area that extended from the living room. Once in the cozy galley kitchen, she poured her drink into her favorite coffee mug, a gift from Jim on their last anniversary and part of a pair that nestled together. He could be such a romantic. She smiled, a feeling of warmth surging through her. She set the mug inside the microwave and pressed the Reheat button.

As the microwave whirled to life, Tammy's voice carried from the other room. "No!"

Dawn stiffened, and her heart palpitations kicked up their heels—-without caffeine to blame. She leaned against the counter. This was Tammy's issue to work out, not hers.

Silence resumed in the other room and the microwave dinged. Dawn retrieved her coffee.

Tammy laughed bitterly. "It was my money, too, Brad. My choice."

I really don't need to hear this.

"I won't be there anymore. You won't have to worry about your wife and daughter. I'll be gone from here, too, probably late summer. My mom has my dad, but Jaycie will need you even more."

What? Where was her daughter going? Although curious, Dawn sucked in a breath and slipped out the back door of the cottage and to the garden near the street. She didn't blame Tammy if she wanted to make a fresh start and move somewhere. As to the money issue, Tammy had brought a lot of cash with her and had opened a checking account locally, something she didn't normally do. Her daughter didn't normally stay so long, either. Tammy had said the local banks charged outrageous ATM fees when she used them so she might as well open a Mackinaw City checking account.

"Dawn?" a deep male voice called out from the street.

Pastor Dave jogging by, dressed in a navy athletic suit, his white terrier at his side. "Hi Dave," she called out.

He paused, bent over, and grasped his thighs, panting. "I thought I'd start jogging again, but I think I'm getting too old for it."

She laughed. Everyone seemed young to her now. "When Jim and I were your age, we started dance classes and never looked back." With her sitting at a desk job most of the day, she'd needed the exercise. "It's a lot of fun, especially the fast dances."

"If I could get my wife to do that, I would."

"I'll put a bug in her ear." Dawn winked conspiratorially.

Dave straightened. "She's so focused on our new grandbaby that I'm not sure it will help."

"Speaking of which—I've gotten your grandson's baby blanket done just now."

"That's great, Dawn. I'm impressed." He slacked his hip. "I bet your VBS talents will be even more extraordinary."

"We'll see." Hopefully it wouldn't be too much like work. She was starting to enjoy this 'practice retirement' just a little too much.

Tamara

Tamara gritted her teeth. Hopefully Dave wouldn't ask why she'd not yet been to church. Right now, she was just too raw to attend the nearby church. Too many people knew her mother there, knew Tamara, too. And she wasn't ready yet to share all her secrets. She'd tell mom soon that she planned to attend church with Hamp, on the island.

She opened the back door and came out, holding her coffee cup. "Hey Dave, how ya doin'?"

"Good, Tam! Glad you, and Jaycie, too, could come spend time with your mom."

The strange way he said 'mom', with a melancholic overlay, made Tamara cast him a questioning glance. Mom was only seventy. She wasn't even technically retired yet. Did Dave know something that she didn't?

"Why don't you two catch up?" Mom glanced between Tamara and Dave, who were close in age. "I'm gonna go inside and reheat my coffee. You know I'm a stickler for having it at just the right temperature."

"If Dad was here, he'd tease you about that, Mom."

"When's Jim arriving?"

"As soon as his torturer of a physical therapist lets him." Mom made a face of mock disgust and headed inside.

Tamara heard Cici bark, inside the house. She and Dave exchanged a look of mutual understanding. "Spoiled," they both said.

"Yeah, I know exactly what your mom is doing right now."

"Giving that dog a treat."

"Your mom loves spoiling people. I bet if she really retires, she'll be working all the time doing volunteer stuff."

"I think you're right."

A teenaged boy dressed from head to toe in black zipped by on a purple bike.

"I used to be like that kid." Crinkles formed around Dave's eyes as he smiled.

"I know." He'd been a bit of a holy terror.

"That's the problem of growing up where you end up preaching. A lot of people know your youthful background."

Tamara swallowed hard. "We've known each other a long time." Not like she knew Hamp. She and Hamp loved each other. Not in a romantic way, although Hamp at one point had thought maybe they could. More like a best friend who was a guy. With Dave, she knew him, but could she trust him?

"I feel like you have something you want to say."

She gave a curt laugh. "More like something I don't want to say."

He looked down and dug his toe in the dirt, looking more like the football player he'd once been. "I heard about your husband. Are you going to divorce him?"

"No." She said that a little too quickly.

Pastor Dave jerked his gaze back up to hers. "But you've left him and have no plans to return?"

"Right." There would be no reason to divorce him, though.

"How's that? I thought he was having an affair."

"Yup. But, actually, I have some other things going on with my, um, health." She pressed her hand to her gut as her stomach spasmed, closing her eyes shut. She couldn't even allow herself to think about her dreaded diagnosis.

"Are you all right?"

No. I'm not.

Chapter Nine

Jaycie
Mackinac Island

Another boring day ahead to file reports with the aggravating Parker. At least upon her arrival today at Fort Mackinac, Jaycie received another sunny smile from one of the young Girl Scout teens. Anna, her black hair pulled into a simple ponytail, waved at Jaycie as she entered through the fort at the ticket counter. "Good morning Miss Worth!"

"Hi there, Anna." Jaycie and the girl had talked about Virginia for about an hour the previous afternoon. Anna's family had only recently relocated to Michigan. She'd been selected as one of the fortunate girls to have summer duty at Mackinac Island for two weeks.

"Feels like home today." The teen's ivory cheeks flushed. "I mean it feels like what used to be home."

"Yeah, today is almost as hot as Virginia." She'd checked her Weather Channel App earlier and both locations were in the mid 80's.

"Have a good day."

"Thanks, you too." Jaycie trudged up the steep hill to the office as the sun beat unmercifully on her. Her Health App on her iPhone registered the climb as over four stairs high. Thankfully, an air-conditioned office awaited her at the top of the climb and beyond the fort.

When she got to their white wood-sided building, Jaycie entered and greeted the secretary. She headed down the hall to their work room. Parker looked up from his state-of-the-art computer, the best one in the office. He turned, grabbed something, then unceremoniously dropped a cardboard box down atop Jaycie's desk with a loud thump. "Jeffries wants these delivered ASAP."

Only a few days into her internship, and Parker now wanted Jaycie to run errands ostensibly for Mr. Jeffries? "Trying to keep me away?"

Parker pinned her with his gaze. "Why would I do that?" A muscle in his jaw jumped.

"You're right, you could have easily done that by accepting the position at Colonial Williamsburg." A spot that should have been hers.

There was something in the way he looked at her. . . something in the way his lips parted, and the fact that he'd refused the Williamsburg position that had her unnerved.

She broke eye contact first.

Parker laughed. "Maybe I want to keep you my minion." His terse laugh elicited a glare from her.

She gritted her teeth. Same old Parker after all. *Inhale slowly, exhale slowly, you must keep this job.*

The director strolled in from the other room, glancing between the two of them and sent Parker what appeared to be a warning look. "I need that package of books delivered to the top of the bluffs, beyond the Grand Hotel to one of our supporters."

"Which house?" Jaycie was familiar with the homes along the bluff but a street number would help.

Her director rubbed his hand along his cheek. "I can't recall the number of the cottage but it's the only lilac one on the West Bluff. The owners call the cottage 'Foiled Again,' but I'm not sure why and there's no sign out front."

"Ok." She hoped that was enough info.

"Oh, and also, it's a three-story Victorian and has several of those spinning black metal dog lawn ornaments that are meant to chase off the geese."

Almost all the cottages were Victorians, so that wasn't quite helpful. "Thanks." And everywhere she went people had those trendy, and useful, lawn ornaments—at least they did in Mackinaw City on the mainland.

In about fifteen minutes, Jaycie trudged past the Grand Hotel and onto the bluff. With each step, the heavier the four tomes—all Mackinaw State Parks hardcover books—seemed to get. They must have weighed about ten pounds total. She should have kept up her workouts in the UK. At least she and Elliott had jogged together and ridden their bikes regularly. But she'd need to start lifting weights again, soon, if this past week was any indication of the demands of this job.

She huffed a sigh. Maybe she'd call on Mom's personal remedy and pray for Parker. She almost laughed out loud. Maybe she'd try to pray him off the island. Yeah, that was it.

"And you need to add a new basket to your bike," she muttered to herself. If she'd done so, she wouldn't be walking right now. She could have positioned the load within a wide basket instead of carrying the books.

Although the winds off the Straits of Mackinac generally kept the island cool, even on sunny days, today was an exception. She shoved her visor up and wiped her forehead. She removed her Saville Row sunglasses which Elliott had received from a modeling job for the British company. Had he been cheating on her even then? She closed her eyes and felt the intensity of his kiss after he'd returned from London and the brief gig. Suddenly, the image was replaced by the memory of Parker's lips melding into hers. She opened her eyes dispelling the mental image and peered down past the many beautiful Queen Anne style homes on the bluff. A yellow one, white, brick, and green but no lilac-colored home.

Jaycie halted and puffed out a breath. A carriage loaded with tourists passed by in the road. The buggy was crammed full of people of all ages. They gazed at her, where she stood on the sidewalk, but she ignored them. About four houses up, a tall man leaned on a shovel so casually that he almost appeared part of the landscape.

He waved at the driver, a young woman. The driver waved back. Probably another islander. The man, a gardener, perhaps, judging by his dirty chinos, wore a white t-shirt with rolled-up sleeves, and navy baseball cap shoved backward on his head.

She continued walking. Maybe she'd ask the yardman where the lilac house was. As she neared, she spied a bit of purple far back in the massively deep and somewhat narrow lush green yard. She took a couple more steps and a breeze lifted branches that shielded a lilac-colored three-story home. This was the place. She wanted to cheer.

Picking up her pace, she continued on to the gate, behind which the man bent over and dug what looked to be a narrow gulley behind a white picket fence. Having watched too many old war movies with Grandpa Jim, she couldn't help herself, "Building a land mine trench?"

Snorting a laugh, the auburn-haired man straightened. He stood well over her tall height of five feet ten inches by yet another handful. Blue-gray eyes sparkled beneath straight reddish eyebrows. His somewhat-generous lips were balanced by a well-proportioned nose. Something in his features reminded her of the Irishmen she'd met in Dublin during one of her weekend trips away from university.

"Don't think that land mines haven't crossed my mind." Laugh lines bunched at the corner of his eyes. She guessed him near to thirty or so.

"My grandfather considered placing some mines for tourists who pull the Milkweeds out in the pocket parks in Mackinaw City."

"The plants placed there to attract the Monarch butterflies?" The man laughed. "They likely see them as weeds."

She cocked her head at him. "The Monarchs and the local butterfly lovers would have to disagreed."

"Yeah, especially since that method is working."

"It is." She smiled. The previous night, several butterflies had fluttered around her mother when she'd sat down on the porch.

"I'm glad for that. But I doubt you're here to talk trench warfare against the tourists, are you?"

"No, I'm not." She shook her head.

He glanced at her arms, which felt heavier by the moment with Dr. Jeffries' books. Then he set his shovel against the fence and pulled off the heavy-looking suede work gloves. He held out his broad hands.

She didn't hand the items over. What kind of trouble would she be in if she passed them off to the caretaker and not the owner? "They're for Mr. Piccard."

The handsome man chuckled, deep and low. She'd not said anything funny, but obviously he thought so. Surreptitiously looking around, Jaycie saw nothing that indicated the owners' name, as some residences did.

"You'll have to excuse my laughter. That's a little joke the. . . owner has about his name."

"A joke?"

"Yes, the owner of this place likes to keep his anonymity and one of his favorite things is to call himself Jean Luc. You know—like Jean Luc Piccard."

"Ah, I guess he's a Star Trek devotee." This was a show her parents enjoyed watching on reruns or used to back when they were still talking.

He raised his eyebrows, nodded, and then took the books from her. "I see Clark sent you over."

"Yes, Mr. Jeffries sent me." Jaycie glanced toward the grand Victorian mansion and the lush grounds. "This place is really beautiful."

The caretaker's lips rolled downward. "Really, a life that is lived beautifully is more important than a handsome home."

The way he looked at her made her feel as though he was judging her. Almost as if his words were meant for her specifically. Jaycie had been told often enough that she was pretty, beautiful even. Her mom had fought her dad to provide her enough allowances to purchase at least a modicum of the latest clothing and styles. Mom had paid for two sets of braces on Jaycie's teeth before she'd turned sixteen. But what about how she was doing inside, in her spirit? What condition was that? Her mother sure asked that question often enough. "I. . . I think you have a point."

She suddenly wanted to turn on her heels and jog all the way back to the fort and her office—even though Parker was there as well as piles of filing to do.

"Are you all right?" The stranger stepped close and firmly clasped her shoulder.

The warmth in his strong grip made her feel dizzy instead of steadying her. His grip was so much like her grandfather's, for some reason, bringing back a rush of memories. How she missed Grandpa Jim being there with them. Hopefully he'd join them in late summer. She took a step away and the man released her. For a moment, she could almost hear Grandpa saying, "You'll be all right, Jaybird. Everything is going to be all right."

But everything seemed out of control. Mom and Dad were on the outs. Gran's heart had gone a little wonkier recently. And Elliott had dumped her at her favorite watering hole. Now she was here working under the supervision of a fellow student who'd probably like nothing more than for her to go back to Virginia. Something dark loomed over her. She could feel it as sure as if a thunderhead of clouds fast drifted in and covered the Straits of Mackinac.

"I. . . I'm fine." She rolled with life. Always had. "I've got to get back to the office."

"Did you walk all the way over here from the fort?" A frown line formed between his brows. He really was a handsome man.

"Yeah."

"No bike?"

She shrugged. "I have a temporarily basketless bike."

He laughed. "Basketless sounds like a dreaded condition for Mackinac."

"Right. But I hadn't expected to be roaming the island."

"No?"

"I'm supposed to be working all day in one place." Nor was she supposed to be running around like an errand girl. Yes, she was a minion, but at least she had a position. Regardless, this wasn't the job she'd thought she'd accepted. It was supposed to be an archeology dig. But roll on, she would, even without wheels.

He jerked a thumb toward the lilac house. "I'm sure the owner of this place wouldn't mind if I gave you a ride back in his vehicle."

She frowned. Cars weren't allowed on the island except for emergency and municipal vehicles. "How?" She pictured the handsome gardener putting her atop his handlebars like Parker had tried when they were both twelve.

He shrugged. "There's a single horse-drawn light buggy in the carriage house."

"Wow, really?" Although intrigued, that might not look too good her returning in a stranger's carriage. On the other hand, she'd save time. "I don't want to keep you from your work." If the owner was as eccentric as he sounded, making up fake names like Captain Piccard, he could give this worker a hard time.

"No worries. He's not a very demanding sort of guy. Knows I have other things I need to do with my time." He grinned. A really warm smile. And a brief image of a magazine cover with his face on it crossed through her mind before being tossed aside by a gust of breeze.

She shivered, despite the heat. "That's nice that the owner is so low-key." Maybe the mansion's owner was okay after all despite his eccentricities.

"He knows better than to blow his emotional energy on the small stuff."

Unlike her dad. She'd never figured out what his problem was, and maybe she never would. At least Mom was a good parent.

The gardener glanced around the yard and then wiped his brow with a red cotton handkerchief, the kind her grandfather used. How could this worker make a decent living on the island if he was a laborer? "Do you take care of other houses, too?"

"Yes, I do." He beamed as though this was quite an accomplishment.

Maybe he was actually a landscaper. They made good wages in this area where a top-notch garden was highly prized. Not that it was any of her business or her concern what this worker bee did. And his dazzling smile didn't need to trip her up.

"There's a shortage this summer of gardeners and landscape artists."

Artist? Interesting way to look at it. "Ah, yeah, that makes sense with. . ."

"Full employment," they both voiced in unison and then laughed.

He seemed like a good guy. She decided right there and then that she liked him.

"I'm Jaycie, by the way." She held out her hand and he stared at it for a long moment but said nothing, before lightly shaking her hand.

That was odd. Some expression of negative emotion warred over his even features.

"I'm Mortimer." His cheeks flushed. "Isn't that an awful name to pin on someone?"

"Yikes! I'd have to agree." She laughed. "But Mort isn't too bad a name." Except that she associated it with death. Having recently traveled to France, she'd immediately paired the name Mort with *morte*, French for dead.

An awful feeling coursed through her. Was this not really another human but an angel? Was this gardener a representation of Jesus? Why was she having such crazy thoughts? Gran and Mom's recent deep conversations about faith must be affecting her more than she'd realized. And she didn't need any encounters of the supernatural kind today. Not on any day really. "You know what, Mort? I think I'll walk back. I'll just take my time." So she didn't get sweaty.

"Are you sure?"

Sure that she wanted to run away from someone who might not be real? Yup. Plus, by the time he got the carriage hooked up and the harness on the horse she could have gotten back to work. "Yes. Thanks!" And she hurried off. Mortimer, ha! She'd ask Mr. Jeffries about this Mortimer.

When she returned to the office, soaked through with perspiration, Parker's chair was vacant. Instead of relief, a tiny trail of regret coursed through her, but Jaycie shook it off as she grabbed her water bottle and threw back the last of its contents.

"Miss Worth?" Mr. Jeffries waved her toward his office. "I want to let you know about some office policies."

She set her water bottle down, hands shaking. "Yes, sir." What had she done wrong?

She followed him and he closed the door behind her. *Uh oh.*

"I want to make sure you understand that office romances have no place here." He crossed his well-muscled arms over his Oxford blue shirt-covered chest.

Jaycie could only stare at her supervisor. "Sir?"

"By your reaction, I'm going to assume this is a one-sided thing." He huffed a sigh.

What did he mean?

He stood only an arm's width away from her looking her directly eye-to-eye. He couldn't mean. No, he must mean. . .

"Parker has already been warned."

Jaycie frowned at him. "Sir, Parker and I are not. . .romantically interested in each other whatsoever. We were academic rivals at

UVA." Except that Parker never worked to earn his grades, as she had.

His lips compressed into a tight line. "I have eyes in my head, albeit older eyes than yours, and I've known Parker all his life. You may not have any feelings for him, but he does for you."

"But he didn't say that?" Jaycie blurted out.

The director slowly shook his head. "No."

She exhaled a sigh of relief. "Sir, perhaps what you think you are seeing is his distress over my being hired here. But I really need this position." Her mouth went dry. "And I would do absolutely nothing to jeopardize that." Even though she'd rather eat nails than keep filing reports every day.

He paced with measured steps until he stood behind his desk. "I believe you."

"Thank you." She drew in a steadying breath.

"Please don't mention this conversation to Parker." He sat in his leather chair.

"I won't." She'd have to be as heavy a drinker as Parker was to attempt that conversation. Not that he'd seemed hungover at work. On the contrary, he'd been to work before she'd arrived, every day. Tired maybe, but not hungover.

"Good. Oh, and what did Dr. Piccard say? Did you get to meet him?" Mr. Jeffries removed his eyeglasses and rubbed the bridge of his nose.

"Oh, no, sir. He wasn't at home."

"I've yet to meet him in person myself, but he often sends for our books. Piccard is a recluse."

Jaycie nodded. Mr. Jeffries didn't act as though he understood the man's name was fake. "His gardener, Mortimer—he accepted the package."

He grimaced. "A gardener named Mortimer? Mike DuBlanc is one of our biggest landscape artists on the island. He's a bit of a prickly pear, though. Still, the ladies love him—they say he looks like that actor who plays Thor in the movies."

Chris Hemsworth? Nope. The man she'd met possessed a totally different kind of look, although he was just as handsome. Jaycie described Dr. Piccard's gardener as best she could.

Jeffries frowned. "I heard there was a philosopher type of fellow house-sitting for him a while back, but I thought that guy had gone back to Europe. Switzerland, I believe."

"Maybe Mortimer is more of a landscaper, like Mr. DuBlanc who you mentioned." Mort hadn't actually called himself one but his allusion to landscape artists might have been a hint.

"I know of few people on the island, no cottage owners, who have been able to procure private landscaping services for homes this summer. Even Mike is only working on commercial contracts as far as I know. I doubt Dr. Piccard would prove the exception. I don't see how he'd be able to hire someone in this current economy where there are no workers to be had."

Then who was Mort? Was he possibly an angel? If so, then why would God put an angel in her life right now? That couldn't bode well. Could it?

Chapter Ten

Dawn
Mackinaw City

Pastor Dave handed Dawn a mug of coffee as his secretary slid a folder chock-a-block full of papers in front of her. "Thanks." She eyed the folder. "I think."

"You're used to paperwork, I'm sure." Dave went to the coffee maker and poured himself a mug.

Maybe she'd gotten unaccustomed to it, since staying home with Jimbo, because that mound in front of her looked about a foot high. In reality it was more like two inches of papers. She sipped her coffee. Crud, she'd forgotten to say decaf, she was so distracted by the crowd of volunteers that now filled half the room. That was another thing that had changed. Being home, and not out in many crowds and not at work, she'd gotten used to the quiet. This was definitely not quiet. People laughed. Someone was singing in the sanctuary. Men nearby talked loudly.

"You okay?" Dave slid in next to her.

"Yeah, I'm just not used to. . ." She wasn't really used to working any more.

"All the noise?" He sipped his coffee. "I imagine you have a private office at your agency."

She laughed. "Yes I have a Head Pumba sign on the door, which I keep closed."

He quirked his eyebrows. "Really?"

"Jim made it."

He laughed. "He's quite the character."

"A lot of fun." And oh, how she missed her better half. "But what all do you have here for me?"

"It's the overall plan, the lists of volunteers, phone numbers, supply lists, and the like."

Her heart must have registered the full-on caffeine intake, because it skipped a full two seconds before it slammed again. Not good. Definitely not good. She pushed her mug away.

Dave opened the folder and pointed to the top sheet. "All of the materials in here are organized by type and sections."

She met his gaze. "Impressive. That will make my work much easier." She grabbed a pen from a cup on the table.

An hour later, she looked up when her phone buzzed. Where was everyone? She sat alone in the fellowship hall. She looked at the message. *Mrs. C I need help. Big group now coming. Call me. KL*

Oh no, no, no. She couldn't finish her task today and do what needed to be done to assist Kay-Leigh. Why now? It was her one last client.

Because you need to let go.

Woah, had that been her or the Holy Spirit nudging her. Dawn usually kept too busy for her to have noticed many of those pushes. It was true, though. She'd have to let go of one of these activities for the other to happen today.

She called Barb. When she got her voice mail, she dipped her chin. She couldn't simply leave her a message about Kay-Leigh. "Hey, Barb, this is Dawn. Please call me back. It's important. Bye."

How embarrassing that would be if she failed the famous young woman and then ran into her on the island. She had to pull this thing out of the fire. She'd thought it had all been settled.

She texted Kay-Leigh back. *Email me the specifics ASAP TY.*

She went back to her work. Normally, at the office, her phone would have been pinging off and on all day, her secretary would have put calls through to her, and her employees would stop by with questions. Plus, Dawn would be making travel arrangements for clients.

Today, though, she had this one task, or had until Kay-Leigh's request. This VBS stuff she'd flown right through. She touched the last document in the folder—which was simply a list of items already ordered and in the storage area at the church. Was this how doing God's work felt? Hadn't Tammy said that's how it was with her and teaching?

Her phone rang. Barb. She answered it. "Hey how are things going there?"

"Great. What's going on there?" Cheerful Barb had the right disposition for working with lots of different kinds of people.

"Well, remember Kay-Leigh?"

Barb laughed. "Your last client—the one you can't release your grip from?"

"That sounds so awful."

"I'm sorry. Anyway, what about her? If she canceled her trip to Mackinac then I've got a couple who'd love to grab up her spot before you release it back to the Grand."

Dawn closed one eye hard. "No. She's still coming. But with an entourage, I guess."

"Have fun with scheduling that one. That'll take hours calling in tons of favors for high season spots."

Flip a coin? Pray? Ask straight out? Or try to do it herself and put aside her VBS work? Dawn closed her eyes and asked God for help. She squirmed, unaccustomed to taking work matters to Him. Hadn't he already nudged her? She drew in a deep breath. The die was about to be cast.

Jaycie
Mackinac Island

Finally—a full day at the dig site. The familiarity of the work settled Jaycie's jangled nerves. For the first time since she'd arrived, she'd finally been where she'd trained to be. Instead of the "woohoo" time she thought she'd have, though, her emotions remained calm, determined. And something about that didn't sit quite right.

After work at the site concluded, she biked to the Little Stone Church. Covered in glacial era cut fieldstone, with a steep roof and a tall bell steeple atop, the church was truly beautiful. Jaycie had always loved this building, situated not far from the Grand Hotel.

Clearly someone was tending the gardens, for a wheelbarrow of rich cedar mulch sat nearby as well as a large shovel. But no one was working on the red geraniums and yellow begonias in the flowerbeds.

She parked her bike then stepped inside the cool darkness of the building. The gorgeous stained-glass windows, portraying some of Mackinac Island's history, and the intricate blue mosaic abstract cross in the front glowed with sunlight streaming behind it made her smile.

Surprisingly, there was only one person inside, a man with a queue of reddish-brown hair. That had to be Mort. Part of her wanted to run, but the curious part of her urged her to stay. He must be their gardener, or landscape artist, or whatever he wanted to fashion himself as. Or maybe he was the philosopher from Switzerland, albeit with a distinctly Mid-West accent.

Mort's head was pressed against his hands, and he appeared to be lost in deep prayer. Jaycie didn't want to disturb him. She was about to slip from the building when he turned and pinned her with his gaze. So much for her much-needed peaceful moment at the church.

He unfolded his tall frame in such an elegant manner that she'd never have pegged him for a laborer. But then again, he was an artist wasn't he?

He grinned, his even white teeth stark against his suntanned complexion. He was one good-looking man, that was for sure. Elliott's handsome face flashed through her mind. Look what handsome had gotten her recently.

"Are those your tools outside?" Dumb question. Of course, they were. Her cheeks heated.

"Yeah." He took a few steps closer. "I'm trying to get those beds spruced up."

"I'm sorry if I interrupted your time with God."

He shrugged and continued forward until he stood right before her. He squeezed her shoulder. "You ok?"

"Yeah." *No.* Dad had laid into her the previous night on the phone, claiming that she'd pressured her mom into closing out her retirement account so that Jaycie had money for grad school. She'd done no such thing. And she really wasn't sure how to bring up the question with her mother, who hadn't disclosed anything about that financial decision. "No, not really."

"Want to talk about it?" He pointed to the empty pews. "We've got plenty of seats available.

Was this guy really an angel? His hands were dirt stained. Angels should be clean. "Um, yeah."

They sat in the pew, angled toward one another. "What's going on?"

"Well," she expelled a long breath. She wasn't going to spill her guts to this stranger. But what if he was an angel? What the heck. "I really want to ask someone something but I'm afraid to. And she's upset a lot actually about this thing I want to ask her."

He flipped his palms over. "You're not in control of how other people feel."

Well, duh. Yeah she knew that. But he did have a point. "But I'm getting blasted by. . . this guy's anger toward my. . .um, friend. And it's really disturbing."

"You have to let that go right through you." He raised his broad hands and waggled his fingers. "Like wind through a screen with wide mesh. Let his anger go past."

She arched an eyebrow at him. "Don't let it stick to me?"

"Exactly." He smiled broadly. "That's something I've had to learn. Let this guy own his anger and you let it blow right by you, don't claim it."

"And don't put it on someone else?"

"Is it really any of your business?" He cocked his head. "Does this choice belong to your. . . friend? Is it hers not yours to decide?"

"Yeah." She felt some relief almost immediately. This was something Mom needed to deal with.

He smiled in approval, his light eyes twinkling. "I better get back to work before my boss complains."

"Oh, sure." Jaycie rose. "Thanks, Mort."

"No problem."

"See ya around then."

"I'll be there if you need me."

Wow, maybe Mom was right with all that asking God for help and He sent it. She didn't know what to say so she gave him a sheepish wave and headed out.

When she stepped into the sunlight, the comfort of Mort's words left her. She tried to blink back her confusion as she grabbed her bike from the stand.

Go to your special place.

The thought came from out of nowhere. Why would she bike all the way back up to the fort and down past it to get to Anne's Tablet area, her special place, when she had to make that trek every day to work?

She hopped on her bike and rode toward Market Street in town, determined to get back to the mainland early tonight. As she passed carriages and others on bicycles, she kept her eyes peeled for the little tea shop where Gran used to take her. She could really use that place right now. *No luck.*

Dodging a fresh pile of horse manure, she turned up Fort Street. When she neared the Governor's Mansion, sitting proudly up on the bluff near the fort, she paused. Two long Great Lakes ore boats passed each other in the Straits, a sight to behold.

The notion to head to the East Bluff kept niggling at her. She continued onto Huron Road and bicycled past the fort and waved to the female reenactor attired in a pink gauzy gown and contrasting white shawl. When Jaycie arrived at her office building she parked her bike in the rack. Exhaling loudly, she gave into the compelling notion to hike onto the trail that led back into the woods.

Anne's Tablet area was secluded. Quiet. Rarely did anyone come up there when Jaycie had gone for her breaks or lunch. It was a great place to calm a mind like hers, that was full of anxiety over the life choices that lay ahead. The hillside by Anne's Tablet had once been a favorite rendezvous place for her and Parker when they were young teenagers. How grown-up she'd felt at being allowed to take the ferry and her bike over to the island by herself.

She walked past the pretty white gazebo from the movie, "Somewhere in Time." A couple of silver-haired ladies were taking selfies. "Can I get a picture of both of you?" she offered.

The two exchanged a quick glance. "Thanks," the taller one handed Jaycie her phone.

She snapped several pictures. "Take a look." Jaycie handed the phone back.

The two ladies bent their heads over the screen, smiling. Both gave thumbs up. "Perfect. Thanks."

She nodded and headed off toward the cliffside retreat. Dedicated to Constance Fenimore Woolson, the beloved author of the novel, *Anne*, set on Mackinac Island, the spot included benches inscribed with her works of fiction, and more. Instead of a solitary retreat, she discovered Parker facing the inscribed sculptural bronze tablet that overlooked the Straits.

Oh no. No, no, no. She pressed her eyes shut for a moment. There was no escape from him.

When she stopped on her descent, he turned. The scowl on his face matched hers. But in an instance the frown flitted away. He smiled, actually looked happy to see her.

"What are you doing here?" she blurted out. Hadn't God been calling her here for quiet reflection?

"Open to the public the last I heard." He gave a curt laugh. "Glad to see you, too."

She exhaled a puff of breath. "I'm sorry. You just surprised me."

"I can leave if you want."

"No." My, she'd said that so quickly. More surprising was that she meant it. "Stay."

"Yeah, we should clear the air." He shoved a hand back through his thick hair.

She finished her descent and he stepped forward, offering her a hand. She couldn't miss the longing in his blue eyes, and something tugged within her heart.

He released her hand and stepped away.

She settled herself on the nearest stone bench. He remained standing.

"Jaycie, I find it hard to talk about this, but I think I should." He rubbed his hand across his mouth.

"Start at the beginning, then." That's what Grandpa Jim always said.

"All right. You know my mom has. . . *had* a problem with. . . I guess you could say addiction, for a long time."

His mother had, frankly, frightened Jaycie the handful of times she'd been around her. To say her moods were erratic was a wild understatement. "I wondered." Mom hadn't allowed her to go to Parker's home any more after Jaycie had shared one of her observations of his mother with her.

His eyes locked on hers for a moment. "I guess I misspoke just now about saying that she *has* had."

She waited. Faint birdsong carried on the breeze.

"I should have said my mom *used* to have, that is. . . when she was alive."

Sorrow clutched Jaycie's gut. "Did your mother die?" Of course she had, hadn't he just said so? She gaped at her old friend. *Oh my gosh.* Why hadn't someone told her? Maybe because Parker was a taboo subject with her family, at her bidding.

He crossed his arms over his chest. "This past year."

While Jaycie was in England. "Oh no. I'm so sorry. I didn't know."

He held up his hand, as if to say it was all right. "I'm. . . we're all coming to grips with things."

"I can only imagine." His situation made hers pale. Mom and Dad might be fighting like two seagulls vying for the same piece of tossed bread, over money, but they'd always resolved the situation in the past and moved on. And Mort might be right about her letting Dad's anger just flow past her like a breeze. She might even hang up on Dad the next time he called so he could find someone else to unload on. But Parker's loss of his mother—that was something he would never get a re-do on.

"You know my father's been a heavy drinker as long as I can remember."

Actually, no, she didn't know that. Her jaw muscles flinched as she sought out a suitable response. "Um, no, I didn't." Her own father didn't drink at all. He'd said his migraine meds and alcohol didn't mix. But she thought her father mostly didn't want to do anything that would affect his control over his emotions.

"He's finally gotten into AA after this." Parker gave a half-smile. "Alcoholics Anonymous."

"That's good." Maybe Parker should join him at the meetings, but she bit her tongue instead of saying so.

"Yeah. Now Carter and I at least have a thirty-something-years-old sober dad instead of two absent parents."

"Thirty-something-years-old, what do you mean? Mr. Parker should be close to fifty. "He's my mom's age."

"His sponsor told him that as long as you're drinking you don't really mature, psychologically."

"Wow, really? But I guess that kinda makes sense."

"Yeah. So, I figure I am maybe eighteen, emotionally, and I don't want that." He made a sour face.

She tried not to gawk.

"I've stopped drinking, but my dad says I'm a 'dry drunk' right now."

"Why does he say that?"

Birdsong and chatter sounded not far from them.

Parker shifted and frowned. "It means you stopped medicating yourself with alcohol to numb your feelings, but all that affective stuff is still there."

"And you don't know how to handle it?"

He grinned and flipped his right palm over. "Exactly."

"Want to talk about it?" She patted the bench beside her.

"Do you have time?"

"Sure." How many times had they sat in this very place, holding hands, and talking about their trials and their hopes and dreams? Mostly she had complained about her father and how impassive he was and what a tightwad he was.

They both sat, their bodies angled toward each other. "I'm sorry, Jaycie, for what a jerk I have been."

Wow, she'd really not expected this. She dipped her chin.

"It's just an excuse, but with our families being so close and our own history with one another, I desperately wanted to maintain a connection with you. In my juvenile alcohol-induced state, I continued to harass you."

"I wouldn't exactly say harass." But she had. Many times.

"I just did. Looking back—"

She chewed her lower lip, guilty about using that term.

"I was looking for affirmation from you, Jaycie, because I couldn't get it from my family." He shrugged. "I felt lost."

"Aren't you close with your grandpa, though?"

"Yeah, thank God for him. And I really mean that—he's great. I don't know what I'd have done without him. But he and Grandma

Kareen lived hours away from us. I only saw him briefly in the winters."

"At least you had the summers." And she now had this summer with her own grandmother. Guilt bit her, as she'd not really spent much quality time with Gran. She usually arrived at the cottage late from the ferry, chowed dinner, got a shower, checked her emails while watching a little tv with Gran and Mom and then went to bed. Then she'd get up and repeat that cycle.

"I did have those wonderful summers. And you were a big part of them. I thank you for having been such a good friend all those years."

Her cheeks heated. They'd been sweethearts at the end of those years. She recalled their recent scorching kiss, and broke eye contact.

"Jaycie, anyway, all I really want to convey is I'm sorry, and I'm going to try harder."

"Do it for yourself, Parker."

"I'm doing it for. . ."

She didn't want him to say he was getting cleaned up for her. Jaycie didn't need that on her.

He exhaled a loud breath. "I need to do it for my brother. Carter is at that age where he could go down the path I followed. When I was at home, I was basically the dad to him all through my teen years."

Parker used to look out for his younger brother all the time. *Too much.* "Your overbearing manner with him makes sense now."

"Mom was often high on something, and Dad was socking back the booze or indulging in his other addiction—addiction to work or workaholism for which my grandmother is the poster child."

Voices carried from near the gazebo. "That's good that you want to be a better role model for Carter."

"I do." Parker grinned.

"I think that's commendable."

He shook his head. "Don't get me wrong, I'm doing this for myself, too. I expect no attaboys for doing this."

"I don't have a sister or brother, so I don't really know what that's like to have someone looking up to you. But I have loved my volunteer work with kids, and I guess I've experienced a little of that. Wanting to do the right thing so they'd see it. But not doing it for, um, I guess the word is aggrandizement. Not doing it to make myself look better. I think that's what you mean."

"Yeah." He laughed. "I always loved how you'd try to come up with a good word to use for a situation."

They smiled at each other.

"Thanks for listening, Jaycie. You're a pal."

"You're welcome."

His smile faded as he looked past her and practically jumped up.

Leaves crunched on the hillside behind them. Jaycie turned to see Mr. Jeffries standing there. Frowning.

She stood. They were off the clock, so why was he here?

"This must be where you two enjoy hiding." Jeffries' dry tone couldn't quite conceal an accusation.

Two more people joined their boss, the petite blond waving at her and grinning.

"Gran, what are you doing here?" Then she remembered. Gran had shared that she'd be on the island that day. *Oh no.*

"Hampy and I rode bikes around the island." Gran gestured to Parker's grandfather, a tall man with a shock of wavy white hair. "Like I reminded you last night, dear. Hampy said we should look for you up here."

Parker smiled and jogged up the hill to pat his grandfather on the back. "Hi Grandpa."

The older man pulled him into a hug.

Gran gestured to Jaycie. "I want one of those, too. Give me a hug."

Jaycie walked up to the top of the hill and complied. Acceptance and peace flowed through her. She wanted to grab onto every bit of that love. No filtering, no flowing past of this emotion—but gathering it all up to hold onto. No loosely woven mesh but tightly knitted, catching every bit of love shared.

Did Mort understand the benefit of doing that, too? Did he understand that with the love embraced, that you had to stand alongside someone in the hard times, too? That to not share in their distress with them distanced you from your loved ones? Dad hadn't engaged with her and Mom, not emotionally, for years. Not in the way her grandparents did with her mom and with her.

She'd let Parker down when they were at college. She'd not been the friend he'd needed. Someone to listen to the hard stuff and not only be there for the fun times. Maybe it was time she grew up. One thing she had learned that day—not all advice, even from spiritual-sounding people was worth taking.

Gran finally released Jaycie and looked at her intently. "You look full of wonder."

"Maybe so." She felt a little older, and wiser, already. And that was a good starting point.

Chapter Eleven

Tamara
Mackinaw City

Seated on the front porch, sipping her cinnamon tea, Tamara prayed for a way to tell her mother and daughter about what was going on in her life. A single Monarch fluttered toward her, and then landed on a nearby hydrangea bush. It was wonderful seeing the butterflies increase in number since her last visit. Dad had helped put in a bunch of the Milkweed bushes in Mackinaw City, to attract them. Her phone rang, and she glanced at the number. She didn't recognize it, although it originated from her same area code. Probably a robocall. *Curiosity killed the cat.* She reached out and accepted the call. "Hello?"

"Mrs. Worth?" The man's voice was low and gruff. "This is Sergeant Michael Hernandez."

Gina's husband. The poor guy had been deployed with the Navy.

She sucked in a breath. How had he gotten her number? She swallowed hard. "Yes?"

"You're gone, I hear, so I assume you know about my wife and your husband."

The events of a month earlier crashed down on her.

"My husband said you and Gina had separated right before your deployment."

"That's not true." He bit out a curse. "Sorry, ma'am."

"That's what people said at one of the departmental parties, too. Gina told people you'd left her before your deployment to the Middle East."

"No, that's so patently untrue." He cursed softly. "Sorry. She lied."

"I'm sorry."

"This puts such another layer of. . . manure on top of what she's already done. She lied and then she went after your husband. You two were together then weren't you?"

"Yes, we were." But they'd grown further and further apart the previous year. "Are you back home now, Michael?"

"Yeah." He gave a curt laugh. "She's gone. Living in your house now, ma'am."

"Oh." Somehow that image hurt more than having seen the two as they'd embraced in the parking lot.

"And my babies are high risk and could come anytime in the next month or so."

She sucked in a breath, unable to speak.

"Yeah, they're mine not your husband's. Not much comfort is it?" He coughed.

In a way it was a bit of relief. "Sergeant Hernandez," most military members in Hampton Roads preferred to be addressed by their rank, "Is there anything I can do to help you?" That must be the reason he was calling.

"If you've got any kind of relationship left with your lousy husband, can you ask him to let me go with my wife to the appointments?"

"As the father, can't you do that?"

"Gina's providers won't let me. She claims that I'll upset her too much."

"They're using that to keep you out?" Tamara had heard of that happening, if the provider felt a parent was detrimental to a child's health.

"Yeah. I really don't want to have to go to court over this. I don't want to upset Gina and have that affect our little unborn daughters." The younger man's voice shook.

"I can try to help. Brad should listen to reason."

"Maybe he can get Gina to let me be there. Shouldn't that be my right?"

"I don't know. But I'll also think of a stick to motivate him if logic doesn't work. Well, maybe a motivator to get him to cooperate."

"If you don't mind me asking, what would that be, ma'am?"

"Maybe I'll return his retirement account savings."

"Woah, are you serious?"

"May not have been my finest moment, but I have every penny he put in there."

"Lady, you got some. . . nerve." He chortled. "Don't be giving me ideas now."

"I'm a believer, Michael, and I don't know why the Holy Spirit didn't stop me."

"Sounds like your anger did an override on that switch, ma'am."

"Maybe. But I'll use that carrot to entice Brad to let you be there for those babies."

"Wow, I feel so much better talking to you. It's almost like I know you."

"Same here. We're sharing the same stress."

"Yeah. Ya know, I was raised by a single mom. She always told me to do my duty as a father. I want to honor her memory."

Chills of conviction coursed through Tamara. After all, her choices now were being made to honor her friend Ruby, and her dying wishes. "I get that."

"Hey, you got my number so call me anytime, ok?"

"Sure thing. And God bless you, Michael."

"Yes, ma'am, thank you and the same back atcha."

Time to at least tell her mother about Brad. About what she'd done in anger. About some of the whys. And to let Jaycie know. First, though, she was calling Brad. At work. He despised calls while he was working. She took a little perverse pleasure in tapping the buttons on her phone.

Dawn

Dawn arrived home to find Tammy arranging a vase of cut lilac blossoms on the front porch table. All around the cottage, the purple blossoms were beginning to bloom, the fragrance a welcoming scent.

"Those look so pretty," she called out.

Tammy offered a tight smile. She finished her task and centered the vase in the middle of the round table.

Dawn joined her daughter on the porch. "How was your afternoon?"

"Eventful." Tamara arched her eyebrows.

"Oh? Do tell." Dawn pulled one of the chairs out and sat.

"Brad's girlfriend's husband called me." Tammy raised her teacup to her lips and took a long sip.

"What?" Dawn's voice emitted as a squeak. Good thing she'd not drank the coffee that Pastor Dave had offered her. Her heart palpitations would have gone nuts right now. "He's been cheating?"

"Yup."

What a scum bucket. If he were here, she'd give him a piece of her mind. "That explains a lot."

"Brad is cheating on me with a very-pregnant-with-twins co-worker."

"What?" She was sounding like a parrot with a limited vocabulary consisting of 'what'. "How could he do that to my precious girl? And to my granddaughter?" If Jim were there, he'd go ballistic.

"The husband, who is active-duty Navy and had been deployed to the Middle East, got home to find her moved out into. . .*get this*. . . my house."

"You have got to be kidding." Dawn punched her fist into her other palm. "Oh, I'd like to show him just what I think of him. I'd give him a big conversation with my fists."

Tammy arched an eyebrow at her. "Mom, you're too tiny."

"Okay, I'd like to spray him with. . ." she grabbed a can of mosquito repellant. "You could hold him down and I could spray him right in the kisser!"

"What would Pastor Dave say about that?" Tammy seemed to be taking this more calmly than she was.

"I need something stronger than tea." Dawn pushed back her chair and rose. "This might be a three wineglasses full kind of conversation."

"At least the babies aren't Brad's. Her husband was pretty insistent about that."

"Big whoop-de-doo!" Dawn made a circling motion with her index finger. How could her son-in-law ruin Tammy's life and those babies'? "So that excuses him having an affair with her now?"

"No."

Tammy must have known for a while. "When did you find out?"

"Same day as I got my award."

"Oh no." Dawn fought back tears and went to her daughter and bent and gave her a hug around her shoulders. "My poor girl."

"Not so poor, actually. I cleared out most of his accounts."

"Oh my gosh." Dawn plopped back into her seat. She fought the urge to cheer her daughter's actions, which could result in some big problems. "Does your lawyer know?"

"I don't have a lawyer."

Dawn cringed. "Baby Girl, I think you're going to need one."

Tammy shook her head then sipped her tea. "Not up for conversation right now."

"Oh, not this again." But at least she now knew what was going on with her rotten son-in-law.

"You can tell Dad, though, if you want."

"First let me have at least one glass of Chablis before I call him. And I'll probably need to put some earplugs in first." She placed her index finger in her ear and swiveled it. "I'm sure my ears will be ringing after that conversation.

The landline sounded.

"I'll get it, Mom." Tammy rose and went inside.

Her poor daughter. What could she do for her? She'd have to lift her up and get Tammy out doing some fun things. She'd distract her. And she'd ask Jim to hire a hit man. Nah, better not do that.

Inside, the phone stopped ringing. Dawn could hear Tammy speaking with someone.

In a few moments, Tammy returned with a wineglass filled half-full. "Mom, is this half-empty or half-full?"

Dawn couldn't help laughing. "You're turning my old trick back on me, aren't you?"

"Yes, I am but I have two right answers."

"Oh?"

"Yes, it's half-full if we're talking about the Brad debacle."

"I'm glad you see it that way." Dawn accepted the glass. "And when is it half-empty?"

"When Aunt Irene comes. Mom, how could you?" Tammy half-wailed her question.

"I. . . I didn't, Tammy."

"You didn't invite her?"

"Heavens, no, don't you remember what happened she came here about a decade ago?"

"How could I forget? I'm tempted to grab that half-empty glass of yours and finish it for you."

Dawn laughed. Her daughter's convictions kept her from drinking alcohol, so this was serious business. She took several swallows. "I think I'll need to buy a few more bottles if you told Irene that we're expecting her."

"Mom, I didn't know what to say other than I'd speak with you about it. But she sounded like she's en route."

"En route?"

"Yeah, she was talking so fast I had a hard time following her."

"Lord help us."

"He'd better. Because frankly, the thought of her descending upon us is more stressful to me than the call to Brad was earlier."

Dawn almost spit out her sip of wine. "You called Bradley?"

"Yup. He's going to 'allow' Michael, the father of those twins, to go with his very own wife to the doctor appointments."

"Mighty nice of Brad, wasn't it?" What a creep.

"I had to buy those visits, but it's worth it."

"What did you do, promise him some of his own money?" Funds that lousy Brad withheld from his own wife and daughter.

"Yup."

Tammy raised her teacup and Dawn touched her wineglass to it.

"Good job. And let's toast to surviving Aunt Irene."

"Sounds like a hurricane name."

"With good reason." They both laughed.

Irene was fine in small doses, which was why Dawn had kept their visits combined to a few days at her home in Chicago or a few days with Irene at her place. The last time "Hurricane Irene" came to town, Dawn and Jim needed a week afterward to decompress. With Tammy in the middle of this divorce crisis, the last thing they all needed was an obsessive-compulsive person like her sister showing up. But it was too late now.

Chapter Twelve

Jaycie
Mackinac Island

My father is having an affair with someone only two years older than me. Jaycie sat numb in her chair at the worktable. Two days after hearing the news, she still couldn't wrap her mind around that bizarre information. Dad had already moved his co-worker into their home. When her mother shared the betrayal, Jaycie had called to confront Dad, but he'd hung up on her.

Other staff members settled in at the table, in preparation for the late afternoon staff meeting which was about to start. How could she focus on work when all she could keep imagining was how her father and *that woman* were packing Jaycie's belongings into boxes and putting them into storage.

Her cellphone vibrated in her right jean's pocket just as Mr. Jeffries took his seat, across from her.

"Do you want to get that?" He quickly lifted then lowered his hand. "It's fine."

She exhaled a quick breath. Did he know about her cheater-of-a-father? Not unless Gran already told him, which she might have. "Thanks." She grabbed her iPhone and glanced at the screen. "It's my Gran."

He pointed toward the door. The man was a stickler for privacy with family business despite the fact that he probably knew more about Gran than Jaycie did.

"Hi Gran!" Jaycie rose and walked to a quiet spot behind the office.

"Oh, Jaycie, thanks for picking up!" Gran sounded breathless.

"Is everything all right?" She chewed on her lower lip.

"Well, yes and no. My sister showed up unexpectedly, your great-aunt Irene."

"I thought you'd called her, and Aunt Irene said she wasn't coming."

Gran snorted a laugh. "Well, she arrived in Pellston an hour ago."

"Really?" Jaycie rubbed the back of her neck, where a knot was beginning to form.

Gran exhaled a sigh. "But she says she has reservations at the Grand Hotel tonight, and well. . ."

And Jaycie was on the island. She recalled a very straight-backed, white-haired, great aunt Irene fussing at her because Jaycie hadn't worn a dress to church, when the stern woman last visited. "And you want me to do what?" She anticipated Gran asking her to escort the bossy old harridan to the hotel. "You know they have a taxi she can call to take her up there." Granted that wasn't very hospitable of Jaycie.

A long silence met her ear. Jaycie waited. One of the fort reenactors swaggered by in his blue uniform, clutching a mug of coffee in one hand and a wickedly good-looking cinnamon roll in the other. Jaycie's stomach growled. She'd forgotten to bring lunch and had spent all afternoon at the dig site. "Gran? You there?"

Another big sigh. "I'm concerned. She doesn't hear so well. And well, this is embarrassing but my heart palpitations are kicking up and your mom is threatening to take me down to see Dr. Zaitoun this afternoon if they can get me in."

Jaycie stiffened, concerned for her grandmother. "Gran, you've been overdoing it."

"I know, I know."

She exhaled a big sigh. "You want me to make sure Aunt Irene gets to the Grand, right?"

That was a definite sniff on Gran's end. "Yes." The sound of a rustling tissue. Gentle nose blowing.

Gran could sure crack a girl's defenses. "All right, Gran."

"She'll be on the seven o'clock ferry tonight."

"Seven?" That didn't give Jaycie much time.

"Right. Irene forgot to bring some stuff, so she's is running to Cheboygan to pick up a few things."

"Cheboygan?" That was a half hour away from Mackinaw City.

"That's the closest place to get everything that she claims she needs."

"Wow."

"Right. Well, at least the Walmart should have it all." Gran coughed. "We hope."

"There's always Doud's Market here on the island."

"Right. I'll call you later, Sweetie."

"Ok, Gran."

A nearby hiker paused. An easy grin spread across his handsome face.

"Mort? What are you doing up here?"

"Oh, I have some free time and I like to hike back in this area."

But hadn't he claimed he was busy with landscaping jobs? "It is pretty back there."

"I'm glad they restored Fort Holmes. That's one of my favorite places on the island." He smiled more broadly.

Once again had the feeling of recognition, as though she'd met him before or seen him. "You seem to know where to find peace."

He blinked, as though considering her comment. "I find nature very soothing, don't you?"

Her mom liked to say that God made the beautiful things, that it was Him in those creations that brought the peaceful feeling. "Probably depends on what kind of nature it is. I don't think reptiles are very soothing." She wasn't really sure why she'd challenged his blanket statement, but it slipped out.

His light eyes pierced hers. "I think it depends on who you're with, too."

His words unnerved her. Was he flirting with her? Or making a statement?

He pointed toward the trail. "For now, I guess I'll have to enjoy it on my own."

"I better get back to work."

He headed off and she went inside the office. Something had just shifted between her and Mort, but she couldn't be sure what that was.

After the meeting, Jaycie went into Doud's Market and grabbed a slice of pizza and a Coke and headed for the library. She sat behind the building, the prettiest library she'd ever seen, and enjoyed her food while she waited for the callback about her great-aunt.

After a while, Jaycie checked her phone. 7:55 pm. *Oh no, did I miss the call?*

Jaycie phoned her mother.

"Hey Jaycie."

"Mom. Where is Aunt Irene?"

"Oh my goodness, you wouldn't believe this afternoon. She just now got on the ferry."

"I have to catch the last ferry back at nine." How was she supposed to manage that?

Mom let out a long weary sigh. "Could you just make sure she gets into a taxi headed to the Grand, Jaycie?"

"Sure." She knew her voice sounded clipped. It wasn't Mom's fault. "How's Gran doing?"

"She's lying down, and her palpitations have calmed but now she's exhausted from them."

"Did she see the doctor?"

"Nope. But they gave us an appointment for next week and said she should go to the hospital if they don't stop."

"I'm glad she's doing better right now."

"Yeah, she didn't want to go to the hospital. Your grandpa would have had to be notified about that, so keep Gran's stuff on the lowdown okay? She wants him to complete his PT before he heads up here."

"Okay, I'll keep it quiet, but if she has another bad episode maybe you better call him."

"We'll see."

"All right, Mom." She sounded snarky, but she couldn't help it. "See ya."

She packed her things and headed to Shepler's dock. This time of night, an oxymoron since it was still light until after ten, there weren't as many passengers coming over from Mackinaw City.

Toward the back of the dozen or so passengers, a woman looked around distractedly. With her spun-sugar-looking white hair upswept in a bouffant style and wearing turquoise capris, a floral tunic, and a shorter hot pink leather biker jacket, her great-aunt wasn't hard to spot. She gave "style" and "flashy" a whole new spin. Since when had she traded in her dowdy duds for this new look?

"Aunt Irene?" Jaycie waved and moved forward. She was blocked by the queue of returnees from the island who were bunched to the right at the dock and divided into two lines. Those headed for St. Ignace lined up on the left and for Mackinaw City on the right of the ropes. Jaycie moved past them, still waving her arm high.

Her elderly aunt looked at her, unrecognizing. Then when Jaycie got within a few feet of her, the older woman's expression suddenly transformed from confusion to pleasure—a look Jaycie had never witnessed in regard to herself and it took her aback.

Irene removed her sequin-studded sunglasses and looked at Jaycie. "Oh, it's so good to see you! Why it's been years and years, hasn't it, Jackie?"

When she opened her mouth to correct her, Aunt Irene turned away and raised her hand to her eyes. It was still light out, even this late. The sun wouldn't begin its pink descent until closer to ten o'clock.

"Is my carriage here from the Grand Hotel?" She offered a tight red lipstick-smeared smile.

Jaycie pointed back toward the ferry terminal's exit. "I called a taxi."

Irene frowned but then her features relaxed. "Yes, a car might get us there faster."

Car? There were no cars on the island, other than for emergencies, as Aunt Irene knew from growing up in the area. "I called a taxi, a horse-drawn carriage, when I got here."

But her great-aunt ignored her and dug out a printed piece of paper from her large brown leather satchel. "The Grand has a prestigious suite ready for me. It's new. And for the prices they charge, we shouldn't have to take a taxi."

Having stayed at the Grand Hotel with her parents and with Gran on occasion, Jaycie had subscribed to their emails. In fact, they did have some new suites available, but from what she knew of her great-aunt's situation, the cost would have been out of reach for her since she supposedly lived on a fixed income. But maybe the elderly woman had decided to splurge. "I don't know, Aunt Irene, but the carriage should be here soon, and then we can go, okay?"

"Jaycie!" Parker strode through the crowd toward them. "Mr. Jeffries told me he thought you were here. You're going to miss my library presentation tonight."

"I know." She gave him a cautionary look. "I'm sorry."

Irene scowled and surveyed Parker from head to toe. Attired in a slim-cut fashionable blue suit with a bright white oxford shirt and bow tie, Parker could have stepped from the pages of GQ. "Who is this young whipper snapper?"

"Aunt Irene, this is Hampton Parker the third."

"Surely not! Mother told you to stay away from him." Irene crossed her arms over her chest.

Parker cleared his throat and leaned in. "We work together."

"Walk together? No? I'm waiting on my Grand carriage." Irene shook her head, her jet earrings bobbing furiously.

Jaycie touched her aunt's shoulder. "We work together," she said slowly and with more volume.

"Oh. Well, all right then." Irene uncrossed her arms and wiped some imaginary substance from the front of her shirt.

Parker extended his hand. "I'm Hampton Parker the third, ma'am, but I go by Parker."

"You're Hampy's son?"

"Grandson." Pride reflected from his shining face. A self-satisfaction that Jaycie certainly didn't possess.

"Humph! Always thought those Parkers had some terrible secrets."

A muscle in Parker's cheek jumped.

Jaycie, tried to change the subject, hoping to save him further embarrassment. "You better go on, Parker, so you're not late for your important presentation."

He continued to stare gape-mouthed at Irene. Finally, he spun on his heel and strode off from the dock.

"Well, there was good riddance to bad rubbish if ever there was! My grandparents told me all those rumors about the Parkers and that dead maid from the Grand."

Jaycie stared at her aunt. Obviously something was wrong with her. How could Mom and Gran dump this problem on her? "We need to get you up to the hotel. Come on."

Irene followed her.

A carriage driver pulled up by the curb. "Grand Hotel!"

Jaycie waved. She turned to see Irene eyeing the dock porters, who were stacking luggage onto portable racks. "They'll deliver them for you, Aunt Irene!" she called but the woman didn't hear her. Obviously her hearing problems had grown worse.

She went to her aunt's side, took her elbow, and steered her away from the luggage carts. "They will bring them."

"What?"

"The luggage." Jaycie pointed. "They will transport it."

Fury etched the older woman's features. "Of course they will, I told you so!"

Jaycie sucked in a breath. She had only thirty minutes until the last ferry for the day returned to the island. But she couldn't let her elderly relative go to the Grand on her own. Not like this. Something was seriously off. Jaycie made her decision. She'd have to accompany Irene.

Fifteen minutes later, she left the taxi and paid for both herself and her aunt when Irene imperiously descended from the cab and ignored the driver's request for payment. Fortunately, Jaycie had heeded her mom's advice to always keep cash on her. "Thanks!" She wished she could tip the driver, but that wasn't possible on an intern's low salary.

She raced after Irene who had already headed into the hotel. She caught up with her at the registration desk. Jaycie checked her watch. Fifteen minutes. She'd have to make sure the reservation was okay and then jog all the way back to the wharf. Still might not make it.

What would she do if she missed it? Aunt Irene would have to let her stay with her at the Grand Hotel, pure and simple.

At the desk, a pretty Asian girl about Jaycie's age, offered them a tight-lipped smile. "Reservation name?"

"Irene."

"Last name?"

Her great aunt blinked her light blue eyes several times. Her hearing loss must be severe.

Jaycie, leaned in. "Last name is Aylsworth."

Her aunt nodded. "Of course. That's what I said. I have the Presidential Suite."

The Presidential Suite? Jaycie frowned. Then cringed. When the clerk cast Jaycie a sympathetic look, reality struck her. Her aunt wasn't operating on all of her cylinders, as Grandpa Jim would have said. Irene may not have a booking after all.

"We don't have a guest under that name, ma'am."

Irene stared.

Jaycie touched her aunt's arm. "Do you have your registration paper?" She pointed to her aunt's satchel. *Please God let there be something in there.*

"Oh. Yes!" Irene dug into the depths of the purse and pulled out the printed page and shoved it across the counter to the young woman. She tapped hard on the image of an opulently decorated suite. "There."

The worker's small features tugged in concentration. She held it up to Jaycie. "This is an email about one of the new suites. It's not a registration."

Jaycie took the print-out and scanned it, as her aunt shifted from side-to-side in her black ballet flats, looking around the lobby. Jaycie swallowed hard. Someone else was waiting in line behind them. "Let me see if I can sort this out."

"Of course. And the Presidential Suite has been occupied this week by your country's Vice-President.' The Asian girl again cast her a knowing look and waved the next guest forward.

Jaycie took her aunt's arm and led her away from the counter. "Aunt Irene, do you have something else showing your registration details?" In her heart, Jaycie knew that the woman didn't. But she hoped and prayed that somehow she'd pull out another sheet.

"That was it! All I had." Irene's face once again crumpled into anger.

From somewhere a grandfather clock chimed nine times.

No way to get back to the mainland.

Chapter Thirteen

Dawn
Mackinaw City

"I feel a little guilty for unloading Irene on Jaycie." Dawn wiped down the kitchen counters.

"She'll be fine." Tammy sipped peppermint tea at the dining room table.

"Do you think she's that tough, though?" What would Jim say? She sighed. "Your dad would have a cow if he knew that we sent her over there to his granddaughter."

Tammy pressed a hand to her aching stomach. She seemed to be doing that a lot recently. Maybe it was the hard water they had because of all the limestone shelf in the area. Maybe it was her cursed disease.

Dawn rinsed the washcloth out. "I didn't realize Irene's hearing had gotten so bad."

Tammy nodded. "She needs some hearing aids, that's for sure."

"She'll never get them."

"Too vain."

"Yup."

"She sure has changed her style from what I remember. But then we haven't seen her in quite a while."

Dawn grabbed a towel and dried the wet countertops. "She was still certifiably dowdy the last time I saw her. Maybe her daughter is trying to get her to branch out more."

"I don't think so. Aunt Irene claims she's always dressed this way—all her life."

"Which is patently untrue, Tammy."

"I know."

"Oh boy." Irene must have far more problems than her hearing loss.

Tamara
Mackinaw City

Tamara's cell phone rang. She answered it. "Jaycie?"

"Yeah, Mom, it's nuts here."

Tamara's gut squeezed. "What's going on?"

"Oh my gosh, something is really wrong with Aunt Irene."

"Did you get her checked in?" If her daughter could get Irene settled then maybe that would help.

"She doesn't have reservations, Mom!"

Oh no! "What do you mean?"

"There's nothing on the books for her."

"Oh my gosh. She said she printed out her itinerary." She knew her voice rose in frustration, and she tried to regain control. She took a deep breath.

"It was just an email talking about the new suites, Mom! That's what she had. It's bizarre."

"What? Oh my goodness. I'm so sorry, honey." Tamara heard a man's deep voice in the background, and Irene's throaty laugh.

"Mom, I think maybe she has Alzheimer's or dementia or something."

"Oh, good heavens." If Brad were here he'd be cursing up a blue streak.

"Yeah."

She glanced at the clock, panic gripping her. "Oh my gosh, honey, the last ferry has left!"

"Yeah. I hate to ask but if they have a room, could I put it on the emergency charge card?"

"Oh," She drew out the word. "Oh. No, honey, I'm so sorry. Daddy canceled all our credit cards since my last phone call to him, and I don't have my new ones yet. They haven't come in the mail." She should have kept one of them, but she'd not been thinking about financial emergencies. She had a lot of cash on hand.

Silence on the other end.

"Are you there, honey? I'm sorry. Let me ask Gran if she has an idea. Maybe you can use her MasterCard."

"Okay," Jaycie sounded defeated.

Mom moved closer to the phone. Tamara covered the receiver. "Can you cover a night at the Grand with your Mastercard? I could reimburse you."

"I can ask the Parkers to have Jaycie and Irene stay over there." Mom shrugged.

If only Tamara's nausea wasn't becoming more of a problem. She could have taken Aunt Irene over to the island herself and Jaycie wouldn't be in this predicament. When she finally saw Dr. Austin, the doctor she'd been referred to, she'd demand medications that could manage her symptoms better. After all, if they weren't going to treat her condition, they could at least try to manage it. Was that all that was going to be left now? Managing? Maybe so.

Jaycie
Mackinac Island

A man's familiar deep voice caught her attention while she was on the phone. The "gardener" stood attired in a suit even finer than that sported by Parker earlier, enhancing his muscular form. Her heart seemed to stop in her throat when he'd joined them. He was clean-shaven and his auburn hair was cut short and styled. He was surrounded by other guys about his same age, similarly attired in clothes that screamed "money." A couple of the men had checked her out, appreciation shining their eyes.

Mort strode toward Irene and Jaycie. "Hello, ladies. What's going on?"

Irene gawked up at him. "They've given my suite away."

Standing behind Irene, Jaycie shook her head. Mort extended his arm to Irene and she took it.

Tonight, Mort looked so good. Too good. She was not going there. She was not going to give her heart out again in a place where she had no intentions of staying. And especially not to a guy who could probably do modeling assignments if he wanted to, like Elliott had done during his university breaks. No wonder the so-called gardener's face looked so familiar. She'd seen him in some magazines, probably ads for businessmen.

"What happening?" Mom asked.

Mort walked Irene to the reservation counter and appeared to be chatting up the staff.

"I'm not sure."

"Your grandmother says to take Irene to the Parkers' hotel."

Not a chance. She was not going to be indebted to Parker and his family.

Mort slipped something to the reservationist and walked Irene back over to join Jaycie.

"This nice man got me my suite back!" Irene beamed up at Mort.

"Mom, I think a. . . friend of mine got Irene a spot here."

"Call me back later, okay? Let me know what happened." Mom said her goodbyes and Jaycie ended the call.

Jaycie tapped Aunt Irene's bony shoulder. "I called my mother."

"I don't need to call my mother. I'm married now!"

Mort winked at Jaycie. "Your Aunt Irene is all set."

"Are you sure?" Only a few minutes early Jaycie had no ferry ride, no room for the night, and an irascible great aunt who couldn't be reasoned with. Now, though, Irene seemed as happy as an archeologist who'd just found a prized Etruscan artifact. "You can get us into a room?"

Mort grinned at her. "What are friends for?"

Irene peered up at him. "You two are friends, are you?"

"Yes, and I'll let you in on a secret." Mort leaned in toward Irene's left ear. "Castle Suite is much better than the Presidential Suite," he whispered loudly, in a conspiratorial tone.

"Where would the Castle Suite be?" Jaycie's voice came out a squeak.

"Top floor in one of the new turrets." Mort extended his arm to her. "Come on, ladies, I'm offering an escort."

His friends, who had lingered in an alcove, must have realized they'd lost him because they now waved and one called out, "Meet you in the Cupola later!"

Mort shook his head as his buddies departed toward the elevator. "Maybe."

"Have you got the key?" Aunt Irene gazed expectantly at Mort.

"I do." He reached inside his jacket and pulled out a large old-fashioned looking, but new, shiny brass key.

Okay, who was this guy? How could he simply produce a key to a new suite at the Grand? "We're not taking your spot are we, Mort?"

"Oh, no. *Dr. Piccard* keeps it for special occasions or emergencies." His tone was teasing. Was he the mysterious Dr. Piccard?

Irene glanced between the two of them, her white eyebrows knitting together. "Don't argue in public, it's unbecoming."

Jaycie simply nodded but Mort replied, "Yes, indeed madam."

"What?" her aunt demanded loudly.

Mort bent over her. "I said you are quite right."

"Of course I am. And where is my luggage?"

"Oh no." Jaycie cringed. "They won't have known what to do with her luggage."

"Let me handle this. Excuse me, madam." Mort slipped his arm free from Irene's and Jaycie's and went to the bell captain's desk. A salt-and-pepper haired man with a substantial girth spoke with him and accepted what looked like two twenty-dollar bills from Mort. How was Jaycie going to pay him back? She had no clothes of her own and not even a toothbrush with her. And there was no tipping allowed at the hotel so why had he done that?

A young man with short cropped dark hair and café-au-lait skin pushed a cart past them, the scents of roast beef and yeast rolls and something vanilla and sweet wafting up from beneath the silver domes that covered the room service plates.

"That smells delicious." Irene reached out as if to lift a cover, but the young man stared at her and she stopped. "I haven't eaten all day."

"Really? Didn't Mom or Gran feed you?"

Irene waved her hand. "I'm watching my figure."

When the woman's stomach growled loudly, Jaycie was inclined to believe her that she hadn't eaten. "We'll get room service to send something up." Jaycie could cover that limited expense tomorrow.

Mort rejoined them. "Luggage all straightened out. They'll bring it straight up."

Soon they'd gone up in the elevator and Mort led them to the suite. He opened the door and waved them inside the beautiful room, decorated in shades of lilac, hot pink, and bright green.

"This will do very well." Aunt Irene reached into her purse and pulled out her wallet.

When it became clear she intended to tip Mort, Jaycie's cheeks blazed.

Mort waved his hands. "No need, madam. No tipping at the Grand."

"That's right." Irene scowled at Jaycie. "I told you that earlier."

Why hadn't Mom and Gran picked up on Irene's mental problems? Why did they send her to the island unaccompanied?

Someone knocked on the door and Mort opened it. The bellman brought Aunt Irene's luggage inside. Two large cases, the size of Jaycie's entire summer wardrobe were rolled inside, all for a one-night stay.

Irene clapped her hands. "I'm all set. Thank you, both."

Mort pulled the luggage over to the bedroom door. "There's a king-size bed in here. You should be very comfortable."

The two of them should be able to fit in there. If Irene didn't want to share, Jaycie could always sleep on the comfy-looking pale pink sofa in the room's center. "Thanks so much, Mort."

He bowed. "Happy to be at your service. Sadly, I'd better catch up with my friends. Otherwise, I'd stay and visit some more with you two lovely ladies."

He left the room, gently closing the door behind him.

Aunt Irene motioned to the phone. "Order us up some room service, will ya honey?"

"Sure." Jaycie complied, wondering what she was going to do in the morning. She used the hotel phone on the nearby bureau. A framed picture of a beautiful raven-haired woman smiled down from the wall. The international supermodel known only by her first hyphenated name—Kay-Leigh. She was Gran's client. She had made it big about a decade earlier and had been going strong until recently, according to the tabloids that Jaycie sometimes read. Something niggled at Jaycie about the woman, maybe because Gran had some kind of issue with Kay-Leigh's upcoming travel plans.

She pushed thoughts of the supermodel aside and made the call to Room Service.

Forty-five minutes later, Irene had devoured a steak meal while Jaycie watched. She rose and stretched. "I'm really tired and I've got to go to work tomorrow morning."

"Goodness, I've kept you too long." Irene made a shooing motion. "You better get home now."

Jaycie stared at her aunt. "The ferries have stopped for the night."

"Oh my. Well, you cannot stay here." Irene gestured around the place as if she owned it. "This is my room."

"Aunt Irene, I can sleep on the sofa."

"This is my special vacation. I've looked forward to it all year." Irene made a petulant face. "You don't want to ruin it for me, do you?"

"I cannot get back to the mainland." Jaycie said each word loudly and clearly so that her aunt would catch each one. "I have to stay here with you."

Her aunt rose and grabbed the ice bucket. "Go get us some ice would you?"

"All right." And while she was at it she'd call her mother and tell her what was going on. She took the ice container and headed out hoping to find the ice machine. As she walked the corridor, she called her mother.

When Mom answered, Jaycie hurriedly explained everything.

"Oh no," Mom groaned. "Let me get Gran in on this conversation."

Soon Gran and Mom were on speaker phone and Jaycie reiterated her concerns.

"We'll come over on the first ferry in the morning and I'll call Lenet tonight and fill her in on things."

Hopefully her aunt's daughter could help them get her safely back home. "Take a carriage straight to the Grand."

"Will do."

Jaycie spied an ice machine and headed toward it. "I'll stay with her until then."

"Sorry, honey." Mom sounded exhausted. Lately, she's seemed pretty wrung out. And no wonder, with Dad cheating on her.

"Sooo sorry, Jaycie." Gran's voice was pathetic, which was unlike her. "If your grandpa was here he'd have helped out."

But Grandpa Jim was in Chicago and her useless father was in Virginia, likely readying her room for the twins. "I'll see you tomorrow. Goodnight."

She filled the bucket with ice and returned to the room. When she tried the door, it was locked. She knocked. No answer. She tried again. Still nothing. She pounded one more time and called through the door, "Aunt Irene, open up, I have the ice."

She heard footsteps on the other side. "What's that?"

"It's Jaycie, I'm back, I have the ice."

"I don't need it, honey."

"Let me in, please."

"You go home now and let me enjoy my vacation."

A couple strolled by, hand-in-hand, eyeing her with suspicion.

Jaycie blew out a breath. She must look a sight. She'd been at the dig earlier and traipsing all over the island since then. She leaned in toward the door. "Aunt Irene, I can't get home because the ferries have ended."

"You're not my problem, dearie."

She heard footsteps heading away from the door.

What in the world? She stood there, gaping at the door.

Tears threatened but she was too angry to release them. She couldn't make herself go down and search for Mort. She'd be too humiliated. She pulled her phone from her pocket, hands shaking. She'd call the one person who absolutely would come help her out. Who would stay at her side, if need be. Something about that realization sent shivers through her from head to toe.

"Jaycie?" Parker's sleepy voice croaked out.

She almost hung up. "Parker. . ." She sank to the floor.

"What's going on?"

She stifled a sob.

"Where are you, Jaybird?"

Trying to make her voice work, she sucked in a deep breath.

"Listen to me. Whatever is going on, our Higher Power is bigger than this."

That got her attention, and she almost laughed to hear Parker refer to his Higher Power. "You. . . mean God?"

"Yeah. Tell me what's going on."

"Um, my great aunt. . ."

It sounded like Parker was rustling around. "I'll get our boat and come straight across to you in Mackinaw City."

"I'm here." She sniffed.

"On the island?"

"Yes, at the Grand."

"The Grand? What are you doing there?"

"Locked outside my great-aunt's nonexistent room." She choked out a laugh.

"Ok." He sounded so calm. "What floor has this nonexistent room? I'm coming over right now but let's keep talking."

"It's the Castle Suite. A new turret suite."

He whistled. "She must have some cash to burn."

"Nope, wait till you hear." She was already starting to feel better. She inhaled the scent of sweet geraniums, set on a nearby cherry console table.

"Should I get my dad or grandpa to help?"

She blew out a long breath. "Let me tell you about it and then you decide."

"All right. Shoot."

She told him about the whole ordeal.

At the end he whistled again. "Ok, definitely rounding up Grandpa and Dad to help. Grandpa knows your Great-aunt Irene, I bet, from what she spouted earlier."

"Probably so."

"Some benefits of multi-generational family friendships."

"Yes." How she'd missed *this* Parker. This guy who always had her back. And maybe, in some way, that's what he was trying to do at college. But he'd been so beyond annoying at UVA. Maybe he really had meant to look after her, before things went haywire for him.

"Okay, I'm gonna sign off now, and I'll be there soon."

"Thanks, Parker."

"That's what friends do for one another." When he said it, something rotated and clicked within her. Mort had spoken the same words earlier. But Parker's affirmation immediately soothed her angst.

Dawn
Mackinaw City

If Hampy, his son Hamp, and grandson Parker, didn't deserve medals, then Dawn didn't know who did. The three men had watched over Irene's hotel suite, taking turns two nights earlier. The Parker men sat by the door, in case her poor sister came out and began wandering. They'd also put Jaycie up at Hampy's beautiful old white Victorian house on the East Bluff—the original Butterfly Cottage previously owned by Dawn's parents and sold to the Parkers. Then they'd ferried Irene back over to the mainland.

Today, Hampy and Parker had returned to give Irene an escort to the airport in Pellston when she'd refused for Dawn to drive her. Thank God Irene had a direct flight home, and her daughter would meet her at the airport.

Dawn let Cici outside in the back yard then returned to the kitchen.

Tammy stood staring inside the upper cabinets.

"Are you looking for something?"

"Mom, I bought more coffee filters. I put them right where they always are."

Dawn groaned. "We've been 'Irened' I believe."

"Irened?"

"Your aunt Irene must have snuck in here put everything in what she thought was perfect order."

"Did you ask her to?"

Chuckling, Dawn opened the cabinet with the plates, bowls, and saucers. The bowls, used on a daily basis, were up so high that it would require a footstool to reach them.

"What the heck?"

"Indeed. Despite her mind being so disordered right now, Irene saw fit to put everything in her idea of perfect order."

"Without asking and without permission?" Tammy, ever the teacher, had a big thing about someone messing with her stuff.

"Correct. But I think she could have done much worse, based on what she did with Jaycie." Dawn tore off a paper towel and place it in the bottom of the coffee basket. "I'll keep using the paper towels until we can buy some new filters."

"You haven't found them either?"

"Nope." She scooped out a half cup of medium-ground Michigan Cherry coffee that she'd purchased from her friend, Laurinda, at the Bakery. She inhaled deeply.

"That stuff smells heavenly."

"Tastes even better. I grabbed this yesterday while you were napping."

Tammy stretched. Her pink sleep shirt, with a multi-colored moose printed on it, made Dawn smile.

"I'm glad you like that sleep-set, sweetie. When I saw it, I wasn't sure if you or Jaycie would want it."

Tapping her chest, Tammy quirked an eyebrow. *"Moi, ma mere, moi!"*

"I can see that, darling. It's all yours." Dawn poured filtered water into the coffee pot. They'd not used tap water because of the heavy amount of lime in it.

The doorbell rang.

She went to the door and opened it. Chris, a teen who was a regular summer resident, held a massive bouquet of peonies, lilies, roses, carnations, and ferns. *Lord help me, all I can think of is – where's the funeral?*

He thrust the heavy crystal vase at her, and Dawn struggled to balance the thing, which must have weighed over five pounds. She should give him a tip.

"Wait a moment, Chris."

She brought the arrangement inside and set it on an entryway table, then pulled a fiver from her wallet and handed it to the teen. He towered over her now. "Goodness, you must have passed six feet already."

His cheeks turned pink. "Yes, ma'am."

She loved his Southern politeness. Like how things used to be done back in the day even in the North. "Tell your mother to come over sometime and visit."

"She's busy on another story, ma'am." He rolled his dark eyes. "You know how that is."

His mom wrote murder mysteries. The family resided in South Carolina and spent summers by the Straits. "She didn't do an effigy in the yard this year did she?" The woman done some outrageous things to promote her work, including showing up at Fort Michilimackinac dressed in Native American clothing, covered with what looked like blood.

"No effigy, ma'am, but Dad went home early when she began using him as the inspiration for her next victim."

Dawn patted the boy's arm. "I'm sure she doesn't plan to literally make a victim of him."

"No." Dimples appeared in his tanned cheeks. "She intends to 'literarily' make him a victim."

They both laughed.

"I'll see you later, Mrs. Charbonneau."

"Thanks, Chris."

She closed the door and locked it for good measure. A little shiver coursed through her, and she shook it off. Simply thinking about some of the writer's outrageous shenanigans was enough to creep her out.

"Mom?" Tammy came around the corner. She stopped when she neared the flowers. "Who are these from?"

"I imagine they're from my husband."

Tammy pulled the tiny envelope free from its hard plastic holder and opened it.

Maybe Jim misses me. Maybe he, like she, had found romance stirred by their nightly chats.

"Yup. These are for you."

Something fluttered in her chest. The last time she'd had flowers they'd been because of Jim's surgery, a time when she'd been pretty stressed out. Both she and Jim had appreciated the flowers, sent by Tammy.

Tammy thrust the card at her.

"Thinking of you." Dawn read the card aloud. "Your Sugar Boy, AKA Mickey of Minnie & Mickey's Diner." That's what they teasingly called each other when they were cooking together.

"Someone has an admirer."

"Yes, for almost fifty years." Dawn grinned

"Oh, I almost forgot." Color drained from her daughter's face. "It's not for a few more months."

"November."

Tammy's eyes suddenly filled with tears. Her poor daughter. Tammy would never have a fiftieth anniversary to celebrate.

"Oh, sweetie." Dawn opened her arms and went to her only child and held her close. "Things will be all right. And we're here for you."

Tamara

Her mother's words earlier that day echoed in Tamara's mind as she walked up the street. Things would not be all right. Things were about to change. Terribly. There'd not likely be any fiftieth wedding anniversary celebration that included Tamara. And that made her even sadder than she'd been.

She entered the Mackinaw Bakery, the scent of sweet freshly baked items attempting to tease her senses but failing. Was this how life would be now? She took her place in the long line. A twinge started in her side, and Tamara pressed her hand over the offending area. Her physician had warned her there would be more of these pains.

In a few days she'd finally see the cancer specialist in Petoskey. The oncologist, Dr. Austin, had fit her into his packed schedule.

Earlier, after she'd discovered Brad in the parking lot, she'd had a visit with Dr. Forbes. Although his wife was her distant cousin, he'd been Tamara's family practitioner for years. He'd been concerned about her recurring symptoms and ordered blood tests. Then he made an oncology referral.

Pancreatic cancer.

The dread disease that had killed Ruby had come for Tamara. And wasn't it just like the devil to bring this on when Tamara was already struggling with Brad's infidelity?

Although the oncologist in Virginia wanted to proceed with surgery, Tamara felt convicted to refuse. With what had happened to Ruby, she rejected a Whipple procedure. She'd prayed on it.

Of course, she probably should have prayed about clearing out her and Brad's retirement accounts, too. She'd been in such a crazed and distressed mindset that she did like she usually did—set into action to do something about her situation. Since she wouldn't be alive in about six months, it hadn't seemed like such a bad idea. And Brad would receive punishment for all the years he'd kept their finances separate. At least that was what she'd told herself.

She scanned the workers behind the high glass bakery case, which was filled with all manner of goodies. Three of the five women were the regulars whom she'd enjoyed chatting with over the many summers she'd come to the cottage.

Tamara examined the rows of pastries. She touched the hem of her too-loose polo shirt. Normally she'd fret about the calories. Now, with ten pounds already gone, with her pancreas troubles, she should be able to eat anything in the case and not worry—if she could work up a better appetite.

A dark-haired man with crinkles around his eyes held his toddler aloft to better survey the entire case. The chubby boy pointed to a gooey bear claw.

A space at the counter opened up and Tamara stepped forward. Her mother's long-time but younger friend, Laurinda, smiled at her. "How are you doing today, Tam?"

"Good." A blatant lie. A million mixed emotions roiled in Tamara's gut. Joy in seeing her familiar faces at the shop. Sadness that this would be her last summer on earth. Fear of what these last days would be like. Doubt about how to tell her family. The pain of knowing her husband had another woman. She blinked rapidly. She'd not break down. *Not here.* She forced brightness into her quavering voice, "I get to spend the whole summer with my mom and daughter." If she lived that long.

"What a blessing."

"It is." It truly would be. Was it selfish to not want to ruin this last bit of happiness with her mom and Jaycie? *Lord give me the right time to tell them.*

Chapter Fourteen

Jaycie
Mackinac Island

"Thank you, Miss Worth." The school kids who'd visited the dig site that day waved at Jaycie as their leader led them away and off to their next adventure.

Parker rubbed his arm across his forehead and grinned at her. "I don't know how you do it, Jaybird."

"I love working with the kids. All the excited questions. All the silly things they think." Jaycie pulled off her work gloves.

She'd run into Mort on her lunch break. Once again she'd been struck by what a handsome and philosophical man he was. And like the other times when she'd run into him, even briefly, like at Doud's coffee counter, he always offered up pithy advice. Today's offering was that it was pointless to search for inherent meaning in her work, because it was unlikely that she'd find any.

"Those kids value your work. And you should, too."

She straightened. Parker's words contradicted Mort's. "So, you believe it's okay to think we have some usefulness?"

"Of course." He shot her a quizzical look. "Not all work brings joy, though."

Since when had Parker joined the philosophical crowd? "What's your example?

He took a quick swig from his water bottle. "I've watched out for Carter all my life. I don't share your same enthusiasm for working with kids."

"For me, I wasn't happy being an only child." She leaned in toward him. "Although now I guess I'll have stepsiblings who are two decades younger than me."

"It'll be like being their aunt. And you won't be living with them."

Jaycie shook her head. "I don't know what it'll be like. Although I thought I was ready for the next adult phase of my life, it really bugs me that Dad is already making over my room for the twins."

Parker frowned. "Your dad is making some bad choices, but it doesn't mean he's a bad man."

"Yeah, maybe so."

Miles, one of the main muscle men on the job, joined them. He swiped his red handkerchief over his sweaty brow. "You ready for us to shut down and secure the site for the day?"

Parker offered the deeply suntanned man a mock salute. "As you wish."

"Want to ride our bikes back, or wait on the dray, Jaybird?"

"Quicker to ride."

"All right. Let's get back to the office and finish our paperwork."

"Gotta get cleaned up before I meet my mom at the Pink Pony for dinner."

He cocked an eyebrow. "The Pink Pony? And I don't get an invite?"

"I bet she wouldn't mind if you joined us." A smile tugged at her lips.

They retrieved their bikes. "For smoked whitefish dip I think I'd do almost anything."

She laughed. "I'd forgotten how awesome that stuff is until I grabbed a little box of it from Doud's for my lunch the other day."

"Pink Pony's is best, but they get some decent stuff at Doud's. What did you eat with it?"

"Nothing." She cocked an eyebrow at him. "A plastic fork, some smoked whitefish and voila—Nirvana."

He chuckled but then his expression became serious. "Hey, ask your mom if we can help her with anything tonight while she's on the island."

That question flew at her out of left field. "Help her?"

They mounted their twelve-speeds and headed off toward the fort.

"Well, yeah, Carter says he's assisted her with a few things lately."

Jaycie almost lurched from her bike. "What do you mean? When does Carter see my mom?"

"When she comes over to the island."

Mom hadn't said anything to her about coming over to the island. Not until today. They rode on in silence, beneath the canopy of tall pines and maples.

"Jaybird, your mom visits with my dad every handful of days or so."

"What?" Her heart slammed into her chest, but she kept peddling.

He glanced over at her. "Do you really not know?"

"Know what?"

"They've been friends all their lives for one thing."

Mom had always been pretty vague about her friendship with Parker's father, but she'd suspected they'd dated in high school.

"My dad asked your mom to marry him, and she said no."

She shook her head. "I don't think so."

"Yes. He even kept the ring."

She twisted her lower lip to the side in a doubtful expression.

"Dad was rebelling against Grandpa, and he enlisted in the military against Grandpa's wishes. Your mom refused him because she didn't want that lifestyle."

"But my grandfather retired from the Coast Guard, so she grew up with that."

"Exactly. Your mom didn't want a life where she'd be moving around from place to place like she had her first eighteen years."

That actually made sense. "Wow. If that had happened, if they'd married, then neither one of us would be here right now." They both cast a quick glance at each other.

"Yikes. I guess you're right." Parker sped forward and was soon cycling ahead of her.

Jaycie pedaled faster and caught up with him. "So, are they. . . like. . . seeing one another?"

"I don't think so. Dad is working out his recovery. He's making amends to your mom."

"Amends?"

"He apologized because his rebellion ended their relationship."

"Is that like those step things that you have to do?"

"Part of the AA plan."

"And yet my mom has still kept coming to the island even after he did that?"

"Dad says that your mom has some things she needs to share."

"Such as?" Probably about how awful Dad was.

"Don't know. But Dad seriously needs a sympathetic shoulder since Mom died."

"Are they like besties again or something?"

"Maybe."

"Wow, and I'm just now hearing about this." A rush of Straits of Mackinac breeze chilled her cheeks.

"I doubt it's personal." Parker laughed. "Her not telling you."

But it felt like it.

Soon, they arrived back at the office and settled into their post-dig rhythm of completing necessary nightly paperwork.

"What time's your mom coming?"

"She said six."

Parker tapped his phone screen. "We better get going—it's a quarter till."

They both rose from their desks and headed out.

"I wonder why she's finally deigned to include me on this visit to the island?" And why had Carter had to help her mother?

Tamara
Straits of Mackinac

Tamara held fast to the back of the ferry seat ahead of her. Nausea bubbled up. If she could reach into her purse, she could pull out one of the medications for that, but she was afraid that if she released the seatback that she'd buckle and fall off her seat. All around her, the latecomers from Mackinaw City disembarked the ferry. She had to get off. She practiced Lamaze breathing, which had gotten her through the difficult delivery with Jaycie.

"Mrs. Worth?" Carter moved alongside her seat, attired as usual in his navy Shepler's work shirt, a polo, and khaki cargo shorts and white dock shoes. "Are you getting off, ma'am?"

She drew in a long slow breath. "Yes. Sorry." She smiled at him, but he stared back at her in concern.

"You all right?"

She opened her purse, pulled the top of her pills, and took one out and then swallowed it. "I'll be all right in a minute."

His gaze darkened and his features tightened. "You know, you need to be careful with medicines even if they're prescribed by a doctor."

Poor kid. He'd lost his mother to prescription opioids. She opened her mouth to say something reassuring to him, but he'd spun on his heel and walked off the boat. If she wasn't mistaken, that was an expression of disgust and anger that had flitted across his face before he'd turned. She followed, moving as fast as her roiling gut would allow.

When she got onto the dock, the sun burst from behind fluffy white clouds and suddenly she felt better. It was as if God himself was giving her a reassuring "hello." Smiling, Tamara headed down the long dock and then onto the sidewalk on the main street. Up several blocks, she'd meet her daughter. Tonight, she'd tell Jaycie about her diagnosis, and what it meant. All about the decisions she'd made. First, they'd have a nice dinner, and she'd do a lead up. Then she'd take her precious daughter shopping and tell her some things she'd like to do that summer—stuff on her bucket list of items to do before she died. Then, they'd catch a ride to the Cupola, and over a virgin frozen margarita, Tamara would tell her daughter that she had maybe three months to live.

Her hands began to shake. She could do this. She had to do it. As she wove through the tourists on the sidewalks, Tamara spied Jaycie ahead of her. With Parker. From the looks of things, the two both planned to dine with her. *No, no, no.*

She reached them.

"Hi Mom." Jaycie pulled her into a quick hug. "You don't mind if Parker joins us, do you?"

Yes, I do. She didn't want to lie but she also wasn't going to be rude. "Sure, come on." They could speak privately later. *And please, dear God, don't let me get sick on the island tonight.*

They went inside and were seated by a spunky teen with pink spiked hair. Before he sat down, Parker's mouth dropped open. He walked over to the bar. Hamp was seated at the bar, apparently alone as both seats on either side were empty.

Should she go over there, too, to make sure her friend got away from the bar?

Parker returned with his father. "Mrs. C., you don't mind if Dad joins us, do you?"

"Of course not." Tamara gave Hamp a sharp look. "I'd much rather that than you sitting there at the bar by yourself."

Her old sweetheart had the decency to blush. "I got the brilliant idea to see if I could sit there and order something nonalcoholic and drink it."

"How'd that go for you?" Parker sat down next to his father.

Hamp shook his head. "Not a real good plan." Sweat broke out on his brow.

Parker scowled. "Didn't think so."

Tamara couldn't help but grin at Parker's words to his father. He was a good kid. No, he was becoming a thoughtful young man. And he'd been put through the wringer of life.

Splaying his hands, Hamp looked around at the three of them. "I've been rescued."

Hours later, the four were still together, having forgone a visit to the Cupola Lounge at the top of the Grand Hotel, and instead went from fudge store to fudge store, the other three sampling fudge while Tamara tried to not breathe in too deeply lest her nausea ramp up.

"Listen, guys, I've got to get home." Tamara shrugged apologetically.

"Coming back over on Friday?" Hamp tried to hand her a piece of peanut butter fudge, but she refused.

"Yes, I'll be there." If she didn't get any sicker. This was all an unknown journey now. "And we'll plan out the bucket list of Upper Peninsula spots I want to hit next week."

Jaycie exchanged a quick glance with Parker. "You know we'll have to work, Mom."

"Gran and Hampy will be coming with us." By then, Tamara planned to have told her mother about her condition. "But I'd love to do some things with you that last week before you go off to grad school."

If she still could get out of bed at that point. She'd add a request to her friend, Susan, her pastor at home, Larry, and her Prayer Group for specific intercession for these trips. And for healing. God was in the business of miracles, wasn't he? Even if He didn't give her one, though, she'd trust Him.

Jaycie
Mackinaw City

Jaycie gathered all her work clothes and loaded the washer in the basement. It seemed strange to be in a basement since their home and most in their Tidewater area of Virginia didn't have one. The cottage's basement housed the sump pump, the washer and dryer, and a line for indoor drying when it rained. In the winter, Gran and Grandpa stored the bikes there and all the outdoor equipment and gardening stuff.

Her cell phone rang. *Dad.* She hesitated but then answered the call. "Hello."

"Jaycie, it's Dad."

Yes, she'd seen his ID on the phone. "Yup."

He sighed. "Listen, this hasn't all been me, you know."

She was tempted to hang up on him. "What do you want?" She loved her dad, but right now, he was on top of her "Bad List."

"I wanted to let you know that Gina and I want to make you comfortable when you come home. We decided to leave your room alone after all."

"Um, yeah, like I'll ever be staying with you." Yes, that sounded caustic, but danged if Mort wasn't wrong—this keeping stuff in or letting it flow right through without feeling it was unnatural.

"Well, that's harsh."

"Harsh? You wanta hear harsh? Running off with another woman is." Jaycie couldn't help herself, she pushed the red circle to end the call.

She puffed out a few long breaths. When the phone rang again, she glanced at it. Dad again. *He can leave a message.*

The door to the basement creaked open. "Jaycie, are you down there?"

"Yes, Gran. Dad just called. He's such an idiot."

"Agreed, but he's still your father."

"It doesn't mean I have to listen to him spouting nonsense. I mean really. I don't."

"Okay, okay. I just wondered if you want to come for a hike with me. I'm done with my VBS work."

"Yeah, sure. We've been talking about going out to Mill Creek for a while. Can we go there?"

"Great minds think alike. That's exactly my plan. I've started packing a picnic lunch."

"Let me get this laundry started, and I'll get some sneakers on."

"Yeah, those aren't going to work." Gran pointed to Jaycie's sparkly sandals, an impulse purchase she'd made in the UK before she'd left. Before Elliott had betrayed her.

Painful memories flashed through her mind. Walks around the university hand-in-hand, stolen kisses in the hallways outside their classes, late nights noshing at the pub and laughing, and those intimate moments at his apartment. At the rush of shame and hurt and longing, she was reminded of the Bible verses that cautioned against such relationships before marriage. It was like she'd lost a part of herself in losing Elliott.

"Jaycie, are you all right?"

"Yeah, yeah, sorry, I was just thinking about something."

"Thinking about Parker?" Gran's teasing tone startled her.

"Oh, no, why would you say that?" Parker was as different from Elliott as a seventeenth century set of armor was from a modern-day Ermenegildo Zegna suit. Elliott had been so thrilled to receive the most expensive men's suit in the world, on his last job. And why was she thinking of this comparison? Instead of putting Parker in a knight's armor, she should have been thinking of him in khakis and a polo shirt.

"Well, your mom said you two seemed like two peas-in-a-pod at the Pink Pony."

"Um. . ." Her thoughts veered to mulling over just why she'd spent so much time in England comparing Elliott to Parker. Why had she wasted so much time doing that? She was no psychologist, but even she knew she shouldn't be spending so much time obsessing, yes obsessing, over someone who'd harassed her through her first three years of college.

"Jaycie?" Gran shook her head. "I think you need to get more sleep. But for now, let's get going soon, okay?"

"Yeah." And do a "Mort" and leave her thoughts of Elliott and Parker in the basement, locked away, instead of letting them flow through her and be gone.

Chapter Fifteen

Tamara
Mackinaw City

"I'm heading out, Mom." Tamara grabbed her purse. This was it, the real deal, as she went to her first appointment with Dr. Austin, the oncologist in Michigan. She closed her eyes. *God help me now.*

"You sure you don't want me to come?"

This wasn't the day for Tamara to have her mother's company. "I'm going to catch up with Wendy after her show is over."

Her friend, Wendy Shoults, had an artist's exhibit that day, but that wasn't the main reason Tamara needed to go on her own. She wasn't ready yet to let go of things and tell people. Soon, though. "Next time I go to Petoskey you come with me, ok?"

"Sure thing."

She *would* have to tell Mom soon because that schedule of hers would be taking a hit with Tamara's own needs, soon, as her condition worsened. "See you later."

"Bye, honey."

Tamara headed out the door. Several tourists walking past the house gawked at her. Sometimes strangers visiting the area would stop her and ask, "What's it like living here?" Would they ask her things as her condition deteriorated? As she became sicker, as things progressed, no doubt people would avoid her.

She kept her head down and headed toward her car parked on the street. Soon, she was on interstate I-75 heading south, and then took her exit for Petoskey. *Dear God, give me a good doctor, who will understand my needs and really listen. You've already spoken to my heart and told me what to do, now help those around me to support me in this decision.*

Peace enveloped her. Ever since her diagnosis, and the conviction God had given her, she'd known this was the path to follow.

Once her GPS announced she was at the medical center, she pulled in and found a spot. She went into the building, filled out their paperwork, and waited to be called to the insurance counter.

Ten minutes inched by until her name was called. A petite Hispanic woman with silver-streaked hair looked up at her and smiled. Her nametag had Maria imprinted on it.

"Have a seat." The woman's voice was lightly accented.

Tamara climbed onto the tall stool across the counter from the woman. She passed Maria the insurance paperwork and her cards.

"I'll scan these." Maria pushed the cards through a small scanner on her counter. She passed the cards back to Tamara.

"Thanks."

The woman then copied Tamara's paperwork before going into her computer and entering information. She'd been silent for a couple of minutes before she suddenly stopped typing.

"Your husband's name is Bradley X. Worth?" She rapidly blinked her heavily mascaraed brown eyes.

"Yes, the X is for Xavier. His parents were a bit eccentric." That was an understatement. His mother insisted that Brad refer to them by their given names not as Mother and Father. Her mother-in-law was a highly sought-after Manhattan psychiatrist, and her father-in-law had just retired from his job as a tax attorney. "They thought that with such a common last name it would be helpful."

Maria's red lips remained parted, and color drained from her deep complexion. She reached for a mug embossed with *Mamasita* and took a long swig. "His birthday is in March?"

"Yesss," Tamara drew out the word, wondering why the hospital insurance worker appeared so distressed.

"This man. He is my *brother-in-law*." Maria's dark eyes fixed on her. "Bradley X. Worth."

What in the world?

Maria stood, tears in her eyes. "And he *killed* my sister and nieces." She stood and walked away from her desk, her co-workers calling after her. Another woman slipped into the spot that Maria had vacated.

"Sorry." The slim blond shrugged and stared at the computer. "I've never seen Maria so upset. But she's only been here a few months. I don't really know her situation."

Tamara dipped her chin slightly in acknowledgement but clamped her lips together. Her world had already been flipped upside down, but Maria's words sent her spiraling down into a dark hole that left her dizzy. What did the woman mean? Surely Brad hadn't killed anyone. Nothing made sense anymore.

She finished up the insurance intake with the other worker, who looked as uncomfortable as Tamara felt. She returned to the waiting room, reeling emotionally.

Tamara sat down and logged onto the hospital's Wi-Fi then texted her mother-in-law a message, asking for a phone call later. Brad had lived in Texas during an extended internship. That's where he'd had his accident. Since he'd kept Gina a secret from her, had he also conveniently failed to mention that not only had he been previously married, but he'd killed his wife? But if he had, wouldn't he have served jail time?

The maple wood door to the offices opened and a nurse holding a clipboard peeked out. "Mrs. Worth?"

Tamara grabbed her purse and rose.

She was brought back to a masculine office, the rectangular matte black desk piled high with files. She settled in the brown leather chair, where the nurse had indicated for her to sit. "He's not examining me?"

The nurse's lips compressed, and she shook her head. "He'll be in shortly. He likes to speak with his patients first and review their cases."

"Thanks."

Framed licenses and degrees occupied almost every inch of the wall. She stood and took a few steps to examine the closest ones. Medical license from Texas. Residency in Obstetrics also in Texas. Obstetrics? He was supposed to be a cancer specialist. Had someone messed up his license or had he really switched specialties?

The door opened and a tall man with golden hair and light blue-gray eyes entered. He took two swooping steps toward her and extended his hand and gave it a firm shake.

"Dr. Tom Austin." His voice held a warm Texas accent.

"Nice to meet you. Well, that's not exactly true." To her dismay, her hands and arms began to shake. Everything was becoming too real. Obviously her nervous system recognized it to betray her like this.

"No need to be nervous, Mrs. Worth, I don't bite." He winked at her. "At least not at the first visit."

She almost laughed. "I don't either. Not until we get to know each other better."

He grinned.

"But in my case, doctor, we won't have the benefit of that much time. As I'm sure you know." She pointed to her file, on top of his desk.

His eyebrows drew together. "Unless I can convince you to let science do it's very best to save you."

What had science done for Ruby? She'd still died, and the treatment had made her last few months sheer misery for her and her family. "I have peace that my God will get me through this."

"Not without treatment."

So, this Dr. Austin wasn't a believer. She clutched her hands in her lap. "The specialist in Virginia explained my options, but I'm not planning on being a slice-and-dice case."

"We have some excellent surgeons here and state-of-the-art science for saving people."

"I'm not going that route." She hoped her firm voice conveyed her conviction.

"That's one reason we're sitting in here and not in one of the examining rooms right now." Dr. Austin slipped some reading glasses on and opened her file. "I understand you want palliative care, and if I can't convince you to undergo the best option for survival then we need a plan."

All the while he was speaking, 'Brad's a killer' kept swirling through Tamara's mind. She rubbed her head and bent forward. What a bombshell Maria had dropped on her.

"Are you all right?" The oncologist rose from his desk and came around.

"I. . . I had a bit of a shock before we met." That was an understatement.

Pancreatic cancer was enough of a shock, but she'd had peace about her decisions. Until this morning. She'd even had peace that no matter what, besides her maternal grandparents, Jaycie would still have her father to turn to for help when Tamara was gone. But if he really had been involved with his first wife's death. . . His parents could have won an award for being the most absentee grandparents ever. She couldn't count on them, either.

Dr. Austin pressed a broad hand to her shoulder. "I'm finding it hard to imagine something more shocking than the diagnosis you have, Tamara." He sat down in the chair beside her.

She drew in a shaky breath and faced him. "What if you found out that your wife had killed someone?" she blurted out.

His blue-gray gaze locked on hers. "My wife died last year." His Texas accent made the words sound even more pitiful, like a cowboy's lament. "So, I'd actually welcome that announcement as long as she was still with me. Because then I could still visit her in jail." His lips twitched as if he was forcing himself to be quiet.

"I'm so sorry." Tears poured down Tamara's face, and she stifled a sob.

Dr. Austin handed her a box of tissues from his desktop.

"Thanks." She wasn't crying for herself. Or was she? Her peace seemed to have fled.

"You want to tell me about it? About everything?"

And to Tamara's surprise, she did.

Dawn
Mackinaw City

The phone rang, and Cici barked. Dawn grabbed the phone. "Charbonneau residence."

"Mom?" Tammy's breathless voice seemed a million miles away.

"Yes, are you all right?"

"I've been better." It sounded like her daughter was rifling through her purse.

Dawn glanced at the wall clock. It was almost dinner time. "Gee, I thought you were coming home sooner than this. Did something happen?"

Tammy exhaled a long breath. "I've been at the library in Petoskey. Wendy has been helping me do some research on Brad."

"On Brad? Why?" Her heart palps kicked up, and Dawn pulled a kitchen chair closer so she could sit.

"Mom, he was married before." Irritation tinged her daughter's words.

Dawn cringed. "Really?" How the emotionally constricted man had been married even once, had surprised her. Her sweet Tammy and that stuffed shirt were opposites.

"Not only that but his first wife died in that bad car wreck he was in."

"Wow." More palps. *Breathe normally.*

"The intake worker at the hospital, Maria, was his sister-in-law and she saw Brad's info in my records. She gave me an earful. She called Brad a murderer."

Dawn sat there, considering this information. No doubt that information likely aggravated Tammy's digestive problems further.

"You there?"

"Yeah, yeah, I'm just shocked." What a thing to find out at a doctor visit.

"Brad was driving the car that crashed." Tamara exhaled loudly. "I'll tell you more about it when I see you. I'm just glad that I've finally stopped shaking.

Dawn's shakes had just begun. "Be careful driving home after this."

"I'm okay now. Wendy let me unload my angst."

"She's a good friend."

"Yup. Hey, Mom, I was wondering if you'd like to go out for some whitefish tonight at the Keyhole. I really need some comfort food." Tammy gave a sharp laugh.

"No kidding." No wonder her daughter turned to food for comfort, it had been one of Dawn's bad habits, too. "But what did the doctor say about your stomach problems? Do you have to change your diet?"

"We're, uh, gonna try some new meds. And I can eat anything that doesn't bother me."

"How far out are you?" Cici circled Dawn's feet, tail wagging. She'd walk her later. It was light outside until ten, so she'd fit in a long walk after dinner.

"Ten minutes or so I'll be there. Do you mind getting in line for us?"

The Keyhole was very popular, and a half hour wait was the usual minimum. "I'll head out in a minute as soon as I get my lipstick on." *If only Jim was able to be here, he'd know how to handle this Bradley situation.*

"Oh, and Mom, if I get a call from my mother-in-law, I'll want to take it, ok?"

"Sure. I can't believe she wouldn't have known about this. Especially with her being a psychiatrist."

"She's a workaholic. I'm not sure she ever really listened to Brad, nor did his father."

"That's sad." She and Jim had worked hard to give Tammy lots of attention.

"You reap what you sow. That's what the Word says, and it's true."

"Yup." Dawn rose and headed to the bathroom for her tube of Revlon *Fire and Ice* lipstick. "Hey, what if Jaycie comes home early? Do you want her to come?"

"Nope." Tammy's voice was so emphatic that Dawn flinched.

"Ok." She needed her husband's advice, though. She wasn't going to ask if her daughter minded if she shared with Jim. "See you soon."

When Tammy ended the call, Dawn phoned her husband.

"Mickey and Minnie's Diner, but only Mickey is in right now," Jim cracked.

Their little joke made her sad. "Golly I miss you, Mickey."

He made a kissing sound. "I miss you, too, Minnie."

"If you were here I'd hug you so tight."

"Hmm, I like that idea. And guess what?" He'd lowered his voice.

"What?"

"Yee ha! Brianna might cut me loose soon."

"Hallelujah for that!" He'd be by her side, he'd help her, and he'd be snuggling her every night.

"I am a happy camper. But what's going on there?"

She exhaled a heavy sigh. "Oh, Jim, Tammy found out today that Brad had been married before and had never told her."

Jim blurted out a mild profanity. "No kidding."

"No kidding. And he caused the accident he was in, which killed his wife."

"Woah. No wonder that. . ." Jim launched into some colorful language and Dawn held the phone away from her ear. "That no good bum."

"She's going to tell me the rest of all that tonight over dinner."

"Oh man, I wish I was there. I'd have the four of us call old Brad and give him a ration. Then we'd go over to the Keyhole, the whole family."

"Jaycie doesn't know and don't you tell her." Dawn shook her finger, as if Jim was with her.

"All right." He groaned. "I hate keeping secrets."

"Speaking of that, I'm pretty sure our daughter is losing weight and dressing differently to impress a certain young widower."

"Her and Hamp?"

"I've seen her coming back from the ferries when I've come home early from VBS work."

"Come on, Dawn. She probably was over there shopping or out to lunch with a friend."

"When I innocently ask her how her day was, she'll say it was quiet. Or good. Doesn't tell me she'd gone over and back in the course of six or so hours."

"She's not used to sharing her every move with you."

"This feels different." She nibbled her lower lip. "And I found an envelope full of ferry tickets on top of her bureau.

"Snooping?"

"I call it motherly concern investigation tactics. And they were paid for by Hamp Parker—it showed that on the envelope."

Jim huffed a sigh. "Now we're both sighing over our daughter."

"Like we used to do."

"Well Sneaky McSneakers, keep your eyes open."

"I will. And do your exercises every day so you can get here sooner."

"Sounds like my girls need me."

"We do." She made a kissing sound, and he did the same before they hung up.

Thirty minutes later, Tammy and Dawn were seated at a small table in the center of the rustic dining room at the Keyhole. A crew of reenactors from Fort Michilimackinac were laughing at a nearby long wooden table. Dawn leaned in and pointed to them. "Seems so strange to see them out of costume, doesn't it?"

Tammy snuck a look and nodded. "They've time-traveled a couple of hundred years forward."

Dawn waggled her eyebrows. "No real, red-coated British soldiers in Mackinaw City for a long time."

"And it seems weird to see the girls in skinny jeans and not those long skirts."

Skinny jeans. Tammy was wearing those tonight. Jaycie's clothes. What was that all about? Was she already looking for a new husband and not yet divorced?

"It does." Dawn bit her tongue and refrained from asking why her daughter was wearing her granddaughter's clothes.

Their server arrived, David, a young local who often waited on Dawn. "Where's Mr. Charbonneau?"

"All the ladies in Chicago wanted me gone this summer so they'd get a chance to dance with Jim at our club." Dawn delivered her fib in a deadpan voice.

David's dark eyes sparkled. "I've seen you dance at the festivals around here, and he's not gonna find a better partner."

Dawn playfully touched his sleeve. "Jim's recovering from foot surgery, so all those ladies will have to wait."

Tammy rolled her eyes upward. "My dad is letting us girls hang out up here by ourselves until his evil physical therapist releases him."

"He says his therapist is a cross between Arnold Schwarzenegger and Miss America, and he's not sure which side will win out— Terminator or the sweet beauty queen."

"Well, I'm lookin' forward to seeing him here when she cuts him loose." David winked at her.

He offered her the menus, but Tammy raised her hand.

"No need to look. We want two whitefish platters."

"That's easy." He grinned. "I'll be back in a minute with water. Do you want anything else?"

"A glass of Chablis for me and an Arnold Palmer for my daughter."

"Ok." David headed back toward the bar.

Tammy huffed a sigh and placed her hands atop the table. "So, when I called you earlier I told you about that woman, Maria, and what she said."

"Yeah, what a shock."

"No kidding. Wendy and I searched the internet at the library, and we found that Brad had caused that terrible accident."

"He'd admitted that to you already, hadn't he?"

"No. He would never discuss it." She made a sour face. "Now I know why. The article said that Brad ran a red light and a semi hit his car, killing his passenger."

"Then it was his fault. But an accident. But that's different than murdering someone."

"Maria said killed, not murdered, and I guess she was sort of right. The articles we found said his wife was only *eighteen*, Mom." Someone nearby cackled loudly, their emotion contrasting strongly with the sadness in Tamara's heart. "His wife was so young."

Dawn tapped her fingernails on the wood tabletop. "Too young to die."

"And pregnant."

"Oh my. Really?" Dawn wasn't an especially empathetic person, but she'd been doing better with that now that she wasn't working all the time. And she felt for Brad's young wife and baby.

"Pregnant with twins is what the accounts said."

"What?" Dawn pressed her hand to her mouth. Could Brad's story get any worse?

Tammy's iPhone rang as the adjacent table erupted in another round of raucous laughter. She glanced at it. "It's my mother-in-law. I better take this." Her daughter pushed back from the table and gestured that she was going outside.

"Sure."

Tammy slipped past David as he arrived with the water glasses. "Thanks."

"I'll be back with the other drinks in a minute."

Dawn lifted her glass of ice water to her lips and sipped. She watched the other guests in the restaurant. Normally, she'd be distracted by Jim's conversation and by that of the other guests.

They'd come here with fellow golfers, church friends, and with out-of-town guests. How strange to be sitting here by herself. And while dealing with such distressing news. But having spoken with Jim earlier, and knowing they'd have their nightly phone call at bedtime, helped lower her anxiety.

David slid her glass of wine in front of her and placed Tammy's soda at her spot.

Another few minutes ticked by as Dawn sipped her wine. How could Brad keep such information from his wife? *Poor Tammy. What a shock.*

The server returned with a basket of rolls and a dish of butter. "You lose your dinner partner, Mrs. Charbonneau?"

She turned and looked at the door. Tammy was striding toward her. And if she wasn't mistaken, several men at the bar were appreciating how good she looked in Jaycie's skinny jeans. Dawn looked hard, trying to take in her daughter's appearance. With her tunic flapping against what appeared to be a now-flat stomach, it was pretty clear that she'd lost quite a bit of weight.

"Here's your beautiful daughter, now." David stepped back. "The meals should be right up."

Tammy slid into her seat; her face flushed. "His mom didn't know."

"No?"

"Not about any of it." Tammy shook her head.

"Oh boy."

"I'm betting that Brad will be getting an earful tonight from his mother."

Dawn took a long swig of her Chablis. "He deserves it."

She reached across the table for Dawn's free hand. "But no one deserves to lose their wife and unborn children."

"I meant he's earned the scolding he'll get from his mom."

"I think she contributed to the problem."

"How?"

"She kept repeating that she and my father-in-law told Brad that he was not to get married until he'd finished his master's degree and landed a good job near them." Tammy drank some of her Arnold Palmer.

"But that didn't cause his wreck."

Tammy set her drink down. "Mom, the way she kept repeating it—heck it was like she was saying if he'd listened it wouldn't have happened. As if she was trying to sweep the information away."

"Really? How do you do that?"

"She was saying Brad must have 'compartmentalized' what happened and then locked it away. And it felt like that's what she's trying to do right now." Tammy unrolled her napkin and utensils. "I can't believe I am saying this, but I feel a little sorry for him."

"How?"

"Well, his mother and father weren't going to fund his master's degree if he got involved with someone. So here he is out-of-state, marries someone really young. Doesn't tell his folks. And when it all blows up in tragedy, I think he shut down emotionally."

Dawn reached for a roll and the butter. "You know them far better than I do. Is that what you think?"

"I bet he couldn't deal with facing them, Mom. So, his brain put all that stuff in a compartment and boxed it off."

"Oh my. I've heard of stuff like that, but I've never known anyone who'd had that happen." Jim was gonna get the lowdown on all of this when she called him that night.

"And Gina is Hispanic like his first wife. And Gina's also pregnant with twins."

Chills coursed down Dawn's arms as she set her roll on a bread plate. "And he's trying to save his first wife, isn't he? This is really about her."

"I think so."

"I think you're right to not tell Jaycie just yet."

Her daughter's facial features tugged in several directions. She opened her mouth as if to say something but then clamped her mouth shut and nodded.

Chapter Sixteen

Jaycie
Mackinac Island

Trisha, the office's pretty blond secretary, strode to Jaycie's desk, trembling. "Jaycie some gorgeous—I mean absolutely gorgeous—British guy is out there looking for you!"

Jaycie shrank in her seat. *No, it can't be. Just relax.*

"Elliott is his name." Trisha practically glowed with excitement.

"Tell him I'm not here." Jaycie squeezed her eyes shut.

From behind her someone cleared his throat. "But I can see you sitting there, love."

Irritation and a little dose of fear shot through Jaycie. She wasn't afraid of Elliott so what was that terror all about? *Be honest with yourself—you're afraid he can make you fall for him again.* She'd finally stopped loving him. Now he had to show up here.

"I told him to wait." Trisha winked at Jaycie. "I guess he was anxious to see you."

Parker, oh Parker, where are you? Jaycie remained seated but finally turned to look at him. A frisson of unchecked emotion shot through her. He was gorgeous—that was still true. Dressed in dark slim jeans and a dark clinging tee-shirt that showed off his muscles, he'd have made her weak in the knees if she wasn't already sitting. "I'm working, Elliott, so this isn't a good time for your unannounced visit." She crossed her arms over her chest and scowled at him.

Elliott glanced around the room. Only Jaycie was there at the moment. "Your fiancé isn't here right now?" He pulled out a chair from a nearby desk and sat down across from her.

"Very funny. Do you think I'd have been in a serious relationship with you if I had a fiancé elsewhere?" To her surprise, pain flitted across his strong features.

"I certainly didn't think you were, Jaycie, until Isabella told me about you and Parker." With the smoldering sadness he projected, it was no wonder Elliott had been hired for modeling jobs that needed that specific look.

She stiffened. "I believe Lady Isabella probably told you that after you'd already begun stepping out with Phillippa."

He shook his head emphatically. "Isabella told me about you and this guy, Parker, coming over to sweep you back to America and I thought—that's just unbelievable. I thought you and I had something special. My ego was hurt. She told me that night you saw us. I knew you'd show up at the pub eventually, so I took Phillippa there. And that was wrong."

Should she believe him? She grabbed her water bottle, threw back a swig, and swallowed hard. "And continuing to see Phillippa when you could have had this conversation with me there?"

He raised his broad hands in surrender. "Hey, I saw how you kissed him. The two of you obviously had some chemistry."

Her cheeks burned.

Elliott leaned closer. "As far as Phillippa goes. *Mea culpa.* I never should have kept that up as long as I did—which was until you left the UK. I feel badly about that."

"That's not what Phillipa says." She gave a harsh laugh. "She's sent a message via Lady Isabella that you two were traveling to Majorca together soon.

He barked out a laugh. "Where do you get this information? From Parker?"

Her expression must have given away the truth. Elliott shook his head. "Don't you think he might be making some of this up?"

Jaycie pressed her eyelids shut. In her spirit, she felt a check, as though there was some truth in Elliott's words. She might not trust Elliott, but she did believe in that gentle whispering to her soul. She opened her eyes. Elliott leaned even closer, his brows drawn together, his eyes yearning.

He covered her hand with his, his touch warm, his calloused fingers strong. "I still love you, Jaycie. And I think I always will."

"Oh, Elliott. What a mess." Tears pricked her eyes.

"I know. Right?" He kissed her forehead then pulled away. "I want to tell you how I ended up here, though. Because we wouldn't be having this conversation if it wasn't for some work that brought me here."

She swiped at her eyes. "Are you coming in on the dig?" Part of her wanted that to be truth but a larger part rebelled at the notion.

"No. It's my side job. A little modeling assignment and part-babysitter duty. Not exactly since no baby is involved, but some oversight for supermodel Kay-Leigh who wants to give her husband one last chance. I guess he's here vacationing."

"Wow. Seriously?"

"Yes. And it's Kay-Leigh who has inspired me to try to settle things with you."

"Really?" Jaycie sipped her water and set the bottle back down.

"Indeed, she says something worthwhile means facing your unresolved struggles."

"Wow, no kidding." Pretty much a far cry from Mort's notion of letting the stuff float away.

"No kidding." He smiled that gentle smile that made his lips irresistible.

For a moment she considered kissing him. That same sense that prodded her to believe him now held her in check. "Where are you staying?"

"We're at the Grand Hotel all week doing a shoot for the new owners."

"And her husband is here, too?"

"Yes, he lives here during the high season. Then he returns to Europe part of the year and to Montana to their place in the mountains."

Jaycie laughed. "Surely they must have a tropical island place, too?"

"Probably. But she didn't mention that." He pulled his phone from his pocket and glanced at the time. "I've got to get back to babysitting her. The agency doesn't want her with too much free time, and they don't want her husband causing her to have a setback."

"A setback?"

He glanced back through the office door. "Kay-Leigh's been severely bulimic in the past. Her husband was a real control freak and the agency felt he was making her situation worse even though he claimed he was trying to get her into treatment."

"A food control freak with a control freak husband. Yikes."

"Yes, but she wants to give him a chance. He's been on some year-long spiritual journey, he claims."

Her own journey for her plans in archeology were ending up leading her in other directions than she'd planned—like doing something with kids.

"Jaycie, she makes more money in an hour than we'll make as archeologists in a year."

"But you've always claimed it's been about the joy in our work." Not that she'd been truly enjoying the actual dig lately herself.

"We had so much fun together, didn't we?"

They had. But was it more the excitement of being with him? Of being in another country doing new things? "Yes, we did."

"We could have that again. We could have such amazing adventures together going on digs. Traveling the world. We could be that team of archeologists—the researcher lovers."

Footfall sounded behind them.

"You're sitting in my chair." Parker's voice held more than a simple challenge.

Elliott stood and Jaycie pushed her chair back. She rose and caught Parker opening and closing his fists.

"I don't know what you're doing here, man, but if you hurt her again. . ."

"That's rich, coming from you. Considering you fabricated a story about being her fiancé to keep us apart."

Parker's features tugged in disbelief.

"I have to go, Jaycie. But call me." Elliott pulled her to his side and attempted to kiss her, but she turned her cheek.

When Elliott walked past him, Parker grabbed his arm. "I mean it. We take care of our own here on Mackinac Island."

"Is that a threat?" Elliott tried to shake off Parker's hand, but he held fast.

"It's a fact."

"Please stop." Jaycie grabbed her purse and water and headed toward them, planning to leave and get some air.

Parker released Elliott and he moved past. When she reached him, Parker cocked his head at her. "You're not chasing after that cheating *tool* are you?"

She exhaled a sharp puff of air. "I'll talk with you later."

"Why not right now. Right here?"

She shook her head. "I need to clear my head."

He shoved a hand back through his hair. "Me, too."

"Right now, I'm going for a walk. A long walk."

"Let me go with you."

"No. I'm going alone."

Outside, the sun shone down from brilliant blue skies. Could be some kind of sign. Was Elliott here part of God's plan for her? She glanced around the area but didn't see him anywhere. Not that she had planned on walking with him, but yikes he hadn't even waited for her. She pulled her sunglasses from her purse. She eyed her bike, parked by the office. She hopped on and rode. Yes, she had to admit she was looking for Elliott. All she saw, though, were reenactors at the fort, dressed in their historical costumes. Other bikers passed by.

Clusters of walkers made it a little tricky to keep pedaling. And then there were the ever-present tour carriages to get by. No Elliott. Jaycie headed down to Market Street, disturbed in her spirit. Her mother and grandmother had been acting very cagey lately. They'd asked her to not speak with her father until they shared something with her about an event that had happened when he was young. They were fact-checking before they told her, which only got her more worried about what he'd done.

She stopped at the post office and parked her bike. If ever she needed the Christy Tea Shop, it was today. Across the street, she caught a glimpse of a beautiful woman whose dark hair was covered by a colorful silk scarf. If Kay-Leigh was trying to go incognito then she was failing miserably. Jaycie quickly crossed the street. She was a half block behind the tall slim woman when suddenly the supermodel stopped, looked to her left and then opened a door.

Jaycie sped up, weaving through the shoppers on the sidewalk. She'd just made it to the coffee shop when she spied a small shingle hanging from a shop two doors down—The Christy Tea Shop. A thrill shot through her. Some of her kin had actually started that shop over a hundred years earlier. Over time, apparently some of the relations had come back and run it again. Other times, it was as if the place had vanished. The last time she'd been able to locate the tea shop, she'd been young. She'd gotten separated from her mother. It was before she'd first met Parker. In fact, it was right after that event that Mom had her meet all of Parker's family. The workers at the tea shop had reminded Mom that she had many friends on the island who would help if Jaycie ever lost her way again. Jaycie sniffed at the memory and blinked back tears. She'd been so terrified that day.

She stopped at the heavy paneled oak door and looked through the window. Inside, Kay-Leigh pointed to an item in the case. *Oh no.* Was the model planning to eat it and then purge? And where was Elliott, who was supposed to be looking out for her?

Jaycie stepped inside. Like many other places on the island, the interior could have been straight from the 1890s. The shopkeeper and his wife were attired in old-fashioned costumes that were incredibly accurate looking. That was an advantage of living on an island where people kept stuff forever and where the Victorian age was continuously celebrated. It was so cool to think that someone in her family had actually helped start this place. Grandpa' cousin, Garrett Christy III, was even named after tea shop owner, his many-greats-grandfather.

Kay-Leigh carried her dessert to a table as Jaycie moved forward.

The glass case shone immaculately. The only nod to modern décor were the tiny sparkling butterflies that dangled from the ceiling on invisible wires. They even had almost-imperceptible movement. Those were seriously cool. Mom and Gran would love to have these at the cottage.

The proprietor, whose dark hair looked almost the same as over a decade ago, flipped his towel over his shoulder. "May I help you?"

No one beside Kay-Leigh and Jaycie were in the place. No wonder—it was incredibly hard to find. Jaycie shook her head lightly. "I've been trying to locate this shop again since I've begun working here. I'm so glad I found you."

The man winked at her. "We're here just when you need us."

The lady working there, likewise, didn't appear to have aged. Some people had all the luck genetically. The woman pointed to the case, a butterfly overhead gleaming silver, then gold, and then orange. "I bet you'd like the angels' wings with heavenly vanilla filling."

"Like last time?" The man reached into the case.

He could remember from when she was a child? Chills shot down Jaycie's arms. This place—this wasn't real.

From where she sat, Kay-Leigh gestured with her fork toward her plate. "That's what I'm having. The Polish have something a little different called angel wings, a fried dough pastry. But I like this better." She took a big bite of the pastry.

The pretty server placed the doughy treat on a pink glass plate and handed it to the man. "Sweetheart, please seat Jaycie by the window, next to Kay-Leigh."

How could they have known her name?

He nodded and came from behind the counter and directed her to sit on a padded pink striped seat at a circular metal table by the large glass window. But looking through the window was like looking through water.

Kay-Leigh appeared completely chill with the tea shop.

Jaycie's sense of the surreal nature of this visit continued as she sat across from the supermodel—People magazine's most beautiful woman in the world. "My name is Jaycie. I'm a friend of Elliott's."

The woman pressed her hands together. "Jaycie? You're a friend of my husband's, too."

Like Elliott had done earlier, she covered Jaycie's hand, but only briefly. "Please tell me how he has been. I've been so worried about him."

"Your husband?" Jaycie took a large bite of her angels' wings. The vanilla filling was indeed heavenly.

"Yes, he's mentioned you."

The lady brought a teapot to the table while the man carried two teacups with saucers. The couple poured tea for them and smiled in approval.

Kay-Leigh smiled broadly. "It smells divine, doesn't it?"

Cloves, cinnamon, nutmeg, black tea, and some indefinable sweetness wafted up from their pretty rose-covered teacups.

Jaycie took a sip and another, as peace flowed through her. She closed her eyes for a moment. This was like being in church. This was sacred ground.

"Tell me about my Mortimer. He says you challenge him and that's good."

"Mortimer?" Although Jaycie thought she'd sputter his name, she didn't.

She laughed. "He and I fought all the time about him pushing me to take better care of myself."

"I think that's what love makes you do." Where had those words come from? Jaycie said them, but they felt put in her mouth. *Holy Spirit.* That's what the Bible said could happen, but she'd never experienced it herself.

Kay-Leigh sipped her tea. "I think you're right. He's been encouraging me to check all these things he's been doing to get free from his need to control me, but it worries me."

The tea must have loosened the gorgeous model's perfect lips.

Jaycie puffed out an exhalation. "Is that why he's always looking for answers in other places than with God?"

"Yes." Kay-Leigh pointed her French manicured nail at Jaycie. "While I've been letting God help me past a problem I have, Mortimer keeps searching through philosophy."

"He's a smart guy, though, your husband." Husband. Mort was Kay-Leigh's husband. *Wow.*

The proprietor returned with the teapot. "Mr. Mortimer has a beautiful wife and a good friend who can both help him to a path his parents' never laid out for him. He's close to making a decision. And Kay-Leigh, you can ease the way."

Kay-Leigh's eyes grew large. As the owner, or whoever he was, poured them the splendid tea, she stared up at him. "I did the right thing by coming here, then."

Outside the window, Mort stood looking in, hard, as though he was trying to see something, but he couldn't.

"Should I let him in?" the lovely server asked in a gentle voice.

"Yes," both women said.

She opened the door, and Mort practically stumbled into the room. "Kay-Leigh?"

The angel pulled a chair over to the table, took Mort's arm, and had him sit.

"What is this place?" Mort looked between his wife and Jaycie. He shoved his hand back through his hair. "I was staring at this wall and then I saw a window appear and then a door. Am I hallucinating?" He squeezed Jaycie's arm.

"Ow!" She pushed his hand away.

"Kay-Leigh are you really here?" Mort grabbed his wife's hands.

Their server brought another angels' wings dessert to the table. She smiled at them. "Don't worry about him. He won't remember this later. Not until after he makes his decision."

"What is she talking about?" Mort glanced between Jaycie and his wife.

"You know all that Existential stuff you've quoted to me over the summer?" Jaycie tried to keep her voice even. "The sayings that I told you weren't really founded on Truth? Not from God but from man."

He compressed his lips. "My wife has communicated a similar message. But I have found help for my need to control others—through focusing on Existential principles to let go of that compulsion."

"That might be true, my darling husband, but you need a bedrock faith—as I do—if we're going to make this work." Kay-Leigh looked around the room, her eyes filling with tears. "I never thought I'd experience anything like this, so full of joy and love, in my lifetime."

"This must be so much bigger than us, that God's allowing it." Once more, Jaycie wasn't sure she'd said the words that came from her mouth.

"As your former boyfriend, Elliott, would say, I have a huge platform. My healing is something I'm ready to share. And God is a huge part of that."

Mort stared at his wife. "I'm so sorry for how hard I pushed you."

"You love me. That's why you did it. But I needed God. You do, too."

"Love is patient, love is kind, love wants that which is best for one another. It always seeks healing." The two voices together intoned the words in a uniform other-worldly voice that sent shivers down Jaycie's spine.

A gentle hand touched her shoulder, and the proprietors led her to the door. The next thing she knew, Jaycie was on the street. She'd gone looking to find help and solutions to her own problems and instead had wound up right in the middle of a divine appointment for an estranged husband and wife.

Still, she felt better than she had in a long time. She sensed that she'd received a glimpse into God's realm. That heavenly visitation was something she wanted to hang onto, that she wanted never to forget. Chills coursed through her. She felt in her purse for her notepad and took it out. This fantastic peace. This promise of eternity. This knowing of God's presence. She found her purple gel pen and clicked it.

"Jaycie?" Parker called from the street as he biked toward the sidewalk. "I'm glad I found you."

"We need to talk." Why were negative emotions creeping into her again? She looked toward Christy's Tea Shop. *Gone.*

"Hey, sure, yes, I'm sorry." Parker dismounted his bike and pulled it into a spot at the coffee house, Lucky Beans. "Want to get a coffee?"

She didn't think so. Hadn't she just drunk something hot? "Umm. . ."

He pointed to her hands. "What do you have that out for?"

"What?" She was holding a notepad and her favorite pen. "I don't know." She tried hard to remember. It had to do with something important.

"Making a list of all of Elliott's fine points and my deficiencies for comparison?"

"No." Hadn't she just seen Elliott a half hour earlier or so? Why did it seem as though it hadn't even happened?

"You're pale. Come on and sit down. I'll go and get you a mocha frappe."

"Thanks." She sat on the ornate metal chair. It looked very similar to somewhere else she'd been recently, as did the round table.

"Hey, Jaycie, thanks." Kay-Leigh strode toward her, pulling Mort, who grinned from ear-to-ear. Jaycie exhaled in relief. That's right, she had stopped at the tea shop down the street and while there she'd met Kay-Leigh, and then Mort had come in and the two had a joyful reunion. The rest of the stop was a haze. She rubbed the side of her head.

Mort stood in front of her, blocking the sunshine. "Thanks for helping me and my wife consider what's really important."

"You're. . . you're welcome," she stammered.

Kay-Leigh tapped out something on her cell phone. "I'm texting Elliott that we're doing great."

"We should all take a nice long ride in my," Mort paused and smiled at Kay-Leigh, "that is, in *our* carriage, around the island."

Kay-Leigh smiled at Jaycie. "If you join us, that might give you time to spend with Elliott."

But she had no desire to do so. First of all, she wanted to give Parker a piece of her mind about his lie to his cousin Isabella. Then she wanted to. . . She didn't know. "I think I better pass."

Husband and wife exchanged a meaningful glance.

"See ya around then." Mort patted her shoulder and then took Kay-Leigh's hand and headed in the direction of the Grand.

I should be texting Elliott to catch up with me. I should take the day off and spend with him. She pulled out her phone and stared at it.

The café's door opened, and Parker backed out, holding two large frappes. He grinned at her and brought them to the table. "Jaycie, I want to tell you that my cousin knew I was just messing around when I said we were engaged. I explained to her about the candy ring pop things when we were teens and before I flew over. So, either Elliott's lying—"

Jaycie raised her hand. "He's not. I can tell." She patted over her heart.

Parker slid into his seat. "Which means Lady Isabella deliberately wanted to mess with him."

"Do you think so?"

"I wouldn't be surprised. I think she had a thing for Elliott that wasn't reciprocated."

"Her and half the female population at the university, no doubt." Something that frankly, if she were honest with herself, Elliott encouraged in many ways.

"Sorry she did that."

"Me, too." She wrapped her hands around the cold drink. "Especially for Phillippa."

"I know. That's lousy for her, too, to get caught in the middle." Parker sipped his drink.

"Collateral damage."

"I plan to call my cousin and yell at her."

"I don't think it would do any good." Jaycie had never seen Lady Isabella flustered. "She'd probably laugh."

"Or lie about it."

"Yeah." Jaycie took a long sip and reached out to take Parker's free hand.

He tentatively grasped her fingers in return. "You don't hate me?"

She loved him. She couldn't lie to herself anymore. She might even be falling *in* love with him. But she needed to make things right with Elliott, too. What would have happened if Parker had never teased with Isabella about their childhood "engagement" and she'd used that to interfere? What if Elliott had come directly to her and asked instead of reacting as he'd done? But she understood that need to react when humiliated—she'd done it herself with Parker.

"We've been friends since we were like five or six years old, right?"

"Right."

"I want what's best for you. I messed things up, and I'm taking responsibility. I'm going over to the Grand. I'm going to grovel to Elliott and ask him to forgive my part. I'll do what I need to get Isabella to confess, too. Regardless, I know you really loved this guy."

She nodded. *Loved, as in past tense.* She still cared about him. "He's not the bad guy we thought he was."

"And he's going to be a great archeologist who can share that passion with you." Parker squeezed her hand. "Whereas I'm at heart a businessman. Won't be going to grad school. No archeologist deep down in my soul."

"What?" She pulled her hand free from his.

He locked his gaze on hers. "Any day now, you'll get a letter indicating that the original recipient of the fellowship will not be attending the program."

"You?"

He nodded. "And the letter will grant you the monthly stipend and the assistantship."

"No." The word slipped almost silently from her mouth.

"I thought that's what you would want." His expression looked pained. "Encourage Elliott to apply to transfer to the program. There's a spot open now, and he might be on that waiting list."

Parker would not be in grad school with her. Elliott would be or could be. And she'd have a full ride to attend. Why then wasn't she happy dancing?

"I'm not going." Had she really said those words?

"This has been your dream. I just grabbed your coattails, Jaybird."

"No." She shook her head slowly. "I wanted to prove something to my father."

He frowned. "I know he wasn't keen on it."

"You know how you say your AA program is making you grow up?"

"Yeah. I figure maybe I am at the sophomore level, as much work as I've been doing with my sponsor. But it's gonna be a while."

"Well, maybe I need to grow up and realize that stupidly rebelling against my dad for my career choice is pretty immature. I need to find my. . . calling." That felt right, saying those words out loud. Weird, but right. And definitely not a fit with Mort's Existential beliefs.

"You're awfully good with those kids, Jaybird." Parker's hand trembled as he grabbed hers.

"Thank you."

"I want to let you know something." Parker's cheeks flushed, and he averted his gaze. "I'm dating someone, and I made sure our boss knows. That'll get him off your back."

Jealousy ripped through her, but she willed it to vanish. "Oh."

"Dayla is in recovery, too." He still wouldn't look at her.

"Do you think that's such a great idea? I mean considering your mom and all."

"She understands my issues." His defensive tone reminded her of the Parker from UVA.

"You don't have to have the same problem to understand someone's issues." She couldn't help herself from challenging him. It had become second nature at some point.

"But it helps."

She forced a smile. "I pray it works out as God wills." That sounded like something straight from her mom's playbook, but she meant it.

Parker returned his gaze to hers. "That's exactly what my sponsor said. And my dad."

"Your dad?"

"Yeah. Since he's gotten sober, he's also gotten back to his faith."

"My mom mentioned that he'd invited her to a church service here on the island."

Parker shrugged. "You're certainly welcome to come, too. I'll save you a seat."

"Sitting beside you and Dayla?"

Confusion washed over his face. Maybe Dayla wasn't a believer. Or maybe, just maybe, Dayla was someone Parker chose to get Mr. Jeffries off *his* back, too.

Her cell phone sounded, and she looked at the screen. A text from Elliott. *Come up to the Grand Hotel for dinner?* She stared at the message, vacillating. Then she texted back—*what time?*

Chapter Seventeen

Jaycie
Mackinaw City

Light evening breeze drifted toward the house from Lake Huron, carrying the scent of daylilies, roses, and hydrangea as Jaycie walked back from her favorite "pocket park" to what almost seemed like home. She smiled when she spied a cluster of milkweeds that her grandparents had planted there. Sure enough, two Monarch butterflies flitted past, en route to a nearby cluster of daisies. How amazing that the little pollinators had come back from the brink of death.

Jaycie patted her midsection, remembering the delicious meal the night before. She'd better watch her diet, or she'd be overfed, unlike the butterflies. Her dinner with Elliott the previous night had gone well—too well. Charming, intelligent, and dressed to perfection in the clothes from his and Kay-Leigh's photo shoot, Elliott drew all of the female staffers' attention. When he'd invited her up to his room, it would have been so easy to have said yes to the man who'd been her only serious relationship. But she'd kissed him goodbye on the covered Grand Hotel porch and caught the ferry home.

Truth was, she'd felt like she needed to run from him as fast as she could.

From two blocks away from the cottage, '60s music blared from Shepler's Boat Docks, interrupting her thoughts. "I Wish They All Could Be California Girls" by the Beach Boys was one that played repeatedly throughout the day on Huron Street. If Gran had the windows open tonight to catch the Straits of Mackinac breezes, then Jaycie would be subjected to the noise for the next few hours—unless she switched on the window unit in her bedroom or jacked up her Pandora music on her iPhone.

Gran and Mom sat on the covered front porch, sipping tea. Did Elliott's mother and grandmother do the same back in England? She'd never been invited to meet his family. She frowned. If Elliott really had been serious about her, which he'd repeated last night, why hadn't he introduced them?

"How do you stand that nonstop soundtrack from the last century?" Jaycie pulled a face.

Her mother laughed and waved her hand as if dismissing the noise.

"Want a cuppa?" Gran pointed to the electric tea kettle plugged in on a wicker table on the covered porch. "Your mother may have finally converted me to tea."

"Isn't that Downton Abbey Christmas tea fantastic?" Jaycie had chugged down a huge mugful the previous evening when she'd returned from her date with Elliott. "It's like Christmas in a cup."

"Sure is. I'll get you some." Gran made as if to rise but Jaycie gestured for her to sit. "I'll go grab it from the cupboard, and a mug and some honey."

"Can you bring us a couple of danishes? They're on the counter." Her mother beamed up at her.

Jaycie stopped midway through opening the screen door. Mom had been on some form of a diet all her life, yet in the past few weeks, she'd kept bringing back bags of treats from the wonderful bake shop. Or someone was. She felt a check in her spirit. "Is that *you* who keeps bringing these in, Mom?"

"Yes," Mom's penitent-sounding voice made Jaycie regret her question.

"I simply wondered—didn't plan to do a guilt trip." She gave a curt laugh, hoping her mom wouldn't feel called out. Hadn't Jaycie stopped at a sweet spot herself yesterday? She rubbed the side of her head, trying to remember where she'd been.

"Your mom has been getting me anything I want these days." Gran smiled benevolently as Jaycie went inside.

What was that supposed to mean? That phrase didn't sound right—sounded more like something used for a prisoner on death row or something dying. Gran's heart issues weren't serious…were they? The world wouldn't be the same without Gran. There'd be a shift. A terrible shift in time that didn't include one of the most wonderful women she'd known. Jaycie blinked back tears as she headed to the well-stocked kitchen. But hadn't Grandpa Jim said that Gran's heart problem was minor? *Ugh, I'm overtired and hormonal, I need to get my act together and not overreact.*

The screen door creaked open and then slapped shut again as she gathered her materials. Jaycie waited, expecting someone to have come inside, but no one joined her in the kitchen. Maybe one of them had just peeked in. Soon she had a tea bag and two heaping teaspoons of honey in her Lilac motif ceramic mug, and she headed back outside to add some hot water.

Her mother's space was vacant. That must have been her that the screen door had squeaked open for.

Gran looked up from reading the paper. "Your mom is lying down for a bit. I think she was a little stressed from my heart appointment in Petoskey yesterday. I'm so glad they could fit me in. But I think she worries about me too much. I'll be fine."

Would she be? Her color was great, though. "You look pretty perky despite those nasty palpitations." Perkier than Jaycie felt after her emotionally grueling day yesterday.

She should tell Gran and Mom about Elliott, but she knew how they'd react. And it wouldn't be good. She also didn't want to share Parker's part in what had happened. Best to leave it alone. For now. Especially since Gran was struggling and mom was so tired.

"I think the new medication is already helping." Gran offered a tight smile and then raised her teacup to her lips and stared down at the table.

Ugh. She'd just stepped in it again. Gran obviously didn't want to discuss her condition. Time to call Grandpa and ask him. Jaycie pressed the electric kettle switch.

"Shouldn't take too long since we recently had it on to full boil." Gran still wouldn't meet her gaze, looking past her to the steps.

Jaycie turned.

Carter, Parker's younger brother, stood there. He brushed his long sandy hair back from his brow with one hand and in the other clutched a lovely rose, lily, and greenery bouquet.

"Wow, this must be bouquet season at the Mackinaw Cottage." Jaycie stepped toward Carter. "Twice in a week."

At least she knew Parker hadn't sent Carter here with flowers. Her old friend would be buying them for Dayla, not her. That shouldn't bother her, but it did. The memory of twelve-year-old Parker making a lilac bouquet for her, at his family's Victorian home on the East Bluff, left her misty-eyed. He'd been such a sweet boy.

The seventeen-year-old extended his arm. "These are for your mother."

"What's this, Carter?" Gran cast him a quizzical look.

"These are for Mrs. Worth." The boy offered the flowers to Gran.

"Tammy will love these, but she's resting right now."

"Please tell her I'm sorry about what I thought." He stared down at his shoes.

Gran motioned with her hands as if dismissing the thought. "What could you have done to offend Tammy?"

"Um, she knows, Mrs. Charbonneau." He cast a quick challenging glare at both Gran and at Jaycie, which surprised her.

Jaycie forced a smile, eyeing the plastic wrapped stems which needed to be taken care of. "Those are pretty. Let me get a vase and some water."

"All right, Carter, I'll ask my daughter about what horrible, awful, heinous thing you did that merited you bringing her some posies." Gran motioned for Carter to sit down but he remained standing. "Bring the kitchen shears, Jaycie. I'm gonna put Carter to work fixing these for your mom."

Gran bent her head over the bouquet and inhaled. "They smell amazing."

"That's what I thought." Carter made a sheepish face.

"Where'd you find them?"

"Walmart Shopper." Carter made a W with his hands, flipped them over to make an M and then twisted his fingers sideways into an S.

Gran laughed. "They're very colorful, too."

"Like the clothes she wears on the ferry." Carter scratched at the light scruff of golden beard on his chin.

"She's been wearing some of Jaycie's clothes, actually." Gran laughed. "And sweet Jaycie is the color-loving one in our household."

Jaycie came back through the door. Mom was borrowing her clothes. Was she trying to recapture her youth or something? "I wondered what was happening with my clothes." Granted, they were always returned clean and fresh, but out of order in her closet and drawers.

She shot the boy a quick glance and set a half-filled vase in front of him. She produced a pair of kitchen shears that could cut through bone and in the other hand she held up a plastic grocery bag. "We can put the bottoms of the stems in here."

Carter's features tugged together. "Do what with the stems?"

Jaycie tapped the flower preservative packet and passed it to the teenager. "Read this."

He squinted at the packet and read, "Mix the powder in warm water. Cut one to two inches from the bottoms of the flowers." He looked at Jaycie. "Did you know about doing this?"

"Yup. When I was in the UK, I'd buy a bouquet at the market once in a while as a little treat."

A bemused expression flickered over Carter's face. "I think I can handle this."

Gran patted his hand. "I have every confidence in you, young man."

His blue eyes fastened on hers. "Do you?"

"Why don't you sit down for a minute, Carter? Please." Gran gave him the guilt-inducing Mommy-eye which she'd perfected over the years.

Jaycie tapped the chair beside her, and Carter finally sat.

"Can I get you a soda?" Gran gestured to a tub of drinks on ice, nearby, that they kept out for the postman, the UPS driver, and soda loving friends who stopped by to chat.

"No thanks. I'm good, Mrs. Charbonneau."

"A danish?" Gran pushed the tray at him.

Carter picked one up and held it tentatively in his hand. "I'm so embarrassed about what I did." He took a big bite of the pastry.

Gran made a sour face. "What happened?"

Jaycie had to fight the urge to laugh. Gran was gonna get the info out of Carter one way or another. Goodies always helped.

Carter swallowed and wiped his hand across his face. "Coming back on the ferry, I thought she was drunk."

"Drunk?"

"Or on something, ya know? Like my mom used to get."

Jaycie stiffened, leaning back in her seat. "My mom is a teetotaler."

"Yeah, I know that now." Carter shoved the rest of the cookie into his mouth.

"Let me get you a pop." Gran turned and pulled a drink from the ice.

Jaycie leaned in. "Carter, what on earth are you talking about? What happened?"

Gran handed the boy a can of Orange Crush soda.

"Thanks, Mrs. Charbonneau."

"You're welcome."

Parker's brother gulped down his drink for several long seconds. "Wow, I didn't realize I was so thirsty."

Gran patted his hand. "It's all right. Now tell us what happened."

"I called the cops on Mrs. Worth."

"What?" Grand and Jaycie exclaimed simultaneously.

"I felt I had to."

"Why?" Gran squeaked out.

"We have a rule," Carter explained, "that if someone is drunk or high or whatever—which happens more often than you might think—

then we have to report it if we think they might be driving home. It's a Shepler's rule, but I also think it's the law."

"You thought she was drunk?" Jaycie frowned.

"Um, yeah," he pushed blond strands of hair off his forehead. "She was kind of staggering when she got off the boat, and then. . ." His face flushed.

"What happened?" Gran asked.

"Ya know." He glanced between the two of them. "She got sick."

"Sick?" Jaycie repeated, imagining her mom throwing up at the dock.

"Happens sometimes and we clean it up." He shrugged. "And with those pills I've seen her popping."

"Pills?" The only thing Mom took were vitamins.

"Yeah, in that little red box in her purse."

Auntie Zara had sent Mom a red satin pill box from Asia the previous winter. At the time, Mom put it aside, saying she didn't have a use for it.

Carter pressed his eyes closed and then opened them. "My mom would sneak drugs. Be sick. We'd get a call. I guess I was re-playing that in my mind. But I was so embarrassed when the cops came, and Mrs. Worth explained that she's sick." He glanced between the two of them.

"You mean like she got sick from something she ate?" Jaycie narrowed her eyes at the teen.

"I don't know. I just know she was sick."

"Oh, I feel terrible about making her drive me to my doctor's appointment." Gran pressed a hand to her chest. "Especially after she's been sick this week. I had no idea."

"I'm really sorry I jumped to conclusions." Carter pushed his chair back and stood.

Speaking of drawing conclusions, something began niggling at Jaycie's subconscious mind, but she couldn't grab ahold of what it was.

"I hope the flowers make up for it a little bit."

Gran smiled warmly at Carter. "That was very thoughtful of you."

"I better get back to the dock and get home. Dad and I are riding bikes around the island tonight."

"Counter-clockwise I assume," Gran said wryly.

Carter grinned. "That's the only way to do it, Mrs. Charbonneau. It's the opposite way that the tourists usually ride."

"I know."

"Ah, that's right. You and my grandpa get out there at least once a week don't you?"

"In between my VBS duties, yes." Gran stood and gave Carter a hug. "I've known your grandfather all my life, and I bet we've put thousands of island miles on our bikes in that time."

He laughed. "Please tell Mrs. Worth that I hope she's feeling better soon."

"Will do." Gran assured him.

Mom was resting now, she'd lost at least ten pounds, she wasn't eating well, and she'd been so ill on the ferry that Carter had reported her, thinking she was drunk. Furthermore, Mom's own clothes were so loose that she was wearing Jaycie's clothes. Something was really wrong. As soon as Carter left Jaycie would check on Mom.

Tamara

Tamara pulled up the YouTube video of The Afters singing their beautiful song, "Live On Forever," and played it on her iPhone. *Gonna live on forever.* How could she explain to her mother and daughter that she had complete trust that, like the song said, she was gonna live on forever in heaven, and that she wasn't afraid. Heaven was real. If she didn't get a miracle, she was going to her eternal home.

Someone knocked on her door. Mom popped her head inside. "You ok, Tammy?"

"I still feel a little queasy, but. . ." A sharp pain in her side caught her by surprise, and she rolled over and was sick in the plastic waste basket by her bed. Sweat broke out on her brow and she exhaled slowly and closed her eyes.

"Oh no." Mom left the room.

Tamara laid her head back down on her pillow. *Oh Lord, is this how it's going to be now?*

Mom returned in a moment. "I've got a damp wash cloth." She pressed the cool compress to Tamara's brow.

"Thanks."

"Do you think it's the flu? Carter told us about you being sick on the ferry."

Sick was an understatement. She'd been violently ill on the trip from Mackinac Island. And then the Shepler's staff had called in the police, thinking she was drunk. "Mom, I need to talk with you."

Jaycie stepped into the room. "Carter just left." She held up a vase of beautiful flowers. "I arranged the flowers that he brought."

Mom chuckled. "I guess they didn't need to worry about a DUI since you were only walking home."

"Carter is so sorry about asking them to call the police." Jaycie set the vase on the bedside dresser.

"They have sick people on the weekends who are drunk and it's for their safety." Tamara felt another wave of nausea and closed her eyes, pushing her head against the pillow.

"Right. I've seen that." Mom pressed a hand to Tamara's brow. "Now what did you want to tell me?"

"I want you two to listen to this song."

"What is it?"

"Listen." Tamara lifted her iPhone and pressed play. After a brief commercial, The Afters began singing *Gonna Live on Forever*. She closed her eyes as tears streamed down her face.

Jaycie sat down beside her and took her hand. "Mom?"

"Shhh. Listen."

"Gonna Live on forever." The Afters' beautiful anthem about heaven continued.

"Mom, I believe that song. I'm a believer."

"Shhh."

When the song finished, silence reigned.

"We were made for another place. Eternity in heaven." Tamara sniffed.

"Oh honey, do you feel that bad about Brad?"

Jaycie squeezed her hand hard. When Tamara opened her eyes, she saw tears streaming down her daughter's face and recognition in her eyes.

"Mom? Oh, no. Mom?" Jaycie bent her head over their locked hands. "You're really sick aren't you?" She began to sob.

"I'm going to heaven soon." And the tears flooded out. Not for herself. She knew where she was going. The tears were for those she was leaving behind. For her daughter. For her mother and father. For her friends and extended family.

"How long?" Mom squeaked out.

"God only knows." That was true. But reality was maybe a few months. But she'd make them count—or rather God would make whatever time she had left count for something.

Dr. Austin hadn't offered her many options. When she'd explained that she'd been convicted in her spirit to not have the Whipple procedure, he'd blinked at her as if she'd said she was an alien. In a way she was—since her eternal home was with the Lord. He kept speaking about science as though that was the temple where he worshipped. He genuinely seemed like a good man, but without God in his life, he was lost. His last-ditch effort for her, he'd said, was to get her into a clinical trial. She told him she'd pray about it. And she had—and she'd prayed for him, too.

Mom exhaled a long sigh. "At my age, most of my pals have talked about what we'll do with our last years. But I never expected. . ." Mom's startled features morphed into an expression of genuine compassion. "We're gonna help you, and give you a great time, no matter how short or long that is."

"What have you got in mind?" As pained as her abdomen was, what could they manage?

Chapter Eighteen

Jaycie
Mackinac Island

Staring blankly at the computer screen, Jaycie willed her fingers to move but they remained like twin sentinels hovering over her laptop's keyboard. What was she supposed to be typing anyway? The screen showed a Microsoft Word document in need of much revision. She puffed out a quick breath. *That's right, I'm supposed to fix all those errors so the Board of Directors will realize that we're accomplishing a lot at the dig site.*

Her hands shook as she tapped the touchpad, scrolled down the document, and began searching for the cells which needed the numbers changed. She stared and stared. She'd worked on the same report all morning. But the only thing running through her mind was—*Mom's dying.*

Someone tapped her on the shoulder, and she jumped.

"I didn't mean to startle you." Trish, the secretary handed her a message. "I was asked to give this to you."

Jaycie nodded dumbly and took the memo. She tried to make her eyes focus. *Mr. & Mrs. H. Mortimer request the pleasure of your company for dinner tonight in their private dining chamber at the Grand Hotel at seven pm. Regrets only.*

She dropped the note onto her desk. Regrets? She had regrets aplenty. And she didn't want to compound them. She didn't want to kick herself later for spending her mom's last months working and then studying for a career that no longer felt right for her.

"Are you ok?" Trish cocked her head and frowned.

Her head jerked almost involuntarily into a 'no.'

"Can I do anything? Get you anything?"

"Um. . ." Jaycie pushed back from the desk and stood. "No."

Trish stepped aside as Jaycie closed her laptop shut and grabbed her backpack. "Where are you going?"

Shrugging, Jaycie strode out of the office. Mort's platitudes sure weren't enough to help her now. Once outside, the fresh breezes stirred the leaves of the nearby maple trees. *God. Oh God. My God, I need Your help now.*

A sob squeezed past Jaycie's lips as she hopped on her bike and rode off to a church that she knew would be open. Mackinac State Historic Parks kept the big white Mission Church open for tourists from noon until four each afternoon. She'd take a seat there and pray. And cry. And pray some more.

The afternoon passed in a wet-Kleenex blur. Following her hour of sobbing at Mission Church and waving inquisitive tourists away from trying to help her, Jaycie had hopped on her bike. She rode around the island, stopping at every spot where she and Mom had made a special memory. At Arch Rock, she'd nibbled on the muffin that Gran had packed for her breakfast on the ferry crossing. She'd not eaten it that morning, too upset still from the events of the weekend. After the bike ride, she looked for the Tea Shoppe but couldn't find it. She stopped at the coffee shop but burst into tears at the counter when she saw they'd put chocolate caramel frappe up as the special—Mom's favorite. Covering her mouth, she'd fled and gotten back on her bike.

She rode up to the school and sat on one of the swings, the voices of nearby children like an echo from someplace far away. She powered on her iPhone, finally ready to deal with whatever the fallout was from her running off from her job. She took a deep breath as the phone powered on. The white apple logo flashed and in a moment she opened her text messages.

The text from Elliott she ignored. Being brutally honest with herself, she had to admit she didn't want to deal with him at the moment. Then she was angry with herself for feeling that way. She scanned the messages. Nothing from Parker. That stung. Mr. Jeffries' message was one she had to force herself to read.

'I know about your Mom, Jaycie. Please take whatever time you need.'

She hiccupped a sob.

Jaycie closed the text message. Her thumb hovered over Elliott's text. Shouldn't she want to reach out to him? To tell him about the deep pain scorching her soul? She looked away from the screen. Overhead, seagulls swooped. A young father, with a tiny red-headed daughter, tossed bits of bread onto the schoolyard for the birds to scoop up.

She drew in a deep breath and then touched the screen to retrieve Elliott's message. There was a link to YouTube. 'How I felt when I saw you in the pub with Parker.'

What was it with people trying to send her musical messages? Her mother had devastated her with her music about living in the afterlife. Jaycie could never again listen to the song "I'm Gonna Live on Forever." Granted, she wasn't the one who played K-Love nonstop at home—that was Mom. Jaycie walked away from the swings. A couple wearing matching navy and gold University of Michigan t-shirts left a nearby bench, holding hands. Jaycie's legs trembled. She already needed to sit down again.

She touched the link that Elliott sent. Lewis Capaldi's "Someone You Loved" showed on the screen. She stiffened. She'd never have associated that popular song with Elliott. The UK singer sang about feelings that she couldn't imagine gorgeous Elliott ever experiencing. Her former boyfriend was a pretty matter-of-fact kind of guy who ordinarily reacted with anger—not the hurt that Capaldi sang about. And Elliott certainly hadn't wasted time finding a replacement for her, even though he protested that it was in reaction to what he thought was her betrayal.

"You're not here to get me through it all," the sentiment that the singer expressed was something she associated with Parker not with Elliott. Although the desire to message Parker warred within her, Jaycie couldn't bother him—not now that she knew he was dating someone. Parker no longer possessed the shoulder she'd cry on. She'd spent an hour on the phone the night before with Hannah, who was loving her summer internship in Boston. Jaycie had hated to bum her out by sharing about Mom. Hannah said she'd call her again on the weekend.

Capaldi's lyrics continued. Unlike Mom's sharing of the profound song expressing her upcoming death, Elliott's attempt to share this song felt more like manipulation. She checked the text again. 'See you with Mort and Kay-Leigh tonight' he'd written. Why did Elliott believe Jaycie would be there when she'd just learned about her mother? *Elliott doesn't even know about Mom—I didn't tell him.* She rubbed her aching head.

She couldn't have dinner with them.

Her phone rang. "Gran?"

"Aw, Jaycie, I was worried about you. You didn't answer earlier."

"I turned the phone off."

"I figured."

"How are you? Besides awful, I mean?" Jaycie certainly felt like roadkill.

"Lousy, but your mom is insisting we come over for dinner with Hampy and Hamp tonight. At the Grand at seven. Can you meet us?"

"Uh. . ." She pushed strands of hair out of her eyes. "I don't have anything to wear." She'd been so in shock that morning. It hadn't even occurred to her to grab onto the perfect excuse to nix the invitation from Mort and Kay-Leigh. And from Elliott.

"We'll bring you an easy popover dress and some dressy sandals."

How could she say no to anything her mom wanted right now?

"I'll change in the bathroom at the Grand."

"All right."

Several hours later, Jaycie stepped into the handicapped stall on the Grand Hotel's entry floor. Gran and Mom watched in case anyone with a real disability needed to use it. Jaycie hurriedly removed her clothes, sprayed on some of Mom's Beautiful perfume, and then pulled the seafoam-green, long summer dress over her head. "This really doesn't go well with my tennis shoes."

Mom gave a soft laugh. "Probably not." How could mom still find humor despite her condition? Jaycie wiped away an errant tear.

"Hurry up, Granddaughter, and put those sparkly sandals on before Hampy has a conniption upstairs. He hates waiting." There was forced humor in Gran's voice. Poor Gran, like Jaycie, she'd been gob-smacked by Mom's disclosure.

Oh, God, I need my mother. Don't take her away. Hot tears streamed down Jaycie's face. *Must stop crying, Must not upset Mom.*

She untied her shoelaces, slipped off her shoes, pulled off her socks and then put the sandals on. "Yikes, I've got ribbed socks feet." She opened the stall door and held up one foot, displaying the imprint of her crew socks, a necessity for days in the field. She bit back the sarcastic thought that Ribbed Socks Feet wasn't a terminal condition—that would surely have been the most insensitive thing she could have said. She grabbed some tissue and blew her dripping nose.

Gran motioned for her to put her foot down. "They're not going to be looking at your feet."

"Let me put on some lipstick." Jaycie pulled a tube of MAC Peach Blossom Cremesheen out of her purse and ran the lipstick over her mouth.

"We'll leave your backpack at the newsstand. I know the guy running it tonight." Gran held her hand out for Jaycie's backpack, and she handed it to her as they headed toward the door.

They crossed the foyer, the lush colorful carpet dense beneath her thin sandals. Gran passed the backpack to the silver-haired man.

"No worries, Dawn, I'll keep watch over this."

"Thanks, Ben. Hey, how're the grandkids?"

He pulled his wallet from his back pocket and opened it. He displayed a picture of three children, all under five, clustered around a tiny Asian woman. "Ain't they cute?"

"They sure are." Gran offered her signature sweet-crossed-with-spunky smile.

He returned the wallet to his pocket. "You ladies have a good dinner. And don't forget to let the gents pay." He winked.

"Thanks." Mom smiled at the man but placed a protective hand over her abdomen.

The three of them moved toward the stairs and then went up to the next level, where dinner would be served.

When they arrived at the maître d's station, Mr. Parker and his son weren't there. Gran peered around the distinguished looking Jamaican man at the desk. "We're with Hampton Parker and his son, Hamp."

The man's dark eyes flashed the slightest look of annoyance. "I'm aware of this, Madame. Please follow me to one of our private dining chambers."

As Mom and Gran stepped forward, Jaycie's mouth opened like a trout as she tried to protest. She'd never replied to Kay-Leigh and Mort's invitation nor to Elliott's text. They, too, would be in a private area. "Gran, I forgot to mention that Kay-Leigh arrived. They'd actually invited me to dinner here tonight, too."

Gran's forehead wrinkled. "I know. I only hope she's okay with what Barb did for her and her crew."

"You passed her off to Barb?" Oh, that came out wrong.

Gran shrugged. "Barb says she pulled it off without a hitch, so hopefully my final client is happy."

Final client? Was she really going to retire? Maybe Mom's news helped flip that switch.

They trailed past diners in suits and dresses, some of the children in miniature suits and gowns that matched their parents. They looked so adorable. One little girl, with hair as blonde as Parker's gave her a little wave. A flicker of joy pulsed through her. Then the sensation passed as she contemplated the loss of her own mother. But wasn't there always hope? Apparently not much chance of survival when it came to pancreatic cancer.

"This way, ladies." The maître D' waved them into an apricot-colored room that could easily have accommodated two dozen people.

At the end of the long table, Mort and Kay-Leigh were speaking animatedly with Gran's dear friend. *Oh no.* So, this wasn't going to be a private dinner where they'd share their thoughts about Mom's illness.

"Hampy, you ran off." Gran's gentle scolding got the older man's attention.

"Sorry, doll. I saw my old friend's son, Mort, here."

"Kay-Leigh, it's so wonderful to see you again!" Gran went to the younger woman and they air-kissed both cheeks.

"So good to see you, too." If Kay-Leigh was irritated with Gran for sending her to Barb, her face didn't show it.

Hampy Parker helped Gran into her chair. "You remember Harry Mortimer, don't you?"

Gran's face brightened. "Oh, yes, Harry was the old coot who used to chase us out of his yard with a broom—up on the bluff."

Mort laughed and extended his hand to Gran. "I'm his grandson." Then he shot Jaycie a meaningful glance and waved at her.

Mom leaned in. "Is that your gardener?"

Jaycie whispered, "Yeah, but he's no gardener, is he?"

Mom laughed. "Also, no angel. From what I understand, he was quite the playboy until he got married. I knew his dad and that man was awful. I mean a real genuine jerk who would make your dad look like a saint in comparison. Truly!"

"Wow, really?"

"Yeah." Mom moved forward to join the others further down the table and Jaycie followed.

Parker's father leaned in and kissed Mom lightly on her cheek. "You're gonna get through this, Tam, and I'm gonna be right by your side."

Jaycie blinked back more tears. She knew Mom had renewed her friendship with Mr. Parker, but to hear him say those words really touched her. And brought relief.

Dad might not be there, but Hamp Parker would step into the gap. He squeezed Mom's hand. "I texted Parker and asked him to bring his date in here—they're out there by the windows right now having a tête-à-tête about something."

No, no, no. Parker was the last person Jaycie wanted to see.

She heard footsteps behind her and turned, expecting to see Parker. Instead, Elliott, attired in a navy European-cut suit, a different one from their previous dinner, strode toward her, a question in his eyes.

Jaycie turned to fully face him. In a low voice, she told him, "I got some terrible news, and I couldn't make myself answer your text to send my regrets."

He frowned. "But you're here now. So, you weren't going to come?"

This wasn't the time or place to explain. "I'm here now, you're right." She smiled up at him.

He leaned in and kissed her. There was intensity in his kiss, and at one time she'd have responded to his touch. Why didn't she? Instead, she simply stared at him, her heart as empty as the crystal wine glass and china place setting before her.

"Parker!" Hampton Parker called out to his grandson.

Jaycie pulled away from Elliott as Parker and his date, a petite redhead with a daring low-neckline on her too-short dress entered the room. Parker's stricken face reflected Jaycie's emotions—like he'd rather be anywhere else in the world right now than in this room.

Elliott glared at Parker.

Parker gestured at his guest. "This is Dayla."

Green eyes narrowed on her. "You must be Jaycie."

"Yes." She ran her tongue over her upper lip. "And this is Elliott."

Dayla's flawless ivory complexion pinked as she fixed her gaze on Elliott. Jaycie glanced at him, noting the twitch of his lips as if he wasn't immune to Dayla's charms either. Then lip curling he glanced dismissively toward Parker.

"Let's sit down," Jaycie encouraged.

"Let's do." Elliott took her hand possessively and pulled her toward the others. He sat beside Mom and introduced himself.

Mom's eyebrows lifted slightly as she took in his appearance, and she cast Jaycie a look that indicated she appreciated Elliott's sterling good looks, too.

Parker headed toward the other side of the table. His date edged ahead of him, taking a seat by Hamp Parker. The young islander greeted Mr. Parker as though they were old friends. A surge of jealousy surprised Jaycie. This was ridiculous. Of course, Parker's date knew his father, given the island was so small and islanders quite close with one another. She chewed on her lower lip. This dinner was turning out all wrong. She could excuse herself halfway through, go get her backpack at the newsstand and call for a taxi to take her down to the ferries and then she'd go home. Absolutely. This was the best plan she had all day. Beneath the table, she rocked her feet slightly in anticipation of her departure. She lifted her eyes.

Parker, his eyes reflecting sorrow and compassion, seated directly across from her, caught her gaze. "You all right Jaybird?"

"That's a dumb question." She almost spat the answer back at him.

Elliott glanced between the two of them. "If you don't want to be around Parker we can go elsewhere, Love."

Parker cocked his head. "I am not the problem, you buffoon."

Sensing Elliott's rising anger, she grabbed his hand. "Parker is not causing me upset. It's. . ." She glanced down toward her mother.

"My mother is. . ." Dying. In maybe four months since she was refusing treatment. "She's very ill."

He leaned in. "What on earth is she doing here, then?" Elliott's low words, although logical, irritated her. It reminded her about how so many times he'd question something she'd stated. Always asking stuff that made her feel like he didn't trust what she'd just said.

Parker exhaled a loud puff of breath. "Mrs. Worth has a right to be here if she wants."

A little wave of comfort buoyed her. Parker gave enough information to silence Elliott without giving away her mother's secret—which was Mom's to share.

Dayla nudged Parker. "Let's not get all philosophical here, okay? I thought we were going to enjoy ourselves tonight."

Parker bent and whispered something in Dayla's ear, and she did the same back to him. When they stopped their exchange, Dayla shot Parker a quelling look and snapped open her menu.

Jaycie strained to hear what Gran and Hampy were discussing.

Elliott leaned in and smiled at them. "You're talking about possible travels across the Upper Peninsula? I've heard it is beautiful."

"Over four hundred miles across." Hampy jerked a thumb. "That's if you're on the mainland over there. Believe it or not, you're already in the Upper Peninsula here on the island."

Elliott glanced between Jaycie and Hampy and both nodded. "How many kilometers is that then, I wonder."

"Around five hundred," Parker supplied, looking rather pleased with himself for the quick answer.

Elliott's dark eyebrows tugged upward. "That's impressive."

From the way Dayla was now staring across the table at Elliott, she must think the Brit was impressive, too. And he was. In his own way—but not in a way her heart needed.

Their server, a young Asian woman attired in a short-waisted, white jacket with black trousers, approached the table. "Perrier-Jouet Belle Epoque Rose Cuvee 2004," she announced, mangling the French pronunciation with her heavy accent. She displayed the gorgeous bottle, which was detailed with large pinkish flowers.

Elliott gave a wry smile; one she knew reflected his distinct approval.

Parker's eyes darkened, and he cast a furtive glance to his left, to his date, who was staring at the bottle.

Mort raised his jacketed arm and waved for the server to bring it to his end of the table. When she reached him and poured into his and his wife's champagne glasses, he made a circle motion with his index finger. "Ask the rest if they'd like some, and add that to my tab."

Wow, Mort was definitely from another world than the one Jaycie occupied. Dad would be having a coronary if he were expected to pay for a round of champagne—especially one that cost around three hundred bucks a bottle.

As the young woman came around, Mom shook her head, but Gran nodded.

Elliott raised his eyebrows. "Of course I will." He leaned forward and gestured a thumbs up in thanks to Mort, who smiled back at him.

Across from her, Parker's lips were compressed in a tight line. A quote from the book of Romans quickly ran through Jayce's mind—about not causing a friend to stumble. Granted, he was here with other people who would be drinking, but she'd not contribute to that. Besides which, she wasn't a fan of champagne, having sampled it only twice at weddings.

Jaycie shook her head. "None for me."

Parker stared at the server as Dayla chewed her lower lip.

Jaycie faced the Grand Hotel worker again. "They're not having the champagne, either."

"Fine. Would you like something else?"

Shifting her gaze again, Jaycie caught Dayla's glare. "Parker and I," she gestured between her old friend and herself, "will have Cokes, please."

Parker nodded, but his cheeks reddened beneath his tan. Had she really just ordered for Parker and herself as though they were the two out on a date, not him and Dayla? Her own cheeks heated in embarrassment. But she'd known him so long—knew what he always drank.

Beside her, she felt Elliott stiffen.

"What will you have, Miss?" The server's soft voice held a bit of confusion, and was that also a bit of censure in it?

Jaycie cringed inwardly.

Dayla's gaze shot daggers at her. "I'd like the champagne, actually."

Parker whispered something in the islander's ear. When he straightened, he said, "Diet Coke for my date."

"Very good. I'll be right back."

Elliott leaned in. "Parker is a controlling bugger, isn't he?"

She pulled away. Parker was trying to protect his fellow alcoholic, but she wasn't about to share that with Elliott. "I really don't think so."

Parker and Jaycie reached for the soft rolls and butter in a chrome basket at the same time, bumping hands. They both laughed.

"You first." Parker pulled his hand away.

"Do you remember when we'd flip a coin to see who got the last roll, when there was a singleton left?" Jaycie grabbed a big soft cloverleaf roll and the butter dish. She transferred the bread to her bread plate, then smoothed some butter over her roll.

When Parker gestured for his date to have a roll, she shook her head. "How long have you two known each other, Parker?"

"Since we were five or so." Jaycie took a big bite of the soft roll and savored the creamy butter. Her stomach growled loudly.

Elliott patted her hand. "That's really the worst kind of carbs. I never eat them anymore."

"Me, neither." Dayla grinned triumphantly. "White refined flour is the worst."

Parker and Jaycie shoved their rolls into their mouths, and he mirrored her own low chuckle as they both chewed.

Dayla glared across the table. "You and Parker have known each other almost all your life then. Wow."

Jaycie swallowed her roll and nodded.

"She was gone to the UK this past year." Parker shoved half of another roll in his mouth, something he did when he was upset.

"That's where I met Jaycie." Elliott aimed his thousand-megawatt smile on Dayla.

Dayla beamed back, running her fingers lightly around her overly exposed décolletage as if to draw attention there. "I'm sure she was delighted to meet you."

Not that Elliott was delighted to meet Jaycie. That was a definite mini jab. Jaycie waited for Elliott to correct Dayla and indicate that it was *he* who had been delighted. But Elliott only smiled back.

Heat singed her cheeks. Beneath the table, someone kicked her. *Parker, if she was correct.* She glanced up at him. He rolled his eyes toward the room's exit. She glanced in that direction, once more running her tongue over her lip, in anticipation of escape. Was he thinking the same thing?

Nearby, Mom, Gran, Hamp, and Hampy were engaged in spirited conversation with Mort and Kay-Leigh. Raucous laughter erupted at one of Hampy's stories. Mom didn't need her there. Jaycie certainly didn't want to be in this place.

Across the table, Parker was pushing his chair back. He patted his pockets. "I think I misplaced my wallet."

Dayla frowned at him. "Well, you better go find it, then."

He saluted his date.

Parker was leaving.

That connection to him, that had been broken at college, had been fused together, again. They knew each other so well. When he wasn't giving in to his alcohol addiction, Parker and her worlds aligned.

She knew he wasn't coming back. Jaycie would go find him.

Now.

Chapter Nineteen

Jaycie found Parker where she knew he would be—on the world's longest porch. At almost seven hundred feet long, the expanse was almost always filled with guests who wanted a spectacular view of the Straits. She pulled in a long breath of cool air as she stepped out from the building. Since it was after six at night, everyone, including a set of adorable triplets, was attired in dressy clothes. The men all looked pretty similar—white or pastel dress shirt, dark tie, and a dark jacket with matching pants or khakis. The women were attired in more colorful dresses and some in pantsuits, jumpsuits, and one in what looked like a harem costume, with the back so low it dipped to her nether regions. Most of the hotel's white rocking chairs were claimed. She headed toward one of the best sunset views on the island. The west end of the porch often allowed viewers stunning pink and orange sunsets off beyond the Mackinac Bridge over Lake Michigan.

One among the cluster of people at the porch rail would be Parker. Somehow, each step toward him felt like a step toward a future. Yes, he'd been with her all the way so far, but this resonated like a new beginning toward a place they couldn't yet see. She shivered. This was ridiculous—he was here with his date. Granted, his fellow AA member was already wanting to order alcohol right in front of him. Dayla was wrong for him, all wrong.

Then who is right for Parker?

She knew the answer to that God-whispered question.

As she neared the group, Parker smiled. Her Parker. He extended his hand as she approached. When she shivered, he pulled her close into his arms. The chatter of the others gathered for the sunset faded with Parker's embrace. All her fears about her mom and this devastating illness fled with that heartfelt hug as she inhaled the scent of his intoxicating cologne. Parker pressed a long kiss into the top of her head.

"I have some things I need to tell you." His husky voice stirred longing in her.

She pulled back and looked into his eyes. "I'm guessing Dayla is no longer going to be dating you."

They both held back a laugh and then released it. "Yeah, I'm guessing that."

He pulled her into his arms again, and something small and square in his chest pocket pushed against her shoulder. He kissed her forehead. The gesture recalled a time long ago right here on this porch in this spot. A time when they both had their mothers in good health, and all seemed right with the world.

Holding him like this was setting her world back on its proper axis.

Parker bent further and brushed a kiss against her cheek. "I wanted to tell you what my cousin Isabella said when I called her this afternoon. And I have something I want to give you."

She stepped back. "You sound pretty serious."

He took her hands again. "I am. It kind of is. You should know what Isabella said today."

"All right." Behind him, the sun's slow descent to the water transfigured the skies to deep pink with streaks of yellow and orange extending as far as the eye could see. With this being one of the first days of summer, it could be close to eleven before it was really dark outside.

"Wouldn't our boss be shocked if he knew this is where I knelt down and proposed to you?"

"Proposed to me?" Was that what he had in his pocket? A ring? But that made no sense. He'd come there with Dayla.

"Yeah, don't you remember when I offered you the very best Ring Pop that Doud's Market had in stock?"

"Oh wow, yes." She pulled her hands away and covered her mouth as she giggled like the young teenager she once was. "I remember it tasted delicious."

He cleared his throat. "That's why I could legitimately tell my cousin that we were engaged."

"What?"

"Back before my Dad sent me over to check on that new hotel in England, I called Isabella. I did ask about you—how you were doing."

She shot him an annoyed look. "I'm not surprised. You were stalking me at UVA."

He hung his head. "Yeah, I guess I did."

She grabbed his hands again and shook them playfully. "I forgive you. We're friends again, remember?"

"Yeah, I remember." He cocked his head. "When I chatted with Isabella back then and asked about you, she'd gotten really quiet. Too quiet for her, which should have been a clue."

"What do you mean?"

"She said Elliott was cheating on you and had been for a while."

"That's not what he says." Was Parker telling the truth or Elliott?

"Well, that's what *Lady* Isabella," he rolled his eyes over his use of her title, "insisted back then. Should have trusted my gut instincts. Being newly sober, though, that was tricky."

"That's what she told you? That he'd been unfaithful?" In her spirit she *had* felt a check.

"Yes. God's honest truth. I got a little irate when I heard. So, I told her you'd already given me a promise of marriage." He waggled his eyebrows.

"A promise of marriage between two young teenagers is hardly an engagement."

"Agreed. But Isabella didn't need to know the specifics." He scrunched his features. "I'm sorry because it wasn't fair to you and Elliott. So, I want to tell you what she said today when I challenged her original story."

"Honestly, I'm not sure I care." Having Elliott there made her realize all the ways his red-flag behaviors had slipped under her infatuated radar.

"Hear me out." Parker lifted his palms and splayed his fingers. "Isabella and Elliott had a relationship, off-the-grid I guess you could say. My uncle would never have approved, with Elliott's background and lack of money. They kept it secret until Elliott broke it off—the only guy to ever dump her. My call this past March gave her a great opportunity to get back at him."

"When were they an item?"

"A couple of years back. Anyway, in that call she'd lied and said Elliott had been seeing Phillippa for a few months. She now admits that wasn't true."

"No?" The space between herself and Parker seemed too distant. She moved a tad closer.

"She told me today. I wanted you to know. And I apologize for telling about our status as an engaged couple."

"We were a little too young to be engaged, weren't we?" They weren't young teens anymore. "Isabella's sharing that not-quite-true information with Elliott still didn't have to serve as a catalyst to pursue Phillippa immediately. That says something about him."

"What did your kissing me at the pub say about you?" Parker's eyes grew darker.

So many thoughts chased through her mind. Yes, she'd tried to get even with Elliott. But that kiss. Wow. It had sparked something in her. "It was wrong, and I've apologized to both you and to Elliott about it." She leaned in and inhaled his cologne; the same one he'd worn that night when she'd run into him at the pub. Nautica Blue might become her favorite scent in the entire world.

His features dissolved into a blank slate devoid of emotion. "My point is that Isabella deliberately set out to break up you and Elliott. And he's now here. It's your chance to—"

She couldn't bear it any longer. Jaycie took a step forward, placed her hands on Parker's cheeks and pulled him toward her. This kiss was slower, gentler. Parker's initial surprise didn't last as long as it had the previous time. He pulled her so close that she wondered if they'd meld into one. He deepened the kiss, and she didn't care if anyone saw them, not even their boss. This was right.

Parker released her and took two steps back, bumping into a lady attired in a flowing champagne-colored dinner gown. As Parker made his apologies to the woman, the chill evening air rushed at Jaycie.

Parker gaped at her for a moment. The sky, blazing behind him, made his golden hair almost glow. He took a pace toward her and placed a hand on his chest. "I'm still only about nineteen, emotionally, remember? I'm still really young for you to be kissing me like that."

She squeezed one eye shut, assessing him, but said nothing.

Parker pulled something from his jacket pocket. He extended his hand and opened his fingers. He held a small gray jewelry box. "I want you to have this."

It could not be a ring. But somehow, deep in her soul, she wanted it—as though it could be a talisman to protect her from the pain and hurt that her mother's death would soon bring. If she had Parker and they had a new life together. . .

"Oh, this was the thing I wanted you to know about today." Parker's face tugged into an expression of shock and remorse as he took in her reaction. "Yikes, it's not. . ." He shoved his free hand back through his hair.

Cheeks heating, Jaycie shook her head. "I wasn't expecting another Ring Pop, I think they're all out of them at Doud's."

He chuckled, chasing away the awkwardness. "I wanted to tell you that I got my one-year sobriety coin at AA today." He opened the case and inside was a bronze disk about the size of a poker chip. "I want you to have it."

"Oh. I'm happy. So glad, Parker." She accepted the box and ran her finger over the imprinted message on the token.

He stepped closer and pressed his forehead against hers. "And of course, I'm in no position to be actually offering a proposal to anybody until I've got at least another year or so of sobriety under my belt."

That sounded like a promise. Her soul certainly swelled with hope inside at that obliquely offered pledge.

He wrapped his hands around hers. "You keep this as a vow of my intentions."

She blinked back tears. This would go in her keepsake box. She wished she'd kept her red plastic Ring Pop remnant to put alongside it. "Well, I *propose* we go to your house. The *other* Butterfly Cottage. I really enjoyed staying there after the Aunt Irene fiasco."

"We were glad to welcome a Welling family member back to the place."

Jaycie's great-grandparents had owned the Mackinac Island white Victorian on the East Bluff and had sold it to the Parker family during World War II when her Great-Grandfather Jack Welling, Jr., had served in the Army. He'd named it Butterfly Cottage, and when he returned from the war he named the cottage on the mainland after his island home.

"Carter would love to see us." He winked.

"I bet." Hopefully the kid didn't have a girl there.

"He helped put in some new bushes to attract more butterflies in the garden."

"I love that big front porch. It reminds me of the old Wellings' family farmhouse." She'd been to it once, in Shepherd, Michigan. A distant cousin of Gran's owned it now.

"Yeah, it's got that vibe."

"And Carter's helping with the garden?"

"Right. He's helping out after Grandma Kareen hired Thor to make sure the gardens are immaculate."

"Thor?"

"Michael DuBlanc, 'Mrs. Hemsworth's missing third son' is what Dayla calls him. The landscaper who our boss thought was Mort, the supposed gardener. But Mike's the real deal."

There had been a tall, muscular, blond gorgeous guy who was filthy dirty with mud who had been landscaping around the Grand earlier. She wasn't going to say anything about that, though. "I don't know him."

He looked her up and down. "Hey, you want to change before we bike over there?"

"I'd better."

Soon, they'd raced each other through the mostly quiet streets.

Parker pulled alongside her. "Your mom likes to have tea on the porch with my dad."

A few days earlier, she'd have been concerned that Mom was hanging so much with Mr. Parker. Now, though, all she felt was gratitude that her old friend was there for her. Mom would soon be gone. Tears threatened. "I'm glad they have each other."

Parker maintained her same steady pace. "There's always hope, Jaycie."

Not much hope for pancreatic cancer. But she couldn't push those words past her lips.

"Don't give up."

She sped past him. Artfully, she dodged horse manure and puddles she knew weren't rainwater.

He caught up. "Hey, Jaycie, why don't we go with them?"

"Huh?"

"Let's join our grandparents and parents on their trip."

If this request had come before her mom's announcement of her condition, Jaycie knew she'd have rejected it outright. Guilt set in. "Sure. If they want us."

"Why wouldn't they? We're young, fun, and wildly attractive." He chuckled. "And physically fit. Race you!"

With an islander's confidence, he raced off, darting his bike around anything and anyone in his way.

He'd tricked her.

When she caught up with him, she laughed. "You forget that I've got a gold medal Olympian in my family tree."

"How can I forget when my dad put a plaque for Jack Welling, Sr., outside the cottage?"

"Good point." Nothing for Jack Welling, Jr., whose exploits during World War II he'd kept closely guarded. Being a sharpshooter and a scout weren't exactly things he'd wanted to talk about, according to Gran.

"Come on, I'll let you win if you want to race to the *real* Butterfly Cottage."

"Hey! I take exception to that." As would Gran. But Parker had already shot down the street.

Before long, she biked past Parker, who'd stopped in the drive leading to the two-story white Victorian house. "I always loved this place." Or had she just loved someone who lived there?

Parker gave her the strangest look. Was he thinking the same thing? "You had butterflies following you." He pointed behind her.

She turned. A dozen or so Monarchs flitted in the drive behind her. "Wow."

The screen slammed on the porch. "That's so cool!" Carter shielded his eyes from the sun.

"You chased them away, you goof!" Parker scowled at his brother as the butterflies flew away.

"Well, hello to you, too." Carter crinkled his nose. "Why aren't you at dinner? With Dayla." He drew Dayla's name out in a mocking manner.

"She got busy ogling Jaycie's boyfriend."

"He's not my boyfriend."

"Ex-boyfriend."

"Better," she murmured.

"Whatever." Carter raised his hands. "Did you eat?"

"Nope."

"Do rolls count? With butter?"

"No. I've got an entire pizza from Doud's that I can reheat."

"Awesome." Parker dismounted his bike and set it near the bushes by the cottage.

Colorful flowers edged the porch. Jaycie parked her bike at the edge of the carriage drive that wound around to a white carriage house.

"Hey, Jaycie, what did Dad and your mom say when you two lit out?" Carter laughed.

"Um . . ."

The teen held up his phone. "Haha, I already know you didn't tell them. Dad texted me to let him know if I saw you two."

As he neared him, Parker attempted to lightly cuff his brother, but Carter ran inside the house.

Oh my gosh. Parker was right. He really was still more like a teenager himself. But Grandpa Jim was the same way. Unlike Dad, whose image could be posted under dour, serious, or humorless in a dictionary.

She called to Parker, "I'll be there in a minute. I'm going to text my mom and tell her we're here." And text Grandpa Jim and ask when the soonest was that he could arrive. She really needed him there. Mom needed him. Gran did, too.

Later, after eating pizza and playing Carter's fun game Beat Saber on Oculus for a while, Jaycie checked her phone. Mom had texted. *We're staying overnight. Got your message about Parker and you. Please let Cici out tonight and in the morning. We return around eleven tomorrow.*

Parker did a face plant with his hand. "If they're staying in our suites, which I assume, I bet I'm gonna be the one to get an earful."

"We've definitely earned this one."

"When hadn't we?" He laughed.

"Got that right." Carter ducked away when Parker playfully swatted at him. "You better watch out big bro, I'm as tall as you now."

"I better go. I gotta catch that last ferry."

"I'll go with you." Parker waved at Carter, who was beginning another game. "I'm riding with Jaycie to the docks."

Carter made the OK sign.

They stepped outside and Parker wrapped an arm around her shoulder. "If our parents had recorded all the lectures they'd given us over the years, how long would that play?"

"Would anyone listen to it on YouTube?"

"Maybe our kids? Or our grandkids?" Parker's low voice sent shivers down her back, warming her despite the chill breeze that had begun.

The pain of the impending loss of her mother combined with this sweet promise was so bittersweet.

She leaned her forehead against his. "This day has gone nothing like I thought it would."

"We only get one day at a time, Jaybird. One hour, really. But I want to be there for you. I will be there, I can promise you that—one hour, one day at a time."

That was a promise she could hang onto.

Chapter Twenty

Dawn
Mackinaw City

"But I really need my husband here." Dawn pleaded with Brianna, the torturer, and now her sworn enemy.

"I'm sorry Mrs. Charbonneau. If your husband's knee went out while he was driving. . ."

"Yeah, yeah, yeah." This was them covering for themselves and liability. She was immediately convicted that of course if it wasn't safe for Jim to drive then he shouldn't do it. "A girl can hope though, can't she?"

Brianna laughed. "If he does everything right, all the stuff I tell him to do, then he will be there very soon."

Cici's ears perked up, almost as though she understood what the therapist was saying.

"How soon?" Dawn squeezed the phone tightly, waiting.

"Mr. Charbonneau made me promise not to say. He wants to share that with you himself."

Dawn crinkled her nose in disgust. "He's trumped me, again."

"Sorry. But be patient and you'll see your sweetie soon."

"Thanks so much." She didn't want Jim having a setback, but the nightly calls, alone, weren't cutting it. She had to tell him about Tammy, no matter that her daughter wanted her to wait.

"No problem."

Why did people say that? It was as if the call *was* a problem in some way. Mixed signals, in her opinion. Maybe she was getting too old to understand why younger people said the things they did. And she really did have a problem.

She slumped onto the overstuffed couch in the living room. She had an hour before she needed to get to the church for a VBS meeting. Tammy was sleeping. Dawn called Jim.

"That you, Minnie?" In the background, Dawn heard Hard Rock barking.

"It's me. Sound like Hard Rock wants to talk to me, too."

"That's our neighbor delivering me a nice hot breakfast."

"Huh?"

"Yeah, Joan and Don have been bringing me hash brown casseroles, French toast, pancakes—you name it."

She hated to rain on his breakfast parade, she really did, but things had to be shared. "Honey?"

"Yeah?" She could hear him shuffling toward the back door. "Thanks, Joan!" he called out.

"Jim?"

"Um hum?" That sounded like aluminum foil crinkling.

"Sit down."

"I am. Gonna eat my breakfast. Will call back."

"No!"

"Huh?"

"No. Sit down and listen to me."

"What's wrong?" She had his attention now; she could tell by his worried tone.

"Tammy." That was the only word she could manage before her eyes moistened.

"What about our daughter?"

"Cancer," she croaked out.

"What?" Jim's booming voice hurt her ears.

"Don't yell. She's really sick."

"Oh, dear Lord."

"Yes, we need Him now. Tammy needs our prayers." And I need you with me. She chewed her lower lip.

"How bad?"

Could she really make her mouth say the words? "A few months."

"Sick a few months?"

She swiped at her eyes. "To live, Jimbo."

"No." It sounded like he'd slapped the table. "I don't accept that."

She told him more about what Tammy had said about her visits with the doctors and about what she'd chosen to do. And to not do.

"Listen, you shouldn't be going through this all alone. My girls shouldn't have to do that." His voice caught. "And I miss you so much."

"I miss you, too."

"I'll make some calls to get some help planning my trip up. Let's talk tonight, okay?"

"I don't want you to undo all that good work you've done."

"I could use my good leg for driving and put it on cruise when I can. That would help. And if push comes to shove, Don would probably drive me up."

"Or drive you halfway and I could come get you?"

"That's an option, too. But I think if you could hold on a few days, and if I wean off the rest of these meds, I could probably do it."

"A few days, even a week—that sounds wonderful." Just knowing he'd be there soon lifted a weight from her shoulders.

"Talk to you tonight."

"Best part of my day."

They exchanged phone smooches and hung up. Thank God she wasn't working remotely. Thank God her husband was coming. *And please, God, heal my daughter.*

Chapter Twenty-One

Jaycie
Mackinac Island

Jaycie concluded her short speech to the visiting group of children, and they all clapped, which was a tad unusual. There were usually the few who stood around looking bored but not this time. The well-behaved kids were from the summer camp program in Newberry, a town about an hour away in the Upper Peninsula. Jaycie slid her few notecards back into their protective case and the photographs into a rigid plastic folder.

"Come on children, you can go ahead and examine the relics." Their teacher, a slim petite woman with a short silver bob pointed to the nearby table. Parker had arranged various items from the dig atop it that Jaycie had deemed safe for the children to touch.

Someone tugged at her elbow. A blond girl with huge brown eyes stared up at Jaycie. "Miss Worth, can I hold your hand? My name's Cassie and I'm five." She held up five little fingers as if to prove her point.

Jaycie looked to where all the other children were gathered. "Don't you want to see the cool stuff we dug up?"

"I do but my mom says don't touch anything while I'm here." Cassie's lower lip quivered.

"Oh," Jaycie made her mouth wide in surprise, "that's because I forgot to put in the parent letter that this is a touchable kind of talk that I was doing."

"Touch-a-ball?"

"Touchable–it means you can touch the things." Jaycie nodded solemnly. "Your mom is very right about not usually touching anything old like this special stuff."

"My mom's real smart."

"I bet she is." Jaycie tousled the girl's silky golden curls. "But this time I promise you, Scout's honor," she held up her hands in a Girl Scout oath gesture, "that you really are allowed to look at and even hold some of the things we brought up out of the earth over there."

She cocked her head. "I'm a Daisy Scout."

"Are you?" Jaycie took the girl's hand. "Come let me give you the special Daisy Scout tour where you peek into the box where we are getting ready to clean up some stuff. And no touching on this one, though, like your mom said."

"Okay."

She and Cassie walked past her colleagues who were busy at work, most down on their knees in the dirt, some actually down in the partially dug-out basement of the old house.

Mr. Jeffries, looking spotless as usual, rolled up his sleeves. "How are you two ladies doing this morning?"

Cassie stuck her index finger in her mouth and stared at Jaycie's boss.

"This is Cassie. She's five and a Daisy Scout and listens very well to her mother's advice." Jaycie raised her eyebrows and nodded seriously.

The director dropped onto one knee—that was going to turn his khaki pants a new shade of grass-green—and held out his hand. "Hi Cassie, my name is Mr. Jeffries, and I was also once five."

Cassie nodded gravely and hesitated. Finally, she pulled her finger from her mouth and held out her hand.

"I think Miss Worth here really likes kids. What do you think, Cassie?"

The child nodded vigorously, and Mr. Jeffries laughed. He stood and wiped the grass from his knees. Yup, definitely going to be some grass stain there.

"Cassie?" The teacher waved for the child to rejoin her group.

The tiny girl hugged her, wrapping her little arms around Jaycie's thighs and burying her tiny head against her abdomen. Then Cassie ran off.

"Well, I think you've made a new friend." Mr. Jeffries laughed.

"She's so cute." And for one of those rarest of moments, the thought of becoming a mother one day raced through her mind. Time for that later, though. Why then, did the thought of a little girl with blond hair like Parker's and dark eyes like hers make Jaycie yearn for a child of her own? Maybe because with her mother dying, the thought of being part of generating new life made sense on more levels that she wanted to consider.

Parker shot her a quizzical look. Her face heated. Had he read her thoughts? No, of course not, that would be ridiculous.

Her boss leaned in. "If you change your mind about starting your doctoral studies next year, I could really use you as one of our educational consultants. We send employees out to the schools to share about history, archeology, about our museums and all that."

"That's tempting." And it really was. With Mom having maybe only a short time to live, the idea of going off to graduate school really no longer appealed.

Tamara
Mackinac Island

Why had she promised Hamp that she'd come to the island? After the walk to the fort with Mom, Tamara wanted to conserve her energy. But she didn't feel tired today. In fact, if anything, she'd felt revived. Still, she didn't want to push it, but she'd promised Hamp. She checked her phone for the time. Mom had already left for a VBS meeting with Pastor Dave at the Church of the Straits.

Mom was a doer, a busy person. At least she was finding with her volunteer work, that she could be active and feel useful. And although her cancer was a terrible thing, maybe Mom could see the benefit of finally selling her business and retiring. Life could be short. Terribly short. Mom and Dad should enjoy their last years without the agency always hanging over their heads.

Tamara gathered her belongings and headed to the ferry dock. Soon, she was underway with a fairly full boat. She sat inside, in the back, at the outside edge so that she could get off quickly. Of course, most people had headed to the top to get unobstructed views of the water, the bridge, and the approach to Mackinac Island. The lower deck was completely full as well. July promised to be a busy month if the early crowds were any indication.

As the boat docked, she texted Hamp that she'd arrived. Tamara quickly disembarked the boat and caught sight of a familiar face as she stepped onto the wharf.

"Mrs. Worth, I didn't see you come aboard." Carter beamed at her but then he looked away, suddenly sad. "I'm sorry you're so sick."

She drew in a steadying breath. This boy had already suffered enough loss. "I feel pretty decent tonight."

His blue eyes met hers. "Great. I'm glad to hear that."

"In fact, I'm going to the Pink Pony with your dad for dinner."

"Tell him to bring home some smoked whitefish dip for me, please." He pressed his hands together in a mock prayer.

She grinned. "Sure thing."

"Do you need any help with anything here on the dock?"

"No." The way the word came out, kind of biting, she instantly felt bad. The furrow on his forehead reflected the sting he must feel. "I'm sorry, it's just that, like I said I'm doing well right now and I don't want to. . ."

"It's all right Mrs. Worth, I think I get it. It's like when my Lupus acts up—I need some help, but when I'm fine, like this summer, then I don't want to be treated like an invalid."

"You have Lupus?" Good gracious, as if the boy didn't have enough to contend with.

"Yeah, but I'm doin' okay." He shrugged.

"Good." Poor kid. She'd keep him in her prayers. And when she got to heaven, she'd keep on praying for him and his family. "See ya later, kiddo."

"See ya, Mrs. Worth."

She strode down the dock, surprised at the spring in her step. She'd heard she'd have great days like this one, and then some others, like the ones she'd experienced where she felt like she had the flu and worse. Until they would all be bad days. She shook her head as if she could shake off the thoughts. When she exited the docks onto the sidewalk she impulsively headed toward the library. Jaycie had told her she was going there tonight after work. She'd surprise her daughter with a quick visit before her dinner with Hamp.

Tammy hadn't walked far when she spied Jaycie's handsome British beau and Mort's supermodel wife posing for pictures in front of the Windemere Hotel. The two were striking against the backdrop of the beautiful yellow building with its lovely front porch and gorgeous, lush landscaping. Standing near the camera crew, Parker's friend Dayla stood on tiptoe, her short dress creeping up so far that if she wasn't careful she'd be giving everyone an unexpected view of her posterior.

Tamara sighed. She and Gran had decided to not tell Parker and Jaycie that both Dayla and Elliott hadn't seemed too perturbed when Parker and Jaycie never returned to the table. That night, about a half hour after it became clear that Jaycie and Parker weren't coming back, the other two left together. When the rest of the group went up to the Cupola a couple of hours later, Dayla was three-sheets-to-the-wind and Elliott wasn't too far behind.

That same night, Kay-Leigh had suggested that Elliott should go up to his room so he'd be in good shape for a morning photoshoot. The handsome young Englishman then invited Parker's date to join him. Dayla and Elliott had left, hand-in-hand. All that information was something that neither Tamara nor her mother wished to share with Jaycie.

Let the young people work it out for themselves.

When the photography crew finished, Elliott came to the fence and playfully lifted Dayla over it, giving Tamara way more than a glimpse of her thong underwear than she'd wanted to see. She cringed. Tamara continued toward the library, hoping to get that image out of her head.

She paused in front of the quaint building. Before she went in, she'd go around back to the special place where she used to come with Hamp. The library's back porch was a great place to watch the ferries and was very private.

She rounded the corner and stopped abruptly when she spotted a young couple locked in an embrace. That could not be. But it was. That was definitely Jaycie with her dark ponytail tucked in a loop and the golden-haired man kissing her was. . .yes. . . Parker.

Tamara took a step backward and then walked away. A slow smile began to bloom. Jaycie would have someone to look after her when Tamara was gone. If that kiss was any indication, Parker was in love with her girl. And Jaycie reciprocated the feelings.

Thank God she had someone to rely on since Brad wasn't someone her daughter could count on for moral support. Or any kind of support for that matter. Tamara exhaled a slow breath.

She and Hamp would have some planning to do tonight. At least their kids could get a happy-ever-after even if they'd both failed in their marriages. Poor Hamp, he deserved better. Heck, she deserved better. But regardless, God had given them wonderful children, and they were a blessing. Who knew—maybe one day the Lord would bless Hamp with grandchildren that he could enjoy. Her own grandchildren, maybe. Tamara wrapped her arms around her middle.

She'd not intrude on Jaycie and Parker's romantic moment. She headed toward the restaurant, determined to pick up a few baby items that she'd pack away for when she was gone from this earth. She'd leave them for Jaycie.

Maybe coming to the island for dinner with Hamp had seemed like a silly idea. But to see Jaycie and Parker together like that—so worth it. She felt a new spring in her step. It gave her hope, in God's goodness, that after she was gone her daughter would be okay. That was a blessing.

And she'd keep praying for her old friend, Hamp, that God would send him a soulmate, a true friend, companion, and comfort.

Chapter Twenty-Two

Dawn
Mackinaw City

Dawn set a mug of hot mint tea on the coffee table in front of Tammy, who still lay prone on the couch in her pajamas. She'd drank a cup of mocha that morning. Sipped soup at lunch. And had nursed a mason jar of Arnold Palmer all afternoon. Not one bite of solid food. *My girl. My dear girl.*

"It's Friday night!" Dawn pointed to the plate glass window facing the harbor. "You know what that means."

Tammy gazed up at her but didn't move to sit up to drink her tea. "Even more tourists than usual peeking in through our windows?"

Sighing, Dawn had to nod. "What else though?"

"Dad will be here soon?"

"Yes, but what else?"

"More VBS planning tomorrow?"

"No."

Tammy tossed a soft pillow at her and Dawn caught it.

Dawn reached behind her daughter and raised the blinds so they could get a better view of the upcoming fireworks. She arched an eyebrow. "But what else happens Friday? Something you love."

"I used to love it." She rolled her eyes, just like she did when she was a teenager. "Now, though, the fireworks make my head ache even worse than it does otherwise."

"I'm sorry my darling." She really was.

"It's not your fault."

"It's nobody's fault. It is what it is. But I'll miss you." How many years did she have herself? The thought sometimes terrified her, making her heart palpitations even worse.

Tammy struggled to sit, and Dawn resisted the urge to assist her. The time would come soon enough when she'd *have* to help.

"If what the Bible says is true, and I believe it is, I won't miss you at all because there's no sadness in heaven."

"Right." Dawn wiped a tear from her eye.

Tammy put her feet on the carpet and then swiveled toward the window, groaning. "At least we can watch the fireworks from right here."

"Yes, we can. And you have to admit the pyrotechnics on the weekends have been spectacular this year."

"Mom, I'm too tired to care tonight." Tammy's eyes filled with tears.

Dawn sat down beside her girl and pulled her into her arms. Tammy's slim frame wracked with sobs. Outside, small clusters of families walked by toward the park and the harbor as the last of the daylight dimmed. A woman about Tammy's age looked in at them from the street. A woman who was physically well enough to stride purposefully with the tall man beside her and two teenage boys dressed in Mackinac Island t-shirts and cargo shorts. Anger coursed through Dawn at the unfairness of it. She averted her gaze. *Jim, I need you here.* Now that her daughter was leaving this earth. And Jaycie, she, and Jim would be left behind to grieve. But Dawn, too, would be leaving earth before too many years as would Jim. That was reality. A decade, maybe two, until she crossed that bridge to heaven.

She held Tammy for a long time. Outside, the sky grew dark. She stroked her daughter's hair. When she went limp, soft snores confirmed Tammy was sleeping. Dawn leaned back against the couch and settled her baby girl a little more comfortably against her shoulder.

The front door creaked open. "Dawn? Tam?" Hamp tentatively entered the living room. He crossed the living room and stared open-mouthed at Tammy. "Is she much worse, then?"

"Only sleeping," Dawn said softly as her daughter began to stir.

"May I?" Hamp gestured for her to move aside.

Raising Tammy's head from her shoulder gently, her daughter suddenly straightened and opened her eyes. "Hamp?"

"I'm here." He sank onto the couch beside her.

Dawn left the room and started the electric teapot. When she returned to the living room, Tammy and Hamp were leaning against one another companionably, like brother-and-sister. Those two had been like two peas-in-a-pod back in the day, like Parker and Jaycie had been. But Hamp and Tammy had always been more companionable and going on double dates together like Dawn and Hampy used to do when they were teenagers. Outside, the night had grown black. She set the tea in front of Hamp and gestured to Tammy's cup. "Would you like me to re-heat your mug?"

Tammy shook her head and lifted the mug to her lips, her hand trembling. She placed her other hand beneath the mug to steady it. This weakness had come on rather suddenly.

A pop sounded outside. A starburst of orange and gold sizzled in the sky. Hamp turned. "Oh wow, look at that!" He elbowed Tam gently. "You wanta go out and watch them?"

Could Tammy handle that right now?

Hamp must have caught her shocked expression because he met her gaze and then glanced between her and her daughter.

"No, thanks, I'm not up to it tonight."

"Oh, fine, fine," his words were rushed together, and he reached for his own cup of tea and swallowed several gulps.

Tammy had complained that one reason she wanted to be in Mackinaw City was to escape any expectations that anyone had of her. These past couple of days even the simplest expectation had begun to wear on her, since she'd finally disclosed her illness. Hamp smiled with affection at Tammy. "This is perfect from right here. We can see them. . . Oh!"

Several fireworks went off at the same time, a blaze of blue, pink, and yellow lighting up the velvet black night sky.

Dawn sucked in her breath and moved closer to her daughter and the man who'd once spent so much time with them in this very room. "Wow!"

Tammy swiveled and placed her arm on the couch back, settling in. Hamp mirrored her, his arm also across the back.

One after another, the muffled explosions could be heard even through the closed windows, blocks from the harbor. One amazing sparkling kaleidoscopic image after another lit up the sky.

Dawn "Ooh'd" and Hamp "Ah'd" but Tammy simply laid her head on her arm and watched in silence.

Another quartet of flares went up. Would it be like that going to heaven? Three wiggling pale pink wormlike flares sped skyward before bursting into glittering pink trails of light, falling through the sky. They were so beautiful. Would angels accompany her precious child? Tammy wouldn't go alone on her heavenly journey—Dawn was sure of that. Not only the loved ones who'd gone before them, but of course her heavenly Father would welcome her.

Tears streamed down Tam's face. "I wonder if it's like that?"

Had her daughter read her mind? Another firework exploded, with zig-zagging gold trails running through a green starburst. "Maybe, darling. Maybe getting to heaven is just like that."

Tammy's gaze locked on hers in understanding, that moment of connection was almost palpable. "I have a feeling that it will be." She squeezed Hamp's arm.

Hamp ducked his chin and sniffed. "I wish we had more time my friend. I wish. . ." He choked back a sob, "I know that God loves you. . .best. And we have to. . . trust Him."

Outside one explosion after another sounded as dozens of colors burst through the sky one after another, too gorgeous to even peel one's eyes away from. The three of them stared in awe.

"I hope it's like that." Tammy's serene face confirmed the truth in her words.

"I bet it is, Tam." Hamp wrapped his arm around Tammy and gave her a quick hug.

Dawn hoped so. "Yup. I think so, too."

In the distance, vehicle horns began to sound in appreciation of the display. She couldn't help but smile at the thought that her daughter's arrival in heaven could have the others there, the angels even, cheering her arrival. And maybe a few would be sounding horns.

Chapter Twenty-Three

Dawn
St. Ignace, Eastern Upper Peninsula

Dawn drove Tammy and Jaycie over the Mackinac Bridge, her daughter with her eyes pressed closed and Jaycie silent in the back. The skies were full of puffy white clouds, brilliant against the intense blue sky. Beneath the bridge, where Lake Huron and Lake Michigan met, small whitecaps bore evidence to the stiff breeze. She took the exit for town and drove to the parking lot where the others would meet them.

When they arrived, Hampy, Hamp, and Parker stood in front of the enormous three-row seater new black Lincoln Navigator. The luxury SUV had to cost over seventy grand.

They got out of the car and Jaycie opened the trunk. Hamp went to Tammy's side.

"Seriously?" Dawn cocked an eyebrow at Hampy. "This is what you're driving now?"

His grandson passed by her, heading toward Jaycie. "Granddad says, 'Go big or go home,' don'tcha know?"

She laughed. Dawn caught the look that Jaycie sent Parker's way—one of admiration mixed with longing for something more. Had she missed some signals between those two? She sighed. It sure wouldn't be the first time she'd missed emotions that had been displayed right in front of her. But maybe it was like Pastor Dave said in his latest sermon—God knew each of us intimately and He loved us as we were, even with all our foibles.

"I need to get in that humongous vehicle, please." Tammy touched Hamp's arm.

Oh no. Her girl was already tiring out, and they'd only just started the first leg of their journey.

Hampy shot her a look. She could almost read his mind. They'd allowed up to three days to do Tammy's bucket list tour of the Eastern Upper Peninsula. "Yeah, we need to get going. We don't want to miss the Paul R. Tregurtha coming through the Soo Locks."

Fleeting sorrow danced across Hamp's face as he opened Tammy's front passenger door.

Score one for me, I saw that sadness on his face.

Hamp opened the driver's door. "The PRT is the Queen of the Lakes."

Parker helped Jaycie into the back of the black behemoth. "The biggest boat to pass through the Soo Locks."

Dawn knew a little about this topic, too. "Longer than three football fields," she shared as Parker jumped into the rear seat.

"It's going through the Locks at eleven." Jaycie's forced brightness was easily discerned by Dawn.

What's happening with me that I'm noticing all these feelings? Was it Tammy's diagnosis? Or was it God at work after she'd asked Him to be stronger in her life? She'd prayed for Him to help her to be less focused on herself and more on others. God was answering this prayer in a way she couldn't miss. And she felt more connected to others because of it. The sensation felt good, comforting. Hampy offered her a hand, and she climbed into the seat in the middle row. Hampy went around and got into the seat adjacent her.

Dawn looked around at the five loved ones traveling with her. She didn't have a bag of knitting to occupy herself. She'd planned to be fully engaged in the moment this trip—another prodding from the Holy Spirit.

"Buckle up," Hamp called out. He started the ignition.

"Roll down the windows," Jaycie called out.

"Yeah, it's hot back here," Parker agreed.

"I'll turn on the air conditioning," Hamp called back.

Hot air blasted Dawn in the face. "Whew!" She raised her hand and Hampy reached past her to adjust the middle row vents.

"Keep your windows down for a minute and let me blow the hot air out, and then let's figger out what we're gonna do with the AC, okay?"

"Sure, Son." Hampy leaned in and patted his son's shoulder.

Tammy turned in her seat. "Mr. Parker, do you mind if I recline a bit? I'll move the seat forward first."

"Sure thing, Darlin'." Hampy's use of one of Jim's favorite phrases brought tears to Dawn's eyes.

Oh, God, I need my husband here. Oh, Jim, how I miss you.

This trip was for Tammy. This wasn't about her. It wasn't about what she needed. Jim would be there in God's good timing. Where had all those thoughts come from? Whew, God really was working on her brain. She rubbed her temple.

Tammy reclined her seat. She'd already closed her eyes.

"Who needs boxes of Tic Tacs?" Hampy pulled a Doud's market bag from his backpack.

"We do," Jaycie called out.

Hampy tossed two containers back to Jaycie and Parker. He leaned forward and touched Tammy's shoulder gently. "Two boxes of Tic Tacs for up front?"

"Thanks." Tammy's soft voice was barely audible. She placed the candy in the console as Hamp continued to adjust the mirrors.

"How about you, Miss Mackinaw City?" Hampy handed Dawn the tiny rectangular box.

"Orange. That's my favorite." She grinned at him.

"How long have I known you, old friend?"

"Before these things were ever made, that's for sure. And the many decades since I was Miss Mackinaw City." She laughed, remembering the ride in Hampy's white convertible down the main drag during the Fourth of July parade when she was seventeen. A lifetime ago. But her daughter, Tammy, wouldn't get those extra decades—not unless God came through with a miracle. Still, didn't her preachers always say that God was in the business of miracles?

Hamp glanced in the mirror. "Everybody ready?"

Parker's shrill whistle from the back seat startled her.

Hampy swiveled around and wagged his index finger at his grandson. "Listen up, buddy-o, I've got my hearing aids in, and if you do that again I'll put you out onto the side of the road. You can jump in the lake and swim home."

She chuckled as Hamp drove the SUV onto St. Ignace's main street. They drove past the water, white caps billowing along the lake's surface. "That's rough chop today, Parker, so maybe listen to your Grandpa."

"Yes, ma'am." Parker's laugh belied his words.

"It's so pretty, though, all that foam." Tammy leaned her head against the window.

"It is. Even when it's rough." Hamp reached across and patted her hand, then gripped the steering wheel.

Pretty, even when it's rough. Life wasn't always easy. Things got pretty rough, like now. But they would take in all this beauty and enjoy this trip. Puffy cumulus clouds dotting a row in the bright blue sky.

Before long they were on the outskirts of town.

"Mom?" Jaycie leaned forward. "There's the hospital over there, like I told you."

Jaycie and Parker had scoped out where the hospitals and medical facilities would be while they were on the trip.

"Thanks, honey."

Tammy briefly looked in the direction of the hospital. "I'm so glad my doctor okayed this trip. But I'd have gone even if he'd said no."

Dr. Austin had prescribed plenty of medications to make this trip manageable for Tammy. *God bless that man.*

They drove up I-75, the brisk winds rocking the huge SUV. "That's some Straits of Mackinac breeze today, isn't it?" Hamp called back to them.

"It is," his father agreed.

"I'm glad it didn't get stronger until we crossed the bridge," Dawn said.

A cellphone began to chime. Tammy's. She reached into her purse and pulled it out. "It's Brad."

"Put him on speakerphone!" Hampy cackled at his suggestion, and Dawn playfully swatted at his hand.

"That's a great idea, Mr. Parker." Jaycie leaned forward. "Gran—make Mom do it."

As if she could manage that.

To her surprise, her daughter took the call. "Brad?"

"Tam, I wanted to share some good news with you."

Dawn stiffened. Her daughter had put Brad on speaker phone.

"Oh?"

"Yeah," her son-in-law continued, "Gina and I are joining a church."

Beside her, Hampy looked like he might swallow his tongue. From the back, her granddaughter and her friend stifled a cross between a laugh and a groan.

A car passed by them in the left lane.

"Well, that's. . . interesting." Tammy raised her seat.

Beside her, Hampy mouthed, "Interesting? Ha."

"Yes, I knew you'd want to hear about it." Brad sounded more animated than Dawn had ever heard him be. "You always wanted me to 'Come to Jesus' as you put it."

"Wow, yes, Brad I did want that for you. I want that for every unbeliever." Tammy swiped at a tear rolling down her wan cheek.

Yeah, my daughter even wants that for you, you cheater.

"We talked with the pastor right away about joining, and he's good with that." Brad exhaled loudly.

"Really?" A spot of color formed on Tammy's left cheek.

Dawn couldn't hold back her ire. She leaned forward and cupped her hands around her mouth. "How about that you're still married and cheating on your wife? Did you tell him that, Bradley?"

"Is *she* listening?" Brad's irritation was crystal-clear.

"Yeah, we're all listening," Hamp spoke up. "You low-life scum. Did you tell your pastor how you dumped your wife and took up with a younger colleague?"

There was a long pause. Then surprisingly, Brad laughed. "I did tell him all about it."

Dawn's stomach filled with acid. She bent and reached for her purse. If ever there was a Rolaids moment, this was it.

Jaycie called out, "And he let you join anyway, Dad? What's with that?"

"Who all have you got in there, Tamara? And yes, he let me, he let *us* join." Self-righteousness tinged Brad's every word.

Hampy raised his voice, "Then he's some kind of idiot, isn't he? Letting a married man, who is living with his lover in Tammy's house, join his church."

"We confessed our sins. God has forgiven us." Brad sounded defensive, however, rather than contrite. "Once our divorce comes through then we'll marry."

"Except there won't be a divorce, Brad." Tears streamed down Tammy's face and Hamp rubbed her shoulder.

"She's dying, you moron." Hampy's face glowed beet red.

Hamp leaned his head toward the phone. "Unless she gets a miracle, you'll be a widower by Halloween. Tell your new pastor that!"

"What?"

"It's true, Dad." Jaycie sniffed. "Mom, end that call, please."

"Goodbye, Brad." Tammy tapped at the screen and returned her cell phone to her purse.

"Can you believe a church accepted that. . ." Hampy let loose a string of profane names for Dawn's son-in-law.

Parker laughed. He leaned in and touched his grandfather's shoulder. "Grandpa, you're allowed to go to church, and yet you still cuss like a sailor."

"Yeah, so what? I ask for forgiveness." Hampy's tone was what Dawn liked to call his mule voice. "Just like Bradley is claiming to do."

"So. . ," Parker drew the word out. "Maybe the church can accept people like Jaycie's dad, too."

Hampy turned and scowled at Parker. "You really do want to swim back to the island, don't you boy?"

Parker raised his hands in surrender.

"He didn't sound too contrite to me." Dawn sighed.

"Me, neither." Tammy shook her head.

"Sounded like the big dope he is," Hampy griped.

Dawn felt a nudge in her spirit. "But I hope he's being genuine in his newfound belief."

A long pause of silence reverberated in the van as they continued down the almost empty interstate.

"I hope so, too." Tammy leaned her head against the window.

"I don't want to believe him." Parker's voice held the wistfulness of youth. "But if he's finally given himself over to his Higher Power, then maybe Brad still has a chance."

Everyone has a chance to be redeemed. Dawn looked around, almost expecting to see something, someone, to affirm the voice she'd felt in her soul.

"As weird as that call was, I am actually happy for Brad." Tammy's low emotion-filled voice tugged at Dawn's heartstrings.

Jaycie
Mackinac Island

Jaycie recounted their trip to Mr. Jeffries, "Tahquamenon Falls, Pictured Rocks, a trip through the Soo Locks, too much whitefish to measure, but we missed out on Kitch-iti-kipi Springs."

Parker's mouth pulled to the side. "I really wanted to see that again. I last went with Jaycie and her grandparents when we were both five."

Mom had run out of steam before they could get to the beautiful clear pool of water near Manistique, so they'd returned home a little early. Jaycie grinned wistfully at Parker. "That was our entering kindergarten trip. And I still remember how you could see through the clear water all the way to the bottom."

"We'll have to go back on our own." The promise in Parker's eyes sent warmth through her all the way to her toes.

Mr. Jeffries glanced between the two of them and from the twitch of his lips, he hadn't missed the emotions sparking between her and Parker. "What was your favorite part, Jaycie?"

Her heart lurched. *Standing under the dark skies in Paradise, the stars twinkling, Lake Superior's waves rushing against the shore—and Parker holding her tightly, assuring her that life would go on for them, that they were part of something bigger.* Parker's compassion had enveloped her as she cried about her mother. They'd found a spot beneath the huge white birches, away from her cousin's large cabin, where they were all bunking out, for a bit of privacy. "Uh. . ." She swallowed hard. "Paradise is such a beautiful place."

"Ah, yes, the Falls are stupendous, aren't they?" Mr. Jeffries smiled benevolently. He pointed to a pile of new paperwork on her desk and then to Parker's, similarly encumbered. "But now you're back."

So much for their mini vacation, albeit one heavy with the knowledge of her mother's illness.

"Is that what I think it is?" Parker took two steps toward his desk. "The airport stuff?"

A muscle in their boss's square jaw jumped. "Yes, it is. Not too many state parks also have control over an airport. It adds further complexity to my job, on occasion."

Good thing Parker was being tasked with the paperwork on that big job. *Yikes.*

"If you need me to have lunch sent in for you, let me know." The director pushed his glasses up on his nose, the conversation clearly over.

"Yes, sir, I will."

When their boss headed toward his office, Parker rolled his eyes at Jaycie. "So, I'll be in here, head bent over these numbers while you're out playing with schoolkids again?"

"Yup." Her heart warmed at the thought of showing their dig site to a group of teens from the Lansing area.

She'd shared her thoughts of a career change with Gran and her mother. Mom had encouraged her to look into what she'd need to do to pursue a teaching certificate. Gran advised her to check out master's degree in education programs in Michigan. She offered to keep the cottage open year-round if Jaycie couldn't bear to return to her home in Virginia. The home that wasn't hers anymore.

"You all right?" Parker leaned in as if he might take her hand, but she stepped back.

She didn't need to jeopardize his position. They'd already been warned, and Parker loved this work. He never looked happier than when he was elbow-deep in the business of running a state park.

"I was just thinking about something." If she stayed in Michigan and worked, she'd be here, but where would Parker be? He'd mentioned possibly pursuing an MBA now that he'd given up his doctoral studies slot. With Mom having maybe months to live, she couldn't see heading off to pursue a career that no longer interested her. That didn't mean Parker shouldn't pursue his real passion of studying business.

He shoved a hand through his hair. "I don't know how you can think at all, honestly, with what's going on."

How she longed to take two steps forward and hold him tight. To have him shelter her in his arms. But he had his own issues to sort out, too. Maybe with time. *God only knows.*

Chapter Twenty-Four

Tamara
Mackinaw City

Tamara replayed in her mind the cryptic phone call she'd received the night before. *"Mrs. Worth, Dr. Austin wants to see you first thing in the morning. Are you available?"*

She'd agreed to drive to Petoskey, and the scheduler had hung up before Tamara had even had a chance to ask why her oncologist wanted to see her. Now, she grabbed her purse and a copy of Guideposts magazine and went to the table, where Mom was sipping her morning coffee. She kissed her on the forehead.

"Are you sure you don't want me to go with you?" Mom squeezed Tamara's hand.

Surprisingly, Tamara felt fairly decent considering the whirlwind trip they'd recently had. "No, I feel a lot better today. I'm sure I can drive. And I want to keep doing stuff for myself as long as I can."

A sheen of moisture shone in her mother's eyes as she released her hand. "I understand, darling. What I don't get, though, is why your doctor is bringing you in for this visit."

Tamara inhaled deeply. "Honestly, Mom, I'm guessing he's going to use his considerable charm to get me to enroll in his clinical trial. I read in the paper that it's been approved." Tears pricked her own eyes and she swiped at them. The pancreatic cancer clinical trial was only for people whose cancer was so advanced that they either weren't candidates for the Whipple procedure or who had refused the drastic measure.

Her friend had survived the excruciating Whipple procedure only to live in excruciating pain afterward, barely able to eat. When the medical staff still required chemotherapy, Tamara and Ruby's family had been shocked. Then the cancer had spread, anyway. Her dear friend, and her traumatized family, had experienced months of devastation.

At least so far Tamara's symptoms were manageable. Thank God that He had helped her be obedient to what He had laid on her heart.

This time with her mother and daughter was the most precious gift of her lifetime.

"Will you do it if you qualify for the trial?" Mom's hopeful expression pierced her heart.

"Yes, Mom, I will. I prayed about it, and I'll share with you and Jaycie when I get back." She'd read that one of the risks of Dr. Austin's clinical study was that patients could die even earlier if they experienced an adverse reaction to the medication. Although she felt the Holy Spirit's direction that she should agree if it was offered, Tamara also felt in her flesh that if she did die then she'd not experience the horrendous suffering her best friend had.

"All right. Now you better be off, or you'll be late." Mom pointed to the door.

Tamara gave a curt laugh and mock saluted her mother. "Yes, ma'am. I guess you haven't forgotten the years Dad spent in the military, have you?"

"Nope. 'Never late and always ready' is his motto."

And all in God's good time. Tamara grabbed her purse and headed out. On the porch, several butterflies flitted in and out of the bushes that edged the railing. She watched, spying one that was the slightly lighter orange of the female and another the more brilliant orange of the male. Another lighter orange monarch flew up and the male followed after her. The first female hovered nearby. Tamara smiled. If she reached out would the lone butterfly land on her fingertips? Suddenly, a cluster of lighter orange and darker orange monarchs swooped in and then all flew off.

No matter what happened to her, she was in God's hands. And if she left this earth, she'd be able to fly up to heaven, when the angels came to take her home. A tear trailed down her face, but she didn't wipe it away.

In under an hour, she'd had driven to the hospital, parked, registered, sat in the vacant waiting room and was finally called to the back. What was left of her limited energy threatened to vanish.

Tamara followed the nurse past several empty waiting rooms. "Not many people here at this time of the day, are there?"

"Only you until about an hour from now."

Only Tamara? The niggle of unease in her stomach transfigured into a stampede of buffaloes. *Hope. Have hope.* The gentle voice that whispered to her heart brought a measure of calm.

She followed the young woman into the office and took the seat across from the oncologist's desk. He stood by the window with his back to her. When the door closed behind the nurse, he faced her, arms crossed over his broad, white-coated chest.

"Good morning, Tamara." Dr. Austin smiled but his eyes looked serious. "Thank you for coming in so quickly."

"No problem." Would he try to use his god of Science to persuade her to participate in his study? They'd had some interesting arguments on her other visits. She always felt that she had won. Not that winning had been her goal. Rather, she wished this kind physician would accept God into his heart.

"I have a lot I want to cover with you in a short time." He glanced at his watch. "First, I have some good news for you, and second, I have some favors. I also have some not so good news that is. . ." He closed one eye and frowned. "Well, it's a consequence of your good news. Which do you want to hear first?"

She sighed. "Hit me with the bad news first."

Dr. Austin came from around his desk and pulled a rolling wooden chair close to her—so close that when he sat his knees almost touched hers. He patted the old-fashioned chair. "This came with me from Texas, it was my father's."

"That's nice to have a family memento in your office." She pushed a strand of hair back from her face, suddenly feeling nervous. Maybe Mom's erratic heartbeat problem ran in the family.

"It reminds me of a lot of things, like how change can happen in the blink of an eye." He snapped his fingers to demonstrate.

Tamara cocked her head at him. "You said this bad news is a consequence of good news—how can that be?" Her heartbeat ticked upward in anticipation—or was it dread?

Dr. Austin laced his fingers together and then flexed and released them. "Tamera Jane Worthe of Williamsburg, Virginia, was misdiagnosed as having pancreatitis when in fact she has, or had, advanced pancreatic cancer."

Tamara blinked at him in confusion. This was why she should have had Mom come with her and not have been so bull-headed. It was always good to have a second set of ears at these appointments, in case something important was missed. She'd taken Ruby to one appointment where, afterwards, her friend had only "heard" about a quarter of what her oncologist had rattled off to her. Tamara shook her head. "Okay, wait—my middle name is Joy not Jane and I live in Yorktown, not Williamsburg.

Dr. Austin nodded solemnly. "Yes. But there is indeed a Tamera—with an 'e'—Jane Worthe who lives in Williamsburg, and she had advanced pancreatic cancer as of the testing you both had in May."

They both had been tested for this dread disease? Did that mean what she thought? Suddenly it felt as though all of the wind had been sucked out of her. *Breathe, just breathe.*

He turned and reached for his office phone. He punched a button and held the receiver to his ear. "Maria? Come in as soon as you get a break."

Tamara cringed. Why was Brad's former sister-in-law invited in with them?

He hung up the phone and swiveled to face her again. "That was the bad news. And I do have a favor that involves Maria."

Mind still whirling, Tamara ran her tongue over her lower lip. If this Tamera Worth of Williamsburg was misdiagnosed, then had she been also?

She was too terrified to ask.

"Maria is responsible for your good news, related to the bad news I just delivered. She got in a world of trouble after fussing at you on your intake. Maria has been here in Michigan on a trial basis. I brought her with me from Texas."

"Oh?" At least her tongue could manage that one word as her mind whirled. So possibly, if she understood right, she didn't have cancer and that was why she was not yet jaundiced and doing well. Was she the one he referenced with pancreatitis and had it calmed? Maybe this was her answer to prayer. But what about the other Tamera? And why had Dr. Austin brought Maria with him?

"Maria felt terrible about upsetting you. I told her what you shared with me at your last appointment—that Maria's outburst had helped you find out more about your husband and what had caused his current behavior." He raised his eyebrows.

Tamara nodded. "It explained a lot. But tell me about Maria. How did she come here with you?"

"She was my secretary in Texas for the past twenty plus years. She lost her husband shortly before my wife passed away." He averted his gaze and rubbed his chin. "She asked about a job here. She also needed a clean start. Her kids are grown."

What about his kids? Did he have any? Strange how that thought seemed more important than definitively hearing her good news. She rubbed the side of her head. "You said Maria helped track down my good news?"

"Yes." His light blue eyes pierced the air between them. "Maria felt so badly about what she'd done. She asked me if there was anything that she could do to make it up to you—and to me. And I asked her to track down your original records for me, not those files forwarded from the oncologist's office."

Tamara could hear her own exhalations and inhalations as she waited for him to continue. "Why did you want her to do that?"

"Maria checked, double- triple- and quadruple-checked because I felt something was wrong with the original diagnosis. And she did some searching on her own time." He touched her knee, his fingers warm. "Tamara, I imagine you've figured it out. The good news is that you—Tamara Joy—have pancreatitis. You do not have pancreatic cancer."

Her conclusion confirmed, her vision suddenly blackened, and Tamara reached out to Dr. Austin. She closed her eyes, and he grasped her hand, his warm strong fingers reassuring. His office door squeaked open.

"*Querido Dios!* Oh, Mrs. Worth are you all right?" Maria's frightened voice accompanied the quick click of her heels over the linoleum floor.

Tamara opened her eyes to look into the woman's warm chocolate brown gaze. "Is it true? They messed up my records?"

"*Si.* Yes." Maria fanned herself with a manila folder she clutched in her be-ringed hand. "I have an extra copy of the corrected reports for you."

"Maria called the medical facilities in Virginia and requested that they correct their files and also inform Mrs. Worthe of Williamsburg about the errors."

The poor woman.

"You, dear lady, to have worried all this time and those *stupido* people—" Maria launched into a tirade in Spanish.

Dr. Austin cleared his throat. "We've done our part and now hopefully they have done theirs."

"And this other woman, is it too late for them to help her?" Even though Tamara felt convicted in her decision to not do a Whipple procedure, that didn't mean the other woman shouldn't have had the time and chance to make her own conclusion about her treatment.

Maria and Dr. Austin cast a long glance between one another, faces grim. The doctor released her hands and pushed his chair back and stood. "We're not allowed to comment on other cases, Mrs. Worth. HIPAA regulations."

Maria nodded solemnly, clasping her hands together.

"Right." Tamara forced herself to breathe evenly. She had a treatable illness. This wasn't pleasant but it was way more manageable than pancreatic cancer. *Oh, my dear God. Thank You, Lord God.*

"I do have a favor, Mrs. Worth." Maria stared at her shoes. "I am on probationary period here at the hospital."

"Would you be willing to write a letter supporting Maria and acknowledging the situation that led to the. . .um. . .little issue you two had when you first met?" Dr. Austin rubbed his cheek.

Tamara waved her hand airily, a gesture she'd not used since her diagnosis. Amazing how much lighter she felt with this news. "Of course, I'd be glad to. You tell me what you need."

Maria smiled shyly at her. "When you're over fifty, it's not so easy to get a job, si? And I don't want to go back to Texas."

"I wish I could have gotten Maria a spot as my own office manager here, like she was in Texas. We're still waiting on that."

"I'll pray for you," Tamara promised Maria. And she meant it.

"*Gracias.*" Maria beamed at her. "I've been praying for you, too, and I am so grateful God could use me to answer those prayers—and Dr. Austin, too."

Tamara cast a sideways glance at the tall man, who exuded such a calm competence, and much more.

"Thank you, Maria, for your due diligence on this." The oncologist dipped his chin at his former office manager, now a receptionist at this new hospital. There didn't seem to be anything between the two, other than a high professional regard. No romantic interest anyways. And why was she thinking about such things?

Maria wrung her hands. "I am so sorry for that melt-down I had. I loved my sister so much. She was the world to me. And I'd so looked forward to being a *tia*, an aunt, to those little girls. To one day celebrate their *Quinceanera* with them and that was all lost just like that." She snapped her fingers, just as Dr. Austin had earlier.

"God was in control and only He could allow such things and we can't know why, Maria." Where had those words come from? Tamara fought the urge to cover her mouth.

"Si, si." Maria wiped at her eyes. "I must finally forgive Brad. Thank you for this reminder."

"We're both working on it." Dr. Austin's comment and the intensity of his words surprised her.

What did he mean?

"Si. And I wish you all the best, Mrs. Worth." Maria left the office.

Dr. Austin walked around behind his desk. He opened a desk drawer and dug through it for something. He pulled out a business card.

When the door closed behind Maria, Dr. Austin handed her a yellowed business card. "Here. I want you to look at this."

Tamara accepted the dog-eared card. *Thomas Austin, M.D., High Risk Obstetrics* was printed at the top, with the hospital and address and phone number printed in a faded but once-glossy heavy blue ink. She pointed to his wall, where the Obstetrics certificate hung. She'd thought she'd misread the specialty printed on the document the first time she'd seen it. She reached to hand the card back to him, but he waved his hand at her.

"I kept that business card for a reason. It reminded me that God could be cruel."

She wanted to object but felt a conviction to keep quiet.

He stood and paced. "I trained to be an obstetrician with high-risk infants, thinking I could help our most vulnerable citizens make it into this world with a better start. My father was an obstetrician, and he'd bemoaned how many premature infants he'd lost because of poor or inadequate medical care."

Realization hit her. Was he the doctor for Brad's first wife?

"I wanted to please my father—and God." He gave her an almost accusatory look. "And I trained hard to gain my credentials. My wife worked with Maria at the hospital—they were good friends. I took on her sister's case when the young woman became pregnant with twins."

Oh my gosh. "You knew my husband's first wife?" And knew Brad too.

"Yes. They were so young. And no offense meant—but I've never seen a guy so besotted with his wife. He worked three jobs to pay for medical expenses and to get ready for twins. I warned him he was overdoing it."

Tamara swallowed hard. Brad had told her that his mother and father had cautioned him repeatedly that he wasn't to get involved with anyone seriously until he could support them. Until he'd completed his master's degree. "His parents didn't even know he was married. But I don't know if they would have helped him even if they had known then about the pregnancy."

"I don't think so. Bradley was judged to have been too physically exhausted on the day he drove through the red light and a semi ran into them. His wife was DOA, and we couldn't save the twin girls—they were too early." He exhaled a long slow breath. "They were on their way to an appointment with me that day." His voice cracked and he faced the window again.

Tamara blinked back tears and Dr. Austin wiped at his eyes.

"Maria blamed Bradley, and I blamed myself and God." He sniffed. "I left Obstetrics shortly thereafter and made science my god. But now, I sense I'm coming full circle. You say Bradley has been running from the past. I have too—to the extent that I switched specializations and made saving cancer patients my goal. I no longer wanted to please my father, nor did I care what this awful God did. Then you came here, and you've upended everything. I've never had a patient be so in-my-face about their faith and with your decision to not let science cure you. Tamara, you've sent me on another journey that I never planned to make—a spiritual journey."

"I. . .I'm glad." Maybe if nothing else came out of this whole ordeal, maybe this man's soul being saved was worth it all. She blinked back tears of conviction as her spirit agreed.

Dr. Austin stared at her for a long time, his lips compressed. He inhaled deeply and then exhaled. "Tamara, I think you understand that you are no longer my patient, right?"

She blinked. "I guess since I don't have cancer. . ."

"Right, I'm referring you to a colleague for follow-up for the pancreatitis." He continued to gaze at her in a most disconcerting manner.

"Oh, um, thanks." She brushed back her hair.

"I like to eat out a fair bit."

Her heartbeat did a little hiccup thing. "Oh? You should come over to Mackinaw City, we have so many wonderful places to eat there. Remember the bakery I told you about? It's right down the street from where I live." Gracious, she was babbling now.

"I will definitely have to come and check that out soon." The slow-spreading smile on his face was not that of a medical provider. In fact, she'd not been the recipient of such an admiring smile and gaze since she could remember. "I won't be your doctor anymore, but I hope maybe one day we can be friends."

Friends? Her entire mind was in a swirl. She didn't have cancer. She'd have to do so many things, make so many decisions. But she had a new friend. A very handsome and caring one, too.

"I'd love that."

Chapter Twenty-Five

Dawn
Mackinaw City

Looking out the front window, Dawn exhaled a long sigh. A red Cadillac convertible, top down, pulled into the space in front of the cottage that was reserved for Tammy. The tourists really should realize they weren't supposed to park in front of residences. Cici barked like a maniac. She ran in circles and then leapt in the air.

A slim blond woman with a bright butterfly-emblazoned scarf tied around her upswept hair, waved her long-fingernailed hands toward a handsome middle-aged man who was hefting a huge bag from the back seat. Dawn went outside onto the porch.

"Mrs. Charbonneau! Why Sugah, me and Bill are gonna spoil you and Tam-baby rotten—you just wait and see!" Although she sounded like Tammy's friend, Zara, Dawn hadn't seen her in many years. The Southern Belle had certainly morphed into a fashionable diva.

With quick but mincing steps in her shiny peacock-blue high heels, Zara reached Dawn on the porch and gave her an air kiss on each cheek. "Why Sugah, you look even younger than at the wedding. What are you doing to keep yourself up so good? I need to *know*," she emphasized and drew out the last word as though it was the secret to world peace.

Before Dawn could respond, Zara cupped her hand around her mouth. "I've really got to wee, can you point me to the little girls' room?"

Dawn waved down the hall.

"Thanks," the drawl was laced with genuine gratitude as Tammy's friend scurried off.

The dark-haired man with a huge open bag bulging with wrapped boxes, approached the porch. "I'm Dr. Bill Bryant, ma'am. Zara's fiancé."

"Nice to meet you."

"You, too."

"Where are you two staying?" The words popped out of Dawn's mouth before she could help herself. Her cheeks heated at her faux pas.

Thankfully the good doctor didn't take any offense. "We're at the Beach Castle here in Mackinaw City tonight and then tomorrow on to Hudson's Retreat on the island and back here to Mackinaw City. Zara had me book an extra suite on the island for your family to come over and stay with us."

"That is so thoughtful."

"Do you think Tamara will be up to it?" The concern in his voice seemed more than simply bedside manner. He seemed like a genuinely nice guy.

Like Jim.

Where on earth was her husband? He should have been here hours ago. "Please come in and let me put the tea on. I'm going to call my husband, too, while I'm thinking of it."

Tammy's car pulled in behind the convertible, distracting Dawn from her task. Zara emerged from inside and ran past Dawn and her fiancé, squealing all the way.

"Releasing her inner teenaged girl, I believe." The doctor's droll tone made Dawn laugh.

The two of them followed Zara to the street.

"Ohmygoodnessgraciousmeohmy!" Zara's words all flowed into one as she neared Tammy's car. "I had to get up here as fast as I could when I heard you were dying."

Dawn was sure her jaw had dropped and bounced off the concrete walkway. What a way to greet poor Tammy. Dawn was about to call out, 'There's always hope,' but Zara launched herself into Tammy's arms.

"I'm not dying," Tammy squeaked as her friend squeezed her.

Dawn froze. Was that what Tammy meant in her mysterious call earlier? She'd said she had good news that she wanted to share in person and was hurrying home from Petoskey.

"Of course, you're not dyin', of course not, darlin'!" Zara released her bear hug and squeezed Tammy's shoulders. "You're gonna beat this thing. Isn't she, Bill?"

Bill nodded.

"We're sure not gonna let a little old thing like pancreatic cancer get you down Tam-bo."

Tamara stared at her friend. "I don't—"

"Don't you worry about anything. Bill and I are gonna take you off to Switzerland for a special treatment. He knows a bunch of folks there who are getting' all kinds of good results. Aren't they Bill?"

Bill nodded.

Dawn put her foot down. "Tammy, what did your doctor say?"

Zara waved away Mom's comment. "We don't care what they've said, do we Bill?"

Once again, her companion nodded.

"We're gonna make sure you beat this thing with the best treatment possible."

Tamara

Tamara gave her mother a wink and a thumbs up. Sooner or later, her dear friend would run out of steam, and she could answer Mom's question.

"I cannot believe that someone as good, as kind, as sweet as you could possibly have that horrible illness." Zara waved her long red fingernails in the air. "It's not gonna get you. Not on my watch."

Tamara clutched her hands together, hoping this was her chance to share her good news. Someone tapped three toots on their car horn, and she spied her father pulling in behind her car. They were sure to get fussed at by the next-door neighbor for taking their spots, but Tamara didn't care. Her beloved father had finally arrived.

"Oh, Jim!" Mom ran across the lawn to Dad's white van. Hard Rock jumped up and down on the passenger's seat, barking. "I'm so glad you're here!"

Dad got out but left his pet in the van.

"I've missed my other half so very much. I thought I would burst." He swooped Mom into his arms right there in the street. Those two had some kind of love. Would Tamara ever have that for herself?

She remained on the sidewalk, allowing her parents a private moment as they hugged and kissed.

When they paused, Tamara called out, "Mom and Dad, I do *not* have cancer after all. There was a mix-up."

Dad quickstepped toward her and hugged her so tightly that her breath left her. "Oh, Tam, that's the best news ever." He pulled away and then kissed her cheek.

"What a relief! Thank God!" Mom came back around and pulled Tamara into her arms. "We're so glad you're going to be all right, honey."

Tamara couldn't stop her tears. What a blessing to get to spend more time on earth with her family.

"I'm glad to be here with my girls." Dad returned to the van, opened the door, and lifted out Hard Rock, who looked like a tiny bundle of fur.

Heels clicking on the sidewalk announced Zara's approach. She joined them and they all circled in a group hug. "I am so happy I could be here for this!"

When they broke free again, Zara leaned back and made a quick sour face. "Sugah, ya should have told me you were ok."

Tamara exchanged a quick glance with her mother.

Mom shook her head. "And take a chance that you might put all those gifts back in your Cadillac? Fat chance."

Tamara good-naturedly elbowed her mother. "I just now found out, Zara."

Dad and Mom wrapped arms around each other again and kissed like a couple of teenagers. "I missed you," they said simultaneously.

Tamara turned away and laughed. She gave her friend another quick hug. "When did you get here?"

"Bill and I just arrived a few minutes ago. It's so exciting to be here to get the good news from you in person."

"I gotta tell you my head is swimming." All those decisions when she had only months to live…now everything was different. New. Reborn.

"Come on and meet my Bill, he's just the best thing ever." Zara linked her arm through Tamara's and pulled her toward a handsome dark-haired man with warm dark eyes.

As they reached him, Tamara extended her hand. "I'm so glad to finally meet you in person, Bill."

Zara released her and instead of shaking hands, Bill pulled her into a quick hug. "We're so glad to make it and happier yet to hear you'll be okay." He released her, compassion in his face.

"You're definitely a keeper, Dr. Bryant."

"Just call me Bill."

Cici barked in the doorway. Dad set Hard Rock down and released him. The little imp ran to the door and barked at his little buddy.

Zara laughed. "She's sayin' come on in everybody and open all these presents before I do it for ya."

"Yeah, I bet Cici is taunting Hard Rock that she'll tear into the paper first before he ever gets a chance." Mom raised her eyebrows. "They are like two little demons together, I swear."

"Well, they might be, Sugah, but they are way too cute."

They made their way inside where both sweetened and unsweetened iced tea was passed around for the Southerners and Northerners. Everyone found a seat in the spacious living room, the sun streaming through the open blinds.

"All right, this is for your little girl puppy-dog. She's the sweetest thing evah!" Zara passed a lumpy wrapped gift to Mom, and she handed it to Dad.

He unwrapped the item—a small monkey that squeaked when he pressed its middle. Cici sprang from his lap. The dog grabbed the toy and jumped down, narrowly missed the bag of gifts. Hard Rock chased after her.

Zara quickly grabbed the tote's handle. "I think she likes it," she drawled out the word *likes* and winked as she reached for another gift. "I thought you had two pups." She tossed another lumpy package to Dad. He caught it in one hand.

"Better open it quickly, Mr. Charbonneau," Bill pointed to the two dogs, chasing one another, "before we have War of the Pups here in your living room."

Dad ripped off the multi-colored paper and revealed a blue ox with a ring by its belly. He squeaked it. Hard Rock's ears perked. "Come here, boy." In a flash, the dog ran across the rug and leapt onto Dad's lap.

Zara clapped her hands together. "Now they'll both be happy."

"Amen to that," Mom agreed.

Bill passed a gift to Zara. She clutched it to her bosom. "This one's for you, Tam-baby. Not that I think you'll really use it, but when I saw this on our trip to Jamaica I knew I had to get it for you."

Her friend handed her the gift. The Caribbean wrapping paper featured coconuts, palm trees, and a beach. Tamara unwrapped the rectangular item and stared at the human figure made of wood and straw.

Zara leaned in. "That's Brad-boy, honey! It's a voodoo doll." She made a scary noise and waved her hands in the air dramatically.

Mom guffawed.

Her friend waggled her eyebrows. "I know you won't really use it, but doesn't it make you feel good to know you could?"

"If you wanted. . ." Bill said. "Although I'm not sure a voodoo doll is the best way to deal with a cheating husband."

Dad reached for the doll. "I'll give it a try."

Tamara shook her head. She'd dispose of the item later. "I don't know about that." She forced a laugh. She'd focus on praying for Brad and Gina instead, even as difficult a task as that seemed.

Bill nodded. "I'm with you, Tamara." Tamara was enjoying her friend's new fiancé. Hopefully this fifth husband would stick. Each successive husband had been wealthier than the previous one, and older. The latest had only lived a year before succumbing to heart failure. At least she'd finally found someone near their age.

"Aw, spoilsports!" Zara shrugged but offered one of her dazzling smiles.

The front door clattered. "Who's here?" Jaycie rushed in and spied Zara, who rose to pull her in for a quick hug. Jaycie looked over Zara's shoulder to Tamara, her eyes questioning.

"This is Bill." Zara gestured to her fiancé, who extended his hand to Jaycie.

"Good to meet you." Then Jaycie ran to Tamara and threw her arms around her. "I got your text on my way over. I'm so glad you're all right. Well, except for that thing you have that you need treated."

"Pancreatitis, but I'll be ok." Tammy inhaled her daughter's vanilla-scented cologne, such a comforting scent. She had her the rest of her life ahead of her, a longer life now, than she'd planned. But what would that be like?

Jaycie

Jaycie had run all the way from the ferry to the cottage, heart hammering. *Best day ever.* Mom had texted her good news. Grandpa had arrived. Now Mom's fun friend, Auntie Zara, was there.

And Parker loved her.

"Grandpa!" Jaycie left her mom and hugged him. Hard Rock tried to get in between them, but Grandpa held him tightly on his lap.

She made her rounds of hugging Gran and Auntie Zara and then shook hands with Bill, whom she'd not yet met.

"Me and Bill are gonna play Santa now." Zara and Bill began distributing the mass of gifts around the room, pulling wrapped items out of a huge bag.

Jaycie faced her grandfather. "How's your knee?"

"Good as gold." Grandpa Jim patted his knee in emphasis. Hard Rock jumped down.

"Speakin' of gold. . ." Auntie Zara paused from handing Gran a big bundle and minced over to her in her high heeled sandals. "I'd bought you something, Jaycie, to distract you from your Mama's terrible news, but I guess we'll change it to a celebration gift. Right, Bill?"

Bill reached into his pocket and pulled out a jeweler's box. He handed it to Zara.

"Sugah, I saw this in Venice when we got the bad news."

"Venice? I thought you were in Jamaica." Gran took a sip of her tea.

Auntie Zara waved her hand. "Honey, we've been to Jamaica, Venice, Amsterdam, and soon we're doin' a safari."

"Zara doesn't let me sit still." Auntie's fiancé blushed. "Not that I want to with such a beauty by my side."

The two bent in and kissed each other.

"You two are so cute," Mom proclaimed.

"Of course we are, Sugah." Auntie Zara winked at Jaycie. "But anyway, back to this gift for Jaycie. I knew you'd need something to remember your sweet Mama by." She shot an apologetic look at Mom. "Not that I was thinkin' you'd really die, Tam-baby. But I thought this would be perfect on a nice gold chain."

Bill pulled another jeweler's case from another pocket.

Zara handed them to Jaycie. "Open 'em, Sugah."

Jaycie opened the first one. A heavy gold charm of a large heart covered with a cup filled with pencils was engraved with *Cuore dell'insegnante*. Jaycie tried to pronounce the word.

Bill said, "Cuore dell'insegnante, it means—"

"A teacher's heart." Zara waved toward Mom. "I figgered you're really your Mama's heart, and she won that award this year but mercy-me-oh-my, she should have won an award for raising such a fine daughter."

Tears pricked Jaycie's eyes. "Thank you, Auntie Zara."

"You're welcome." Zara kissed her and then pointed to the other box.

Jaycie opened it, a thick gold rope necklace with a substantial heart and arrow clasp. "It's beautiful."

"Let's put them together, and you put them on."

Mom was grinning so wide, she seemed to be enjoying this celebration more than anyone—which was as it should be. Mom had so much to be happy for, as did they all.

Zara took the charm and slid it onto the necklace chain. She wrapped it around Jaycie's neck, and under her ponytail, before closing the clasp. Jaycie patted the necklace, which hung heavy against her heart.

"Snack time break in the back yard," Gran announced. "We've got a watermelon just begging to be cut."

They all began to stand.

"Go look at it on you, in the mirror." Auntie Zara motioned toward the heavy oak mirror that hung over the couch.

As the others made their way to the back door, Jaycie looked into the mirror. Her cheeks were flushed, her hair a mess, and she needed a shower, but that gorgeous necklace hanging against her UVA navy t-shirt glimmered with promise.

Bill leaned toward her as he headed to follow the queue. "It actually says Teacher's Heart, not *A* Teacher's Heart. Not sure it makes a difference, but technically that's the Italian translation."

Unbidden tears confirmed the soul-message she now received. Although meant to remind her of her teacher mom, God had more plans for Mom, and for Jaycie, too. Teacher's Heart. Not one in her family.

Two.

Chapter Twenty-Six

Tamara
Mackinaw City

The three days visiting with Zara and Bill had been fantastic but now Tamara's energy reserves were spent. She joined Mom and Dad, where they were enjoying a cup of tea on the porch.

"Good morning, Sleepyhead. I would rise to greet you like a gentleman, but this new knee needs to settle down a little more." Would that she could find a man like that who really treasured her like Dad did Mom. He'd always shown her a multitude of little courtesies over the years.

She raised a hand. "That's sweet, Dad, but not necessary to stand for me." She kissed his cheek. "I'm so very glad you're here."

"I'm relieved that you're going to be okay." He took her hand and kissed it. "You're my sweet girl. Never forget that Mom and I love you."

She circled the table and kissed her mother, too.

"That's right." Mom grinned at her. "Who would get us old folks some goodies from the bakery if you weren't here?"

Taken aback, Tamara stood there a moment before finally bursting into laughter. "Well, now I know your priorities, Mom. I guess I know where I am about to go."

"That bakery has been calling our names." Mom shook her head, and Tamara rolled her eyes at her.

Dad glanced between the two of them and chuckled. "Two peanut butter Long Johns for me, Sunshine. I'll be walking more and maybe even biking around the island. I did six miles on the stationary bike. My therapist said that's harder than regular biking."

"I agree. I did six or seven miles on the exercise bike before the other summers when we were coming to Butterfly Cottage."

"I wish you'd been able to come every summer." Mom sipped her tea.

Her father scowled. "That crumb-bum, Brad, never deserved you."

Anger shot through her at all the summers she'd stayed in Virginia because Brad had protested her and Jaycie going—usually with the excuse that it caused an extra expense. But knowing what had caused his fixation with money, and the way that had likely resulted in his first wife and twins' deaths, lessened her irritation. "Well, I'm here now and ready to take Mom's order, too." She forced a smile.

"Bear claw. I'm gonna heat it and spread butter all over the top. Yum." Mom patted her slim middle. "Then it will be a tuna salad for lunch and skinless chicken and veggies for dinner to offset all that deliciousness."

"All right then, I'm off." Tamara went back inside and grabbed her purse.

"Tell my friend Laurinda that Jim got here, sweetie."

"Sure, Mom."

Tamara had a spring in her step that hadn't been there in months. It made her smile. Still, with Zara gone, she was left to face her future. A divorce to deal with. The return of her emptied retirement account funds if the company would allow it without penalty. Returning to Virginia to tie up loose ends. Making a decision about asking her boss for a contract. But where would she live?

Tamara paused at the corner and pressed her eyes closed. *God help me now.*

At the sound of car doors closing nearby, she opened her eyes as a tall blond man exited a luxury sedan and then went around to assist his passenger out. *Dr. Austin and Maria.* Were those two on a date? Why did jealousy streak through her like a Mackinac firework over the Straits? Tamara sucked in a breath. She should turn around and go back to the cottage. The two looked in her direction. *Too late.*

A broad smile lit the handsome oncologist's face. Maria waved at her and then motioned Tamara forward. Exhaling loudly, she jogged across the street and joined the duo.

Maria pulled Tamara into a quick embrace, "*Bella dama*, beautiful lady you have blessed me with the letter you wrote to the hospital on my behalf. Dr. Austin and I are celebrating."

She looked at Dr. Austin. Twin spots of red shone beneath his Ray-Ban aviator sunglasses. Was that sunburn or was he actually blushing?

"Tamara, that is Mrs. Worth, it's so good to see you." His voice sounded stilted, more like a teenage boy than the confident doctor he was in his office.

"Dr. Austin told me that you raved about this place and told him to check it out if he ever got over here. So, I made sure he did. We both finally got the same day off."

She wasn't getting any romance vibes between the two. Still. And why was that her business anyway? *Because you're attracted to him.* That little voice nudged her. *Okay, let's be honest, he's a good-looking man.* He was kind, intelligent, and his persistence had started the process to reveal that she didn't have pancreatic cancer after all. He and Maria had given her back her life.

He waved toward the bakery's side door. "Shall we go in, ladies?"

Tamara grinned. "You're not going to get in that way, that's for kitchen staff."

"Oh." That was a blush, not sunburn, because his cheeks flamed redder. "Sorry."

"Follow me." Tamara led them to the regular entrance.

Dr. Austin opened the heavy oak door for them. Maria and Tamara entered to the heavenly scents of coffee and sweet baked goods.

This could be awkward. Especially if the two were, in fact, on a date. But at least the line was short, with only three customers in front of them. "I'm just here to pick up some things for my parents."

"Your father has arrived?" Tom Austin's gaze was warm.

How thoughtful of him to remember. "Yes, he got in a few days ago, along with my best friend and her fiancé. We've been in a whirlwind since."

Maria elbowed him. "Maybe it's best we didn't come over before now, then, huh my *amigo*?"

If possible, Tom's face reddened further. He didn't reply to Maria's question but stared fixedly at Tamara, in a way that made her heart rate accelerate.

"Well, yes, then I'd have missed you." Tamara hoped her bright tone didn't betray her confusion.

"We wouldn't want that." Maria grinned and again glanced between Tom and her.

The trio ahead of them paid for their purchases and carried them off.

Laurinda beamed at her. "The usual for you, Tam?"

"Nope, Dad got here finally, so we need two extra Long Johns."

"Hooray, Jim is finally here." She started filling the order. "How's his knee?"

"He says it's doing great."

"I'm so glad. When you get older, it seems like these things take longer to heal." Laurinda hesitated over a cinnamon roll, Dad's second favorite treat. "I'm gonna throw in an extra goody for him, no charge."

"Thanks, he'll appreciate it."

Adjacent to her, a pretty blonde girl took Tom and Maria's order. "For here or to go?"

"For here." Tom's voice sounded a little terse.

"We heard about your lovely bakery from Mrs. Worth." Maria waved her hand toward Tamara, her gold charm bracelet tinkling.

"She's our favorite customer," the young woman told them.

Laurinda winked. "All of our customers are our favorites, so it's true."

"What will you have?" Summerlee pointed to the case.

"If I don't have one of those Long Johns that Mrs. Worth recommended, I might as well go on home." Tom's dry tone and serious expression belied the silliness in his words.

Tamara laughed and Maria rolled her eyes.

Laurinda nodded. "They are a favorite around here."

"Same for me." Maria pointed at the coffee board. "Oh, and I want that Michigan cherry coffee. It sounds *muy bueno.*"

"Straight joe for me." Tom accepted the tray that Summerlee handed him.

Summerlee went to the coffee maker.

"Once you get your coffees, there's sugar and creamer right over there and napkins." Tamara gestured toward the wooden cabinet.

Tom leaned toward her. "Do you really have to go?"

The plea in his blue eyes seemed more than for simple company. He already had that with Maria.

"I could drop these off with my folks and return." The offer flew from her mouth before she could stop it. Heat singed her cheeks.

His shoulders relaxed and he grinned. "I'd be mighty happy about that. Why don't you leave your own treat with me?"

"Good idea." Then she wouldn't have to carry it back. She placed it on his tray.

"Can I order you a coffee, too?"

Tammy called to Summerlee, "Can you add another Michigan cherry coffee to that order?"

"Sure thing." She popped the white tops on the first two coffees that she poured.

"I'm going to come back and sit with. . . my friends."

Tom winked at her. "Since I'm not your doctor anymore, I'm happy to be your good friend."

And more? She might need to fan herself. She was a married woman still. Her mind in a whirl, she shook her head while at the same time saying, "We could be good friends."

He laughed. "Then why are you shaking your head, Mrs. Worth?"

"Call me Tamara." She was Tammy to Mom and Tam to her old friends but that didn't seem right with this man. She was new again after this ordeal. And she'd always loved her given name.

He placed two fingers at his brow as if tipping his hat. "Yes, ma'am, Miss Tamara."

Miss Tamara. She would be single again once she gave Brad his freedom. Goodness knew her husband had kicked her emotionally to the curb years earlier. He probably thought starting over with Gina would give him back the life he'd lost with his first wife. "I'll be back in a few minutes."

Maria accepted the coffee from Summerlee and placed it on the tray that Tom held. She grinned. "Don't we have a handsome waiter, Tamara?"

"We do. I'll hurry back."

The sound of gulls accompanied her. This felt strangely like a date. An almost date. What Maria said made it sound like the two of them had deliberately hoped to run into her at the bakery. Was she really about to become a *good friend* with this handsome widower? What was she thinking? Her life, this life that wasn't heading toward a quick death, was a mess.

She had to stop her negative self-talk.

A ferry horn blasted, the sound meant as both an alert and a welcome. She smiled. Warmth bloomed within her in the recognition that she'd finally found her place again, the sounds of ferries, seagulls, and tourists' laughter the soundtrack for her new life. And here she could settle in and begin anew. She'd pay attention in this fledgling relationship but also accept Dr. Austin's companionship. And who knew, she might become friends with Maria, too.

She walked the sidewalk to her home. Her new home. And she knew she could not go back to her house in Virginia. It was no longer her home even if Brad moved out, which he wouldn't.

"Tam, hey, I just got here." Hamp called to her from the front porch.

"Oh." Although surprised, Tamara didn't want to appear rude by limiting their chatter. But she did want to return to the Bakery as soon as possible.

"Yeah, look what the cat drug in." Dad laughed and pointed at Hamp, who was attired in casual athletic wear.

"Hey, I'm going for a jog over here, later—around Fort Michilimackinac."

Mom took a sip of her tea. "You look handsome no matter what you're wearing, Hamp."

"Thanks Mrs. Charbonneau."

Tamara exhaled a quick breath. How to phrase this? "Hey, I ran into my oncologist—"

"Your former oncologist," Hamp corrected. "You don't have cancer, my friend."

"Yes, Dr. Austin and Maria, the ones who helped track down my correct records, are both at the bakery right now."

"I want to shake their hands." Hamp ambled down the stairs, grabbed her bakery bag, and brought it to her parents. "I'm going back over there with you. Heck I might even hug them."

"I'm drooling." Dad pulled out one of the Long Johns and bit off a quarter of it.

"Jimbo, you're gonna choke. Slow down." Mom pulled her Bear Claw out and took a ladylike bite from one corner.

Hamp took Tamara's elbow and swiveled her toward the street. "Come on, they're enjoying their breakfast. Let's go."

Tamara forced a smile as they stepped onto the sidewalk that paralleled Huron Street. "I promised them I'd come back and sit with them."

"Oh?" He quirked one eyebrow at her.

"Yes," she bit her lower lip and released it. "I'm the one who suggested they come to the Bakery."

"A bit of a drive from Petoskey."

"Not that far."

He made a face and laughed. "I'm pretty sure they've got their own bakeries over there, Tam."

"But this one is the best."

Hamp nodded. "True." A truck pulling a huge motorboat drove by. "Wonder where they are gonna park that big thing?" Hamp whistled. "It's a beautiful boat, though."

"Big enough for one of the inland lakes but I wonder if it could handle the Great Lakes?"

"Maybe. If it's pretty calm out there, which it isn't today. I doubt they're taking it to the marina, but maybe."

Out on Lake Huron, whitecaps churned the water, much like her insides were doing.

In a few minutes they entered the bakery. Dr. Austin waved at her and rose. Was that a scowl forming on his brow? If it was, it had vanished almost as quickly as it had formed. And what a gentleman to rise for her. Brad had never done that. In fact, he'd rarely pulled her chair out at dinner unless she'd shamed him into it. He claimed that women were independent these days and shouldn't expect such old-fashioned niceties. She had to be perfectly honest with herself, one of the things that had appealed to her about Brad was how he'd always encouraged her to pursue her own interests. She'd thought he was supportive of her career because he loved her and knew she loved teaching. Now she wasn't so sure of his true motives.

When they reached the table, where Maria's back was toward them, Tamara smiled at Tom. There was definite tension in his face. She brought Hamp around to introduce him to Maria, so that he was facing her. When Maria looked up from sipping her coffee, she stared at Hamp. Tamara turned toward her old friend, who was also gazing at Maria like a besotted fool. She'd seen that look on his face before—when he'd met his wife.

"Um, Maria, this is my friend, Hamp Parker. We've known each other since we were kids."

Hamp bent and took Maria's hand in his and drew it to his lips. Maria pressed her free hand to her ample bosom. He stared at the Latino woman as if only she and he were in the room. "I wanted to meet the woman who helped save my old friend."

"*Encantado de conocerte.*"

"Delighted to meet you, too." Hamp launched into a string of Spanish. Maria grinned and pointed to the chair beside her, rapidly responding in Spanish to whatever he was saying.

Tom leaned in. "Apparently we're both not here anymore." He chuckled softly. His warm breath on her cheek sent shivers through her.

"My old pal did want to meet you, too, but um…I think he's been distracted." She watched in fascination as Hamp took Maria's hand again and was rattling off something to her.

Maria's cheeks bloomed pink, accentuating what a pretty woman she was. With that red silk blouse and the black and white scarf at her neck, she was truly stunning. And her smile. No wonder Hamp was enthralled. She wore about as much gold on her person as Hamp's wife used to wear.

"Do you think we should sit at another table?"

Tamara laughed. "I don't think so, I don't think they'll pay much attention to us even if we danced on the tabletop."

"Probably not." Tom glanced toward the two. "He's got a ring on, Tamara."

Both Maria and Hamp were twisting the rings on their left fingers.

"His wife died about a year ago."

"Maria's husband, too."

A family entered though the dining room entrance and passed by them. The young mother clutched a baby to her chest while the father carried a toddler with his index finger in his mouth. The older pair behind them resembled the mother. Probably her parents. What would it be like to be a grandmother?

Tom's gaze followed the family. "I sure miss my little granddaughter. They're coming in a few weeks."

He didn't look old enough to have grandchildren, but then again, many of her close friends did. "How many children do you have?"

"Two daughters. One grandchild so far. My youngest daughter just graduated college."

"My daughter did, too. Archeology."

He raised his brows. "That's an interesting area of study. What does she want to do with it?"

Tamara stretched her shoulders. "You know, I'm not sure. We've been spending an awful lot of time lately talking about what it's like to be a teacher. I've been praying God's will if she chooses to walk away from her doctoral program."

"Accepted to a doctoral program in archeology—she must have done well at college."

"She did. How about your daughter? What did she major in?"

His closed his eyes for a moment. "Would you believe me if I told you she seemed intent on pursuing her M-R-S degree?"

"Wow, really?"

"Yes."

"No, I can't say I'd believe it." That was a lot of money to spend on an education that would never be used. But she bit her tongue.

"I think that losing her mother has made her want to emulate her."

"Your wife was a homemaker?" No shame in that.

"Yes, we'd both agreed that once we had kids Sandra would stay home with them."

When, at twenty-seven, Tamara had given birth to Jaycie, her husband had informed her that her taking an extended leave of absence was not possible. They could have afforded it, had their finances been combined. But Brad had insisted, from the beginning of their marriage, that they would keep their income separated. Tears pricked her eyes at the memory of his question, *How would you pay for things, Tam, if you don't have teacher income?* He had been dead serious. Brad had no intention of ever supporting her and Jaycie. She wiped away an errant tear.

"Are you okay?" Tom covered her hand with his warm broad one. A frisson of electricity moved through her.

If she was right, there was a whole megawatt of electricity sparking from Hamp and Maria, too. She recalled her recent wish that Hamp would find love again. Was this God's answer?

"I'm okay, I was just remembering something really hurtful that my husband said."

"The way you've described him, it's hard to believe Bradley has changed much. He was a tender-hearted young man, crushed when his wife and twins died." Tom swallowed a sip of coffee. "He was devoted to his young wife."

Tamara took a sip of the fragrant coffee. "From all I got out of his mother, he was never the same after the accident, but I never knew that old Brad." Maybe that young man had returned now, for Gina and her twins.

"I know this really isn't the place, but would you like to get together sometime? I'm a pretty good listener." Tom took a bite of his Long John.

She nibbled a small bite of hers, not wanting the delicious peanut butter cream to get all over her mouth. Tom, however, had no compunction. She laughed.

"What?"

She pointed to his cheek. "You have some right there."

When he tried and failed, comically to get it with his tongue, she wiped it for him, with her finger. The warmth of his face under her hand sent a shiver through her. What would it be like to kiss those full lips of his? She stared at his mouth for a moment, considering.

"Will you go out with me?"

She blinked. "What? I thought. . ."

His cheeks reddened. "Yeah, I asked about helping you, but can it be dinner, too?"

"I would love that." Part of her wanted to give him a quick kiss to seal the deal. But it was too soon for that. Way too soon.

But hadn't this whole episode in her life taught her that things could change in a heartbeat?

Chapter Twenty-Seven

Jaycie
Mackinac Island

"Jaycie? May I have a word with you?" Mr. Jeffries asked.

Had someone seen her kissing Parker and reported it back to him? Heat washed over her. She pushed aside her report that she'd proofed on a hard copy and rose.

"Come on back to my office." He led the way.

His voice had been friendly, upbeat in fact, so she forced her fears away.

"Close the door." Now that command took her aback.

"Yes, sir." She did so as he took his seat behind his desk.

"Sit down." He pointed to the chair across from him.

She sat on the edge of the hard wood seat and waited as he searched through some sheets on his desktop. He pulled out one, scanned it, and then set it atop the pile. He pressed his hands together, his fingertips steepled. "It's come to my attention that neither you nor Parker plan to begin your advanced studies."

She compressed her lips. Although she'd not yet been accepted for her education classes to teach in Michigan, she'd declined the Archeology Department's offer of admission as a new doctoral candidate. She'd also turned down the doctoral fellowship which would have paid for her training. But Parker hadn't said anything to her about definitely not going on to graduate school.

"...so, I thought this might be a perfect opportunity for you."

She'd missed the beginning of his sentence. "Could you tell me more?"

"Oh, of course. The educator spot, like we've discussed previously, runs about six months of the year. You'd have your position here for five months and a month off for vacation times."

It sounded like he was offering her a spot. "What do I have to do to be considered?"

He cocked his head to one side. "I'm sorry, I must not have been clear. We are offering you one of the positions."

She grappled to understand.

"If you're worrying about salary, it's comparable to a first-year teacher." He named the pay.

She swallowed hard. If she stayed in her grandmother's cottage, she'd have no rent. She could save that money to fund her Master's in Education. And she could take online classes to help her get a teacher's certificate, if the applications she'd put in weren't too late.

"There are also benefits." He detailed the position's benefits, which of course she hadn't received as an intern.

"I don't know what to say."

He raised a hand. "Think about it. Don't say no, like Parker did to my offer of his being our full-time office manager."

Parker hadn't mentioned that to her, either. He'd had plenty of opportunities to do so both here at the office and on-site. Not to mention the night they'd rode their bikes around the island together after work. No, instead he'd asked her a million questions like he used to do at school. Only now she hadn't ignored him. No, she'd spilled her guts while he kept his personal business close, silent. Back to the Parker of college years. Was that because of his recovery program? He used that as an excuse for some things he didn't care to talk about.

It hurt that after she'd opened her heart to him again, he was closing her off.

Mr. Jeffries had said something else that she'd missed. "And you're free to go back to work now." He gave her a strange look, as if he knew she'd missed what he'd said.

She ran her tongue over her lower lip. "I'm sorry, I didn't hear the first part of what you said. I was thinking about. . .this great opportunity."

He dipped his chin. "Yes, this is a big change for you, but I think it's a great fit."

"Yes."

"What I'd said was that Parker wouldn't be in for a few days until he gets back from Switzerland. But you probably already knew that."

Switzerland? No, she didn't, but she wouldn't say so. Pain pricked her chest. Parker was back to keeping his secrets close to his vest. "I'll do my best in his absence, sir."

"I know I can count on you, Jaycie." He smiled then tapped his pile of paperwork. "You can let yourself out."

"Yes, sir." Mr. Jeffries could count on her.

But she sure wasn't going to count on Parker anymore.

Chapter Twenty-Eight

Tamara
Yorktown, Virginia

The week planning this trip to Virginia had flown by as had the three flights today. *Why—oh, why—did I come back to Virginia by myself?* Tamara loaded her small rolling carryon luggage, all she'd brought for the two-day trip, into the back of the rental car and got inside. She could have brought Dad, Mom, or even Jaycie. But no, she'd decided to make this trip herself on a full head of angry steam. She'd gotten almost as hot as Virginia's humid one-hundred-degrees when Brad had posted pictures on Facebook of house renovations he and Gina had completed.

Tamara had only been gone two months and they'd already had contractors in destroying what she'd saved for, over a decade, to accomplish in what had been her kitchen. At least it looked that way online. How were they going to manage a quick divorce, one possible if uncontested in Virginia, if he and Gina were already doing this stuff?

What a weird thing to go from believing Brad would be widowed and could be remarried, to her realizing she would need to give him a divorce—since she wasn't going to die. Since he'd never known about the pancreatic cancer misdiagnosis that had been a confusing conversation with him, one which Mom had finally stepped in on to explain to him. Basically, Mom ended up asking for the divorce. She shook her head at the remembrance.

She started the car and put the air-conditioning onto Max. At least it had been garaged, or it would be hot enough to bake her alive in there until it cooled down. "I sure didn't miss this heat."

A woman walking by gave her a strange look. *Sure, like you don't talk to yourself sometimes.*

Tamara mentally went through her checklist of tasks for the day. Attorney was first thing. Meet with Susan for lunch. Go by the house while Brad and Gina were at work and retrieve some of Jaycie's belongings and some of her own special items. Check on a storage unit and hope that Brad would allow Susan's husband to transport her stuff there until Tamara could retrieve it later in the fall. She wasn't coming back to live in Virginia. Not now that she'd lined up not one but two teaching possibilities. She smiled as she remembered Tom's comment that she could marry him, take a year or more off, and simply enjoy being a doctor's wife. But he was surely kidding, and she'd laughed it off. She wasn't even divorced yet. How she enjoyed spending time with him. The more she got to know him, the more she liked him. And maybe even loved him.

Too soon for such thoughts.

She pulled into traffic and headed up Jefferson toward her attorney's office. He'd already reviewed a few things on the phone that they'd cover today. It seemed pretty straight forward, and she had the documents with her that he'd asked for.

Over an hour later, she emerged from the 1980's era concrete building and back into the stifling heat, with a headache to match Brad's migraines. Delete that thought—the migraines he'd used to have before he'd been started on a new injectable medication. But Gina was enjoying that benefit, not her. She exhaled and climbed back into the steam-pot of a car, cranking up the AC. The attorney, although straight forward in his advice, had thrown around so many legalese terms that she wasn't exactly sure what he'd told her.

Her cell phone rang. Blessedly the AC was starting to kick in. She answered the call. It was Susan. "Hey, I can't wait to see you."

"Oh, no, I'm sorry I can't make it."

Tamara's heart sank. Her best friend had said she could only meet with her today, during lunch. "What's up?"

"John fell and broke his ankle, so I'm taking him to Urgent Care."

"Yikes. I'll pray for him."

"Thanks. I'm so sorry."

"Don't be. It's not your fault." Tamara put the phone on speaker.

"I want to see you, though." Susan exhaled loudly. "When will you be back?"

"Maybe October to get my stuff, if all goes as planned. But you know how that is."

"I do. But I'm so glad you're not going to be in heaven in October. I'm glad I don't have a funeral coming up for you, my friend."

"You're right. Plus, you promised that you and John will come stay with us in Michigan next summer for at least a week."

"Yes, I did. But first we better get him fixed up and on crutches." Susan sighed.

"Or in a boot, hopefully. Those crutches are a pain." *Uh oh, no asking John to help her move things into storage then.*

"Yes, they are."

"All right, my friend, let's stay in touch then."

"See you."

"Love you, Susan."

"Love you, too." The phone went silent.

Her visit with Susan was the one time she had counted on where she could bare her soul about what she'd been going through.

The phone rang again. *Tom.* What in the world? He was at work. He never called her while he was there. "Hello there, Doc."

"Hey beautiful." He'd started calling her that after their third dinner out, and it made her cheeks heat.

"Hello handsome." She'd give him a little of his own medicine. She chuckled.

"How's it going so far?"

She puffed out a breath. "Well, in the midst of all that legal jargon, basically the attorney walked me through best case scenario and worst case and advised me that if I go with the no contest divorce it might mean I'd have to accept a possible worst-case situation."

"I'm sorry."

"It is what it is."

"Let's hope and pray for the best."

"Did you really say that?" She grinned.

"I did. And I really appreciate you taking me to church with your family this week."

"Yeah?" Warmth flowed through her.

"Yes, it felt good to be back in church again."

"I'm glad." She smiled. This man who'd professed science as his religion was coming around.

"I wanted to make sure I know where you're staying. I should have written your schedule down."

"Why?" She drew out the word.

"Well," he went silent for a moment. "I've found it's often good that someone knows the details of a trip just in case."

"Like in case Brad kills me and buries my body somewhere?"

He laughed that rich warm baritone he had, and she laughed, too.

"Yes, ma'am, that's exactly what was on my mind."

"I talked with my neighbors last night, and they know I'm coming by the house today." That she needed to let the neighbors know lest they called Brad with a Neighborhood Watch intrusion infuriated her.

"You sound upset."

"I am." She'd not felt this infuriated since she'd first encountered Brad with Gina at the Wellness Center parking lot.

"You know, I think most people would be angry in your situation but remember—God's got your back."

Wow, had he just said *that*? This man who had argued that Tamara must let science heal her. His words gave her a distinct pause in her thought processes and in her spirit. "You're right. Thanks for that reminder."

"You're welcome." It sounded like he was shuffling things around. "What are you doing for dinner tonight?"

"That's random. Are you hungry?"

He laughed. "I kinda am. Sure wish there was a decent barbecue place here, but I haven't found one yet."

"County Grill Barbecue in Yorktown is pretty amazing. Maybe I'll go there." But the thought of going by herself didn't bode well. She could always get take-out and eat in the hotel room. The problem with such a last minute and brief trip was that most of her friends already had plans they couldn't change. Or they were on vacation to escape the stifling heat and humidity of the Tidewater area of Virginia.

"Are you going to get some lunch before you head to the house? Maybe you're *hangry*—my daughter accused me of that recently."

Tamara laughed. "I don't think I'm hangry—at least not yet. We'll see after I go to the house."

"Chin up. Positive attitude and all that."

"Aye aye, Captain." Tamara closed the moonroof, the AC had finally chilled the car. "I better head out."

"Talk with you later, then."

"Okie dokie. Bye."

"Bye." His voice held a tinge of regret, and it touched her heart. Something was growing between them. Something warm, good, and strong. She felt the promise of the future in his caring.

She headed out of the parking lot and into traffic. She'd definitely not missed this. Lunch traffic was crazy. Hampton Roads residents loved to eat out at lunch time and unlike up North, there were gazillions of places to accommodate them. Seafood, Mexican, Asian, local fare, and any kind of chain restaurant you could think of. No pasties though. No whitefish here.

In ten minutes, she'd driven through the worst of it and headed toward her neighborhood.

It's just a house—not a home. Not anymore. She continued the positive self-talk all the way into the neighborhood until she turned onto what had been her street. She scanned ahead for her house, wanting to rest her eyes on the beautiful crepe myrtles she'd nurtured over the years. She had white, pink, and a purplish tree in the front yard and more in the back. This time of year, the hardy trees flourished in the heat and humidity, giving a spark of color in the yard. She narrowed her eyes as she scanned ahead, near where her house should be. A moment of confusion hit her.

She slowed the car to a crawl as a neighbor drove past and waved at her. She lifted her hand in return. Then she finally got a view of the front yard. No crepe myrtles. That was their brick house, but the entire front yard had been transformed into what looked like a desert. Mouth gaping, she fought for breath.

Every blooming thing was gone. Her huge daffodil and rose garden gone, covered with sand. Her many azaleas vanished. The two Japanese maples, together worth over a thousand dollars also gone. She pulled into the driveway and stared for a long time. She turned off the ignition. She grabbed her purse and exited the car. She pulled her iPhone out and took a bunch of pictures. She'd send those to Jaycie later and to the attorney.

Oh my gosh, how could he? How could they? The yard now was covered with rocks and hundreds of cacti. Tons of sand had been poured over the yard. It looked like a Spanish desert. It was hideous.

Perspiring in the heat, she hurried toward the front porch. It looked much the same except that a small plaque to the left of the door proclaimed, "Gina & Brad's Casa". Really?

Not yet it isn't.

Luckily there was no alarm system. Brad had been too cheap to put one in. The door handle and deadbolt locks looked the same. Her key worked in the lock. She exhaled a puff of relief. She didn't feel one bit guilty not telling these two about coming to get Jaycie's stuff and to check on what was still her house. She'd paid half the mortgage for all these years—as Brad had insisted.

He owed her big time for all of this.

She was greeted by the intense scent of something spicy. Her pale-yellow entryway was now deep crimson. Spanish art decorated both walls, and all of her artwork had been removed. She moved on to the living room. All of the family photographs—gone. Had they kept them? The expensive leather furniture she and Brad had gone halfsies on was still there as were the rest of the furnishings. She hesitated as she checked the corner where her antique secretary should be. In its place, a heavy Mediterranean-style cabinet dominated.

Where had Brad had moved her belongings? She'd search the whole place except...she wouldn't go into their bedroom. Not there. He had said that he'd removed all her clothing and personal care items from the bedroom anyway.

She knew they'd remodeled and desecrated her kitchen. Still, when she looked at it, inhaling the scent of recently cooked tacos or burritos, the mess still on the counter, she shook with anger. Granted, the new contemporary kitchen with its white glossy cabinets could have been featured in an HGTV show, but Tamara had saved for a *decade* for the money to remodel a few years earlier. The thousands of dollars' worth of granite countertops had been replaced by what looked like white quartz. Gina had even replaced the nice stainless-steel stove with a double oven. Brad had refused Tamara's plea to chip in for one.

Tears of anger and hurt spilled over, and she swiped at them. Brad hadn't put one cent into what she'd done so no wonder he'd let Gina do what she wanted. But had he paid this time? Did it matter, really?

She pulled out a padded island chair and sat. With the quartz counter's waterfall edges, Tamara could never have afforded to have done this to the kitchen island, which had also expanded a few feet. Engineers, even younger ones, still made more than teachers did. So, Brad was moving up with this impending marriage, too. She'd been traded in for a younger woman who recalled to him what he'd lost in the first wife whom he'd apparently worshipped. And all Tamara had from him, emotionally, was the stifled man he'd become after his tragedy—a tragedy he'd never disclosed to her nor to his parents.

But he had given her Jaycie, and she'd never regret that.

This was silly, sitting here feeling sorry for herself. *Good gracious a week ago I thought I had only months to live.* To be perfectly honest, if that was still her situation, she would have been happy that Brad had someone to move on with and that Jaycie would have some stepsiblings. Still, even if she were in that situation, she wasn't sure she'd trust those two to be great supports for her daughter. And that was ridiculously sad.

Time to go to Jaycie's room and get her special items before these two got crazy and totally remodeled that room into. . . Tamara opened the door to view a nursery filled with items to accommodate twin girls. Painted a Pepto Bismol pink, pink unicorns cavorted on the walls. The bed and dresser and nightstands that Dad had bought for Jaycie were gone as was Jaycie's cherry-wood bookcase, which had been filled with hundreds of books. The open closet doors revealed multiple rows of little pastel outfits. None of Jaycie's clothing. And the hope chest, passed down from each woman in her mother's family was missing. Within that chest were antique quilts made by her grandmother, great grandmother and great great-grandmother. Bile rose in Tamara's throat. She turned on her heel and hurried to the guest room. Surely she'd find their belongings there.

She opened the guest room door and went inside. Same furnishings, only an additional lamp that had been on her bedside table in their bedroom. No chest. She went to the closet. Boxes were stacked, labeled in heavy red marker: Crystal, China, Silverware. She'd not stopped in the dining room, so she didn't yet know what had been done there. One box read 'Jaycie's books.' Only one box. She opened it. Inside were college texts. Another was labeled 'Jaycie's clothes.' One two-foot cube of clothes from her daughter's over-stuffed closet. She pulled Jaycie's clothes box out. The college books she wasn't going to tackle. Brad could mail them or keep them. *Or sell them.*

A sense of foreboding shook her.

She speed-dialed Brad's number.

"Hullo?"

"What did you do with my stuff and Jaycie's?" Fury shook her voice.

Silence.

"And where are the heirloom quilts and the Hope Chest from my family?"

Over the phone, she heard a door close. As a manager, he had one of the few offices with a door.

"I'll have to talk with Gina, she's been taking care of all of that."

"Taking care of it? Where's our stuff?" Tamara gripped the phone so tightly that her fingers began to shake.

"I. . .uh. . .I think she's donated a bunch of stuff to one of the churches in the area."

"What?"

"There was one having a big indoor garage sale. So, she called them."

"I cannot believe you let her do that!"

"Are you at our house?" His emotion morphed from surprise to irritation.

"Your house? This is mine too, or did you forget that along with your marriage vows? And she better not have donated that chest with the quilts or you two will not be getting that quickie divorce you want."

"Let me call her. I'll call you back."

"You do that!" Tamara jabbed at the end button on the screen. She stomped through the hall and to the garage. Maybe Gina hadn't donated the items yet. She should have checked there before she'd called Brad. She opened the door to the attached garage.

Empty, other than Brads tools, lawn mower, and bikes and sports gear. He still kept it in pristine condition. Two unopened infant seats were stacked in one corner and a double stroller.

She'd check the office, she should have checked that, too. She stormed into the house with a full head of steam. Gone were the matching mahogany desks and bookcases. All of her education books and Christian fiction and Christian nonfiction books were gone. One would think if Gina and Brad were truly committed to a new Christian life together that maybe they would have read some of those books. Or at least put them aside for Tamara. Brad's engineering books, science fiction novels, and how-to books were gone, too. The room had been emptied of all office furniture. In their place were child-friendly pieces of furniture, a large play pen, baby toys, and a rocking chair transforming this office into a playroom. Instead of diplomas and honor certificates on the walls there were posters of circus elephants and giraffes. A bright green circular rug centered the room, the expensive multi-color wool rug, a gift from her parents, gone.

Tamara lifted her phone, longing to call Susan and share with her what had happened. But Susan was with John at Urgent Care. She could call Mom but didn't want to upset her too much. Dad would simply try to calm her down, and she didn't want that right now. She knew that in person Dad would vent his frustration with Brad with some pretty colorful language. But he wasn't big on phone calls. She did speed dial for Mom. The phone rang and rang and rolled over to Voice Mail.

"Uh, hi Mom." She didn't want to leave this kind of upset in a message. "I got here safely. I'll call you later." She ended the call.

Jaycie was at home. She'd try her, too, but the information about what Gina may have done with all her stuff might not be well received over the phone. No, she'd wait until she heard back from her idiot husband.

Thank God he was about to be her ex-husband.

She walked back to the kitchen and opened the new high-end refrigerator. She grabbed one of the water bottles inside. Four steaks marinated in a gallon Ziploc bag. Four packaged crab cakes sat next to them. What were these two celebrating and who was coming over? She slammed the fridge door. Brad never wanted guests over. He always blamed it on his headaches. Were they celebrating that she'd told him she'd give him the divorce? She removed the water bottle's cap with a vicious twist. The cold water tasted so good. She chugged back half of it before she realized her phone was vibrating in her pocket.

She looked at the screen. *Pastor Larry. Thank God.* "Hey, Larry, did you get my message?"

"I sure did, but that's not why I'm calling right now." Caution tinged his words, which was uncharacteristic of her ebullient pastor.

"Oh?" Oh no, had something else happened? "What's going on?"

Chapter Twenty-Nine

Dawn
Mackinaw City

Jim pulled Dawn into a bear hug and kissed her—a long lingering kiss that still had the power to steal her breath after all these years. When he broke away, she pressed a hand to his solid chest. "Why Jim Charbonneau, are you getting fresh with me?"

"I hope so." He pulled her tight against him again. He smelled of Irish Spring soap and the musky shampoo she'd bought for him.

"I love you, Jim," she whispered against his chest.

"I love you, too, Mrs. Charbonneau." He kissed the top of her head.

She laughed. "It seems like my world is finally straight again."

Jim released her, his countenance serious. "I had no idea how hard it would be until you were here and—" he jerked his head to the side "—and I was there in Chicago."

"I know." She closed her eyes as he bent to kiss her again, this time with a tenderness that sent shivers to her tennis shoe-clad toes.

An alarm sounded in the kitchen. "Blasted alarm, I was just gettin' started smoochin' with my favorite gal."

"Well, if you don't want to keep Hampy and Kareen Parker waiting, then we should be leaving within five minutes or so."

Jim snapped his fingers. "Tonight then? We finish our necking?"

Her cheeks heated and Dawn chuckled. "If you say so."

"I do." Jim attempted to swat at her behind as she headed toward the stove to turn off the alarm, but she side-stepped him.

She shook her finger at him. "Now, you need to be behaving yourself this afternoon, young man."

"That's no fun."

"We'll have a lot of fun, and you know it. We always do with Hampy and Kareen."

"Can't believe he got her to take the afternoon off."

"I cannot believe Jaycie got called in to work today nor that Hampy and Kareen were available for this last-minute tee time at the golf course."

"Providential, my love."

Dawn switched off the alarm. "Thank goodness Pastor Dave and his wife have already taken the dogs for a walk or they'd be going crazy with this stupid alarm."

"Yes, they would." Jim grabbed his ball cap from the table and a small backpack with water and sunscreen. "I already put our clubs in the trunk, in case you're wondering."

"Super. Thanks." Dawn rejoined him and kissed his cheek. "And thanks for asking Pastor to puppysit this afternoon, because now I won't be worried about getting back late."

"Yeah, with Jaycie gone, either she'd have had to rush home from work, or we'd have had to skip dinner tonight in Cheboygan."

They were playing at one of their favorite golf courses today. "I'm glad that Clark is letting Jaycie comp out a day tomorrow since she had to work today. The three of us can go hiking, like we planned."

"That'll be fun." Jim rubbed his chin. "I better let my cousin Garrett know that I can't go fishing with him tomorrow after all."

Dawn grabbed her purse and the tiny tote bag she liked to use when she was golfing. She checked to make sure that her pink and white visor was inside. It was. "Aw, you haven't seen your cousin in a while. You should go."

Jim grabbed his keys from the peg and put them in his chino pants' pocket. "I don't want to disappoint Jaycie, though."

Dawn waved her hand at him as she headed toward the door. "It'll be all right, hon, we'll go for that hike next week. I'll find something else for me and Jaycie to do—a girls' day out or whatever."

Jim laughed as they stepped out into the sunlight. He locked the front door. "It sure won't be like when you girls step out when she visits in Chicago, will it?"

"I don't think so, babe, but I bet we can do something other than shop and visit the spa."

"All right, then. I'll go fishing in the Upper Peninsula and you girls have fun down here."

"We sure will," Dawn assured him.

All would be fine.

Jaycie
Mackinaw City

Ferry horns blasted Jaycie awake from her deep sleep and a dream of dancing, dressed in a glittering white gown, with someone whose face she couldn't see. What were the ferries doing making all that noise before decent people woke up? *Ugh.* She rolled over and stared at the alarm clock. *Eleven.* How had it gotten that late? She normally woke at six and took the first ferry over to the island. Even on the weekends, she'd gotten in the habit of going to bed by eleven at night, so that she could get up more easily in the morning. And she had promised Gran that they'd do something special together today.

She got up from the bed and wiped the sleep from her eyes. She slipped into her flip-flops and went out into the hallway. Hard Rock charged at her, with Cici trailing behind. She picked up the bundle of fur and held him near her face, looking into the Yorkie's huge dark eyes. "Hello handsome boy, how are you today?"

Cici pushed against Jaycie's bare leg and whined.

"All right, all right." She gathered the other tiny dog into her other arm. The two dogs stared at each other and panted. It would be only a matter of seconds before one of them yipped in jealousy at the other. The only question would be which one.

Hard Rock wriggled toward Cici and barked. Now she knew.

"Down you go, then. You know the rule, Hard Rock." Did she imagine it, or was Cici giving Hard Rock a smug look?

"Jaycie, are you finally up?" Gran, still in knit sleep pants, rounded the corner from the kitchen, a mug clutched in her hand. It was unlike Gran to not be fully dressed by this time. And by fully dressed, that meant with all her jewelry on, lipstick and makeup perfect, even her casual clothing just so, and usually a huge smile— all were missing.

"Yes, I'm a slacker today." Cici tried to struggle out of Jaycie's arms as she neared Gran, so she set the dog on the floor.

Cici raced to Gran and circled her legs. "Stop, you're making me dizzy." Gran closed her eyes and reached for the wall.

Her grandmother actually looked serious. Although Gran sometimes teased about the dogs doing that to her, today she looked weak. "Are you all right, Gran?"

"I don't know." Gran sank down onto the sofa's arm. "I think I better lie down."

Jaycie took the mug from Gran's outstretched hand and set it on the coffee table.

Gran eased herself onto the couch. "It's these darned heart palpitations."

They usually went away quickly, but Jaycie had never been there when Gran had experienced a really bad spell. "Is this worse than usual?"

"Yes. I feel. . . funny." Gran drew in a long slow breath. "Like something weird around my shoulder."

Jaycie's own heart started pounding. This sounded an awful lot like a heart attack. Although Gran's cardiologist said she was doing well, that didn't mean she couldn't have a serious heart episode. "It's not like those times when I've called you and you've been in bed until they pass—just resting?"

Gran exhaled loudly. "I don't know." She laid down onto her back and put her feet on the couch, knees bent.

"Is there anything I should do?" Grandpa was in the U.P. fishing with Cousin Garett. Mom was in Virginia—what would she advise Jaycie? She'd say call an ambulance. But the closest place that would likely send an ambulance would be Petoskey and that was maybe an hour. If only Parker was there. But he'd not even called once since he'd gone to Europe. His two text messages were terse. She couldn't call on him. "I'm going to call Pastor Dave."

"He's at a seminar in Cadillac today." Gran pressed two fingers to her wrist. "I feel like something weird is going on with my heartbeat. Something different."

God, You know I need some help. "Gran, I'm going to put some jeans and a t-shirt on and get you over to the hospital in St. Ignace."

"No." Gran raised one hand.

"Gran, if you're having a heart attack then I think that's our best bet." Jaycie wasn't about to start arguing with her grandmother but neither did she want to upset her.

Gran groaned and pressed her hand against her left shoulder.

"I'm changing out of these pajamas and then we're going." No shower today but she had spray perfume in her purse. She raced down the hall.

As she pulled on her jeans, she heard a knock at the front door. She zipped her pants and pulled on her t-shirt and was about to run barefoot down the hall to answer when she heard a familiar man's voice.

"Mrs. C., I hope you don't mind that I let myself in." Parker's deep voice sent ripples of relief through her. Tears welled over as she slipped her feet into her sandals.

She grabbed her purse and phone and hurried to the living room. "Parker, thank God you're here."

Gran still laid there, eyes closed, perspiration beading her brow.

"I just got back into the country." Parker gaped at Gran. "We'd better get her to the hospital.

Jaycie threw herself into his arms. He held her close. "I think she's had a heart attack. I'm so scared."

He released her and went to Gran's side. "Mrs. C. do you think you could get in Grandpa's SUV if we help you up?"

Gran nodded.

"Mrs. C. hang on a minute." Parker faced Jaycie

"She doesn't want to go to St. Ignace," Jaycie whispered.

Parker gave her a sharp look. "She might realize how serious it is."

"Maybe."

He drew in a deep breath. "We'll get her to Petoskey."

Jaycie exhaled a quick breath. Heart attack? Surgery? "My mom is in Virginia, Grandpa is out with your granddad, and I was trying to figure out what to do."

"Come on. Let's get her in the vehicle."

"Bring my purse."

Jaycie grabbed it and with Parker's help, got Gran into the big SUV. Jaycie called the hospital in Petoskey and the emergency room was ready for them.

Jaycie leaned forward from the back seat. "Did you take your heart medications, Gran?"

Gran shook her head and opened her eyes. "I don't take any."

Her grandmother had experienced heart palpitations for years but didn't take any medications? That didn't seem right.

"My cardiologist in Illinois said I didn't need to take any until. . ."

Eeeep, until what—a heart attack?

"Until symptoms worsened."

Parker barked a harsh laugh. "Mrs. C. I think you've qualified now."

Soon, he was signaling for their turn for the road that would take them to Petoskey and the hospital.

Jaycie's heart pounded as she sent her mother and grandfather a text message.

"You'll need to drive back, Jaycie." Parker looked up in the rearview mirror at her, his eyes red with dark circles beneath.

"Sure," although she'd never driven a vehicle this large. "Why?"

"I've been awake twenty-some hours."

"What?" she squeaked out the question. "Why are you driving now then?"

"You need me to. I wanted to. I've done this drill a few times before, remember?" A muscle near his eye twitched.

On several of his mother's accidental overdoses, Parker had been the one who'd gotten her to the hospital. For one incident, Amanda Parker had been at a party between Mackinaw City and Petoskey and if her son had been one hour later or they'd waited on an ambulance, she'd have died.

"Parker, you're a good guy."

"No, I'm not. I'm a sinner saved by grace." He'd not referred to God as his *Higher Power* this time.

"Regardless, I appreciate you driving us."

Gran reached across and squeezed Parker's arm. "Thanks."

"No problem. But yeah, you need to drive this tank back. And maybe, Mrs. C., they'll tell us this is a dress-rehearsal for if you don't get those meds they've been holding off on. Sheesh, in some cases they seem to throw meds at people, like my mom, and then sometimes stuff is withheld that could be life-saving."

"I'm glad I'm not a doctor, though. Making all those decisions." Jaycie glanced down at her cell phone. Still nothing from Mom or Grandpa.

"Me, too. I thought I wanted to be a nurse." Gran rubbed her shoulder.

Despite the tension, Jaycie couldn't help but laugh. "Grandpa said you passed out the first time you donated blood, Gran. I don't think nursing was for you."

"Good point." And to Jaycie's relief, Gran laughed too.

"This might not be the time to mention it, Mrs. C., but Grandma Kareen is bugging Grandpa to pull you back into the travel business."

"Really?" Gran and Jaycie asked the question in unison.

"Yup, they think you could help Dad and me with these European acquisitions."

"I enjoyed my years. . . in the travel industry." Gran reclined her power seat back further. She seemed to be taking deep breaths and then slowly exhaling, like women did in labor. "But I think I'm gonna. . . love being. . . retired."

"You okay, Gran?"

"I feel tired. So tired."

Oh my gosh, was Gran dying? This couldn't be happening. *No.*

"You hang in there, Mrs. C. I'll get you there." Parker sped up and began passing a few stragglers.

Jaycie leaned forward. "Do you think you'll be helping your family with their businesses?"

In the rearview mirror she watched as his blond eyebrows drew together. "I don't think so. I love the business aspect of it, but I'm just learning what I really want to do. I love crunching numbers."

She tried to picture him as an accountant and was surprised when the mental image wasn't as incongruous as she'd thought.

Parker signaled to pass.

He headed around a red Prius.

"Virginia plates," Jaycie commented.

"See, there are other folks from Virginia who have the good sense to travel up North for the summer." Parker gave a short laugh.

"I'm glad I'm here." And so glad Parker was, too.

"You doing ok, Mrs. C.?"

Gran dipped her chin slightly.

Jaycie scanned the empty road. "This is so weird. There's like *no* traffic out here." This was high season and normally a logjam of vehicles would be heading into and out of Petoskey.

"Must be a God thing."

Shivers coursed up her arms.

"Ok, Jaycie, the hospital is up ahead about two miles. I'll pull in at the Emergency Room. Can you please contact them again and tell them ETA is in less than five minutes?"

Jaycie made the call and passed on the information. She ended the call and took a few deep steadying breaths. How did they go from Mom heading toward a horrible premature death to Gran possibly having a heart attack?

This wasn't fair.

"I know you're scared, Mrs. C." Parker squeezed Gran's hand. "But God has got this. We have to trust Him."

Somehow, sometime in the past year, Parker had finally entered into maturity. Maybe he was wrong about all the emotional delay he had from his years of drinking, because he sure seemed more like. . . well more like Mom would be if she was there. She checked her messages. Still nothing.

Hospital workers swarmed the SUV transferred Gran onto a gurney, covering her with a sheet. Jaycie raced after them as Parker parked the SUV.

The hospital staff practically ran Gran back to a room.

Dear Lord, please don't let Gran die!

Chapter Thirty

Tamara
Yorktown, Virginia

Pastor Larry gave a curt laugh. "I think your husband's, uh, partner, dropped off a bunch of your stuff for our big indoor yard sale this weekend."

Tamara pressed a hand to her chest. "Really?" What a relief.

"Yeah, one of the volunteers opened a huge box of books, and your name was on the bookplates. Did you tell her to donate them?"

"No!" That came out harsher than she intended.

"That's what I figgered. I told her to put them aside, and that I'd call you. I was here when she dropped them so I can probably cipher out what all is yours, unless she mixed some of her and your husband's stuff in, too."

"Oh, Larry, thanks so much." She'd not even breathed out the prayer to recover their special belongings, but the Holy Spirit had done that, just as the Word promised.

"Oh, and if you can do dinner tonight, I'll check with Jane to see if we can meet up."

"I'd love that. Otherwise, I'd be on my own."

"Ah, we're never really alone, are we?"

"You're right, as usual."

"Any place special you'd like to go?"

Tom's preference came to mind. "County Grill?"

"Yeah, we love that place. That might tempt Jane to not work late tonight. I'll let you know, okay?"

"Sure thing. Thanks." A huge weight began to lift from Tamara's shoulders.

"Talk to you later. Bye."

"Bye."

Some of her anger dissipated. Thank God for her pastor.

Her phone buzzed again. Brad. Why bother answering? She knew what Gina had done. She let it roll over to voice mail. When she finished her water, she pulled another one from the fridge. They could afford it, obviously. She left the empty water bottle on the island and tucked the new one in her purse. She checked the voice mail.

"Gina's coming over to the house right now. She can't believe you had the nerve. . ."

Tamara jabbed at the phone to end the call. Gina was the one with some nerve. How did you come into another woman's house and wipe out every trace of her? She left, eying the hideous Southwest front yard as she headed toward her car. Honestly, this hurt less than if she'd had to say goodbye to her beautiful gardens and trees and bushes. Gina had already said the goodbyes for her.

Tamara got into the car and her phone vibrated, the short buzz indicating a text message. She'd check it again after she got some Chik-Fil-A in her. They didn't have the restaurant up North. She'd go to the church after, but how would she get all that stuff put someplace? Yikes. She'd have to rent a truck or something. How would she move the furniture if she'd donated that? Larry had said the very-pregnant Gina had brought the stuff. Maybe someone at church had unloaded it though.

She parked in the Chick-fil-A lot and went inside and ordered her salad. She looked around the busy restaurant, wondering if she'd see anyone that she knew. Lots of young moms with kids. A few retirees. She placed her order and once she received her food, she carried it to an empty booth. She whispered a short prayer, *help me, God, help me.*

She logged onto the Wi-Fi and opened Safari. She searched for a nearby storage area, in case she needed it. She'd ask Susan, too, if she and John might have a little room. First, she'd better eat her lunch and then see what stuff Gina had donated. And Larry had helped spare. God bless him.

She closed out of Safari. Mom should have called back by now. But she and Jaycie and Dad were supposed to be doing something today. If they were in one of the areas where there was no cell signal, then they might not even have received it. She opened her dressing packet and the little extra goody packets for the salad and spread them on top. How many lunches had she and her friend Ruby enjoyed here before she'd gone home to be with the Lord?

She bowed her head and closed her eyes. *Oh God, thank You that I do not have pancreatic cancer and please help the other Tamera to heal. Bless this meal, Amen.*

She opened her eyes as a little girl passed by. Heart twinging, she thought of the special children she'd taught over the years. How she missed them.

She removed her fork from its plastic covering and dug in. She took a bite and savored the crunchy lettuce and crispy chicken. She missed this for sure. So many things that when she believed she was leaving this world hadn't really mattered to her. She'd felt a little guilty about not really missing the earthly things when she'd had her eyes fully fixed on heaven. But now, it seemed like God was giving her a little glimpse into how it would be when the end really came.

The phone vibrated again. She lifted it and glanced at the screen. Something from Tom. *Flight #1501, 5:25 ETA arrival PHF, we depart in 10 minutes will call during layover.*

She stared at the message. That was not her flight time nor her arrival, but it was the airport abbreviation. What in the world? She opened her messages. There were two from Tom. She scanned the first one. *Can you hold dinner at County Grill until about 6:30 or so?*

She blinked back tears and pressed her hand to her heart. Brad would never have done something so spontaneous for her. Tom had sensed her need and sought to fill it. Wasn't that love? Tingles coursed up and down her arms. Holy Ghost bumps, Susan would call them. And she'd be right.

Tamara entered the County Grill and spied Reverend and Mrs. Jones right away. She pointed in their direction and told the hostess, "I'm with them." She headed to the table in the middle of the room.

Larry rose as she approached. She loved his old-school manners, which Tom possessed in abundance, too.

"Good to see you." Larry pulled her chair out for her.

"We've missed you," his wife, Jane added.

"Thank you for joining me. And for welcoming Tom, too."

"I thought he'd be with you." Larry slid a menu toward her, but she already knew what she wanted.

"Tom insisted on having a cab bring him." She shook her head. Soon he'd be at her side and the anticipation was making her insides hum with a nervous electricity. "He didn't want to inconvenience me because of the other errands I had."

"That's thoughtful." Larry was eying the menu but apparently he was still listening, unlike Brad had ever done.

Jane gave Tamara a sympathetic look. "You know Larry did talk with Brad and Gina's preacher a few days back to let him know the actual situation of the separation."

He gave a curt laugh. "The other minister didn't budge. In his view Brad and Gina could join his church, since they'd accepted the Lord as Savior.

They're baby Christians. That voice whispering to her soul contradicted every logical thought she had in her head about the two.

Jane frowned. "Given what they did with your belongings, those wobbly newborn Christians might need years to get where they recognize the Holy Spirit and follow that guidance."

"How could anyone with any sort of compassion in their heart do their soon-to-be-ex so dirty?" Tamara still felt sick, thinking about it.

"You have a point." Larry looked past her.

Jane set her menu down. "Is *that* your new friend?"

Tamara swiveled around. An almost-white cowboy hat atop his head, thumbs tucked into his jeans and wearing a fitted blue shirt, Tom ambled across the wood floor to them. Most people in the place gawked at him. Could he have looked more handsome if he'd tried?

Tom removed his hat as he neared the table. He bent and kissed Tamara's cheek lightly then extended a hand to Jane and then Larry. "Good to meet you, Pastor and Mrs. Jones."

"Larry and Jane is fine." Larry grinned at Jane. "Unless we have to call him Doctor, right?"

Jane cast him a look that would have chastised most husbands, but the pastor just laughed.

Tom pulled out the seat beside her and sat. "I thought with this being barbecue, that my Stetson would be worth wearing."

"I love it." Tamara patted his hand. He was *her* cowboy.

The waitress came to the table and took their drink orders.

Jane slipped her reading glasses off and frowned. "Oh my. Do you see what I see?"

"Is that her?" Larry's face contorted briefly but then his features settled into a professional mask.

Tamara turned to catch a glimpse of Gina heading toward their table, her chunky heels clomping loudly on the wood floor. *Oh my gosh.* Tamara quickly swiveled around and shrank into her seat. As angry as she was, she'd not cause a scene here with her pastor and his wife, and in front of Tom.

Tom's features tugged in confusion as Gina stopped at their table, facing Larry.

"Excuse me, Pastor, but I forgot to get a tax receipt for the donations." Her accent was more pronounced than Tamara remembered, but it had been over a year since she'd last seen her. Even then she'd had only a brief encounter with Brad's employee.

"The secretary sent me over, she say, she said, that you were here and I should come see you." She gestured broadly with her arms, appearing irritated as she cocked her hip.

Gina's belly was so big that those twins better not make their appearance right here at the restaurant. That's all Tamara needed.

"Well," Larry drew the word out slowly. "Since those donations were technically Mrs. Worth's—" He pointed to Tamara.

Gina gaped. It sounded like she cussed something in Spanish.

Tamara straightened. "That's correct. Those were Jaycie and my belongings. So, under the law I'd have gotten the write-off. That is if I hadn't come to claim my own belongings and that of my daughter."

She was about to rise and really give this nasty young woman a piece of her mind when Tom pushed back from the table. He towered over the petite woman. Larry also made to rise but Jane touched his arm. Tamara pushed her chair back and watched, hands shaking in her lap.

"Listen here, little lady. You've taken her husband. Then you donate heirlooms and sentimental family belongings—"

Gina launched into Spanish, shaking her finger at Tom.

He bent down, face-to-face with her and gave as good as he got—in Spanish.

Larry, Jane, and Tamara all gaped as the people around began to watch, too. Tom continued on, as Gina stood, looking like a child receiving a scolding, which in all likelihood she was.

The manager came over. "Is everything all right here folks?"

Tom smiled broadly and swept his hand toward Gina. "I'm a doctor. This mamasita needs to get off her feet and leave."

"Is that right?" The man looked unconvinced.

Their waitress slipped around them, sliding their drinks onto the tabletop, a bemused expression on her face.

"*No es eso correcto*, Gina?" Tom dipped his chin.

"*Si*." She patted her belly.

The manager's tight features relaxed. "I'll walk you out, ma'am. My wife's due soon, too, and is on bedrest."

Gina departed, the manager chatting animatedly all the way to the door.

"Whew." Jane pretended to wipe her brow.

"I can't believe our secretary sent her here."

"Did she know what Gina had done?" Tamara pulled her chair back in as Tom sat down beside her, his color high.

"Oh yes. She's the one who called me and told me about your belongings having been brought in." Larry sipped his iced tea.

Tom shook his head. "I explained to her how fortunate she was that Tamara hadn't called the police. And that we would inform the IRS if they didn't hand over every item in that home that belonged to her."

We. He'd said we. Was there an *us*?

Jane compressed her lips. "I heard you say a few more things."

"Ah, another Spanish speaker at the table." Tom grinned.

"I heard the word *esposa*, which was the only word I really understood." Larry rubbed his jaw.

Jane shrugged. "Except that the way you used it, I'm not sure I understood it correctly."

Tom closed one eye hard. "You believe in speaking into the future don't you?"

"When something's God's will, you mean?" Tamara leaned in toward him, feeling his shoulder solid against hers.

"We believe that." Larry said, as the waitress returned to take their orders.

The young woman laughed. "And I believe it's time for me to announce the specials and to get your orders in."

"What's the most Texas-like thing you've got?" Tom beamed at the waitress, as if nothing at all had just happened in the restaurant.

"How about a combo with ribs, pulled pork, and barbecue chicken?"

He slapped his hand down on top of the menu. "I'm in."

She'd never seen him ever eat that amount of food. Tamara pointed to Tom. "I'll be splitting that with him—his eyes are bigger than his belly."

Tom laughed and patted his flat abdomen.

The waitress glanced between the two of them. "*Mi esposo y yo también compartimos la combinación.*"

The server took Jane's and Larry's orders, too.

"What did she say to us?" Tamara asked.

Jane glanced upward as if thinking. "'My husband and I share the combo, too' is what I think she said."

Why had the waitress said that? She obviously spoke and understood Spanish. What all had Tom said to Gina? She swiveled to look at him, and caught Tom gently shaking his head, making eye contact with an inquisitive looking Jane.

Tamara
Newport News, Virginia

"Would you mind swappin' me seats?" Tom ramped up his Texas drawl as he offered a megawatt smile to the red-haired woman by the window in Tamara's row. He pointed across the aisle. "I'm by the window on that side and this is my intended." He gestured to Tamara. *His intended?* That was a bit of a stretch. She wasn't even divorced yet. As far as she knew, Tom wasn't even her steady boyfriend or whatever they were called these days. But then again, look at all he'd done for her. He was a keeper.

"No problem." The woman unfastened her seatbelt and rose.

"Thanks." Tamara stood back so that the woman could move across.

"Thank you, ma'am." If Tom had his cowboy hat on, she was sure he would have tipped it. He motioned for Tamara to slide in by the window.

"You know I would have preferred the aisle." She gave him a teasing grin and feigned annoyance. There was no way his six-foot-two-inch frame was going to make it into that window seat, and she knew it.

"Well, thank you for your sacrifice, ma'am," he drawled and winked at her.

They took their seats. Tamara pulled her phone from her purse and made sure that it was on airplane mode.

Tom pulled his phone from his jacket and scanned the messages. "Only five messages since we departed the terminal and got on the plane."

"Don't they realize you're gone? Sheesh."

He laughed as he fastened his seatbelt. "Yup, but they still send me texts. Remember dinner last night?"

Her face heated at the memory of the after-dinner kiss, which had wiped out any concerns over text messages during dinner.

She hurriedly fastened her seatbelt and turned toward the window, lest he see the blush that heated her cheeks.

The stewardesses began their rounds, checking passengers. Soon they were going through the flight instruction drill for the passengers.

"This chapter of your life is almost over, Tamara." Tom took her hand didn't release it. It felt nice. This handholding suffused her with a promise of something more, as had his teasing words about her being his intended.

"We're not quite to an ending. It will take some time to settle things."

He raised her hand to his lips and kissed her knuckles. "As far as I'm concerned those two are past history. Burn the ships and all that."

She blinked at him. "I didn't know you were a Christian music fan. I love that song "Burn the Ships" so much."

His tawny eyebrows drew together in confusion. "I'm a classic music fan. And country music."

"Those two things seem like a paradox."

"Not if you're a physician from Texas." He gave her a warm smile. "I do a mean two-step, even if I say so myself."

"Really?" She'd tried to get Brad to go to the Country Bootleggers studio in Yorktown for years, but he'd always refused. "We need to find some place to go dancing."

"We'll bring Maria and Hamp with us. I hear he's got a wicked West Coast style, even if he's only sipping a Vernors ginger-ale. At least that's what Maria says."

"Hamp probably shouldn't be in any kind of bar, even if it's only to dance."

"We'll have to let Maria work with him on that, right?"

She'd keep praying for her old friend. "One day at a time, and all that, I guess."

"Right. But back to that burning the ships reference, you'll have to decide what you want to leave behind now that we've stopped that young woman from disposing of all of your belongings." He gave a curt laugh.

Tamara shook her head. "I still can't believe Gina did that."

"I can." His facial expression became serious. "Gina is one spiteful gal. And she wanted a tax break from the donations."

"Yeah, well thanks for being there for me."

"Any time, ma'am." He pretended to tap two fingers to a cowboy cap.

"I cannot believe you flew down here for me." This is what love did—it sacrificed for another and wanted only the best.

He leaned in closer to her. "We'll come back in October and retrieve whatever you'd like from the storage facility."

She blinked at him. He'd really meant it when he'd said he would come help her, again. Even though he was a doctor with a busy practice. What had she done to deserve this man? Nothing, not a darned thing. But God had swept in and replaced that devastating diagnosis with an entire new beginning, a new life. Chills coursed through her. Holy Ghost bumps, her friend Susan would call them.

She pictured Susan in a pink bridesmaid dress and a tiny hat and herself in a white sheath, standing up in front of Pastor Larry. Or would it be Pastor Dave? Susan and John would have to make that trip North finally.

"You are really something, Tom." Her heartbeat sped up as she fixed her focus on his lips. A generous mouth that she knew felt strong and right on hers.

He pressed a kiss to her lips, and she closed her eyes as a little shiver shot through her. He kept holding her hand as the lights on the plane flickered and the plane began to taxi away from the airport. Her last flight, maybe ever, away from Virginia. And as the plane headed up the runway for take-off, she squeezed Tom's hand and couldn't help grinning like the besotted woman she was.

"Do you want to know the most important thing I said to Gina?" he asked over the roar of the engines.

She nodded.

It seemed to take forever before the noise in the plane lessened.

"I told her that she didn't want to cross a man from Texas. Especially not since she and I had the same aim."

Tamara frowned. "What's that?"

He squeezed her hand. "To make the one we loved our spouse as soon as possible."

Did he really mean that? "You know an uncontested divorce in Virginia can happen in as little as a month?"

He dipped his chin. "I reminded her. And that if she wants that she better not mess with you again."

"You don't have a white horse waiting for us at the airport in Michigan do you?"

"No, ma'am. But I'd be happy to buy a pair for my intended and myself."

He kissed her. A kiss so tender and full of promise. When it ended, she leaned her head on his shoulder, sighing contentedly.

She must have dozed off, because someone was poking her arm.

"Tam, we're landing in Detroit. There's a bad storm."

Tom was right there beside her. For a disorienting moment, she couldn't recall what he was doing there. "You saved me yesterday."

He chuckled. "I'll save you as much as I can but for right now, be prepared for a rocky landing."

He was right. Thunder boomed outside the plane. They held hands as announcements continued over the speakers.

Dear Lord, please, don't let us crash right here on our way home.

Lightning jagged through the sky. She wished she could push closer to Tom, but they'd been instructed to sit upright.

"I love you, Tamara." Tom curled his fingers more tightly around hers.

"I love you, too." And if he meant it, and wanted to get married after the divorce, she'd do it.

If they survived this landing.

Chapter Thirty-One

Jaycie
Mackinaw City

"Do you think we did the right thing?" Jaycie asked as Grandpa Jim opened the front door.

"With not telling your mom?" Parker pushed her hair back over her shoulder, his touch reassuring.

"Best to wait till they're here tomorrow. Tonight, we all need to get some sleep. We'll get the full news from the cardiologist after his rounds."

Terrible weather downstate had grounded Mom's plane. So they were spending the night in Detroit. Mom had sounded pretty shook-up.

"Parker, you're welcome to sleep in my room instead of on the couch."

Grandpa Jim looked shocked.

"I meant I'd go in Mom's room since she won't be here."

"Oh." Grandpa headed down the hallway. "Have a seat in the living room, Parker and I'll be right back."

Parker sat on the couch and spread his arms wide overhead.

Jaycie went into the kitchen and flipped on the light. She examined the calendar. How could this still be the same day? She rubbed the side of her head. Then she turned the teapot on, intent on downing a cup of chamomile tea before she hit the hay.

Grandpa joined her. "I gave Parker a towel and washcloth and he's showering in the hall bathroom."

Parker had missed the last ferry but there was no way she would have sent him back home in the condition he was in after not sleeping in a couple of days.

"Hope he doesn't conk out in there." Grandpa Jim rubbed his chin.

"Yikes, no."

She and Grandpa recapped the day together, including how she'd interrupted him from catching the biggest fish in his life.

"Garrett Christy will never let me hear the end of it."

"A rematch?"

"It's not exactly like that. It's supposed to be a fun fishing trip for two old cousins."

"Um, sounds like a competition to me."

He tweaked her nose. "That's men for you."

Her dad wasn't like that. But Parker loved to turn things into a fun competition.

Her phone buzzed. Message from mom. She read the text message out loud. "Goodnight sweetie, I hope you had a good day. The hotel is great. We both got great rooms." Jaycie gave a curt laugh.

"Super." Grandpa opened the pack of vitamins and medications that he took after dinner.

"Yes. Should we tell her now? I feel guilty."

Grandpa waved his hand. "Nah, it won't do any good. Let's let them sleep. We'll tell them in the morning."

She thought she heard Parker's footfalls in the other room. But they stopped.

Jaycie prepared her tea.

"Heading to bed." Grandpa kissed her goodnight.

She carried her mug out to the living room, where Grandpa stood looking down at Parker, who appeared sound asleep.

"I'll get extra pillows and blankets from my room for him."

"Good idea. I don't think he's moving anywhere just yet."

Compassion stirred her at how Parker had rescued her and Gran that day. She wanted to reach out and smooth back his hair, but she didn't want to wake him.

"Let me get the good quilt." Grandpa had a strange look on his face as he shuffled down the hallway.

When he returned, he handed the handmade heirloom quilt to her. "He's part of the family, too. Especially after this."

Jaycie hugged Grandpa Jim and he kissed her cheek. As he headed to bed, she gently spread the quilt over Parker. She bent and pressed a featherlight kiss to his forehead. He looked so peaceful. So angelic. *God, help him beat this thing. If not for me, then for him. For his family now and his future family—even if that doesn't end up including me. Amen. And God, I don't know if I'm able to love him one day at a time, but you know. And if you can help me with that. . .then I'd appreciate it. Amen again.*

Tamara
Central Michigan

At least the drive from Detroit promised good weather. With Tom beside her, would this be the first of many trips together? Tamara's phone rang and she answered it.

"Mom?"

"Hi, sweetie. We took off a little earlier than planned. We're on the road."

"Good. You're not driving?"

"No. Tom's got the wheel."

He grinned at her and her heart did a little flip.

"Mom, I wanted to tell you last night but Grandpa wouldn't let me."

Her shoulders stiffened. "What?"

"Gran's in the hospital."

Oh no.

"They think she's had a mild heart attack, but they say she's doing well."

"Oh my gosh." She covered the speaker on the phone, as she spoke to Tom. "My mother has had a heart attack. She's in the hospital." She lifted her hand from the speaker.

"In Petoskey." Jaycie's voice sounded strained.

"I heard that." Tom said. "Can you put her on speaker phone?"

"Sure."

"Hey, Jaycie, we're rarin' to go—only a couple of hours out. Who's her cardiologist?"

"Dr. Zay-something."

"Zaitoun?"

"That's him."

"He's the best. If there's anything else going on, he'll find it."

Tamara didn't want Dr. Zaitoun to find anything else. But he had been the one to insist that Mom take care of her heart palpitations if they became more problematic. "Is Dad with her?"

"Yes, Grandpa Jim grabbed a cup of coffee and left a few minutes ago."

"Good." Tamara exhaled a breath that she'd not realized she'd been holding. "What time will you be going over?"

"Depends on when Parker gets up. He crashed here last night. I'll tell you all about it when you get home."

"Text me when you leave, and I'll do the same when we arrive at the hospital. Okay?"

"Sure thing. Love you, Mom."

"Love you, too."

"Well howdy back to Michigan, huh?" Tom shook his head.

"Yeehaw, huh?" Suddenly all the drama with Brad and Gina seemed minor. Losing her mom, that would have been major.

"Would you grab my phone and call the hospital for me?"

"She's not your patient. Confidentiality and all that." Tamara picked up his phone, though, and dialed then put it on speaker phone.

She listened as he asked for Dr. Zaitoun. When the cardiologist came on the phone, the two chatted like old buddies.

"Say, I've got a Texas-sized favor to ask you."

Jaycie
Mackinaw City

Parker still slept soundly on the couch. With his tousled blonde hair, he looked adorable, his tall frame still covered by Gran's quilt. She was tempted to go and kiss him awake.

Dr. Zaitoun, the cardiologist, was supposed to meet with Gran and Grandpa that morning, and Jaycie really wanted to be there. But maybe there would be something shared that was best they heard by themselves.

Jaycie settled herself into a chair opposite Parker. She covered herself with a fluffy pink velour throw that Auntie Zara had brought for Gran. She'd take it to the hospital later. The throw felt just like getting a big, warm hug.

"Jaycie?" Parker rolled from his side to his back and stretched his long arms overhead.

"Yeah." She pushed aside the throw went to him. "Scoot over."

Parker complied, and she sat next to him, feeling the heat radiating from his body, from beneath the yellow patchwork quilt. She pushed blond strands of hair back from his eyes and he grabbed her hand and kissed her palm. Shivers coursed through her.

"I missed you so much when I was gone." He pulled her into his arms and held her there, her head against his chest.

Parker's heartbeat sounded steady but her own ratcheted up.

"I'm sorry I didn't tell you about the trip to Europe. It was so sudden. I basically had time to pack a bag and get to the airport with my dad."

She sat up and pressed a finger to his lips. "Shhh, it's all right. You're here now."

"I am."

"And thank God you didn't give me a 'Mort-like' diatribe on 'letting my feelings course through me' when we were at the hospital yesterday and I was freaking out about Gran."

He gave a curt laugh. "I'm more of the 'feel your feelings' kind of guy since I got in recovery."

"Well, I'm glad of that. I think if Mort had been there and tried telling me one of his pat lines I would have slugged him."

"Aw, don't be so hard on your 'gardener'. He's had his own stuff to work out."

"I know, I know." She sighed. "I'm glad for him and Kay-Leigh."

"I'm *glad* they're both gone back to Europe." Parker pulled her back into his arms again. "I think they have a better chance of reconciling their difference back in their own home in Switzerland."

Jaycie snuggled in closer, turned, and laid next to Parker. He held her tightly, but his arms began to tremble.

"I think you better get up, Jaycie." Parker shifted away, loosening his grip. "We've got some things to work out."

She felt like cold water had been tossed on her, but Jaycie sat up and averted her face, not wanting him to see her embarrassment. Parker took her hand.

"I'm not going to do a graduate program right now. I'm joining my dad in running the family business."

She swiveled to face him. "Really?"

"We've got to prove to Grandpa that Dad can remain sober and straight and run the business if he and Grandma retire. And I'm gonna help Dad."

"Well, I've decided that I'm going to be a teacher one day. So there." She gave him a saucy grin. "I love working with kids. I accepted a position with the Mackinac State Parks doing educational outreach."

He didn't seem too surprised. Had Mr. Jeffries told him of the offer?

"I'm glad." He kissed her knuckles. "I'll be traveling a lot this year—which could be a bit of a challenge to my sobriety."

"You can do it. I know you can."

"One day at a time. Could you accept that?"

She didn't know. Jaycie compressed her lips. She couldn't honestly promise she could. She'd keep praying about it.

"It's all right. I understand. That's one reason I wanted us to put a hold on our relationship until I've had at least another year's sobriety under my belt in AA. One year for me—another year for you."

She nodded. Another whole year. It seemed like such a long time. It would be worth it though, if they were meant to be together. And she had other things on her life's journey that she needed to get straight, herself, before she was in a committed relationship. Who knew what a year could bring?

Chapter Thirty-Two

Dawn
Mackinaw City

For the first time since her ordeal, Dawn had gotten dressed before breakfast. She'd donned a matching set of peach capris and short-sleeved lacy blouse and some blush-colored espadrilles.

Late summer rain poured down in torrents while inside it was cozy with the scent of cinnamon buns baking in the oven. No treats this morning from the corner bakery, but a can of Pillsbury Grands cinnamon rolls called into use to save breakfast.

With the entire family gathered around the kitchen table, Dawn clutched her mug of decaf. "No way are you going to take my decaffeinated coffee away from me."

"Aw, come on, Gran. You like some of the herbal teas." Jaycie swigged back her large Michigan cherry fully caffeinated brew. *The brat.*

Dawn scowled at her granddaughter. "Traitor."

Jaycie laughed and set down her drink. She poured more creamer into the cup and stirred it slowly. "Did Dr. Zaitoun tell you to quit?"

She ignored her granddaughter.

Jim stared at Tammy's tablet, which their daughter had been teaching him to use. "Looky here, Dawn." He held it up, revealing the image of a muscular man, bulky arms crossed over his wide chest, attired in deep blue and green patterned scrubs.

"He looks like he needs a shave." She couldn't stand the half-shaved look that young men sported these days. "Scruffy, like a poor tramp."

Tammy snorted a laugh but lifted her mug of Earl Grey to her lips.

Jaycie squeezed one eye closed hard. "Gran, he's what mom would call 'a hunk,' and besides, that's the style with facial hair."

Jim lowered the tablet. "I was thinking that since it was my turn to be the nurse at the Charbonneau household that I'd order me a get-up like this to wear." He displayed the image to Jaycie and Tammy again, deliberately ignoring Dawn.

She rolled her eyes as her daughter and granddaughter admired the model.

"Me and that guy look a lot alike, right?" Jim smirked as Tammy and Jaycie nodded.

Dawn's chuckle started deep in her chest before spreading to her belly. After a moment, she stopped. "James Charbonneau if you show up in our living-room in that hideous outfit and with scruff on your face, I'll—"

Her husband hopped up from the table, rounded it, and kissed her square on the lips. Now that was more like it. How she'd missed him. Dawn put her hand behind his head and pulled him even closer.

"Woooeee, Gran and Grandpa have still got it." Jaycie's crowing laughter pulled them apart.

"Yes, we do. And who knows, maybe someday you and Parker will have that, too."

"We're not even dating, so don't say that." Jaycie compressed her lips.

Tammy shot her daughter a look that spoke volumes. "Well, I *am* dating someone, and I pray Tom and I will have what you two have one day." She raised her tea in a mock toast.

Jim returned to his seat "I hope so, too, Daughter. Tom's a genuine good guy. I really enjoyed meeting him at the VBS blow-out."

Her granddaughter laughed. "What a sport Dr. Austin was— putting on that crazy pirate mascot outfit for your theme."

"Poor Pastor Dave would have been high and dry if he hadn't volunteered." Tammy made a silly cringey face.

Dawn considered how many church meetings she'd missed because of her trip and her heart attack. "If this whole VBS gig, that I'd pretty much failed at, wasn't a sign from God about my retirement then I don't know what is."

"Maybe your heart attack?" Jim shook his head. "Was that a clue, too?"

Dawn lifted her nose in the air and tried to ignore her husband's comment. "I think Tom got a kick out of it, too. He really seems to love kids."

"Yeah, I got that vibe, too." Her granddaughter raised her dark eyebrows.

"Well, whether Dad orders a set of those scrubs or not, you've got to follow doctor's orders, Mom." Tammy used her best teacher voice to get her message across.

Dawn heaved a sigh. "If only we could stay here longer. That's my biggest regret."

"There's always next summer, Gran." Jaycie beamed a sweet smile at her.

Jim, in contrast, scowled. "No more arguments of staying here. We've already passed the recovery time that Dr. Zaitoun suggested."

"True. Just barely, though," she protested.

"You need to be back home so we can get you into cardiac rehab."

The oven alarm sounded for the cinnamon rolls and Tammy got up. "Everybody wants icing, right? Because, I mean, I am more than willing to take extra."

"Not a chance, Sunshine." Jim pushed his chair back away from the table, again. "Do I have to come over there and guard the frosting?"

Dawn laughed. "You've gotten your appetite back, Tammy. I'm so glad."

Jaycie pointed at Tammy. "I'm glad, too, Gran. Mom was putting some serious wear-and-tear on my clothes."

Tammy turned, her cheeks pink. "Are you implying I'm picking up weight?"

Jaycie made an impish face. "Draw your own conclusions, Mom, but when you ripped my best pair of jeans. . ."

"I blame Tom." Tammy's wistful tone suggested she didn't mind regaining a few pounds. "All those dinners he's cooked for me."

"You two are pretty inseparable." Jaycie smiled. "Which works for me and my wardrobe."

"Yes we are." Tammy sighed.

Satisfaction bloomed in Dawn's heart. "A doctor and a chef, I'd say you won the lottery with this guy."

"I really like him, even if he's a pirate." Jim nodded. "He's a straight-up fella. Not like—"

"Jim," Dawn put as much warning into her tone as she could.

Tammy brought two well-slathered rolls to Dawn. "Speaking of Brad, my attorney says if we can agree on settlement terms then I could be a free woman in as little as two months. No kidding."

"That's so unreal." Jaycie went to the counter and refilled her coffee cup. "Do you want some more Grandpa?"

Jim raised his hand. "Nope, I don't wanna upset my girl over there. She's had such a hard time staying off the coffee."

"Oh, maybe I shouldn't have any more then." Jaycie grimaced.

"Go ahead. I don't mind." Okay, yes Dawn did wish she could have more, but she wasn't going to say it.

Jim winked at Dawn. "In that case, I guess I will have a re-heat."

"Jim Charbonneau, I didn't say I didn't mind if you had more but if Jaycie had more."

He swigged back the last of his coffee. "No, you didn't say that."

Tammy set two rolls in front of her dad. "Are you two going to keep arguing on your last day here?"

"Nah." Jim shoved half of the roll into his mouth.

Dawn glared at him. He knew she hated it when he did that. She drew in a slow deep breath. *Failing to appreciate one's food isn't a crime*, he'd tell her if she scolded him—just like he'd said for the past fifty years.

"Good thing food valuing isn't what matters in marriage." Dawn kissed Jim. "But valuing each other."

"That's the ticket." He had the nerve to laugh at her.

Tamara

Tamara laughed. "Mom and Dad you are so cute." Brad and she had rarely argued and when they had it was mostly about money. How odd, but maybe fitting, that here at the end of their marriage, it was the final thing that their divorce came down to—a dividing of financial assets. Tom had already said that if finances were what would hold up her divorce, she should know he'd always financially support her. She blinked back tears at the recollection of this wonderful man's words. She wasn't even divorced yet, though, and her heart had already found its rightful place—in the hands of someone who would protect it.

Tamara finished spreading icing over Jaycie's roll and then her own. She brought them to the table.

"Thanks, Mom." Her daughter beamed at her.

"You're welcome." Tamara slid back into her chair. "It's going to be a little strange with only us two single girls in the house."

"I think it will be the first time in decades that there has been anyone in the house being courted." Mom took a bite of her roll and raised her eyebrows in appreciation.

"*I'm* not dating." Jaycie's defensive tone put Tamara on edge.

Tamara took a sip of her coffee. "Tom will be courting me officially once those papers are signed."

Dad chortled. "The man has already asked for your hand in marriage."

"I think he's a few steps ahead of you, Tammy." Mom gave her a knowing look.

Her face heating, Tamara looked away.

Jaycie nibbled at her cinnamon roll. Her grumpy face warned anyone to contradict her about Parker.

Sheesh, what was all that about anyway, saying they weren't dating? No one was pushing Parker and Jaycie at each other. *They'd managed that all by themselves, thank you very much.* Still, she would talk with her daughter later and try to figure it out. Maybe there had been some falling out, but if so, Tamara had not seen nor heard of it.

"This has been quite the summer, hasn't it?" Mom's eyes glistened.

"It sure has, but I am so grateful that you're okay, and that I am, too. If only the Tamera with an 'e' was okay, too." But medical confidentiality being what it was, they didn't know. It didn't seem fair that Tamara got to live while Tamera in Williamsburg might not. She prayed for the misdiagnosed woman every day.

"Thank God for Maria. Mr. Parker says she's like a dog with a bone when she wants to know something." Jaycie shook her head. "Although that's not a very good image for him to have since he's obviously fallen head-over-heels in love with her."

Maria had followed Tom's hunches and tracked down the correct diagnostic information. She was as tenacious as Hamp was. "Those two are a perfect fit. He'll stay on his program, Maria helping him stay on the straight and narrow path."

"I think you're right." Mom sipped her drink.

Tamara looked around at each person at the table, the family she loved with all her heart. A family that would be expanding.

"A year ago, would you have thought we'd all be sitting here together?" Mom clasped her hands around her mug.

"With all my girls?" Dad cast Mom a long glance, moisture glistening in his eyes.

"Only God knew what was to come." Tamara lifted her teacup to her lips.

She'd heard a sermon once by Reverend Larry about how if you knew what was coming in the year ahead you wouldn't want to know it. You wouldn't be able to deal with it. Yet somehow, during it all, God got you through each day. *So true.* She'd have not wanted to know what she'd be facing this year. Just dealing with the lawyer was enough to give her one of Brad's debilitating migraines. Coping with the ups and downs of believing she was going to leave this earth and then to learn she'd be here for a while yet—that had totally absolutely rearranged her world. And to have met a man who could well and truly be the one who was perfect for her.

"Someone's deep in thought. I've asked you three times if you wanted the last roll." Dad cast her a concerned look.

"You know, I couldn't have imagined last year that this year my marriage was about to end. And I'd certainly not seen that train-wreck of a young woman, Gina, taking over what had been my life."

"Mom, she didn't take it over, she demolished our lives."

"Well, thanks for that clarification, daughter." Tamara shook her head and laughed, surprising herself.

The bitterness was gone.

Jaycie

Jaycie cleared her throat. "Okay, enough of that. Let me tell you about my new job."

"Sure, honey." Mom smiled at her.

"I'm excited to be planning out my school presentations."

"Did you figure out how much driving you'll have to do?" Grandpa, ever the pragmatist when it came to vehicles, had asked her to sit down and figure it out using some state maps he had.

"We checked on MapQuest," Mom answered for her.

"I'm so grateful that you're letting me use Gran's car. Thank you, again." Jaycie grinned at both of her grandparents.

"Well, I sure wasn't gonna let your grandma drive home now, was I?"

"You're doing us a favor." Gran winked at her. "Besides, once I figure out how to transfer the title over to you, then your grandpa can buy me that cute Corolla with a moonroof that I've been eying."

"Oh, no, Gran and Grandpa, I don't want you to feel like you have to give me your car." But as guilty as she felt, she'd sure appreciate it.

"We talked about this last night." Gran and Grandpa locked gazes.

"Buying your grandma that Toyota as soon as I get her home."

"We'd previously wanted to offer my little car to you, if you wanted. So, this has worked out for everyone."

"Thank you." Jaycie rose and kissed Gran and then Grandpa. "I'll have to travel quite a bit, and I am grateful."

"I'm hoping Jaycie will drive to Cheboygan for our groceries, too," Mom teased.

She sat back down. "Luckily, I will be doing some online training with school districts so some days I won't be driving at all."

"It's amazing what they can do these days." Grandpa rapped his fingers softly on the table.

"My college education classes will mostly be online this semester. Not my preference, but improving my technical skills is always a plus."

"Did you get the classes that you need to get so you can pursue your teaching certificate?" Mom had just renewed her own teaching license in Virginia that Spring.

"Yes. I want to get my education requirements out of the way and possibly do a teacher internship in Spring. But I might stick with Mackinac for a while and finish a master's degree. . ." And stay close to Parker.

With Parker traveling between the island and Europe, she prayed he would maintain his sobriety and not relapse. If he did, then in all honesty, she wasn't sure she could consider anything further with him. They weren't in a relationship. He was her friend. Maybe this was why Parker had insisted on a year of sobriety before dating because he knew she wouldn't put up with him drinking.

"—Parker?" Grandpa looked at her expectantly, but Jaycie hadn't heard his question.

Her cheeks heated.

Mom cast her a quizzical look. "I'm sure Parker would be happy to help get your bags in the car, Dad. And I'll ask Tom to come by, too." Mom flipped her phone over from the table. "The 'no cell phone' rule at the table is lifted while we send our guys a text asking them to help tomorrow morning."

"He's not my guy, Mom." Not unless Parker stayed on program for at least a year. And only then would they even start dating. But with all the cuddling they'd been doing, and kissing, how could she call them just friends?

"Okay, okay, ask your friend, Parker, to come lend us some young muscle." Grandpa pointed to his knee. "This danged thing is still gimping me up some."

Jaycie flipped her iPhone over and sent Parker a quick text.

In only a few moments, a ding sounded. Mom grinned.

Jaycie loved seeing Mom look so happy. Thank God she was going to be okay, and Gran, too.

"I appreciate how even though he's a doctor, Tom replies to my texts so quickly. I know he really cares about me." Lines formed between Mom's brows as she read the message.

Jaycie checked her phone. Parker had replied quickly, even though he was in a meeting. *Anything for you, Babe.* Her cheeks heated.

Before she could stop her, Mom had grabbed her phone and looked down at the message. Satisfaction, and maybe relief, slid over her pretty features. "Oh, good, he can help." She gave Jaycie a quick conspiratorial glance before she slid the phone back over to her. "That's what friends are for."

Friends? Friends didn't usually call you 'Babe.'

Chapter Thirty-Three

Dawn
Mackinaw City

Dawn watched as Jim rolled up the last of his white t-shirts and set them inside his duffel bag. "I think that's it, my girl."

Jaycie and Tammy peeked into their room. Their daughter grinned at them. "You're leaving, and we're staying behind without you—seems so bizarre."

"Tell me about it." Dad closed and latched their suitcases.

"Don't even think about lifting those, Jim." Dawn wagged her index finger at him.

Jim and Jaycie exchanged a quick glance and burst out laughing.

"What's so funny?" She was dead serious about her warning.

"Grandpa said I sounded just like you the other day."

"Oh." She winked at her husband. "A Mini-Gran?"

"Yup." He winked back.

The front door creaked open and then slammed shut. Dawn cringed.

"We're here, y'all." That was Tom's deep Texas accent. Thank God her daughter had this kind man looking after her.

Two pairs of footsteps sounded down the hall. Parker entered the room and pointed at his brightly tie-dyed t-shirt, which was emblazoned with "Parker Labor Crew" on the front.

Jaycie stepped to his side and poked at Parker's chest. "Where did you get that?"

"I had it made up for us on the island at one of the shops. Told 'em I was starting a new company."

Sure enough, the good doctor sported a matching shirt. Tom flexed his shoulders. "This is a lot more comfortable than what I usually wear to work—and a lot more colorful."

"Not as colorful as your VBS outfit." Parker laughed.

Jaycie smirked. "All Tom needed was a monkey to complete the pirate look."

Dawn cringed, waiting for the oncologist to take offense. Instead, he guffawed. Those two were going to get along fine. They already were.

"No monkeys, but I'm buying us a dog just as soon as we're married." Tom kissed Tammy's cheek and she wrapped an arm around him.

Parker bent and patted the pooches' heads. "I'm buying my brother a golden-doodle. Kind of a service dog for him."

Tom swiveled to face the younger man. "Is Carter disabled?"

"Nah. He has Lupus. When he's feeling bad, I want him to have a pet to cuddle." Parker locked eyes with her granddaughter. "Cuddling is so nice."

Jaycie's blushed crimson.

Dawn wasn't about to comment on whatever was going on there.

"Isn't Carter going back to boarding school?" Tammy picked up Hard Rock.

"I can answer that." Tom grabbed Cici and petted her head. "Maria has convinced Hamp that it's best for Carter to stay with them on the mainland this winter. After they're married."

"Yeah, because of the Lupus." Parker scratched behind his ear.

Tammy held Hard Rock as he attempted to squirm out of her arm. Finally, he gave up. "She wants to work on her mamasita role with him."

"Yeah, she's awesome," Parker agreed.

"So many changes. What a summer. And despite this heart attack of mine, I'm feeling better than I have in a long time."

"Don't get any ideas of over-doing it." Jim wagged a finger at Dawn.

"All right, crew, let's get a move on." Parker squared his shoulders and then grabbed two of her bags.

Tom passed Cici to Jaycie, then hoisted two other bags and followed Parker out. Dawn's daughter and granddaughter followed him out, with the dogs.

Jim squeezed her hand. "Ready?"

"Ready." Ready, even, to really retire and enjoy all that would offer—including spending time with new family members. This summer had given her a clarity she'd not had in quite a while.

They walked through the house, the last time until likely next summer. A bit of sadness pinched her heart.

"How did you feel about letting Kay-Leigh know you were selling the agency?" Jim kissed her cheek.

"I feel great about it. Which is why we're working up those sale papers next month." She made a face. "Kay-Leigh—not so much. I think she might be as rigid as she used to accuse her husband of being."

"Doesn't handle change well?"

Dawn laughed. "She even admitted as much. But she'll transfer over to Barb—said she was a great help this summer when they needed flights and all those extra spots at the Grand Hotel for the crew."

"Good. How about you? Do you think you'll handle your big change well?"

"I get to spend more time with you, Mr. Charbonneau, so how do you think I'll do?"

He pulled her into his arms, right there on the sidewalk. "I think you'll be just fine."

She pulled away. "How soon can we go on our fiftieth anniversary trip then?"

"You haven't even started your cardio rehab and you're talking about a trip to Europe?"

"Minnie's about to be retired, Mickey! So, fasten your seatbelt tight and get ready for the next phase of our adventure."

Epilogue

Jaycie
Lucerne, Switzerland, April 2019

Jaycie's family members all loved Parker. She did, too. But was she strong enough to love him one day at a time? She'd not seen him in over a month, while he was working in Switzerland. She'd missed him so much; it was like an ache. How would things be when she saw him here?

She opened the heavy gold curtains in their well-appointed room at the Hotel Europe and spied the exquisite fountain in the courtyard below.

"This is some kind of wonderful fiftieth wedding celebration, for you and Dad." Mom hugged Gran.

"Maybe it's a good thing that most of the shops are closed because of Easter week." Gran flopped down on Jaycie's queen-sized bed. "Now we can get some more walking and touring in without feeling guilty about letting you girls down with the no shopping rule."

"I'm well acquainted with Dad's rule from all our trips when I was a kid. So, no problem for me." Mom shrugged.

"How can I feel let down?" Jaycie poked Gran's arm. "I'm on the trip of a lifetime."

Mom ceased unpacking her suitcase, which lay atop a fancy gold and leather luggage-rack in their shared room. "Every day is a gift, but I have to say – this place is an amazingly huge present. Thank you, Mom."

"Come out onto the balcony." Gran waved them toward French doors that opened onto a small balcony.

"Oh my goodness." Mom pressed her hand to her chest. "The mountains are amazing."

The peaks of the Alps were illuminated by the sun's glow. "Wow. That doesn't seem real, does it?"

Mom shook her head. "Looks like a Disney movie background to me."

Gran waved her arm. "Wait until we go up to Mount Pilatus and get a close-up look around."

"Flying in over the mountains was fantastic. I almost held my breath, they were so pretty." Jaycie lifted her hand to shield her vision from the afternoon sun. Seeing Parker again, that would steal her breath away, too.

"Grandpa and I are delighted to have you girls here with us."

"Thanks, Gran. What a way to celebrate!"

Gran motioned to the door that led to the adjoining suite. "This was a great idea having the two suites adjacent. Grandpa Jim can nap or read while we girls giggle in here."

"Things really came together, didn't they?"

"I called in every favor I ever had in the real estate business." Gran looked so much more relaxed now that she was retired, even after the long trip across the Atlantic. "This really worked with your Spring Break week, too."

"Providential that Tom's medical conference is at the same time," Mom said.

"So glad he can be at dinner." Jaycie smiled, wishing Parker could be.

"What about Parker and his family?" They stepped back inside and Grand closed the doors. "I know Carter stayed in the states with Hampy and Kareen.

"They can't make it. Parker, Maria, and his dad are meeting with the hotel management to discuss business." She'd been irritated that they couldn't reschedule the meeting, but this was for business. And he'd seemed so contrite, she didn't fuss at him.

"Bummer." Mom looked genuinely disappointed.

Three hours later, after a short nap and a super quick shower, Jaycie put on a summery dress, since it was almost eighty degrees outside. "Do you know what Gran and Grandpa are wearing?"

"I know she's bringing a shawl in case it gets cool later." Mom handed her a blue paisley wrap that went well with the cap-sleeved cotton dress Jaycie wore. "Here's a pretty one you can use."

"Thanks, Mom." Since last summer, her mother was becoming more fashion-forward with her style. Maybe that was because Tom and Mom had fancy medical functions and parties to attend.

"I think you've gotten a few texts while you were in the shower."

Jaycie checked. Three from Parker. "Parker will meet us at the restaurant when we're done. We're going to go for a walk." Joy bloomed within her. She was really here in this beautiful country, and she'd finally get to see more of what Parker and his father raved about here in Lucerne. More importantly, she'd be there with Parker. Had he stayed sober even with all the temptations to drink? He'd shared how hard it was to decline the always offered wine that accompanied each business meal.

Mom blushed. "Tom and I are taking a romantic walk along the water, too. And I think your grandparents have the same plan."

She didn't want to share Parker tonight. "Um, I think he means alone."

Mom chortled. "We're all planning our walks, *alone*, too, sweetheart."

"Oh." Embarrassment heated her cheeks. "Sorry."

"Grandpa has a special new ring he bought for their fiftieth, and he's planning to give it to her on that old medieval bridge with the paintings."

"The one we'll see tomorrow?" The iconic bridge that Parker wanted her to see, too. She could already imagine how wonderful his hand would feel in hers.

"Right. And I think Tom may officially propose tonight." Mom lifted her bare left hand.

"Really? I thought you might have already secretly married him." Jaycie couldn't believe she'd finally said that out loud.

"He's a keeper, Mom."

"Yup. I know it."

They all left soon after, walking on the bricked walkway alongside the lake, sun gleaming on the Alps in the distance. Dinner was spectacular. Seating was posh and intimate, and the multi-course meal was the best she'd ever had.

If only Parker had been there. When they finished, she texted him. *When are you getting here?* Maybe she punched the question mark too hard because Mom gave her the side eye.

On our way, he texted back, and it felt like she could breathe again.

Her heartbeat accelerated. Why had one month felt like six? One year ago, he'd arrived in England and she'd had no idea that he'd come to rescue her from Elliott's humiliation of her. He'd really done that. Despite all the flack she'd given him in college. Had he really put his party boy years aside?

They stepped out of the restaurant. There he was, so handsome, dressed in a slim cut suite. But Parker hung back hand in his jacket pockets, with his dad and Maria beside him. *Uh oh, they must not have gotten the memo about the romantic walks.*

Mr. Parker and Maria greeted everyone. He jerked a thumb toward the water. "Maria and I rented a boat for while we're here. We're taking a romantic ride tonight.

That was a relief.

"But we'd love to take you all out tomorrow on Lake Lucerne to celebrate the golden anniversary."

"Fantastic," Grandpa agreed.

"Thank you." Gran gazed up at Grandpa. If only Jaycie and Parker could look at each other like that after fifty years.

She met his sea blue eyes and her face heated as she saw the intensity in them. They'd known each other almost all their lives. But instead of the friends that their grandparents and parents had all been, they were destined for something more. No more digging around at Archeological sites—they'd finally found their career paths. And hopefully no more self-medicating for Parker, who was dealing with the dysfunction and loss in his life directly rather than through avoidance.

Parker slowly met the eyes of the others there. "I'm going to steal my old *buddy* away for a bit, if you don't mind."

"What if we do?" Grandpa asked and stood to his full height, which was several inches shorter than Parker's.

Parker shrugged. "We'll make a run for it and see if your bum knee can hold out for the chase, Mr. Charbonneau."

Grandpa guffawed. "Young people these days."

Gran whisked her hands for them to leave. "We all have our own plans, so you young people go ahead and run off."

Dr. Austin took Mom's arm and they headed in one direction while Gran and Grandpa went off toward the bridge.

"I have someplace I want to show you." Parker took two steps toward her and linked arms with her.

The sun had set, and she hadn't realized how chilly it had gotten until she pulled a little closer to Parker's warmth. "How's it been going with your business stuff?"

"Great, can't complain. I love this place." He gestured around them.

She suddenly felt a little shy with him. Seeing Parker here, halfway across the world, felt different. "Me, too. Lucerne seems so unreal. It's so clean. The people are so nice."

"And most of the Swiss speak perfect English." He laughed. She'd missed that laugh.

"Yeah, that's handy." The thrumming inside her ratcheted up a bit. Shouldn't it have calmed down once she and Parker had been reunited?

They strolled back toward the hotel. There were quite a few people out this Easter week. Parks along the walkway held couples with small children sitting on blankets. Older couples sat on the benches that lined the thoroughfare, many holding hands.

"So, what is this you want to show me?" Jaycie leaned in toward him, pressing her side to his.

Love shone in his eyes. "You're gonna be surprised. Shocked even." A tiny smirk tugged at the corner of his lips.

Parker suddenly stopped in front of a gorgeous gray stone three-story mansion that sat immediately off the walkway, near the water. The interior glowed with multiple multi-tiered chandeliers lit with hundreds of lights each. Massive, mullioned, Palladian windows fronted the building which was the size of a federal building in Virginia. A couple danced beneath the crystal chandeliers.

She stood on tiptoe. Gilt-framed mirrors and paintings covered the walls of the massive ballroom-sized room. "Is that a dance hall of some kind?" But Jaycie didn't see anyone else inside.

"No. It's their residence." Parker pointed as the couple danced closer to the windows.

The two danced in perfect unison, mesmerized by one another. "They are really good, aren't they?"

"Don't you recognize them?" Parker leaned in and pressed his cheek against her hair.

The tall man and the dark-haired woman stopped their dance and embraced. The man kissed his dance partner. Jaycie looked away from the tender moment. "Who are they?"

"That's Dr. Piccard, or Mort, or Mr. Mortimer and his wife, the supermodel Kay-Leigh or Mrs. Mortimer. She's officially retired from modeling now and doing international work to help people with eating disorders."

"Oh my gosh. That's absolutely amazing." That was an understatement. "And to think I believed he was a gardener."

Parker laughed. "I bet that hot shot island landscaper, Mike DuBlanc, wishes he had a place like this instead of a little house in Harrisonville."

Jaycie frowned at him. "You sound jealous of him." The noted island landscaper was incredibly busy and impossibly handsome. But he was inconsistent in his interactions with her and others. DuBlanc was what Mom called "touchy" and Gran would call "a crank in the making."

"I kept my eye on DuBlanc last summer and kept you away from him when I could." Parker sounded serious. "When you started talking about the gardener, I was so concerned it was him that I made sure it wasn't."

"You're pretty ridiculous, doing all that."

A cool breeze gusted from the lake. Jaycie shivered and Parker pulled her close. She stared at the Swiss mansion that belonged to Mort and his wife. It could have been left empty. Cold. Like she'd been feeling. If Mort and his wife hadn't honestly tried to work on their issues and reconcile their marriage. If Mort hadn't accepted that his wife would have a lifelong struggle with bulimia. If Mort hadn't worked on dealing with his own feelings. Tears pricked her eyes. If she'd helped them at all, she was grateful and happy for the couple. The touching scene she'd witnessed bore evidence to their love—as did the baby bump Kay-Leigh sported.

"How would you feel about living in something this size but with about a hundred or more people living there with you?" Parker's voice grew low.

"A hundred other people?" Jet lag must be catching up with her.

"You know. Like in a hotel."

"Here?"

"Maybe."

They stood there, hugging for a long moment.

He drew in a breath. "There's this amazing Valley of Butterflies here in the Rhone River Valley of Switzerland. Your whole family might enjoy seeing it sometime. All these amazing endangered species of butterflies are sheltered there."

She pulled away and looked at him. "Really? That sounds incredible."

"My dad said it would make an amazing setting for a wedding." He took her hands in his and stroked the top of her hands with his thumbs.

"Hmmm, too bad we're not even officially dating."

"Yup." A mischievous glint shone in his eyes.

She took a step back closer. "I have a question for you, Parker."

He cocked his head at her. "Okay."

"How would you feel about ditching the one-year ban, and we start dating now?"

Parker shrugged nonchalantly, but then his smirk returned.

"You know, Mr. Smugness, I looked at the AA Two Year Sobriety Coin. I could get one made up early through Etsy."

He mock scowled at her. "That's cheating."

"We could order it now and hold it for your official two-year anniversary this summer."

"Only if you'll kiss me, again, like you did at that pub in the UK, to kick off our official courtship."

"Agreed." Jaycie committed herself fully to her task. The same electricity that had coursed through her in England surged through her, and then some.

When the kiss ended, Jaycie looked up at the man she wanted to spend the next fifty years with. A honeymoon at a Swiss Butterfly Cottage might be the perfect way to start.

The End

Author's Notes

My mother's final wish was that I'd tell anyone who'd listen to "Not have the Whipple procedure done." It turned the last few months of her life into a nightmare. I've published many books since then, although none about this topic. My writing is for God, and for a period of maybe seven months I discerned no direction—other than to rest in the Lord as far new projects. Then, in prayer I felt led to honor my mother's memory, and her last wish. And God gave me encouragement to begin this novel. The amazingly talented musical legend Aretha Franklin died of pancreatic cancer the summer I began this project. As I was completing this novel, beloved Jeopardy host, Alex Trebek, succumbed to this dread disease. The Pancreatic Cancer Action Network group exists to support people struggling with this diagnosis, and for their friends and family members.

I stopped writing for a while, again, after my dear friends, and readers, Cheryl Baranski, Bonnie Roof and Regina Fujitani (my Personal Assistant) passed away. Ann Lacy Ellison, a wonderful reader friend and prayer warrior died of cancer during that time, too. My dear friend from Michigan, Dr. Laura Vann, departed this earth not long after. I also lost Cousin Jackie Williams, Aunt Wilda Fancett and teacher Avis Fretz who had all strongly encouraged my writing. To have so many losses in a short time had me kicking this project to the virtual curb. I appreciate the terrific author Debbie Macomber sharing about a similar experience while writing a recent novel. Thank you, Debbie, for your beautiful words of encouragement in the personal message I received from you on Facebook. You spurred me on.

This is a fictional account, but I have "borrowed" many names. The real-life Director of the Mackinac State Historic Parks in 2018 and until recently, was Phil Porter, who retired after a long and illustrious career there. He has many wonderful nonfiction books about the island. The Director would not have archeology interns working in his office, however. And any internships are awarded via a special committee. There are a number of actual dig sites going on at the parks every summer, in various locations. Always a joy to watch.

There really is a Pastor Dave! Pastor David Wallis is the minister at Church of the Straits in Mackinaw City. I was blessed to be able to

attend there during the summers when I was renting a cottage down the street. He's a great preacher and this is a lovely church with a huge
VBS outreach program, too, like in the story. Fictional—Dave can't be friends with Dawn Charbonneau because she's just a character, and the pastor is portrayed in fictional situations. My Virginia pastor, Reverend Larry Jones and his wife Jane, are also on the page in a fictional scene. Larry, like his fictional counterpart, goes above and beyond to reach out to members of the congregation at Northside Christian Church.

Dr. Zaitoun, a wonderful cardiologist practices in Virginia not in Petoskey, Michigan.

The Afters' song, "Live on Forever", was my inspiration song for Tamara's journey. If you or a love one is facing a short time on earth, I encourage you to listen to this beautiful song—repeatedly. The song, "Amen", by For King & Country is another beautiful inspiration song and even references the butterfly transformation in the lyrics!

There truly has been a movement to save the monarch butterflies at the Straits of Mackinac. Those milkweeds planted in public places may be ugly weeds to us, but they are food for the butterflies and have brought them back. Also, there is a real Valley of Butterflies in the Rhone River Valley of Switzerland.

I wrote three endings to this story. In one, Tamara dies with dignity—that was my original, and literary, version. The second ending was Tamara entering a research trial, with the ending showing her alive after five years but with it being unknown if the cancer will remain in remission. The final version, in this book, is what you've read. I'd had a case, as a psychologist, where I'd been sent the wrong information—the previous psychologist's results didn't remotely line up with mine. They had accidentally embedded another client's results within my client's report! I spoke with a friend about this new ending. There was a long pause. Her son had recently been diagnosed with a Then she said, "This just happened with my son—they gave him the wrong diagnosis."

Acknowledgments

I always thank God for anything that He gives me to produce. I thank the Lord that he spared my wonderful critique partner Kathleen L. Maher, who was in the hospital when she suffered a life-threatening event and my friend, Cynthia Howerter, who was in a horrific car accident that she survived.

Tamara Tomac, manager at the Island Bookstore on Mackinac Island, whose first name I "borrowed" for my heroine has given me a lot of support and excellent feedback with this story. She's a genuine and lovely person.

Dawn Bobay, whose name I also "borrowed" for my grandmother character. Dawn actually became a first-time grandmother during the time since I started this book! She was my amazing neighbor at the Straits and suggested using the butterflies, symbolic of life after death, in this story. Butterfly Cottage had several different titles until I came back to this original idea. Thanks, Dawn!

Mary Jane Barnwell, the owner of the Island Bookstore, on Mackinac Island, has been very kind in supporting my work and allowing me to sign books for the store. She's a gem!

Laurinda and crew at the Mackinaw City Bakery, on Langlade Street in Mackinaw City. Wonderful folks, wonderful food! And yes, like in the novel, their long john pastries are the best ever! If you're making a trip to the Straits be sure to stop by.

My in-laws, Joan and Don, for taking us to Europe and in particular to Switzerland, which I used in this novel. Joan is an avid reader and has been a big support.

Dr. David Buck and his team for keeping me in the proper eyeglasses. Since the start of this project that would be well over a half dozen pairs.

Dr. Lyzette Velazquez, my neurologist (and not a special ed teacher like in the story), who has helped me with my migraines. Her knowledge and use of the new injectables helped me develop the migraine recovery for Brad in the story.

Wendy Shoults, who is indeed a talented artist from Petoskey and has art shows in the area.

My agent, Joyce Hart, who brainstormed with me and gave suggestions. She's a real trooper and helped secure a contract for

Behind Love's Wall (Barbour, November 2021) which includes some characters from *Butterfly Cottage*.

My best friends Tara Mulcahey and Susan Mullen who aren't fiction readers but have put up with me talking about my stories and have encouraged me.

Friend and author Pegg Thomas (also my editor for this book—thanks Pegg!) and my friend and early critique partner for the first version of this story, author Debbie Lynne Costello. Your insights helped changed the path of this story.

Friends Sue Pentland, Jan Koivisto, Janet Labron, and Rosemary Wellington who shower me with their friendship and love when I am "home" for the summers up North!

Family members have been so good to me. Thank you to my son, Clark Jeffrey Pagels, a fellow writer and so helpful—and a name "lender" too. My brother, Gary Lee Fancett. who brainstormed with me about the possible scenarios for my character diagnosed with pancreatic cancer. Cousins Susie Carey, Karen Blank, Kareen and Scott Davis, who encourage me.

My fantastic Pals reader group, my Promo group members for Butterfly Cottage, especially professional Beta reader Jennifer Forbes (thanks for letting me borrow hubby's name Dr. Joseph Forbes, too!) early Beta reader Sherry Moe, and Beta reader Sally Dennis Davison. Much thanks also to Advance Readers: Bonny Sommert Rambarran, Betti Mace, Sonja Hoeke Nishimoto, Tina St. Clair Rice, Teresa S. Mathews, Chappy Debbie Mitchell, Brenda Murphree, Teri Geist DiVincenzo, Anne Payne, Deanna Stevens, Susan Johnson, Nancy McLeroy, Gracie Yost, Wilani Wahl and Deanne Patterson.

Thank you to the Addicted to Mackinac group for sharing about my books and for loving and promoting all things Mackinac Island year-round. Thank you especially to leader, Linda Borton Sorensen, who does a great job and is a wonderful person.

Melinda Evans is a talented dancer and instructor as well as a lovely person. She teaches at the fantastic dance studio Country Bootleggers now renamed CB Dance Studio, in Yorktown, Virginia, and let me "borrow" her name.

Upcoming!

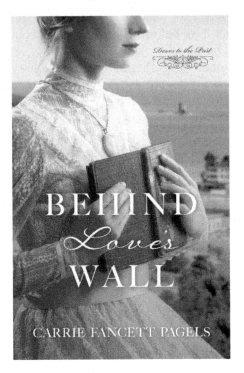

My upcoming *Behind Love's Wall* novel (Barbour, November 2021) has characters in it introduced in Butterfly Cottage. I hope you'll read this dual-timeline novel, part of the "Doors to the Past" series and spend more time on Mackinac Island with my characters from the twenty-first century as well as many from my nineteenth century stories. In the 1895 section, you'll read the sequel to my award-winning and Romantic Times Top Pick novel, *My Heart Belongs on Mackinac Island: Maude's Mooring*. Lily's story takes place during the same summer as Maude's.

In the 2020 part of the novel, modern-day characters are influenced by events from the past—in particular a mysterious death of Lily's maid from the Grand Hotel in 1895. Heroine Willa Christy and hero Michael DuBlanc were both referenced in Butterfly Cottage! All of the stories in the Doors to the Past series have a mystery in them and some, like mine, also have romance.

Excerpt from *Behind Love's Wall*

Yellowstone, June 2019

"Are we in 2019 or 1895?" Willa removed her favorite oversized cheap sunglasses—so unlike the designer cats' eye Chanel pair she'd chosen for this year's television season—and stared up at the large cabin-like structure of the Old Faithful Inn.

Her assistant, Sue Pentland, parked their rental Subaru Outback and then the two of them unbuckled their seatbelts. Sue pushed her fringed blond bangs back. "It's not bad. Probably much nicer on the inside."

"Maybe there's a reason they don't show many pictures of the interior of the Old House rooms." Experiencing the old lodge rustic vibe, had been their aim, though.

"Check-in time doesn't start until five. Outrageous for what you're paying for that room." Sue touched the liftgate button to release it and the two of them exited the vehicle.

Sue grabbed her bag, an oversized black leather monstrosity she'd bought on their recent business trip to Dubai.

Willa pulled her own super-lightweight nylon rolling bag from the trunk. "One of the benefits of traveling incognito is only having one teeny tiny bag this trip."

Shaking her head, Sue touched the button to close the hatch. "If I never see another lime-and-blush camo ensemble on you, I'll be happy."

Willa elbowed her. "Hey, you helped me pick that look."

"It's certainly memorable." Her assistant began pulling her bulky luggage toward the stairs, which led up from the parking lot.

"I should've dropped you out front." After the long flight from Virginia to Wyoming and the many hours driving into the park, her brain wasn't exactly functioning on fully charged capacity.

"Tell me again why we've come here." Sue sighed as she lifted her bag up one step and then another.

"Rustic chic inspiration for the new line." As one of the country's rising stars in hotel design and redesign, Willa had longed to get a look at one of the oldest rustic hotels in the country. "I've never been here."

"Um, yeah, me neither." Sue continued her slow sojourn upward.

"Let me help." Willa grabbed the handle, too. She tried to lift, but the suitcase seemed full of bricks. "What have you got in here?"

Her friend's cheeks flushed pink. "I heard the weather can change fast out here. I brought boots, winter clothes and everything in between."

"Seriously?" Willa cocked her head at her. "It's in the seventies today and I'm warm." Dressed in cargo shorts and a subdued off-white Polo shirt, Willa desired to blend in with the other tourists.

"Can I help you ladies?" At the top of the stairs, a handsome golden-haired man stood alongside an equally attractive woman, two blond girls standing between them.

What a beautiful family. Willa stared up at them. She didn't normally allow herself to think about what she was missing behind the walls she formed over her heart. Her stellar career was enough, or so she told herself.

The broad-shouldered man quick-stepped down the stairs and soon stood two steps above them. "Looks like you could use a hand."

Sue gaped at the man and Willa bit back a chuckle. This guy really was a little too perfect in all the right ways.

When Sue didn't answer, Willa nodded. "Thanks, that would be great."

At the top of the stairs, the stranger's wife pulled out her phone and appeared to be checking something. The two little girls held each other's hands and swung them back and forth. They were adorable.

The stranger grinned at them, dimples forming in his suntanned face. "Let me take them both, eh?"

Willa stiffened. The man's distinct Upper Peninsula of Michigan accent triggered the anxiety she always associated with that place. She swallowed hard but allowed him to take her bag. She pulled her sunglasses back down from where they rested atop her head.

The man bounded back up as though Sue's luggage held only down feathers.

"What's the matter, Willa?"

She shook her head. "Let's catch up with him."

As they neared the top, Sue slowed and grabbed Willa's arm. "Oh my gosh, do you know who that woman is?"

Willa narrowed her eyes, taking in the woman's lovely profile. "As you know, I don't watch television unless it's about hotels or resorts, or go to movies, so just tell me."

"That's Bianca Rossi, one of those Housewives of Beverly Hills."

Drop-dead gorgeous with an equally attractive family, Bianca likely enjoyed showing off her fantastic life for all the nation to see. Her husband sure looked like a happy man, with that huge smile on his face as he rejoined his family.

When they reached the top, Sue reached for her suitcase. "Thanks so much but I can roll it on in from here."

Bianca's silvery blue eyes locked on Willa. "I know you, don't I?"

"No." The numbers were improving for her HGTV segment, but without her makeup, Willa's crazy hair thanks to wigs, and her outré clothing, how could this woman know her?"

"Yes, yes I do."

Her handsome honey glanced between the two of them. Mr. Yooperman with Hollywood Glamour Gal? How had that happened? Still, they looked awesome together.

"You're Willa Christy."

She dipped her chin in acknowledgement. Willa had taken her grandfather and birth mother's surname as her professional name. Willa Forbes was her adoptive and legal name.

"You re-designed my father's resort in Jamaica last summer. He raved about you. And I love your new segment on HGTV!"

Ohmygoodnessgracious, Bianca Rossi is having a fangirl moment. Too bad that Willa couldn't return the favor.

Sue leaned in. "And I love watching you on tv, too. Bianca."

Bianca raised a perfectly manicured hand and feigned locking her lips. "Mums the word for all of us while we're here, right?"

Hunky Yooperman grinned. She didn't care how good-looking he was, if she had to listen to that accent every night she'd be a nervous wreck, even though she'd never been able to say why. Her sweet grandpa was a Yooperman, albeit an elderly one and he didn't make her feel that way.

Bianca glanced around as if making sure no one could overhear. A bus of tourists, most of whom were speaking an Asian language, arrived at the front of the lodge. "So, are you researching something here?"

Willa caught the twinkle in the other woman's eye. "Nothing your father could have used in Jamaica, believe me."

"I know. This look would never have worked for Pops." Bianca laughed.

The older of the two little girls tugged at her mother's navy patterned tunic. "Let's go, Mom."

Willa briefly locked eyes with Mr. Rossi. "Thanks again for your help."

"No problem." Was it her imagination or did he suddenly look sad? Did it bother him when Bianca talked shop?

"Nice to meet you two." Bianca beamed at them.

"Us, too," Sue gushed.

Soon, they'd made their way inside, registered, and headed to their room.

Willa unlocked the door and opened it. Sue had specifically chosen one of the original rooms of the structures to obtain a more genuine rustic feel, and this certainly was that.

Sue stepped in behind her. "Oh my."

"Yikes. Where's the bathroom?" Willa looked around the spartanly furnished room, as though a bathroom might show up if she looked hard enough.

"Um, it's down the hall."

"Down the hall?" A fact Sue had apparently forgotten to share.

Her friend chewed her lower lip. "You wanted the rustic experience."

It wouldn't help to complain. Willa would put on her big girl pants and deal with the situation. "At least the windows are pretty."

"And old, very old." Sue crossed to the window.

Willa joined her. "Look at that, a geyser is going!" Willa pointed out. "Wow, that's pretty cool."

The two of them watched as the geyser continued to erupt.

"Don't see that every day, do you?" As the geyser stopped its flow, Sue reached to turn the window's locking mechanism to open it. "Oh, this was already unlocked."

"Maybe that's why it's so cool in here."

Sue struggled to lock the window again. "Hmm, this might be original equipment here."

"Let me try." On work sites, strong-handed Willa was the one who could often get things unstuck. She tried repeatedly but failed to connect the brass pieces to latch. "I think we needed Mr. Yooperman for this."

"Huh?"

"That guy is from the Upper Peninsula."

"How do you know?"

"His accent." And her reaction to that distinctive dialect.

She rubbed her arms. Although Willa began her life as a Yooper, she'd grown up in Virginia with her adoptive parents. This was silly reacting in this way. "Let's try together to get this thing to close."

The two of them leaned into it and finally succeeded.

When they woke the next morning, Sue went to the window and drew the drapes back. "Good thing we got that window shut tight."

"Why?" Willa stretched beneath the covers.

"Come look."

She rose and took a look outside, where a winter wonderland had replaced the sunny summer's day. "This is the first day of summer."

"Mother Nature doesn't care."

More snow swirled around and in the distance, pine trees were covered in white.

"It looks like a Hallmark Christmas movie."

Willa trembled, shaking where she stood. *It looks like death.*

Connect with me at:

www.carriefancettpagels.com

While you're browsing my website, be sure to sign up for my newsletter via the Contact page. You can also send me messages via the Contact page form. You can see some of my other books on my Amazon author page.

Bio:

Carrie Fancett Pagels, Ph.D., is the award-winning and bestselling author of over twenty Christian fiction books. Twenty-five years as a psychologist didn't "cure" her overactive imagination! A self-professed "history geek," she resides with her family in the Historic Triangle of Virginia but grew up as a "Yooper" in Michigan's beautiful Upper Peninsula. She loves to spend time in the summer at the Straits of Mackinac—where this novel is set!